Love of the Summerfields

Other Historical Novels
by Nancy Moser

- *Masquerade*
- *An Unlikely Suitor*
- *The Journey of Josephine Cain*
- *A Patchwork Christmas* novella collection (*The Bridal Quilt*)

Biographical novels about Women of History
- *Mozart's Sister* (Nannerl Mozart)
- *Just Jane* (Jane Austen)
- *Washington's Lady* (Martha Washington)
- *How Do I Love Thee* (Elizabeth Barrett Browning)

And to commemorate the 250th anniversary of the end of the Civil War:

A Basket Brigade Christmas novella collection (*Endless Melody*)

To find information about all 27 of Nancy's novels go to her website: www.nancymoser.com

Love of the Summerfields

a novel

Book One
of the
Manor House Series

Nancy Moser

Overland Park, Kansas

Love of the Summerfields

ISBN-10: 0986195200
ISBN-13: 978-0986195204

Published by:
Mustard Seed Press
PO Box 23002
Overland Park, KS 66283

This story is a work of fiction. Any resemblances to actual people, places, or events are purely coincidental.

All Scripture quotations are taken from The Holy Bible, King James Version.

Front cover design by Müllerhaus Publishing Group

Printed and bound in the United States of America
10 9 8 7 6 5 4 3 2 1

Dedication

To my sister, Crys Mach
Thank you for helping me
give birth to the Summerfields.

To my daughter, Laurel Conrad
Many thanks for helping
the Summerfields reach their prime.

Chapter One

Summerfield, England
Late July 1880

"They're back!" Fidelia Hayward burst into the Summerfield Mercantile, one hand to her heaving chest, the other steadying her bonnet, which tipped precariously over her left ear.

Her daughter, Lila, looked up from the stack of tea towels she was folding. "I assume you mean the Westons."

Mother yanked her hat off, getting both her chin and her words tangled in the bow. "Of course I mean the Westons. Summerfield Manor is abuzz with news of their return."

"So you've been to the manor?"

"Of course not." She pointed to the village square where every nuance of village life was collected, dissected, and directed. "But if you'd care to walk outside with me, you'll hear the news yourself."

Lila patted the top of the stack and handed them to their clerk, Rose. "You can be our correspondent, Mother. I'm content to get the news secondhand."

"As am I." Papa winked at Lila, then shared a smile with Rose, completing the usual relay of responses to Mother's flutter and flurry.

Mother dug her fists into her hips. "Your lack of curiosity is abominable. And since you're *not* curious, I shall not tell you the latest gossip about Lady Clarissa."

"As you wish," Lila said, turning her attention to a messy stack of handkerchiefs, the need to hide her smile finding refuge in busyness.

Papa nodded toward the stack. "It appears our inventory is low. How many should I buy, next trip to London?"

Lila counted the men's larger handkerchiefs, then the women's smaller ones. "We could use six more of each, I think."

"Very good. I'll—"

Mother strode to the handkerchiefs, grabbed the entire stack, and tossed it into the air. "Listen to me! There's news!"

As the last handkerchief floated to the floor, Lila suffered an inward sigh. They were used to histrionics, but the act of throwing things elevated Mother's news beyond the usual gossip. Yet to concede by giving Mother full attention was not in her nature.

When Rose knelt to retrieve the fallen handkerchiefs, Lila joined her. If they didn't do it themselves, it wouldn't get done.

"Stop!" Mother put a hand on Lila's arm. "Listen. To. Me." She turned to her husband. "Jack, make them listen."

"If it will calm you." He nodded at Lila. "Give your mother your full attention, so the world can move on."

Lila stood shoulder to shoulder with Rose, and they each took a breath and smoothed their skirts. "All right. We're ready. Tell us your news."

Mother peered at them suspiciously. "I'm not sure I want to, what with all the trouble you've put me through."

Lila sighed. Her mother was a mistress of hoops—making people jump through them for her own entertainment. Lila did her duty. "Please tell us. We're dying to know."

Mother set her hat on the counter and smoothed the ribbons. "I heard it on good authority that Lady Clarissa did *not* find a match during the London season. It's been three years since she's come out, and three years without a betrothal."

That was it? That was the news? It was like hearing that the night would be dark.

And Lila wasn't surprised by it. Lady Clarissa was fickle

and rebellious. Word had returned to Summerfield that during Clarissa's presentation to Queen Victoria, she'd refused to wear the three-feather Prince-of-Wales plume with her sweeping veil, wanting instead to wear a tiara — an honor reserved for married women. Cooler heads prevailed, but everyone knew Lady Clarissa pressed her own wishes above all others.

"Obviously she hasn't found a man to love," Rose said.

"What's love got to do with it?" Mother asked.

"Fidelia!" Papa said.

"Yes, yes, love *should* be important, but we all know the gentry set usually marries for title, money, or status, with love a distant fourth."

"Then I feel sorry for them," Papa said.

"Me too," Rose said. "I loved my Ben for the entire twenty years of our marriage, and now that he's gone, I still love him. If Lady Clarissa doesn't love anyone, then she shouldn't get married."

"Hear, hear!" Lila said, more as an affirmation of her own views than care for Lady Clarissa's happiness — which no doubt would be achieved by some ancestral entitlement whether she married for love or not.

Mother pointed a finger in her direction. "You're as picky as she is, and it won't do either of you any good. Timothy is a fine man, and you ought — "

As if summoned by his name, Timothy Billings walked in the mercantile. When he removed his cap, a shimmering of sawdust sprinkled to the floor. He immediately stopped when he saw four sets of eyes upon him. "Am I interrupting something?"

Mother slipped her arm through his and led him over to Lila. "Not a thing, Timothy. Lila was just telling us how eager she was to see you."

His eyebrows rose, and he looked to Lila for affirmation.

She hated that Mother had put her in this position. She found Timothy quite affable but knew his feelings for her ran far deeper than her own. Yet not wanting to hurt him, she offered him a smile. "Mother just shared the news that the Westons are back from the London season."

"They are," he said. "And I've just been summoned to the manor to speak with the dowager countess about some special letter box she saw in London. She wants me to build a similar one for her."

"Good for you," Papa said. "Your carpentry skills will take you far."

"And make you a fine living," Mother added. "Soon you'll be set to assume full responsibility of your father's shop."

Mother's version of subtlety was like too much pepper in a soup, and Lila felt her face grow hot, but Timothy took it all in stride. "There's time enough for that. My father's in very good health and works harder than I do," he said. "And there's still much to learn."

"That's the right attitude," Papa said. "Believe it or not, our generation does have a thing or two to teach the younger set." He gave Mother a pointed look.

"I know what you're implying, Jack," Mother said. "But I still think it's important our own son gains a formal education away from Summerfield."

"A useless one," Papa said. "Morgan doesn't need extra schooling to run a mercantile."

"But—"

"When is he coming home?"

Lila was glad for Timothy's interruption. She wasn't up to enduring another argument regarding her brother, whose attributes, flaws, and future were juggled daily whether he was present at the juggling or not.

"I expected him by now," Papa said. "His term is long over, and he was instructed to stop in London and bring home a shipment. Save me a trip."

"So he lingered in London for a holiday," Mother said. "A well-deserved one after his hard scholarship. Although I can't wait to see him, I don't begrudge him his fun."

Of course not. In their mother's eyes, Morgan was king, prince, and emperor. If he weren't such a self-deprecating man, Lila could have easily hated him. Instead, she allowed her resentment to flow toward his enabler.

Timothy leaned close to Lila. "Wish me luck at the manor."

"Good luck," she said, meaning it. Whether or not she and Timothy ever married, she wished him the best. Getting a foot-in with the Westons was important. Since those who had money were willing to spend it, they might as well spend it within the boundaries of the village rather than ordering from London.

As Timothy left, Mother moved to the windows that served as her personal window to the world of Summerfield even as it displayed the goods of the mercantile. Once at her post, she mumbled her grievances to the bins of buttons and combs. "Lila, you need to snatch him up before you lose him to some other Summerfield girl."

"I don't plan to snatch anyone," she said. "Finding a mate deserves contemplation and care."

"For those who have time for such luxuries. At twenty, you're much too choosy. I still don't see why you ignored Andrew Smith the last time we were in London. His father owns a bank. Andrew has to be worth a thousand a year."

"And he has a nose as hooked as one of those puppets in a Punch and Judy show." Papa said, smiling at Lila. "I wouldn't want my daughter peering at such a face for the rest of her life."

Lila appreciated his support. Andrew's face was but the half of it. A woman could overlook an unfortunate nose. It was Andrew's eyes that provoked shivers. The man didn't look at her, he leered.

"Beggars can't be choosers," Mother sniffed.

"Fidelia, enough!"

Mother let out a breath but quickly drew in another, her voice indicating she was about to favor them with another bout of sarcasm. "The Taylors hired a new farmhand," she said. "Perhaps he'll find a mature shopkeeper's daughter to his liking."

Mature. Lila turned toward the shelves and busied herself

by restacking some porcelain bowls lest Mother see her tears. The cool touch of the china was a balm to the heat of the moment.

Rose stepped close. "She didn't mean it," she whispered.

Yes, she did. In spite of Lila's attempts to ignore her mother's barbs, they left a fresh mark. And it was clear she was being sarcastic, for Mother was all about status — constantly decrying her lack of it and clamoring for more. She might pretend Lila should marry a hired hand, but if Lila were to actually fall in love with such a man, Mother would lock her in her room and drop the key inside her bodice, never to be found again.

If Lila was honest, she *was* concerned about her unmarried state and her prospects in tiny Summerfield. Beyond Timothy, the pool of eligible men was lacking. Chances were that Lila would have to find a husband in London during one of their buying trips. But the thought of a city man . . . He'd never find her witty or worldly enough. And Lila hated the noises, smells, soot, and commotion of London.

She stopped stacking and closed her eyes, repeating a well-worn prayer. *Pick me a mate, God. Choose a good man for me.*

At the sound of a customer, Mother retrieved the smile she saved for public eyes. "Good morn—"

When she stopped mid-sentence, Lila turned toward the door.

"Nana!" Lila ran into her grandmother's arms.

"Oh, my sweet, sweet girl." Nana released her from the hug. "You are a vision."

Lila felt a rush of warmth. Nana always made her feel special.

Papa greeted her with a kiss to each cheek. "Mama, what a wonderful surprise! How good it is to see you." He took a step toward the door. "Is Pa getting the luggage?"

Nana's brow furrowed. "Didn't you get my letter?"

Papa immediately gave Mother an accusatory glance.

But Mother shook her head. "There was no letter."

Papa continued toward the door. "No matter. We're glad

for the visit. You're always—"

Nana put a hand on his arm. "Jack. Your father is dead."

Papa froze, and the color drained from his face. "But how? When?"

"Three weeks ago. He took ill. I tried everything, but even the doctor said there was nothing to be done."

Papa opened his arms to his mother and she cried softly against his chest. He squeezed his eyes shut against his own tears.

Rose wrapped her arm about Lila's shoulders and leaned close. "I'm so sorry."

Lila wanted to feel sadder than she did, yet she'd never had the opportunity to know Grandfather well. When they'd visited her grandparents in London, Grandfather was often out, and during the few times her grandparents had visited Summerfield, Grandfather had spent most of his time off in the woods doing who-knows-what, or over at the Fox Run for a pint. Or two. But whether Lila felt deep sadness for her own loss didn't stop her from feeling bad for Nana and Papa. Nana had lost her husband. Papa had lost his father. Their pain made her own tears flow.

Mother took a position close by as if needing to be a part of the grief, if only by proximity. Did she feel sorrow? Lila had never heard her say a single nice word about Grandfather, or Nana.

As if answering Lila's query Mother said, "Well, I'm sorry too."

At her words, Papa nodded, returning as much sincere emotion as she'd offered.

Nana gently pushed herself free of Papa's arms. "There's one more thing. Oh, how I wish you'd received my letter . . ."

"What is it?"

She looked at Papa, then Lila, then Mother. "I've come to stay with you."

"You've what?" Mother asked.

"Of course you're welcome for as long as you'd like to visit," Papa said.

Nana bit her lower lip and wound the ribbon from her bonnet around a finger. "I'm not here merely to visit, but to live with you. I can't be in London any longer, not without Stanley there. The pain is too much, and . . . there are reasons . . . I am so sorry. I had to come."

Lila couldn't stand seeing Nana's discomfort and went to her side to take her hand. "I'm glad you've come to live with us."

"Where is she going to sleep?" Mother asked.

Papa gave her a stern look. "She can stay in Morgan's room."

"But he'll be home soon. He'll need his room."

Heaven forbid anything might inconvenience Mother's beloved son.

But it wasn't worth arguing about. And so, Lila offered Nana a smile. "You can stay with me, in my room."

"I hate to be a bother," Nana said. "But without Stanley . . . you're my only family." She looked at her son. "Truly, I did send a letter. I had no wish to surprise you like this."

"But surely you must have wondered why there was no reply." Mother pressed.

Papa pointed a finger at her, his usual warning that he'd reached his limit. Mother bobbed her head and moved her lips, the additional words she wanted to say straining for release.

Since there was no guarantee she'd remain quiet, and since Lila did *not* want Nana to hear more squabbling, Lila linked her arm through hers. "You must be exhausted from the journey. Come upstairs and rest in my bed. Later, we'll set up a cot for me."

As they climbed the stairs leading to the bedrooms which were situated above the living quarters behind the store, Lila heard Mother's harsh whispers about the inconvenient timing, the cramped space, and the gall. Lila hoped Nana didn't hear.

Unfortunately, as they reached the top of the stairs, Nana said, "It appears I've set a pot to boil."

"It's not your fault," Lila said. "Mother is always on simmer."

"Would you like to rest, or would you like help unpacking?" Lila asked once Papa had brought Nana's trunk upstairs.

Nana sat upon the bed and her shoulders rose, then fell. "I'm heartily tired, yet I don't want to rest." She shook her head as if dispelling the stress of the journey, then held out her hands.

Lila took them, surprised by their strength.

"Look at you, my little Lila. Not so little anymore."

Was she also going to comment on Lila's age? Lila never imagined the age of twenty could be so burdensome.

"You are a rare gem, sparkling in the sun."

She felt herself blush. "Maybe a river rock."

Nana took hold of her chin and forced Lila to look in her eyes. "A rare gem, I say. And don't let certain people make you feel otherwise."

Lila felt tears threaten. "How did you know I needed that?"

"Because it's my job to know." She pulled Lila's face close and kissed her forehead. "Now then, let's get me unpacked." She nodded toward the trunk on the floor. "One mangy trunk to show for a lifetime. Testament to a woman who has lived little and accomplished less."

It was Lila's turn to encourage. "You were a wonderful wife to Grandfather, you're a wonderful mother to your son, and you are a grandmother with impeccable taste in granddaughters."

Nana laughed. "It appears I am quite accomplished." She motioned toward the trunk. "Open it and let's release my meager treasures."

Folded on top was a green day dress. Lila ran her finger along the frayed hem and cuffs then hung it on a wall peg. Next was a dress of plum gabardine. The fabric was in better condition, but it was missing a button on each sleeve.

"Besides a nightgown and undergarments, that is the extent of my wardrobe," Nana said. She dusted off the skirt of her traveling dress. "I know I should wear mourning, but purchasing widow's weeds does not fit into my budget."

"We could order you something."

"I don't think your mother would appreciate the expense."

Nana caught sight of her reflection in the mirror above the dresser and stood for a better look. "Oh dear. Look at me. My hair was black as yours at one time. And now it's gray and matted from the bonnet." She tried to fluff it with her fingers, but gave up. "What does it matter? Without Stanley, there's no one to look pretty for." Her eyes welled with tears.

Lila stood behind, and wrapped her arms around her. "I'm so sorry he's gone."

Nana leaned her head against Lila's cheek. "I'm not just mourning the man, I'm mourning my youth." She ran her fingers across the spray of lines at the corner of her eyes, and touched the creases on her forehead. "Where's the feisty woman with the bright eyes and eager laugh? Where did she go?"

Lila hated to see Nana's pain. What was it like to grow old? Did a person feel it come upon them a little at a time, or did they wake up one morning, surprised that decades had passed?

"I know you've had a hard time of it," Lila said. "Papa has told us a little about how hard Grandfather tried to make a go of things."

"And how he failed." Nana shook the thought away and removed a daguerreotype from the trunk. "This picture is my prized possession. It's your father when he was fourteen."

Lila held the image toward the light of the window. "He was handsome, even then. The strong chin, the laughing eyes."

Nana took it back, touching her son's face. "The only way we afforded such a thing was because Stanley had been hired by a daguerreotype artist who set up shop during the Great

Exhibition, selling likenesses to commemorate people's visit to the Crystal Palace."

"People still talk about the Exhibition."

"It was utterly grand. And with his earnings, Stanley splurged by taking us into the Exhibition itself. I'd never seen him more proud than when he paid the three shillings for the admission. He even gave me a penny to experience the new-fangled public toilets. It was the best and happiest day of our lives, a day when we could forget the pressures of survival and be amazed at what the world created without us."

"It must have been exciting."

"It was perfect." She set the image on the dresser, leaning it against a vase. "Soon after, Jack found a job in a dry goods store, which was how he learned the business. It was mainly due to Jack that we kept a roof over our heads and food in our stomachs."

"Wasn't Grandfather working too?"

"In his own fashion. While Jack worked his way up the ladder of responsibility, Stanley floundered. The more Jack succeeded, the more Stanley failed. I think Jack's success made him feel less of a man. And he acted up accordingly."

Acted up. What exactly did that mean?

Nana flipped the subject away. "Look at me, blubbering one minute and complaining the next. It does no good to brood over the past. It is what it is." With that, she let the lid of the trunk fall closed and moved to the bed. "I think I will take a little rest."

Lila fluffed the pillow and helped Nana get comfortable, covering her with a quilted throw. "Let me know if you need anything."

Nana nodded, but then she raised herself onto her forearms. "I do need one thing."

"What's that?"

"I need you, my precious gem of a granddaughter, to allow me the privilege of polishing you to a fine sheen."

"It's far too soon to do any polishing. Don't I need to be cut and shaped first?"

"Absolutely. And with my encouragement you will be cut into a many-faceted jewel. And *then* I'll do the polishing."

Lila laughed. "I can think of nothing better."

And no one better to do it.

Chapter Two

"There," Molly said to the room. "Thirty-four dresses unpacked. One to go."

She wiped her brow with the sleeve of her blouse, not wanting to soil her hands with perspiration lest it transfer to the clothes of her mistress. For any stain added was a stain Molly herself would have to remove.

She hung the final dress on its padded hanger—a peach-colored satin with Belgian lace—and scanned the countess's dressing room. The floor was knee-high with tissue paper, and Molly began the task of smoothing and folding each sheet to reuse for their return to London next spring. She was heartily glad the social pilgrimage was just once a year.

Yet as she gathered the tissue, Molly perused the dresses. Of the thirty-five costumes, there were more than a dozen that had never been worn. Not for a lack of invitations, but for lack of courage. Although the Countess of Summerfield had done her duty by being seen on her husband's arm, she'd taken every opportunity and exercised every excuse to stay behind at their London flat. Which meant the earl and their daughter, Lady Clarissa, attended the balls, dinners, parties, and theatricals without her. It was saddening and maddening to witness. The countess was as beautiful and charming as any other socialite—or at least she was behind closed doors. Molly had never been privy to witnessing her mistress in public, but her reluctance to attend social events led Molly to believe that the private countess and the public one were two very different beings.

Unfortunately, while in London, Molly had heard rumors of the earl receiving the attention of a certain Lady Carlton. There were no details about whether her master had encouraged or reciprocated the attention, but the situation did not bode well for his marriage. The countess simply had to stop hiding out in her room and start participating in daily life. If not, she might lose her spouse.

Oh, the problems and intrigues of the rich.

If Molly had been offered the chance to go to London parties, she would have danced every dance, laughed at every witticism, and turned heads when she entered a room, with onlookers overcome by her beauty and confidence. Not that she was beautiful. Her chin was a bit too weak, and her hair a bit too red. But acting beautiful could take a girl a long way. So could clothes. As a lady's maid, Molly might not have to wear a uniform, but neither could she dress to her heart's desire. Occasionally she received the countess's castoffs, but they were simple pieces, nothing luscious like the gowns before her.

She spotted a pink, plumed headpiece on the floor beneath some tissue and placed it on her head. From her experience in dressing the countess's hair, she knew its best angle and set the combs in place to secure it. Then she curtsied to her companion. "Why thank you, Mr. Hayward. I would love to dance."

She placed her arms in a dance position, accepting his lead, and whirled around the dressing room, causing the tissue to take flight and float around her. If she closed her eyes, she could even see Morgan's dark eyes and saucy smile.

You've captured me, Miss Wallace. I am at your mercy.

She laughed at the memory of his words — for as impossible as it seemed, he *had* said them. To her. And though they hadn't been at a grand ball but only sitting on a bench in the Mall near Buckingham Palace, her heart had danced, and she'd felt as dizzy as if she'd truly waltzed across a ballroom in his arms.

That she'd run into Morgan in London — stopped off from

school on his way home to Summerfield — was an odd twist of serendipity that crowned everything that romance should be. How much better to fully fall in love with a local boy in London rather than in stuffy old Summerfield. And how remarkable that Morgan would be home soon, so their love could grow deep roots.

With Molly home and Morgan home, with only a ten-minute walk separating the manor from the mercantile . . . It would be a luscious late summer and autumn.

"Ahem."

Molly stopped dancing and saw the countess in the doorway. She yanked the headpiece off, causing the combs to pull a good hank of hair free in the process. She hid the plume behind her back. "Sorry, my lady."

"It's quite all right, Molly. You've been working ever so hard, you deserve a bit of fun."

Molly returned the headpiece front-and-center. "It is a favorite of the ones I made for you," she said.

"Too bad I never wore it. Your talent is wasted on me."

"Next time, my lady."

"Perhaps." The countess took a tentative step into the dressing room, as if *she* were the intruder, as if all these beautiful things belonged to someone else. "I am glad to be home again," she said with a sigh. "London is not for me. I belong here in the country where I can enjoy my solitude."

Where you can hide in your suite.

"Carry on," she said, turning to leave. But then she turned back again. "You're a fine dancer, Molly. You'd do even better with a real partner."

My thoughts exactly.

"Did you have anyone in mind?"

Molly hesitated, but only for a moment. "No, my lady. Just the man of my dreams *in* my dreams."

"Those are always the best men."

As soon as the countess left, Molly found her mouth dry. As a lady's maid she was not allowed a suitor. If she was found out, she could lose her position.

And to be more particular, Molly could not have Morgan Hayward as her suitor. For his mother was her mistress's least favorite person in the world. Molly wasn't certain about the details of the antagonism between the two women, but she had quickly learned never to speak Fidelia Hayward's name.

Whether Mrs. Hayward reciprocated the animosity, Molly didn't know. The only contact Molly had ever had with Morgan's mother was during assorted transactions at the mercantile. But reciprocated or not, Molly knew it was imperative the countess never know of her romance with Morgan.

At least not until he proposed.

She smiled at the thought.

Ruth Weston, the Countess of Summerfield, stood before the bay windows in her bedroom suite, and watched the commotion on the estate grounds. Wagons laden with trunks and supplies made the transfer from their London flat back to Summerfield Manor. It was all rather silly. Moving an entire household from here to there and back again, all for a few parties. All to be *seen*.

She didn't want to be seen.

Not that she wasn't proud to be on the arm of her husband and be presented as the Earl and Countess of Summerfield. It was every woman's dream to be the mistress of a grand, ancestral estate, to wear gorgeous gowns and lavish jewels. To hobnob with members of Parliament. To have Queen Victoria and her heir, Prince Edward, greet her by name. To have no cares, no needs.

But many worries.

There was a knock on her bedroom door. "Come in."

Upon seeing her husband, she stood taller and smoothed her skirt. "Frederick."

"Just checking on you, my dear. I hope the journey wasn't too strenuous?"

"Strenuous, yes, but not too. And you?"

"Tis a bother to be sure, but what must be done, must be done, yes?"

She nodded. "For our daughter's sake, if for no other reason."

"Hmm," he said, strolling to her windows. "Nice view here."

"Yes, it is."

He turned to her. "Speaking of Clarissa . . . although she had many suitors, once again, she did not secure a proposal."

"She is impetuous and totally charming. I do not blame her for freely enjoying the attention."

"That was fine when she was young, but now that she is twenty-one, it's time for her to temper herself and marry."

By the furrow in his brow, she could tell this weighed heavily on him, and knew it *should* weigh heavily on herself. "Do you have someone in mind?"

"Actually, yes. I've been talking with Mother about it, and she agrees Joseph Kidd would be the most suitable match."

"Isn't he rather . . . serious?" she said.

He looked surprised. "I'm glad he's a serious young man. His father is setting him up to run for a seat."

"A seat in Parliament will make him very serious indeed."

"Clarissa needs a strong hand."

But not an iron one. "She needs someone who appreciates her . . . exuberance."

"Excessive exuberance."

Ruth couldn't argue. "She's much like I was," she said quietly.

Frederick paused, as if trying to find a long-forgotten image of the young Ruth. "Yes, well. There's a time for exuberance and a time to leave frivolities behind."

Did he equate exuberance with frivolity?

But he was right. It was time for Clarissa to grow up. Yet the thought of it made her sad. "It is not as if she is an old maid. There is time enough for —"

"There is *not* time," he said, his voice rising. "I need this settled. I need her to stop playing games and act her age." His face had grown red and splotchy.

"Frederick . . . what's going on? Why are you so fervent about this?"

He strode toward the door. "It is just time, that's all. It is time to change a lot of things."

Was he talking about their marriage? In London she'd seen him laughing and flirting with Lady Carlton. Her fear of seeing them together had provided an extra incentive for her to stay behind while he went out. To not see was better than seeing. To not be there when people whispered behind closed hands was better than pretending there was nothing wrong. Now, with him talking about change, she feared . . .

She pushed the thoughts aside. She had to focus on Clarissa. "Don't you want our daughter to be happy?"

"A person must make her own happiness." He paused at the door. "You know, my dear, now that we're home, you needn't fall into your old habit of closeting yourself away."

"I do not closet —"

He threw up his hands. "Suit yourself. Whatever makes you happy." He left her.

Happiness was a foreign concept.

Frederick deserves better than me. Always has. If he knew what I did to win him . . .

The admonitions never left her. That she'd won the prize yet felt inept while living the life that accompanied it was a punishment from God. What was achieved by ill-gotten means could never flourish and thrive.

She moved to her embroidery, a needlepoint seat for her rocker. As soon as she took the first stitch, up and back, she felt herself calm. The tug of the wool through the mesh, the soft *whoup* sound of another completed stitch . . . yes, it was good to be back in Summerfield where she could live out her penance in solitude and peace.

That others had to suffer with her was unfortunate.

Perhaps someday she could make it up to them.

She said that a lot. Someday, something would change. But

when was that elusive someday? They'd been married twenty-two years and she was still dogged by the past.

Then change. Set down your needlework and involve yourself in all aspects of your family. Be a better wife, a better mother, a better countess.

Frederick's words came back to her: *"You know, my dear, now that we're home, you needn't fall into your old habit of closeting yourself away."*

She shook her head. "I don't know how to do otherwise."

You'd better figure it out. Think of Lady Carlton and all of the other women who find Frederick attractive. You must change, or you'll lose him.

It was their first day home. It was the perfect time to start fresh.

She felt a stirring inside and sensed it wasn't nervous insecurity, but a rush of energy that was meant to propel her forward. "Yes. I must try. I must."

And so she set her needlework aside and went to the door of her suite. She opened it and took a single step into the upstairs hall. There was commotion downstairs, and she heard the butler's voice, giving directions.

But then it was quiet. The faint ticking of the clock in the foyer matched the beating of her heart.

She stepped to the railing and peered down to the marble floor below. With more than sixty servants employed to care for the manor, the silence was astonishing. Yet they were all adept at working behind the scenes, below stairs, making a point of not coming in contact with the family unless they were bidden.

I am the mistress of the manor.

In name only. For the responsibilities of her station still belonged to Ruth's mother-in-law, the dowager countess. Although Ruth should have assumed those duties when Frederick became earl, with her mother-in-law stepping aside, the latter woman possessed a dictatorial manner and an ability to do all things well. Consumed with self-doubt and guilt, Ruth had willingly abdicated her duties to the better woman.

She had no place in this household. She was a title without a position and a woman without a role.

It is your own fault.

She let the rebuke wrap around her like a shroud. She had no excuse.

And no way out.

This is ridiculous. Walk down those stairs and live your life with people instead of setting yourself apart.

Her heart beat in a faster rhythm than the clock, and she pressed a hand to her chest.

But then thirteen-year-old George burst out of his room, racing to the stairs. At the sight of her, he skidded to a stop. "Mamma?"

"Hello, George."

"What are you doing out?"

He said 'out' as though she'd escaped from a prison. "I was just . . . getting a book."

"I'm going to help curry the horses, and Johnny wants to see my new riding crop." He raised it for her inspection.

"Good for you."

That is all I can say? Why can't I have a proper conversation with my own son?

He ran past her, and in his wake she felt like a statue being bypassed without a second thought. Perhaps she should extend a graceful hand like a Grecian woman affecting a pose.

His footfalls echoed in the foyer. The front door slammed shut, keeping her in and all else, out.

The world didn't want her to intrude and certainly didn't need her.

She turned her back on it and returned to her room.

Prison or not, she felt safe there.

Besides, where better to suffer for her sins?

Where is that girl?

The dowager countess spotted the butler giving instruction to the hall boy. "Dixon?"

He stopped their conversation, and the boy stepped away. "Yes, your ladyship?"

"Have you seen Lady Clarissa?"

"I believe I saw her go upstairs. Shall I get her for you, my lady?"

"That will not be necessary." She ascended the sweeping staircase, feeling every day of her sixty-six years. The confined spaces and inactivity of travel always made her bones ache. What she really needed was a long walk across the grounds or through the gardens to make sure they had been kept to her standards while the family was gone.

But first things first.

At the top of the stairs, Adelaide walked down the long corridor to her granddaughter's room, rapped twice, then opened the door.

Clarissa sat on her bed, reading a letter. "Grandmamma. You startled me."

Adelaide made a quick survey of the bed, which was scattered with letters and notes. "Counting your conquests, I see."

"Just taking inventory."

She noticed some torn paper on the rug. "A few rejects?"

"One. A very wordy one. He was attentive but did not rise to my standards."

Adelaide selected a note, scanned it, then tossed it back on the bed. "Perhaps your standards are too high. Three London seasons, Clarissa. That is plenty of time for any girl to find a husband."

She sighed. "Can I help it if I enjoy the game?"

"Games must be finished. Games must have a winner."

"I want to be married as much as the next girl. But in playing the game, I do not wish to be the loser."

"Neither do we."

"We?"

Adelaide turned back toward the door. "Your father and I wish to speak with you."

"About?"

"Come to his study. We will be waiting."

Clarissa slid off the bed, her forehead tight. "Surely you won't force me—"

"We will be waiting."

"You must be strong, Frederick," the dowager countess told her son. "You know how Clarissa can manipulate—"

When he glanced toward the door, she let the sentence go.

"Clarissa, my dear," Frederick said. "Come join us."

Clarissa swept in the room and flowed behind him like the tide drowning a pebble. She wrapped her arms around his neck, kissing his cheek. "Are you glad to be home, Father?"

"Yes and no," he said. "For there's always much to do to get caught up with the business of the estate. Thank God Mr. Collins has handled it while we've been gone."

"Sit, child," Adelaide said, from her chair on the other side of the desk. "We have something to talk to you about."

"Ooh, so serious," she teased. "That's one of the reasons I hate coming home. In London I can be carefree and breezy, but back here in Summerfield I am confined and trapped."

"You are not trapped in Summerfield," Frederick said. "It is your privilege to live here. Are you trapped being my daughter too?"

She flipped away his challenge. "Of course not. But you must agree that the three months in London are a lovely lark."

"They are not a lark," Adelaide said. "There are duties to be done there too. Your duty was to find yourself a mate."

Clarissa sat in the chair near her grandmother, leaning back as much as her bustle would allow. She draped her arms over the carved arms of the chair. Too nonchalant. Too unconcerned.

"I'm all for marriage, but I'm in no rush. Let me be young

and merry while I can."

"The time for being merry is over," Adelaide said.

Clarissa looked at Adelaide, then her father. "I don't like the sounds of this."

"Actually," Adelaide said, adjusting the cuff on her sleeve, "it does not much matter whether you like it or not."

Clarissa traced the curve of the chair's arms. "I suppose if you want me to choose . . ."

Frederick cleared his throat. "Toward that end, we have chosen for you."

Her hands stilled. "*You* have?"

"*We* have," Adelaide said.

Clarissa sat forward, and for the first time Adelaide saw a flash of fear in her eyes. And anger. But to the girl's credit she pressed those emotions down and smiled. "I do hope he's handsome, dashing, and terribly rich."

"Actually, he is."

Her laugh was forced. "Do I know him?"

"Very well. It is Joseph Kidd."

Her face fell. "A neighbor. Someone I have known my entire life."

"That can be an advantage."

"Out of all the men in the world."

She had a point. "You have spent a great deal of time with the man. I wager some of those notes you were perusing were from him."

"One. One note. I had forgotten a fan in his carriage."

Is that all the contact they had?

Clarissa smoothed the piping on the drapery of her skirt. "Joseph is a nice boy. But why him?"

"It does not matter why," her father said. "Just know it has been arranged. His father agrees and we agree, and so —"

The smile left her, and she stood. "I have no say in it at all?"

Frederick looked to his desk, and Adelaide could tell he wanted to give in.

Now was not the time to waver. "We have waited for you

to gain a proposal, but it never happens. You never seal the deal."

"The deal? Marriage is not a deal, Grandmamma."

Adelaide shook her head. "Do not be naïve."

Frederick looked at her imploringly, and Adelaide knew he wanted her to handle the situation without him. She gave him a stern look. *Be a man. Be an earl.*

With a sigh he said, "Be reasonable, Clarissa. You were told before we went to London that it was time for you to settle down."

"But I have no desire to settle down, be married, and get fat with children. If you would let me do what I want, I would spread my wings and fly. I would sing and act on the London stage, and—"

Adelaide raised her eyebrows. "What's this about the stage?"

"Nothing," she said.

Adelaide couldn't let the subject pass so easily. "Women of breeding and circumstance do not perform on the stage."

Clarissa lifted her chin, but the act of defiance was weak. "Even if they have great talent?"

"Dramatic and musical talent can be shared in the drawing room. That is enough for well-bred young ladies."

"But it's not enough!" Clarissa quickly looked at the floor.

Adelaide could tell Clarissa regretted her outburst. She was not one to show her hand. Actually, it was rather fascinating to watch her granddaughter's face struggle to move from anger to appeasement, but within seconds Clarissa smiled and strolled to her father's side.

"But, Father, Joseph Kidd?" She shuddered. "He is just a boy, and so utterly proper."

"He is headed for a chair in Parliament."

Clarissa made a face, as if she had smelled something offensive.

"The decision has been made. You will marry Joseph."

"But we don't love each other."

"You enjoyed his company in London," Father said.

"I enjoyed the company of many young men. I may have flirted with Joseph and he with me, but that's all it was. It's what we do. It doesn't mean I would ever want to marry him—or would even consider such a thing."

"It is not for you to consider anymore. He comes from a good family. His father is a viscount and an advisor to the Queen."

"Good for him. I need—I want someone with more fire."

Adelaide shook her head. "You are fiery enough on your own. You need someone to quench the heat of you."

"But I don't want to be quenched!" She knelt beside his chair and touched his arm. "Father, please."

"I am sorry. It is all arranged."

He avoided her gaze and moved his arm toward some papers, letting her hand fall.

The decades faded and Adelaide remembered kneeling beside her own father, begging him not to make her marry Samuel Weston, the tenth Earl of Summerfield. Even now she felt a hitch in her stomach. But since memories and regret were useless commodities, she forced the thoughts away.

Clarissa rose to her feet, stumbling as her heel caught in her train. "This isn't fair! I thought you respected me more than this. I thought you wanted me to be happy."

Frederick's voice was soft. "I do respect you, and of course I want you to be happy. But I need you to do this. For me." He looked up at her, touching her hand. "Please, Clarissa. Marry Joseph for the good of the family."

She shook his touch away and rushed toward the door, pausing long enough to glare at them both. "I can't believe you're asking me to do this."

Adelaide rose. "But we are. And that's the end of it."

Clarissa tilted her head left, then right, and then Adelaide saw a change come over her. A decision was being made.

Why did that make her nervous?

Clarissa let out a dramatic sigh. "All right. I suppose Joseph is as good as any other. He does have his own appeal, and an intriguing smile." She bounced twice on her toes.

"Very well then. Joseph it is. I shall send a note to Crompton Hall and ask him out riding."

"That's a marvelous idea," Frederick said.

Adelaide wanted to point out that Clarissa should wait for Joseph to extend the invitation but wasn't up to risking another argument.

"Ta-ta then," Clarissa said, heading out the door. "I am off to tear my other love notes into the tiniest of pieces. If I am dedicated to Joseph, then I dare not let my mind stray elsewhere."

"Very commendable, my dear," Frederick said.

"Yes it is, isn't it?" Clarissa strode from the room, pulling the air out with her.

Adelaide released the breath she'd been saving. "Something is amiss."

"Why do you say that? She agreed."

"It was too easy. She moved from nay to yay too quickly."

Frederick leaned back in his chair and pressed the palms of his hands against his eyes. "Perhaps. But we must focus on the fact she did agree."

Adelaide shook her head and muttered, "Too easy. . ."

"I do hate making her marry Joseph, I hate making her marry anyone."

"We don't have a choice."

He nodded. "But to risk my daughter's happiness . . ."

"Such is duty."

He expelled a long breath. "At least I married for love. As did you."

Even as Adelaide congratulated herself for putting duty above all else, she mourned the same.

"My lady," Dixon said when Adelaide returned to the manor house after checking the flower beds. "A gentleman stopped by and left his card. I am sorry we couldn't find you."

"I have been hiding in the garden, Dixon. Trying to catch a

breath of breeze."

"It is rather warm today." He handed her the calling card, bowed, and left her.

She held the card at arm's length, squinted, brought it closer, then away again. There. Now she could read —

Colonel Grady Cummings.

Her heart skipped. Grady?

Adelaide hurried after Dixon, waving the card. "Dixon! The man. This card. What did he say? How long ago did he leave?"

"He left right after arriving, my lady. But he did say he would come to call tomorrow morning."

"Did he say where he was staying?"

"No, my lady. Would you like me to send someone after him?"

She forced herself to calm down. A deep breath helped her regain her countess composure. "That will not be necessary."

She was left standing in the foyer, with her heart beating out of her chest. Grady was here. He was back. Grady. Her darling Grady.

Tomorrow couldn't come too soon.

But as quickly as the thought was born, she forced it to die.

Grady? What did he want with her? He was from another life and knew another Adelaide — one that no longer existed.

She shook the memories away.

Unfortunately, tomorrow would come too soon.

Chapter Three

Lila Hayward watched through the open doorway of the mercantile as her mother gossiped with two of her friends about some stranger in town. A colonel.

Apparently he'd known the dowager before she was married, a fact which added to all sorts of speculation. A few of the oldest villagers seemed to remember him, but all suffered a disappointing lack of detail.

Papa came up behind her, sharing the view. "The village grapevine is losing some leaves."

"If the dowager wasn't titled, no one would think twice about the appearance of an old friend."

"So you're saying there are a few benefits to being ordinary folk?"

"A few." It was fascinating to witness all three ladies talk at the same time.

Father nodded toward the flowers Lila had just arranged in a vase. "Those are pretty."

She felt a bit guilty for getting sidetracked by the gossip. "I thought they'd brighten Nana's morning."

"That's my Lila. Always thinking of others."

She didn't argue the compliment, but knew it wasn't true. She *wished* it were true. She took the flowers upstairs and found her grandmother standing at the washbasin, splashing cold water on her face. "You're up," she said.

Nana dabbed her face with a towel. "I didn't realize how tired I was. I went to bed early and slept late." She saw the flowers. "How pretty."

Lila set them on the dresser and adjusted a daisy stem to reach the water. "I thought they would make the room more pleasant."

"The room is pleasant enough, but thank you." Nana leaned close to the flowers and inhaled the scent. "Did your beau get his commission for the letter box from the dowager?"

"He's not my beau."

Nana looked taken aback. "I'm sorry. The way your mother talked about him . . ."

"Mother wants me to marry and doesn't much care who it is." She turned to leave.

"Oh no you don't." Nana sat upon the bed and patted the place beside her. "What's making this fine day foul?"

Lila had to smile. "I see you far too seldom for you to know me so well."

"I'm your nana."

Lila sat beside her. "Mother never senses my moods — or has care of them." She stood. "I'd better get back to work."

"What's his name?"

Lila put her hands on her face. "Am I that transparent?"

"Only partially. I expected a man might be to blame."

"He's not to blame. Actually he doesn't even have a name."

"Now *that* might be a problem."

Lila sank onto the bed. "It's the thought of a man that plagues me. A bosom friend and partner who holds me up as his one and only. Of course, I'd feel the same about him."

"And Timothy is not that man?"

She shook her head. "He is kind and polite and loyal."

"Sounds like a puppy."

Lila laughed. "I know he *would* follow me wherever I go."

"So you don't wish to lead?"

She pondered this a moment. "Perhaps a little. I want a strong man who can inspire me, who can work beside me and with me to create a wonderful life."

Nana put an arm around her shoulders and squeezed. "He's out there."

"Is he?"

"Don't you think he is?"

Lila's nod had no power in it. "I pray I recognize him and we live happily ever after."

"Then I'll add my prayers to yours. Someday your prince *will* come."

Lila laughed softly. "But what if he's a frog?"

Nana made a face. "No frogs. Their legs are too skinny."

Lila leaned against her. "I'm so glad you came to live with us."

"As am I, sweet girl. As am I."

After greeting her mother in her family's cottage, Molly marveled at how tall her brother had grown in the three months she'd been away in London. Ten year-old Lon had sprouted a good two inches. She tapped the boy's freckled nose. "You're going to be tall as me soon."

Then she winked at her sister. Dottie, though only twelve, was showing signs of womanhood. Yet the sight of her blossoming figure made Molly nervous.

"How's yer job?" Ma asked. "The countess still locking herself in her room?"

"She does no such thing, and I don't want you spreading such gossip."

"I'm just repeating what you told me."

"I've only said she prefers her own company."

"And yours, I hope." Ma took the second of Lon's shirts from the washtub and pinned it to the clothesline. "You have a good time in jolly ole London town?"

Molly felt herself blush. "Actually, I did."

Ma gave her a good study. "There's a man behind that blush, don't I know it."

She was bursting to tell someone. "It's Morgan Hayward."

Ma's brow furrowed. "Ain't he off at school?"

"He's on his way home after the term. He stopped off in

London. I saw him there."

"And?" Ma raised and lowered her brows.

Her sister took sudden interest. "Is he your beau?" Dottie asked.

Molly tried to smooth the back of Dottie's hair, which needed a good brushing. "We started seeing each other before he left for school, and since then we've been writing. He's coming home soon. He said he'd send me a letter before then. I checked at the manor, but there was nothing. Did you get anything for me here?"

Ma nodded to Dottie, who ran in the house. "Picked it up this morning, I did. You owe me pence for the post."

Dottie returned with a letter in hand. Molly wanted to rip it open and read it right there but realized discretion was a better choice. She put it in her pocket.

"Having a beau is fine and good," Ma said. "But don't lose your position over it. You know the Westons won't look kindly on romance between their servants."

"He's not a servant."

"But you are." Ma tugged a tendril by Molly's ear. "You've risen from under-housemaid to lady's maid, a feat seldom done. I won't have you throwing that away for nobody."

"But I don't want to be a lady's maid forever."

Dottie ran a hand along the sleeve of Molly's voile blouse. "I want to be a lady's maid. I want to wear milady's hand-me-downs like you do."

Molly pulled her arm away from her sister's grimy fingers. "It's properly said 'my lady', not 'milady.' And you'll need to learn how to brush your hair and scrub your hands before you can do scrubbing at the manor."

Ma's expression clouded, then she nodded at Dottie, "Go with yer brother and check the chickens for eggs. Go on now."

When the children had left, Ma slipped her hand around Molly's arm. "I needs you to get Dottie a job at the manor."

Molly watched Ma glance toward the village, where she saw her da laughing with his cronies in the square. Her nerves tingled. "Has he . . . ?"

"Not yet. But you see how she's growed."

Horrific memories surfaced. Going into service at twelve had been more than a job for Molly. "Why don't you leave him, Ma?"

"And where would I go? I've never been five miles from Summerfield. Besides, who would believe me? Who would believe you?"

They watched Dottie and Lon chasing the chickens, laughing and teasing each other.

"What about Lon?"

Ma looked at her, confused. "He's a boy."

Molly hoped that would keep him safe. But evil was evil. She wanted the conversation over. "I'll see what I can do. There *is* one under-housemaid who's been complaining a lot. If she gets the sack. . ." Molly thought of something. "Dottie would need a black dress and a white apron, and another plain dress and apron for the hard work."

Ma nodded. "I already got the black one made — thanks to you sending some of yer wages to me. And the other one's cut out."

"So you assumed I could get her a position?"

"She's got to get away."

The butler appeared in the doorway of the morning room as Adelaide attended to her correspondence. "There's a Colonel Cummings here to see you, my lady."

Adelaide's stomach flipped. She thought about telling Dixon to send him in, for the morning room would provide privacy. But she wasn't sure she wanted privacy.

"I will join him in the drawing room."

"Very good, my lady."

She rose and adjusted her skirt and bustle so it draped to its best advantage. She paused at a gilded mirror and captured the stray hairs near her ears that always found their way free. Then she pinched her cheeks, bit her lower lip, and suffered a wave of embarrassment for the actions. She wasn't some ingénue, trying to impress a man. She was Lady Summerfield greeting a guest. It was pure and simple. Or so she kept telling herself.

At the sight of Colonel Grady Cummings standing near the fireplace, Adelaide's heart suffered an extra beat. The breadth of his shoulders was much appreciated, and his height commanded attention. But his wavy hair had turned gray. *As has yours, you silly woman.*

"My, my. It is you," she said.

When he turned and smiled, the years evaporated. "It is me."

He went to her, his hands extended. His grip was firm, yet gentle. He kissed her cheeks, and they stood there a long moment, connected through touch and history.

Touch. No one but family touched her. Propriety declared it so.

She pulled her hands away. "What has brought you here to Summerfield, Colonel Cummings?"

"You, my dear Addie. You."

She suffered the need to swallow. "Will you have a seat?"

He settled on one end of a settee, leaving room for her beside him. Adelaide sat in a chair nearby.

His gaze swept the room. "Nice little place you have here."

She took advantage of his question. "The manor was built by the fourth Earl of Summerfield in 1640," she said. "The wings were added fifty years later, with the back sunroom added by my father-in-law soon before he died."

"I did not come here for a history lesson." Grady looked at her straight on. "As I said before, I came here for you."

What exactly did he mean? "Colonel, I —"

"Grady, Addie. You must call me Grady."

I must not call you Grady, because if I do, it will all come rushing back. "There is protocol for such things, Colonel, and I can not, I will not . . ."

"You can and you will be my Addie again."

Her heart stopped. Only by willing herself to breathe did it start again. She managed to stand but found her legs weak. "You have gone too far."

"I have come too far. All the way from India. All the way from the past into the present. Our present."

He'd always had a way with words. "You can't walk into my life forty-seven years after you left it."

"After you sent me away."

Adelaide tried to calm her breathing. "I did not send you away."

"You rejected me. You succumbed to your parents' wishes and married an earl."

"He wasn't an earl yet."

He cocked his head at the weakness of her point, then continued, "I couldn't stay in Summerfield and watch you love another man."

I never loved Samuel. Not wholly.

Finding it impossible to hold his gaze, she strolled to the mantel, giving her attention to the clock. *Tick tock. Tock tick.* The pendulum swung. Time moved on.

Grady's voice softened. "I left Summerfield, trying to outrun my pain."

She knew about pain and squeezed her eyes shut against it. "Did you succeed?"

"I was diverted." She heard him take a fresh breath and clap his hands upon his thighs. "But now that I'm retired, I have been pondering what to do with the rest of my life."

Her throat was tight, wanting, but not wanting him to say it. "And what did you decide?"

"Look at me, Addie."

She turned around, trying to apply her best countess face, chin high, gaze strong.

He moved close. She knew she should step away, but couldn't. Seeing his blue eyes, like the blue in a moonstone . . . against her will she felt her countenance soften.

Grady didn't touch her, but leaned close enough to whisper. "I decided that we've wasted enough time being apart. I have loved you my entire life. It's time we do something about it."

She could feel his breath upon her cheek. She wanted him to kiss her. She wanted him to move away. She wanted —

Dixon cleared his throat from the doorway. "Excuse me, your ladyship, but the housekeeper desires direction in regard to the inventory of some dishes."

She was pulled back to the present in all its practical glory. "Certainly, Dixon."

She took a step away from Grady, but before she could say her goodbyes, he strode to the butler, clapped him on the back, and stood beside him. "Did you know that yesterday when I came to the manor, Charles and I discovered we were once mates? He opened the door and I recognized him. How long has it been, Charles?"

Dixon stood stiffly, staring straight ahead. "I left the army thirty-two years ago, sir."

"Don't call me *sir*. We were friends."

"If I recall, I was a private and you had just made lieutenant. Sir."

Adelaide could tell Dixon was uncomfortable with the entire conversation. She vaguely remembered when he'd applied for a job as under-footman he'd mentioned being in the army for a time.

"Would you get the colonel his things, Dixon?" she asked.

He returned with Grady's walking stick and hat, then retreated to a position by the door. Luckily there was no way to give Grady anything but the most proper goodbye, so Adelaide held out her hand. Grady nodded and drew it to his lips.

"Good day, Colonel," she said.

"Good day . . ."

Please don't call me Addie in front of Dixon.

". . . Lady Summerfield," he said, but sealed his exit with a wink. "Until two tomorrow, then."

Two? Who'd said anything about two? But she didn't contradict him. "Tomorrow."

Dixon let him out, and Adelaide escaped toward the back of the house to meet with the housekeeper. It was either that or risk Dixon seeing her blush.

Molly replied to the countess's summons. "Yes, my lady?"

Ruth threaded an embroidery needle with orange wool, trying to act nonchalant. "I saw a very handsome older gentleman arrive at the house. He just left, but I wondered who he was."

"I don't know, my lady. Would you like me to find out?"

She pulled the thread through her needlework of a bird of paradise, then added a sigh for effect. "I *would* be interested."

Molly nodded and began to leave. Ruth called after her, "Discretion, Molly."

"Yes, your ladyship."

Molly spotted Nick readying the dining room for the mid-day meal. The footman looked up from aligning the knives and forks with a rod. "Hello there, pretty Molly."

She smiled and picked up a sterling fork, pretending to admire the intricacy of its pattern. "Who was the man who came calling?"

"What'll you give me for the information?" He winked.

"A good slap if you don't behave yourself."

His charm left him. "Don't get all hoity-toity with me, *Miss* Wallace. We all know your first job here was emptying the chamber pots."

He'd hit a sore spot. But the countess was waiting. "If you don't want to tell me, fine." She turned as if to leave.

Nick shrugged. "It was a Colonel Cummings, asking to see the dowager."

"I've never heard of him."

"No one has." He moved close. "But I couldn't help but hear them talking in the drawing room, and it appears they have a history."

"History?"

"Forty-seven years was mentioned."

Molly wasn't certain of the dowager's age, but knew that amount of time would place her back in her youth.

"And he called her Addie."

That bit of information was more shocking than the other. Molly couldn't imagine anyone calling the dowager by her first name—and a nickname, no less.

Nick huffed on the bowl of a spoon and buffed it with a towel. "Whoever he is, he came today and he's coming tomorrow at two. And . . ." He drew the last word out, crooking his finger to get her to move even closer. "He knew Mr. Dixon before he was Mr. Dixon. They were both in Her Majesty's."

"The colonel was a servant?"

"Not that kind of service. The military. Can you imagine old Dixon *taking* orders?"

There was movement in the hallway so they stepped apart. Dixon walked in, and raised an eyebrow at Molly's presence.

"Good morning, Mr. Dixon," she said.

"Good morning, Miss Wallace. May we help you?"

"I was just checking the day's menu from Nick—for the countess, sir."

"Will she be joining the family?"

As if she ever came down to dine. "Probably not, sir."

"Very well then." He glanced at the doorway.

As she moved to leave, he cleared his throat. "Does the countess require the use of a fork, Miss Wallace?"

She felt herself redden, handed it to him, and fled.

"Colonel Cummings?" Ruth said. "I've never heard of him."

"Apparently he knew the dowager when she was young."

The way Molly looked away indicated there was more. "And?"

"He called her by her first name. Actually, a nickname: Addie."

Ruth was taken aback. Adelaide an Addie?

"He's coming to call again tomorrow."

Curiouser and curiouser.

Molly was waiting to be excused. "Thank you for your help. That will be all for now."

As soon as the door closed behind her, Ruth stepped toward it. She desperately wanted to find out more about this man and his relationship to her mother-in-law. She put her hand on the knob, but as she began to turn it, she hesitated.

Even if she did venture out of this room, who could she turn to for information?

The dowager?

As if she'd give me the time of day.

Clarissa?

Why should she do anything for me?

Frederick?

Never mind.

Something new and interesting was going on in this house. But it might as well have been a state secret for all the chance Ruth had to tap into it.

Molly left her mistress in her room, glad for some free time to mend a blouse. It was a beautiful ivory organza with tiny tucks down the bodice and delicate lace at the neck and cuff. The lace was so fine that it had ripped when the countess caught it on the tightening-screw of her embroidery frame.

But on the way to retrieve the blouse from her second-story room, she spotted Bea, an under-housemaid, sitting in an alcove on the first floor, right outside the dowager's bedroom. As soon as Bea saw her, she popped up and began dusting the chair. It wasn't the first time Molly had caught Bea slacking. Plus, it was rumored the girl was homesick.

Bea nodded at Molly as she passed.

"Working hard, I see?"

"Yes, Miss Wallace."

Molly walked by, then turned back. "You don't like your position here very much, do you, Bea?"

"Of course I like it. Of course."

Molly gave her a knowing look. "You miss your family, don't you?"

Bea hesitated.

Molly leaned closer. "You can tell me."

Bea looked both ways down the hall. "Truth be, I wants to go home."

"I don't blame you."

"You don't?"

"Why should you be unhappy? I'm sure your family misses you horribly."

"I *was* thinking of leaving."

Molly's heart beat faster. "Again, I don't blame you."

"You don't?"

Suddenly, Molly feared that Bea would blab and say that Molly had urged her to quit. That would not help her sister's chance of getting the position. "I do understand your feelings, but working at the manor . . . having a position here should not be taken lightly. It's a privilege."

Bea let out a laugh. "Getting up at five and working till dark. Some privilege."

They both looked toward the end of the hall. Gertie, the head housemaid, strode toward them, her jaw set.

"What's going on here?" Gertie asked.

"Bea and I were just having a discussion." Molly looked at the girl, hoping she'd walk through the door Molly had opened.

"I'm giving me notice," Bea said.

Gertie looked from Bea to Molly.

"It appears she's unhappy here," Molly said.

Gertie glared at Bea. "Since when is your happiness my concern?"

"I wanna go home," Bea said. "The work's too hard. I needs me sleep."

"So you're going to run home and sleep till noon? Your family farms. You'll be up to your eyebrows in chores."

"Maybe so, but I'd rather do chores there than chores here."

"Stupid girl," Gertie hissed.

Molly was thrilled the situation was progressing so nicely, but she needed to cover her own culpability. "Perhaps if Mrs. Camden spoke with her?"

Gertie rested her hands on her ample hips. "So yer saying I can't handle it?"

"Miss Wallace understands," Bea said. "She'd let me go."

Molly pressed down a wave of panic. "I never said I'd let you go. You made a commitment to the manor. You should do your job to your fullest ability."

"But I don't fancy the job." She pressed her dust cloth into Gertie's hand. "And I won't do it." With no further ado, she ran toward the servant's stair to gather her things from her room in the attic.

Gertie's head wagged and she stared at the dust cloth a moment before stuffing it into the pocket of her apron. "What am I going to do with one less? And I do *not* relish telling Mrs. Camden about it. She just had to hire a new scullery, and now this?"

"I'm sorry for your inconvenience. I know how hard it is to get good help."

"Near impossible, if you ask me."

"I was on my way to speak with Mrs. Camden about something," Molly said. "If you'd like, I could tell her about Bea leaving. Pave the way."

"Well then. That would be right nice of you, Miss Wallace."

"I'm happy to help."

More than happy.

Molly found Mrs. Camden in the dish room speaking with the dowager countess, who was just leaving.

"Your ladyship," Molly said with a curtsy.

"Miss Wallace."

As soon as the dowager was gone, Molly approached the housekeeper. "May I have a word?"

The housekeeper was consulting a list. "How the dish inventory can change in three months when the family's been gone . . . I have a mind to go room to room and even house to house to see who's been pinching our dishes." Mrs. Camden looked up with a sigh. "Well then, what is it?"

"I'm sorry to be the bearer of bad news, but we are now short one under-housemaid."

The older woman rolled her eyes. "What's Bea done now?"

"She quit. Gertie tried to get her to stay, but the girl desperately wants to go home."

"Good riddance. If a girl can't do the work, she doesn't belong at the manor." She set the list on the ledge of the floor-to-ceiling dish cabinets. "But why are *you* telling me?"

It was the perfect opening. "I know a girl who might fill the position."

"Do you now."

"She's a hard worker, eager to be taught, and comes from a good family."

Mrs. Camden tilted her head, clearly suspicious. "I'm listening."

"It's my little sister, Dottie. She's twelve — which was my age when I came to work at the manor in the very same position. I could keep an eye on her and make sure she does the work properly. She's a respectful girl who'd be eager for the opportunity."

The housekeeper gave a small, knowing smile. "This sounds very convenient. Are you sure you haven't been urging Bea to leave so there'd be an opening?"

Molly hoped her face wouldn't flush with guilt. "It's common knowledge she's homesick and hasn't been doing her work. Many a time I've caught her sitting down on the fancy furniture, or lollygagging."

"Don't I know it."

"If you'd like, I'll write a note to my mother and ask her to send Dottie over for an interview."

The housekeeper took up her list. "Have the hall boy run it over. Tell your sister to be here tomorrow to speak with the dowager and me."

Molly returned upstairs, letting her feet tap a happy rhythm step to step. Dottie would be out of the house, away from their da.

She'd be safe.

Chapter Four

Reverend Lyons cupped Nana's hand between his own. "We're glad to have you join our parish, Mrs. Hayward. Your son is a marvelous man. You must be very proud of him."

"I am, Reverend. And he's the best of sons for taking me in."

"Toward that, I am sorry for your loss. To lose a spouse is devastating." The vicar's gaze lowered.

"When did you lose your wife, if I may ask?"

Lila was impressed with Nana's sensitivity.

So was Reverend Lyons. "It appears you have a talent for perception, Mrs. Hayward. My wife passed away four years ago. A finer lady never lived." He seemed to momentarily leave them for his memories before returning to the present. "And your granddaughter, here, is well on her way to being just as fine."

"For that compliment I'll happily bake you a blackberry pie," Lila said.

"And I will happily eat it." He looked at Nana. "Can we expect you at services this Sunday, Mrs. Hayward?"

"I . . ." Nana seemed nervous. "I'm not sure. Lately I prefer to do my worship in private. I mean no offense."

"None taken. The Lord will accept all offerings. Just know you are welcome here." He removed his spectacles and polished them with the bottom of his jacket. "Now, Lila. When is your brother due home from school?"

"Soon," Lila said. "Though as usual his exact arrival date is unknown. He likes to keep us guessing."

"Ah, to be young and carefree," the vicar said.

Lila took offense. "Begging your pardon, Morgan is not carefree. He's a very hard worker."

"Then I stand corrected." When he smiled his eyes twinkled, revealing his good nature. "And how lucky he is to have such a loyal sister."

"He'd do the same for me."

"Good for him." He led them to the entrance of the church. "Give your father and brother my regards. And I hope to see you on Sunday, Mrs. Hayward."

As they walked away, Nana shared an observation. "Reverend Lyons didn't include your mother in his regards."

My, she's perceptive. "They don't get along."

"Why?" Nana asked. "From what I've seen, Fidelia is kind and approachable to *others*, and I would think she would be on her best behavior towards the vicar."

Lila was reluctant to speak ill of her mother. "Let's just say that Reverend Lyons also possesses the gift of perception."

To curtail village speculation about Nana's identity, the two women spent the rest of the morning bisecting and dissecting the town, with Lila tirelessly making the introductions. Most villagers were friendly and welcomed Nana, but a few seemed wary. Not many strangers came to Summerfield.

"How was your morning, ladies?" Papa asked once they made their way back to the mercantile.

"Very fine," Nana answered. "The people of Summerfield were quite welcoming. But it got me thinking . . . since I am now a member of their community, I'd like to do my part by working in the store with all of you."

"But you're in mourning," Papa said.

"And I will continue to mourn. But I feel useless sitting around *in* mourning while the rest of you do all the work. Give me something to do, or I will go mad."

Fidelia stepped out from the storeroom. "I forbid it. It's not proper."

Lila suffered a silent sigh. If Nana declared the sky blue, Mother would argue its shade.

"I know I'd be stretching the bounds of propriety," Nana said. "But is it proper to be idle when there's work to be done? Idle hands are the devil's workshop."

But Mother wasn't through. "We were just going to order you some mourning clothes. The dowager countess wore mourning a full two years after the earl died. Only then did she graduate to lilac and dark mauve."

"Then thank goodness I'm not a countess."

Mother looked as if she'd been slapped.

Nana tried again. "I know I should wear mourning, but to spare the expense and to help my family in a more practical way . . . I simply wish to help."

Rose stepped forward. "I would be happy for your help, Mrs. Hayward."

"Of course you would, Rose," Mother said. "For it would mean less work for you."

"And you," Lila said.

"For all of us," Papa said. "If you feel up to it, we'd be happy to have you."

"Thank you, son."

Nana removed her bonnet and went to Rose. "Please. Put me to work."

With a huff, Mother retreated to the storeroom.

Lila had to get out of the store. Although she was supportive of her grandmother working there, the tension between Nana and Mother was palpable.

When Mother slipped out on an errand, Lila asked her father, "May I go riding? We're not busy, and with Nana's extra help . . ."

"It has been weeks, hasn't it?" he said. "I know Raider would enjoy a proper gallop."

Lila kissed his cheek and quickly escaped before Mother returned and stopped her. She hurried across the square toward the blacksmith's stable where they boarded Raider.

"Morning, Mr. Reed," Lila said when she saw him at the forges.

"Morning to you, Miss Hayward. Going to take Raider out?"

"We both need some fresh air."

"Indeed you do. And I know he'd rather have you take him for a gallop than pull your father's cart."

"Will you help me with the saddle, please?"

"Gladly." He secured the sidesaddle on Raider's back and stroked the leather. "'Tis nice of your father to buy you such a fine saddle."

"It may be fine, but I miss riding astride as I used to."

"Being grown up does have its drawbacks." He helped her up and adjusted the stirrup. "Now then. All set. Ride fast but ride safe."

"I'll do my best."

She held Raider to a trot near Summerfield, but once away from its boundaries and curious eyes, she set overland, across meadows and fields, letting Raider have his way. She could feel the miraculous movement of his muscles and let his joy meld with her own.

There was something incredibly freeing about the wind rushing through her hair, the sun upon her face. She'd seen Lady Clarissa riding while wearing a fancy habit and a hat with a veil, but Lila didn't envy the contrivances.

She eased Raider to the left, then to the right, relishing the choice.

So many choices had been taken from her lately. Although she adored Nana, having to share a bedroom was a strain. With Morgan away, Lila was used to solitude. Her bedroom was her haven, her place to escape the public setting of the mercantile and Mother's exasperating personality. But with Nana around, with her privacy gone, she felt like a colt in a very small pen.

But not now. Now she was free as the wind, flying like a —

Raider whinnied and pulled up short as a horse came barreling out of the woods. He reared up.

Lila felt herself slipping off . . .

She held out her hands to curb the fall, but upon hitting the ground, felt instant pain and rolled to take the weight away.

The man on the other horse leapt down and ran to her aid. "I'm so sorry, so sorry. Are you all right?" He knelt beside her. "Miss Hayward."

It was Joseph Kidd. Lila's first response was to make certain her skirt wasn't revealing too much. Unfortunately, when she'd rolled, it had become twisted. She pulled and tugged with her good hand, trying to cover her calves and ankles.

Mr. Kidd kept his eyes on her face, allowing her a few awkward moments to make her skirt behave. But when it still wouldn't cooperate, she ended up flat on her back. "I surrender," she said, laughing. "I'm a tangled mess."

Mr. Kidd smiled. "If I may be of assistance?"

"Please."

Before he tackled her skirts, Mr. Kidd removed his coat and rolled it into a makeshift pillow for her head. "Rest now. I'll take care of everything."

It was awkward having a man kneel over her, taking hold of her skirt and petticoats, untangling them. To his credit, he did his best to tackle the task with speed and modesty. With pain in her wrist and throbbing in her head, Lila had no choice but to trust him.

"There," he said. "Now. How are you feeling?"

"My head hurts and I landed on my wrist."

"May I?" he asked.

What was a wrist compared to tangled skirts?

His touch was gentle. "Can you move it?"

She winced. "It's not unbearable."

"I don't think it's broken, only badly sprained. But we ought to get you home where Dr. Evers can take a look at you."

Just as she was ready to agree, another horse and rider burst out of the woods.

Lady Clarissa rode toward them. "Well, well, what have we here? A damsel in distress?"

"I nearly ran into Miss Hayward, and she fell when her horse reared. I should get her home."

Lady Clarissa peered down from her perch above them. "Will you be all right, Lila?"

"Of course." She looked to Mr. Kidd. "If you'll please help me up and onto my horse?"

He helped her stand, and she tested each leg. Fortunately, her wrist seemed to be the only casualty. She started to walk to Raider, but Mr. Kidd intervened. "You are in no condition to ride alone."

"My wrist will be all right."

"But you've also hit your head. We must be cautious. I'll tie your horse to the back of mine, and you can ride with me."

"Oh, Joseph, how gallant," Lady Clarissa said. There was a teasing, almost mocking tone to her voice.

Mr. Kidd lifted Lila to the front portion of his saddle and then deftly mounted. "I am sorry, Lady Clarissa," he said. "We will resume our ride another day."

"By all means, complete your heroic duties," she told him. I have had my fill of the outdoors." To Lila she said, "I hope you recover sooner rather than later, Lila." With that, she turned her horse in the opposite direction, toward Summerfield Manor.

Mr. Kidd headed toward the village. The feel of his arms around her, keeping her safe . . . Lila was shocked by how much she liked it. She even found herself thanking God for rearing horses. If she were a heroine in a novel, she would rest her head against his chest and listen to the beating of his heart.

Her own heart was beating double-time.

"I have seen you out riding before," he said.

"And I have seen you." *Many times.* "I do love the out of doors."

"As do I. When I ride, my thoughts take to the wind."

"And what do you think about, Mr. Kidd?"

"Many things and nothing at all. It's just very . . ." He took a deep breath and let it out. ". . . liberating."

"Do you need liberating?" she asked.

"Sometimes."

She pointed toward the river. "Papa used to take my brother and me fishing."

"Used to?"

"Morgan is away at school, and I'm grown. It's been too long."

"Are you a good fisherman?"

"I hold my own against them."

"*Them* being the fish or your father and brother?"

She laughed. "Both."

"Perhaps someday I'll put you to the test."

Really? The thought of spending time with Joseph Kidd was too much to fathom. They'd known each other their entire lives, yet their paths had rarely crossed beyond a simple greeting or a transaction at the mercantile.

"But alas," he said. "The fishing will have to wait. For now, let's get you home where you belong."

Oddly, sitting within his arms seemed home enough.

"Oh, my dear girl, what happened?" Papa exclaimed.

Mr. Kidd helped her into the store, an arm around her waist.

"She fell from her horse," he said.

"I'll be fine. It's nothing."

"She fell on her wrist and also hit her head," Mr. Kidd explained.

"Rose, go get the doctor," Papa said.

"I'll make some tea," Nana said.

"Tea?" Mother said. "What good will tea do?"

Mr. Kidd handed Lila into Papa's care, and as she grieved

his absence, she noted the common strength they shared as well as the intrinsic compassion. "Thank you for taking care of her, Mr. Kidd," Papa said.

"I am just sorry for my part in the accident."

"How so?"

"I came riding out of the woods with little regard to who might be in my path. Your daughter is the victim of my recklessness."

"I'm as much to blame," Lila said. "For I too was riding while preoccupied with my own thoughts. No matter who is at fault, I thank you for your care. You have made my injuries bearable."

"May I come and check on you, Miss Hayward?"

Yes! "That would be nice."

He bowed and started to leave, and she yearned to call him back. *Please stay. I may never get another chance to be with you.*

For once, Mother's impulsive actions were of benefit. "Please stay for tea, Mr. Kidd. And scones. I do believe we have some scones left from breakfast."

"That sounds enticing, but really, I must get home." He tipped his hat to Mother, then Lila. "Until later then?"

"Until later."

Once Mr. Kidd left, Papa led Lila back to the living quarters. "Thank God you're all right. A fall from a horse can cause serious injury."

"I'll be fine. The doctor will care for me."

"As will we all," he said.

"Rest today so you can work tomorrow," Mother said.

"Fidelia!"

Mother shrugged. "She herself said it was just a sprain. Then again . . . don't get well too quickly. It would be nice if Mr. Kidd was forced to call again and again."

It *was* a thought.

But Father would hear none of it. "So Lila's to feign the degree of her injuries to gain Mr. Kidd's attention?"

"Attention is attention," Mother said.

"He's not my beau, Mother."

"If only he were. If you don't like Timothy, then you might has well set your sights on a gentleman."

"Fidelia! Really. Enough."

Papa helped Lila up the stairs. "She *is* genuinely concerned."

Concerned less about Lila's injuries than about romance — even if it was impossible.

Lila couldn't think about that now. Instead, she focused on the memories of sitting within the warmth and safety of Joseph Kidd's arms.

Lila heard her bedroom door open. When there was no other sound, she opened her eyes. Nana was quietly placing a cup of tea near the bed.

"Thank you," Lila said.

"I'm sorry if I woke you."

"I was only dozing."

Nana sat on the edge of the bed. "How are you feeling?"

"I'll be fine."

Nana smiled. "I could see you were fine when your handsome hero brought you home."

Lila felt herself blush. "He was very kind."

"A man who leads, I would guess?"

Lila remembered their previous discussion, where she'd mentioned wanting a man who would be strong and lead. "He's a gentleman. By action and birth."

"Gentlemen have feelings too. Very deep ones, or so I've heard. Even passionate ones."

"They do not have feelings of any kind for the daughters of shopkeepers."

"Not yet, perhaps."

"Not ever." Lila sat up in bed. "It does no good to think about what can never be."

Nana patted her hand. "Never say never. Not where love is concerned. Do you care for him?"

Lila thought a moment. "I care about the idea of him."

"Perhaps one day the idea will become a reality. Dreams *can* come true."

"Even in Summerfield?"

"Dreams know no boundaries."

It was a nice thought.

Chapter Five

"And who is this, Miss Wallace?"

Molly sat with her little sister in the passageway outside the housekeeper's parlor, awaiting instructions. She stood to answer Mr. Robbins. "This is my sister, just hired on. Dottie, this is Mr. Robbins, his lordship's valet."

"You dress 'im and all that?" Dottie asked.

Molly swatted her arm, but Mr. Robbins smiled. "Indeed I do—and all that. Just as your sister helps the countess with her dressing toilette."

"Toilet?"

Molly wanted to die. "Please excuse her, Mr. Robbins. She has much to learn—especially about keeping her questions to herself."

He winked at Dottie. "There is nothing wrong with a little curiosity. Good luck to you, girl."

Molly returned to her chair, her heart beating a frantic rhythm, hoping and praying that Dottie would do a good job. Her own job might depend on it.

She kept her voice low. "Be respectful at all times, and work your very hardest. And no complaining. That's all the last girl did: complain and be lazy. My room is on the second floor, just below yours in the attic, so there will be no saying you're homesick. Yet when I'm in with the countess, I cannot be disturbed unless it's an emergency, and even then . . . you'll report to Gertie with your questions—which you will keep to a minimum. She's the one directly in charge of you. Do you understand?"

Dottie's legs swung up and back and Molly stilled them with a hand.

"Do you understand?"

"I ain't stupid."

"I'm not saying you are, it's just —"

Mrs. Camden and Gertie came out to the corridor. Molly rose to her feet.

Dottie just sat there.

"Stand up," Molly said under her breath.

She did so, but with an attitude that implied it was an imposition. Dottie clearly had no notion of the pains that had been taken to get her here — or the other sort of pains she would have endured if she'd been left at home.

"Well now, Dottie," Mrs. Camden said. "Has your sister advised you of the great honor it is to work at Summerfield Manor?"

Dottie looked confused. "I guess so."

Molly put an arm around her shoulders. "She's ready, willing, and able, Mrs. Camden. She won't let you down."

"Won't let us down, Miss Wallace." She nodded at Gertie. "Tell the girl her duties."

Gertie glared at Dottie with narrowed eyes. "Each morning you will get up at five, wash yourself and dress, then quietly — quietly, mind you — go downstairs and clean the ground-floor rooms. You will scatter damp tea leaves on the carpets and sweep them, and scrub the tile in the foyer and hall. You must make the public areas presentable before the family comes down for breakfast at nine." She waited for Dottie to respond.

Molly nudged her.

"Yes, ma'am."

"When the family awakens, and when you are called, you will bring hot water from the kitchen to their rooms for their bath or basin."

"All that way?"

Gertie ignored her and continued. "After the family quit their bedrooms, you will hurry upstairs and clean their rooms.

For the first few days I will let you work with Prissy or Sally, but then you will be expected to handle the chore on your own."

"I make their beds?" Dottie asked.

Gertie sighed deeply and glanced at Molly. "Is she always so vocal?"

"I just asked a question," Dottie said.

"Before I was done giving your orders."

"Shush, Dottie," Molly said. "Listen to Gertie."

Gertie seemed somewhat appeased. "On nice days you throw open the windows to air the room, place two chairs at the foot of the bed, and carefully pull the bedclothes over them so you can smooth each layer properly. You will empty the hipbath or the basin and wipe them out, and . . ." Gertie paused for effect, as if it brought her pleasure to leave the worst for last. "You will empty the chamber pots into the slop bucket and wipe —"

Dottie made a face. "Ugh."

Molly touched her arm. *Please don't talk back.*

Mrs. Camden looked at Molly, her head shaking. "I hope this insolence isn't going to be a problem."

"Not at all, Mrs. Camden."

Dottie looked up at her. "Chamber pots are foul. Isn't it all right to say so?" Molly touched a finger to her lips and Dottie turned back to the women. "Sorry."

"Sorry what?"

Dottie hesitated, but only for a moment. "Sorry, Mrs. Camden. Sorry, Gertie."

Both women's faces lost of bit of their edge.

"As I was saying," Gertie said, "You empty each chamber pot into the slop bucket and dispose of the contents —"

"Out back?"

Mrs. Camden shuddered, and Gertie answered. "Don't be crude. Down in the basement, in the cesspit."

"When do I get breakfast?"

Molly was dying inside and wanted to clamp a hand over her sister's mouth.

The housekeeper shook her head. "The staff has breakfast at eight in the servants' hall." She pointed to the far end of the corridor, near the kitchen.

Dottie looked up at Molly. "Do they have good food here?"

Molly felt her cheeks flush. "Behave yourself."

"I was just asking."

"Anyway. . ." Gertie extended the word. "After those chores I have described, you will do whatever I need you to do: scrub floors, dust, help with the laundry, and . . ." She looked to Mrs. Camden. "I heard Mrs. McDeer's new scullery could use some help."

Mrs. Camden nodded. "I do think it would be best if Dottie's time was split between the two."

"She's going to be a tweeny?" Molly asked, knowing that the girls who split their time "'tween" upstairs and down were worked the hardest.

"She will be used where she's needed."

Dottie looked up at Molly. "I have to work in the kitchen too?"

Gertie threw up her hands and turned to the housekeeper. "Really, Mrs. Camden. How can I be asked to work with such an impertinent girl?"

They both looked to Molly, spreading the fault. "I apologize for my sister, ladies. I will have a stern talk with her, after which, she will do her job well and with a good attitude."

"I hope so," Gertie said.

"We will give her a week." Mrs. Camden gave Dottie a look that made even Molly shiver. "Understand that, girl? You are on trial. One week. If your work is not up to snuff, you'll be sent home, with your chance at Summerfield Manor gone forever."

Thankfully Dottie seemed to understand the seriousness of the moment and nodded. "Uh-huh."

Mrs. Camden raised an eyebrow.

"Yes, ma'am. I mean yes, Mrs. Camden."

"Now then," Gertie said, "Come with me and I'll show you

the proper way to sweep the rugs."

The two of them marched down the hall toward the back stairs. Dottie glanced over her shoulder at Molly as if wanting to be saved, a female Daniel being led into a lion's den. She looked so small, so young, and so ill-equipped.

"I fear she's trouble," Mrs. Camden told Molly.

In trouble perhaps. In over her head.

"She's a hard worker at home."

"How do you know? Haven't you been living at the manor for seven years? By my calculations, the last time you lived at home your sister was five."

Molly bit her lip, realizing she was right. But this had to work out. Dottie's future depended on it.

Grady visited the manor at two. Prompt as usual.

"For you." He handed Adelaide a bouquet of wildflowers. She inhaled their sweet scent.

He plucked a buttercup from the bunch and held it under her chin. "It reflects yellow on your chin, which means you like butter." He leaned close. "Which I know to be a fact."

"I haven't played that children's game since — "

"Since I last brought you wildflowers?"

A gust of memories blew over her and collided with the present. "I don't know what to do with you, Grady."

He smiled. "You called me Grady."

She sighed. "What do you want from me?"

He relieved her of the flowers and placed them on a table nearby. Then he took her hand and led her to the settee, angling to sit knee-to-knee beside her. "One day a few months ago, as if smacked with a log, I realized we don't have all the time in the world. I am old. And as I accepted that fact, one thing became clear. I could not leave this world without seeing you again."

His words resonated with her own private thoughts on age and the relentless momentum of the passing years. "So you just want to see me?" Even as she asked the question she was unsure of how she wanted him to respond.

"No," he said with a sharp shake of his head. "That isn't all I want. If you want me to give you more details, I will, but—"

Suddenly panicked, she shook her head just as sharply. "That won't be necessary."

He reached for her hand, but she pulled it out of reach, grieving the wrinkles and age spots that had appeared since he'd held it last.

When he spoke, his voice was low, as if something sacred was being shared. "Our love is forever, Addie. Let us start living forever now."

With his words the past caught up with the present and rushed forward into the future.

"Do you want me to stay in Summerfield?"

She put a hand to her chest and tried to press the surge of emotions back where they'd lain dormant for decades.

"Addie . . ."

With a blink she was at a crossroads. In one direction was the life she'd been living, and in the other . . .

Was lovely, witty, delectable Grady. The thought of him leaving again caused her physical pain. To have him walk away now would be as permanent as death. She was receiving a second chance. There would be no third.

And so she offered him a nod and a single word that represented everything she could feel and think and perceive. "Stay."

He drew her fingers to his lips, and his eyes lingered on hers. Where they belonged.

As Adelaide headed downstairs for dinner, she passed Clarissa coming out of her room. The girl was wearing an off-the-shoulder party dress.

"That's a lovely dress, dear, but isn't it rather formal for dinner?"

"Not when the dinner is at Crompton Hall."

It was good to see evidence that the match was moving forward. "So the Kidds are entertaining. How pleasant."

Clarissa eased her gloves over her elbows. "It fits well into your plan, doesn't it? But I am not the only one invited. It's a party for a group of young people from London." She smoothed her gloves around each finger. "But I am not supposed to care about anyone other than Joseph. Is that not correct?"

"Clarissa . . ."

She let out a huff and rolled her eyes. "You needn't panic, Grandmamma. I shall behave."

"It is imperative you do."

Clarissa smiled wickedly. "I will behave if you will."

"Whatever do you mean?"

"I saw you with the colonel. Sitting close."

Adelaide didn't know what to say. She couldn't deny it. "He is a dear friend."

Clarissa leaned close and said, "I think it's marvelous."

"You do?"

"Absolutely. 'Let us start living forever now.' Isn't that what he said?"

Now she had gone too far. "It is not polite to eavesdrop."

"Don't scold me. I am very impressed by your feelings for each other."

Thank you?

"But I was wondering . . . if you've known the colonel for so long, does that mean your marriage to Grandpapa was arranged?"

It sounded like a trick question.

"Even though you loved the colonel?"

"I . . ."

"Not ideal, was it?"

"Well no, but—"

Clarissa kissed her cheek. "Have a nice evening."

Ruth stepped away from her bedroom door. She hadn't meant to eavesdrop, but when she'd heard Adelaide and Clarissa talking in the hall . . .

Adelaide and the colonel had met and exchanged verbal intimacies? In this very house?

Let us start living forever now.

She leaned her shoulder against the door, closing her eyes, imagining what it would be like if Frederick would embrace her and tell *her* such a thing.

But in her mind's eye, Frederick's face faded.

She shook the emptiness away and went back to her embroidery.

It was nearly ten when Molly knocked on the door to her sister's attic room to say good night and ask about her first day.

But when she received no answer, she opened the door. The light of her candle revealed an empty room as tiny a closet. The air was stale.

The memories assailed her like a bitter wind. This had been Molly's room when she'd come to the manor as an under-housemaid. There was no window, no air, no light except that which came from the stub of a candle. There was only a bed, a dresser, a chair, and a hook on the back of the door for clothes. The absence of a window had been the hardest thing to get used to. At home, even though she'd shared a bed with Dottie, and their sleeping space had been just as tiny, they'd had a window. Many nights Molly had hugged her little sister close and gazed out into the night. She'd taught Dottie her numbers by counting the stars.

There were no stars here, and no way to know whether it was morning or night.

Molly remembered her first night in this room, longing for home and regretting the reason she'd *had* to leave. She'd cried herself to sleep and had prayed for strength to do a good job so she could stay at the manor.

Molly spotted something on the bed. Victoria. Dottie's ragdoll lay against her pillow, its very royal name belying a very unroyal doll. Molly had made for Dottie's third birthday. Some of her yarn hair was missing, and the rest was tangled. Her faded blue dress was tattered from the doll being held by one arm and dragged on the ground. That Dottie had brought her here, as her one tie to home . . .

Hearing feet on the attic stairs, Molly pulled back into the hallway, holding her candle high. It was Dottie, negotiating the final stair as if it were a cliff to be scaled. Staggering down the hall, her feet barely rose from the floor, and her head seemed too heavy for her neck. When she saw Molly she mumbled, "Seventy-nine steps. Seventy nine."

Molly rushed toward her. "My poor little polka dot." She helped her into her room and set the candle on the dresser.

Dottie fell onto the bed, immediately curling on her side.

Molly silently cursed Gertie and Mrs. Camden. Had they no compassion? Or had they worked Dottie especially hard *because* she was Molly's sister?

She removed her sister's shoes, stockings, and apron. Molly had to pull her upright in order to remove her gray dress. "Arms up," she said, as she dropped a nightdress over her head. Then Molly pulled back the covers and helped her in. Dottie immediately snuggled against the pillow.

Molly placed Victoria close, and Dottie pulled the doll to her chest. She looked so small, so vulnerable.

"Scoot forward," Molly said.

Dottie moved toward the edge of the narrow bed and Molly lay behind her. The years fell away as Dottie pulled Molly's arm close, bending her knees so Molly's could lock in place behind hers, the sisters fitting together like two spoons.

"It'll be all right," Molly whispered. "I promise."

Dottie offered a weak nod before falling to sleep.

Molly stroked her sister's hair and prayed the promise could be kept.

Chapter Six

Molly was awakened by knocking. She opened her eyes to blackness and leaned back, barely catching herself from falling off the bed. It took her a moment to remember she was in Dottie's room.

She whipped around as the door opened, and the light of a candle flickered in the room. "Up girl, it's time —"

Molly managed to stand, nearly losing her balance as her heel caught in her petticoat.

"Miss Wallace."

"Gertie."

Gertie peered around her, looking for Dottie. "Get up. There's carpets to sweep."

Dottie moaned. "I'm coming."

Gertie started to leave, then looked at Molly, "Does it bring back memories, Miss Wallace?"

Her question did not deserve an answer. Molly looked at her sister. "I'll see you later, at breakfast."

Dottie nodded as she retrieved her stockings.

Molly brushed past Gertie. "If you'll excuse me. I must see to the countess."

"You do that."

She hurried downstairs to the second floor. Once inside her own room, she saw that it was still dark outside. The clock on her dresser read ten-past five.

First up, last to bed.

Poor Dottie.

The housekeeper placed a napkin in her lap and looked down the row of servants seated at the table. "And where is your sister, Miss Wallace?"

Molly glanced at Gertie. "I assume she'll be here." Dottie was never one to miss a meal.

With an exaggerated sigh, Gertie pushed her chair back. "Last I checked she was sweeping the carpet in the morning room. If she can't handle the duties . . ."

Molly stood. "I'll find her. I'm sure she's—"

There was a crash in the corridor. "Blast!"

It was Dottie's voice. Molly rushed toward the door along with many of the others.

"Now she's in for it," Nick said as he surveyed the scene.

"That'll cost her," said the kitchen maid.

It was worse than Molly could have ever imagined. Dottie knelt beside a scattering of broken porcelain. The handles of two broken chamber pots told the sad story. The white cloths used to cover them were spotted with yellow, and the smell of urine . . .

"Disgusting!" said a fellow housemaid, wrinkling her nose.

Mrs. Camden pointed down the hall. "Be quiet and fetch a broom, dustpan, and a mop." To the kitchen maid she said, "Go get a pan of water and rags."

"And add some soap to it," Gertie added.

Mr. Dixon herded the others back inside. "Sit down now. The show is over."

"I didn't mean to drop them," Dottie said amid tears. "I was trying to be careful."

"What are you doing carrying chamber pots around, Dottie? You empty them into the slop bucket," Gertie said.

"And it's not time to clean the family's bedrooms. That's after our breakfast, while *they're* at breakfast," Mrs. Camden said.

Molly couldn't believe how wrong her sister had gotten everything. And then a horrible thought formed. "Where did you get these pots?"

"From the pretty lady's room and . . . I think it was the old lady's—"

All three women gasped. "Certainly you didn't wake Lady Clarissa and the dowager countess?"

"No, Mrs. Camden. I snuck in while they was still sleeping."

Gertie crossed herself.

"Oh, Dottie," Molly said. "You never do that. Everything in its proper time and order."

"But I was behind and you were all at breakfast, and I didn't want to be late."

"Well, now you'll miss it entirely." The housekeeper pointed a finger at Molly, then Gertie. "Someone didn't do a proper job explaining to Dottie the details of her tasks."

"But I did," Gertie said. "I told her every step."

"What do you have to say for your sister, Miss Wallace?"

Not much. "She's just nervous. I'm sure it won't happen again."

"No. It won't. Or she won't be here."

"Yes, Mrs. Camden."

Mrs. Camden returned to the servants' hall, and Gertie glared at Molly. "I assume you'll oversee the cleanup of your sister's folly, Miss Wallace? If I remember correctly, you're quite familiar with chamber pots."

At the insult, Molly's jaw tightened. Gertie—who had trained Molly when she was under-housemaid—had never forgiven Molly for rising in the ranks. Yet the truth of it was that Molly's position was now higher than Gertie's, right beneath Mrs. Camden herself. No other lady's maid would ever be asked to handle this odious task.

Yet, it *was* her sister. She didn't want Dottie to suffer because of her own pride.

"Of course."

"Very good then. My breakfast is getting cold." Gertie gave Molly a satisfied smile before retreating inside.

The housemaid came back with a broom and pan, and the

kitchen maid with a bucket and brush. "Thank you, girls. Go get your breakfast."

"But I want breakfast too," Dottie said.

"Shush! And finish picking up the bigger pieces."

Dottie plucked porcelain from the puddled floor. "I'm really sorry."

Molly rolled up her sleeves and got to work.

An hour later Molly walked into Lady Clarissa's bedroom to find Dottie filling two pails of used bath water from the hipbath to be carried downstairs. Another housemaid, Prissy, had chosen the easier job of making the bed.

Molly pulled a breakfast roll from her pocket and handed it to her sister.

"What about me?" Prissy asked.

Luckily, Molly had suspected Dottie wouldn't be alone. "I brought you one too."

Prissy's eyes widened. "Thank you, Miss Wallace."

Dottie broke off a piece, then put the rest in her apron pocket. "I thank you too."

Molly gave her a wink and left to help the countess with her morning toilette.

Mrs. Keening, the baker's wife, handed Lila two loaves of her famous brown bread, then nodded at Lila's wrapped wrist. "Your parents working you too hard at the mercantile?"

"I fell off my horse."

"That's not like Raider—or you."

"At least it's my left hand." Lila refused to mention Joseph Kidd. "I hope to make blackberry preserves soon. I'll bring you a jar."

"Maybe you should save a jar for your hero."

So that's how it was. Lila tried to act nonchalant. "Hero?"

"Mr. Kidd. You didn't think you could ride into town with his arms wrapped around ya without no one seein', did ya?"

"His arms weren't *wrapped* —"

"And your mother being your mother . . ."

Ah.

She hoped Mother hadn't colored the situation to make it seem as though Mr. Kidd was her beau. Yet the limits of reality wouldn't stop Mother from implying and suggesting there *should* be a romance.

"Mr. Kidd was a perfect gentleman," Lila said, choosing her words with care. "I highly commend his kind attention."

"Ooh," Mrs. Keening said, obviously reading into her words.

She wondered what Mrs. Keening would think if she knew Mr. Kidd was coming back to check on her. Unfortunately, the odds were good that her mother had included that bit of information with the rest. Yet if Mr. Kidd *didn't* follow through, Lila's romantic, ridiculous daydreams would be judged as folly.

It was folly. But that didn't mean Lila wanted people to go back to thinking of her as a girl with no prospects.

"Good day, Mrs. Keening."

"Let us know how things progress."

Mother would take care of that.

Lila's wrist didn't bother her half as much as her stomach. For whenever someone came in the store, her insides grabbed.

Yet not one of them was Mr. Kidd.

She even volunteered to man the store through the noon meal — a task that usually belonged to Rose. If only he'd come now, while her family and Rose were back in the kitchen, eating. How much better to have a few minutes with him away from Mother's eyes and ears.

Not that their conversation would progress beyond small talk. Mr. Kidd would ask after her injuries, they would discuss the weather and perhaps their shared love of riding, and he would leave.

As she wrapped a new teapot for Mrs. Reed, the blacksmith's wife, she tried to think of some subject that could prolong her time with him. Something witty or profound perhaps? She'd heard Papa talking to a few of the men in town about some disastrous battle in the Afghan war. Perhaps if she mentioned—

And then, as if materializing from her thoughts, he walked through the door left open to let in the summer breeze.

"Good day, Mr. Kidd," she said.

He removed his hat and nodded at Lila and then Mrs. Reed. "Good day, Miss Hayward. Ma'am."

Lila handed over the teapot. "There you go. I hope it serves you well for years to come."

Mrs. Reed hesitated, and it was clear she longed for a reason to stay. To be able to feed the village gossip by *being* there was a feather in any woman's bonnet.

But then Mr. Kidd stepped forward and asked, "I was wondering if you have any match safes? We are in need of a new one."

"I think we can accommodate you. Step over here and I'll show you our selection." Lila nodded at Mrs. Reed. "If you'll excuse me?"

"Of course," the woman said. She glanced at Mr. Kidd, sighed, and having no other recourse, made her exit.

Mr. Kidd laughed. "She seemed reluctant to leave."

Lila set two match safes on the counter. "Your presence has caused a stir."

"But I've come into the mercantile many times."

"But never the day after . . ." She didn't want to be too direct.

"The day after I carried you here on my horse?"

She felt herself blush.

He sighed, then offered a grin. "I suppose I should have made you walk."

"Not at all. But in a village where gallantry has been buried in an unmarked grave . . ."

He absently examined a match safe then set it down. "How are you feeling, Miss Hayward?"

She held out her wrist. "I am on the mend."

"But it is bandaged."

"Dr. Evers did the honors. Apparently a wrap will give it support." She carefully bent her wrist, but feeling pain, stopped the demonstration.

"So it's not broken?"

"Just a sprain. As we suspected."

"It needn't keep you from riding, I hope?"

Lila's heart flipped. Was he asking her to go riding? "Not at all."

He picked up the second watch safe. "I think I like this one."

Is that it? The subject of riding is over?

Lila heard voices. Her time alone with him was also over.

He must have heard them too. "Put it on our tab please."

"Mr. Kidd," Mother said, sweeping into the room. "How nice to see you."

"As it is nice to see you, Mrs. Hayward."

"Come to check on our Lila?"

"I have. I am exceedingly glad she is mending well."

"Not so well," Mother said. "Just this morning I heard her moan when she was forced to use her injured wrist."

Lila instantly recognized Mother's attempt to manipulate Mr. Kidd into further visits, but hated the lie. "I will be fine. Fine enough to soon ride again." Mother had her methods, and Lila had hers.

Mr. Kidd smiled and gathered his purchase. "I hope to see you out riding then."

With a nod, he was gone.

Mother rushed to Lila's side. "You're going riding together?"

Lila could *not* let that bit of gossip gain legs. "Not together. He simply meant that we might see each other when either one of us is out riding."

"That's it?"

Papa laughed. "If you had your way, you'd have the two of them ride over to speak to the vicar."

Hearing her father's words emphasized the absurdity of the entire situation. By keeping the fire of the fantasy alive, Lila risked getting burned. The wise thing would be to douse the flame, the spark—whatever it was—and spread the ashes so it could not flame again. She looked at her mother, hoping her steady gaze would indicate her own seriousness. "Joseph Kidd is the son of Lord Newley, a viscount. The Kidds are one of the wealthiest families in the county. He is not—and can never be—interested in me, a shopkeeper's daughter."

"There are worse things than being a shopkeeper's daughter," Papa said.

"Don't take it wrongly, Papa. I only meant—"

"I take no offense." He crossed the store and flicked the tip of her nose. "But I won't have you thinking less of yourself. Understand?"

She nodded to appease him. Unfortunately, she was what she was. And there was nothing she could do to change it.

When Molly stepped out of the countess' room, she nearly ran into the dowager and Lady Clarissa. "Excuse me, your ladyship, my lady. Good evening."

The dowager paused and asked Molly, "Will Lady Summerfield be joining us for dinner tonight?"

"No, my lady. Not tonight."

Lady Clarissa rolled her eyes, and they moved on.

Then Molly spotted Dottie dusting the railing at the top of the staircase. When the ladies passed her, Dottie looked up from her dusting and said, "Hello."

What? No!

The ladies nodded and went down to dinner, but as soon as their voices faded to a distant murmur, Molly raced to Dottie's side.

"What do you think you're doing?"

"Dusting."

Molly took her arm and pulled her further down the hall, out of earshot and view of the foyer. "You do not say 'hello' to the family."

"Why not? You did."

The intricacies of servant-master decorum raced through Molly's mind. "You are an under-housemaid, and a tweeny at that."

"Don't I know it."

"As one of the under-servants, you're invisible."

"I'm not invisible."

Patience, Molly. "You're to appear invisible to the family."

Understanding fell across Dottie's face. "This is that face-the-wall thing Gertie was telling me about."

"Yes, it is. When a family member approaches, you are to stop what you're doing and face away from them. You become invisible to them."

"That's silly. I'm working for them, but they want me to disappear? If I disappear, none of the work's gonna get done."

Molly rested a hand upon her shoulder. "I know it doesn't make sense. I remember feeling the same way when I was an under-housemaid."

"If it doesn't make sense, then why's it done?"

Molly looked into the air, retrieving the only answer she could find. "Tradition. What's always been will always be."

"*I* think we have to turn away so they needn't look us in the eye and feel embarrassed that we have to do the dirty work for them—like dumping their chamber pots."

Molly smiled at her logic. "Whatever the reason, you must follow the rules, all right?"

Dottie nodded once. "But when I'm not a tweeny anymore, then can I tell them hello?"

"You work your way up and we'll talk about it." Molly checked the time on her watch-pin. "I've got to get dinner for the countess."

"And I must turn down the beds."

"I'll see you later, for *our* dinner, all right?"

Dottie grinned, then turned toward the wall.

"What are you doing?"

"You're family, aren't cha?"

"Smartie pants." Molly swatted her sister's behind and headed down to the kitchen.

Chapter Seven

Lila saw Nana studying the basket of ribbon.

"Is something wrong?"

Nana tidied a spool. "To display these best, they need to be hung."

"No, they don't," Mother said. "They're fine."

"Perhaps on a long stick?" Nana moved to a shelf. "If we rested the stick horizontally on some sort of bracket or nail attached to the shelves . . ."

Lila nodded, seeing her vision. "That would keep them untangled."

Nana smiled. "Want to go with me to the woods and find the perfect stick?"

"I'd love to."

"You can't both go," Mother said.

Papa intervened. "Of course they can."

"Quick!" Lila whispered. "Let's make our escape!"

Nana giggled, and the two of them gathered their bonnets, walked through the square, and strolled down the road toward the forest.

"Are we really looking for a stick?" Lila asked.

"Actually, yes," Nana said, linking her arm in Lila's. "But I do like the chance to go walking with you."

At the edge of village, they veered down a path, but it soon disappeared, and they had to lift their skirts against the budding undergrowth, fallen twigs, and branches. Their eyes were forced downward, stepping this way and that, negotiating a woodland gauntlet.

Soon out of breath, they stopped and looked around. They were deep in the forest with no evidence of human life anywhere. Lila's heart took an extra beat. There were wild things in the forest: deer, wolves, and boar.

She started at a sound to her right. A rabbit hopped from behind a tree, then paused to wiggle its nose at her.

"I'm not afraid of you," she said. "It's your bigger brothers I'm worried about."

"Oh, don't be worried," Nana said. "The woods can be a marvelous place. Listen." Nana closed her eyes and raised her face to the canopy overhead.

Lila heard a chorus of birds, and watched a brown squirrel leap from tree to tree. "It is rather peaceful."

"I used to live here."

"What *here*?"

Nana opened her eyes and spread her arms wide. "Here. In the forest. Before moving to London, your grandfather and I lived in these woods."

"I don't understand."

Nana turned in a circle, as if looking for something particular. "Come on. I think it's over this way."

"What are you talking about?"

Rather than answer, Nana hurried off.

"Nana? Where are you going?"

"Home."

Nana's pace was erratic as she paused to look up, then turn, as if she were indeed looking for some particular location.

"There!" she said, pointing.

Before them lay the remnants of a shack, overgrown with ivy.

Nana stepped over fallen logs to reach the front door — what little remained of it. She fingered the rough peg used as a knob. "Oh, the times I stepped through this door."

Lila shook her head in disbelief. "You lived in this shack?"

Nana peeked inside the door, but didn't enter. "We lived here for the first years of our marriage."

"Years?"

She nodded, stroking the door as if it was much more than a piece of scrap wood. "We didn't have any money so your grandfather made this shack from scraps of lumber he stole." She paused and glanced at Lila. "Yes, stole. Stanley did odd jobs, and I gleaned from harvested fields and made baskets from reeds to sell at the village market. And Stanley poached off the Summerfield estate."

"He could have been arrested."

"He was, more than once. Running from the law often made us move deeper into the forest. But we always returned here." She laid a hand to her stomach as though the memories made it hurt.

"You ended up in London."

"After your father came along."

"He was born here?" Lila couldn't imagine having a child in this shack.

"All my children were born here."

"Children?"

Nana hesitated, then pointed to her right. "Come with me."

Lila followed her a hundred yards deeper into the woods.

Suddenly, Nana fell to her knees at the foot of a huge tree with a crooked trunk. She dug through the layers of leaves and twigs and brambles.

"What are you looking for?"

Nana's fingers froze, and she hurriedly swept the debris aside, revealing one stone. Then another. And another.

Lila stared at the three stones, carefully set in a line, a foot between them.

"One baby, two, three. My three dead babies."

Lila knelt beside her, staring at the stones. "You lost three babies?"

"Howard, Hester, and Fanny. My babies. My dear babies."

Nana began to cry quiet tears, and Lila put an arm around her, pulling her close. "I'm so sorry." She couldn't imagine such pain and loss.

Nana picked up the stone that marked the first grave. "Howard died at birth, never even seeing my face." She set his stone in her lap and took up the second. "Hester. This beautiful child lived three weeks before succumbing to the January cold." She set Hester's stone beside her brother's and took up the last. She cradled this one as if it were the baby it represented. "Little Fanny. She lived two months. Her smile lit up my world."

Lila cried with her, feeling her heart break. To think that her father had three siblings, that he was the only one who'd survived. "Why hasn't Papa ever said anything?"

"These babies came first. And we left when he was little. He doesn't even know about his siblings. I certainly didn't tell him."

Nana took a deep breath and set the three stones back upon the graves. "Three babies dead, and two others who died before they were born."

"More babies?"

"Two others."

It was too much to bear. Lila fully embraced her grandmother, and together they keened forward and back, sobbing over the awful loss.

At least Nana had Papa. Thank God for that.

Molly entered the sitting room down the hall from the housekeeper's quarters, which was especially allotted to the three lady's maids. She'd hoped to have time alone, to fully read the newest letter from Morgan. Luckily, Agnes and Bridget were occupied elsewhere.

She set aside her mending, removed the letter, and sat in her favorite rocker.

> *My dearest Molly,*
> *I am counting the days — nay, the hours — till I*
> *see you. Though I have tried to commit your face to*

*memory, to gaze into the depth of your blue eyes, to
revel in the softness of your cheek, to wallow in the
feel of your lips against mine . . . I know my
memories pale when compared to the breadth of
your actual beauty. I hope to be home on the tenth.
I'll meet you at the arbor after dark.*
> *Yours forever and always,*
> *Morgan*

Molly leaned back and closed her eyes, holding the page
close as if his words were a surrogate for his arms.

"Well, well, what have we here?"

Molly started. In her reverie both Agnes and Bridget had
come in.

She quickly folded the letter, trying to fit it in her pocket.
But seated, the opening wouldn't cooperate, and it fell to the
floor.

Agnes rushed forward and plucked it from the rug.

"Give that back!"

Agnes scurried out of reach.

"Give it to me," Molly pleaded as she lunged for it. But in
her desperation, she bobbled a tin of straight pins, only
catching it at the last moment. "Please, Agnes. It's private."

"I can see that." Agnes began to read the letter out loud. "'I
am counting the days—nay, the hours—till I see you . . . I
know my memories pale when compared to the breadth of
your actual beauty.'"

Bridget brought her hands to her chest. "That's lovely. I've
never had a man say such things to me, about me."

Agnes folded the letter. "I did. Once."

"Who?" Bridget asked.

"You don't know him. He died in a wagon accident."
Agnes opened a tin of biscuits, placed one between her teeth,
and put another in her pocket.

"I'm sorry for your loss," Molly said.

Agnes shrugged. "It was ten years ago."

"At least you had a beau," Bridget said.

The idea of the elderly Bridget ever even thinking about

courtship was odd. "How long have you been a lady's maid?" Molly asked her.

"I became the dowager's maid soon after she became the countess." She looked to the ceiling. "Eighteen-thirty-seven, I believe."

"That's forty-three years," Agnes said.

Molly thought of something else. "Were you here when that Colonel Cummings was around?"

Bridget shook her head, placed a blue voile blouse in her lap, and adjusted her spectacles to thread a needle. "I do remember some rumors about her caring for some other man before she married, but she certainly never mentioned him to me. And I was new and had other things to worry about."

The notion of being a lady's maid until she was old made Molly shudder, but she didn't say anything. For Agnes was also on her way to being a lifer.

Agnes returned to the letter, mumbling the last words of it around the biscuit in her mouth. But when she reached the closing salutation she looked up. "Morgan? Your beau is Morgan Hayward?"

Molly's stomach churned. The fact they knew his identity was far worse than knowing his sentiments. She tried to shrug it off by simply nodding and returning to her chair.

Bridget made a *tsk-tsk* sound, shaking her head. "Does the countess know?"

"Of course not."

"She *can't* know," Bridget said. "Any suitor is against the rules. And the simple fact he's Fidelia Hayward's son makes him totally unacceptable. Surely you know that."

"Of course I know that. But I can't help that Morgan Hayward loves me." Molly thought of a fib that might ease the issue. "It's not as though I reciprocate his feelings."

Agnes gave her the letter and sat down. "What is it between the countess and Fidelia, anyway? Everyone knows they hate each other, but no one ever says why."

"I'm sure I don't know," Molly said, as she threaded a needle with green thread.

"You should know," Agnes said. "You always boast about how close you are to her."

"We are close—as close as a countess and lady's maid can be. But her ladyship doesn't confide in me about her past."

"I know the reason," Bridget said.

Both Molly and Agnes snapped their heads in her direction.

"Then, tell," Agnes said.

Bridget squirmed in her chair, obviously not accustomed to such scrutiny, yet judging by her smile, not disliking it either. "The way I remember it is they both had eyes for the earl—for Master Frederick *before* he was earl. He was a handsome young man, and many girls in the county were keen on him."

Molly tried to wrap her mind around this. "The countess came from a wealthy family. Her father was a baron. But Fidelia? She's a shopkeeper's wife."

"Now," Bridget said. "Now she's a shopkeeper's wife. But back then she was Miss Fidelia Breton. Her family had an estate north of Summerfield. The Kidds bought it when her family left."

"Why did they leave?"

Bridget removed her spectacles and cleaned them on the edge of the dowager's blouse. "That, I don't know. It was all hush-hush with rumors flying far and fast about losing their fortune. And soon after, his lordship proposed to the countess, and no one ever saw Fidelia again—until years later when she and her husband came back to Summerfield to run the mercantile."

Molly tried to let this sink in. "If there was a competition between Fidelia and her ladyship, it's obvious who won."

Agnes retrieved the second biscuit from her pocket and took a bite. "That explains Fidelia's hatred of the countess, but why does the countess hate her? As the victor, she shouldn't give Fidelia another thought."

"Out of habit?" Bridget suggested.

For the first time, Molly felt a kinship with these ladies. Usually when they sat together, the other two chatted among themselves, rarely giving Molly a second glance. Perhaps Agnes snatching the letter was a good thing.

Molly settled the countess's dress in her lap and began her stitching. "Back to the letter . . . since we all know the consequences, I would be especially grateful if you'd keep Morgan's feelings for me between us. As a favor."

"Of course," Bridget said.

Agnes sighed deeply. "All this talk of love . . . I suppose you've heard that Lady Clarissa and Joseph Kidd have been matched."

Bridget nodded, but Molly shook her head, and her thoughts coursed back to their time in London. "I wasn't aware she spent much time with him during the season."

"She didn't. And he's not *her* choice. The dowager and the earl have decided."

Molly wondered if the countess knew about it, or if she'd even been consulted.

"You don't seem too keen on the match," Bridget said.

"It's not me who needs to be keen," Agnes said. "I know for a fact Lady Clarissa has little care for Mr. Kidd."

"Then why is she agreeing to it?"

"She hasn't told me straight out, but her obsession with London is well-known. It appears Mr. Kidd is headed for a seat in Parliament, so that would give the two of them time in the city." Agnes shook her head in short bursts. "Lady Clarissa does *not* like country life. She thrives in London and is infatuated with the theatre. I believe she'd perform if she had her way."

"I'm certain her parents and the dowager will heartily forbid that interest," Bridget said. "Attending a performance is one thing. Performing is quite another. Everyone knows all actresses are. . . "

"Whores," Agnes said.

"Shh!"

"It's just us three. I can say it aloud. I won't be struck down." Agnes leaned forward confidentially. "I am quite certain she agreed to the match to appease them so she's free to use the situation for her own purposes. If they knew about half the people she spent time with in London, they'd faint dead away. She's quite adept at sneaking out to cavort with whomever she pleases. Actors. Musicians. All sorts of unsavories."

"So she truly has no interest in Mr. Kidd?" Molly asked.

Agnes harrumphed, then said, "Lady Clarissa has no interest in anyone but herself."

Molly knew Agnes wasn't Lady Clarissa's champion, but she'd never heard her so disparaging. "If you don't like your mistress and don't approve of what she does, then why do you stay on as her lady's maid?"

"Because someone else took the position that should have been mine." Agnes stared at Molly.

It took her a moment to understand. "You wanted to be lady's maid to the countess?"

"I certainly had more experience than you."

Bridget intervened. "Now, now, Agnes. Her ladyship had the right to choose anyone she wished, and she chose Molly because . . ."

"Because why?" Agnes asked.

Molly was interested in the answer too. She'd never been certain why she'd been chosen.

Bridget's eyes flit from here to there, as if looking for any answer. "I would guess it was due to Molly's sweet nature."

"Are you saying I'm not sweet?"

Bridget shrugged.

"Well then." Agnes gathered her sewing and left the room, letting the door slam shut behind her.

"A tempest in a teapot, that one," Bridget said.

"Thank you for defending me," Molly said. "And for the compliment. I've wondered why her ladyship chose me."

Bridget laid a hand on Molly's knee. "She chose you because you had proven yourself a hard worker, loyal, and kind. When Mademoiselle DuBois left her ladyship's service because she felt her fashion expertise was wasted on the countess, Agnes was next in line, and she *did* make her wishes known. It was the dowager who stepped in. She knew Agnes and the countess were not a match."

"Thank you for telling me that. But from what we've just heard, I'm not sure Agnes and Lady Clarissa are much of a match either."

Bridget sat back and adjusted her eyeglasses, ready to sew. "Actually — and mind, she's never clearly stated as much — I think the dowager likes having Agnes and Lady Clarissa together. Sometimes those who prickle must be prickled in return."

Molly wasn't sure about the logic in that, but who was she to argue?

The dowager had chosen her to be Lady Summerfield's lady's maid.

That knowledge was a gem of great worth.

Molly paused on the back stairs and listened.

There *was* laughter coming from the upper floor. She recognized young George's laugh, but the other —

No!

She lifted her skirt and rushed up the stairs and found Dottie talking with Master George. Laughing with him.

"Dottie!"

Her sister stepped away from the Westons' son and dropped her jar of brass polish.

George picked it up for her and held it at arm's length. She giggled.

This would never do.

Molly held out her hand to George. "Master George, if you please?"

He handed it over. "She's funny."

"I'm sure she is. But she also has work to do."

"I'm going out riding," he said.

"I've never ridden a horse," Dottie said.

Molly gave her sleeve a tug.

"Well, I haven't."

"Go on now, Master George," Molly said. "Have a nice ride."

As soon as he left, Molly yanked Dottie into an alcove. "Don't force me to keep telling you that when the family comes by you must turn toward—"

"I *was* turned toward the wall. But then he pulled my hair and nabbed my polishing cloth. *He* talked to *me.*"

Molly let go of her arm. "That doesn't mean you should respond."

"How can I not?"

It was a good question.

"He's a nice boy."

"He's not a boy, he's the heir, the next earl."

Dottie's eyes grew large. "Really? He doesn't act like an earl."

The conversation was going in circles. "Get back to work."

Dottie made a face. "I didn't do anything wrong."

The innocent blue of her sister's eyes made Molly's anger fade. She touched Dottie's cheek.

Master George and her sister . . . the two were nearly the same age.

This could be a problem.

Chapter Eight

A third meeting in as many days. If Adelaide wasn't careful, the gossipmongers of the manor would take flight with new fodder.

Actually, this time, Grady had requested they move their meeting outdoors. "My horse is lame and I need to take him to the smithy. Would you care to join me?"

Adelaide pointed toward the stables. "I'll call someone to attend to him in no time."

"No, thank you." Grady winked and spoke for her ears alone. "*No* time would not be enough time in your presence. I would rather extend our time by walking to the village together."

"Walk?"

He made a walking motion with his fingers. "One foot in front of the other?"

She ignored his barb. "I will call for the carriage and—"

"Walk, Addie." He offered her his arm.

He was moving too fast. As dowager countess she did not simply walk to town.

Grady saw Dixon and gave him instructions. "Dixon, old boy. Would you fetch her ladyship's hat, for we are going to walk to town."

"Walk?"

Grady rolled his eyes. "Is this aversion to walking contagious?"

Dixon looked to his mistress. "Would you like your hat, my lady?"

To end the discussion, she nodded. "The straw one with the yellow flowers on the brim."

Dixon nodded and left, and they heard him speak to Bridget. There were footsteps up the stair.

Grady grinned. "My, my. All for a hat."

She gave him a pointed look. "You started it."

Minutes later, Bridget appeared with the hat. Adelaide sat and Bridget pinned the hat to her hair, and tied and fluffed the bow beneath her chin. "Anything else, your ladyship?"

"No. Thank you. That will be all."

Bridget bobbed a curtsey and left.

Grady offered her his arm. "Shall we?"

Adelaide and Grady walked arm-in-arm down the country road leading from Summerfield Manor to the village, with Grady leading his horse.

Adelaide raised her face to the summer sky and drank in the warmth and the breeze. The birds sang from the trees that lined the road, and the smell of lilies and lavender washed over her like a wave.

She stopped.

"What's wrong?" Grady asked.

Put on the spot, she found no words. "Nothing. Nothing at all." She took a cleansing breath.

"It is beautiful out here, isn't it?"

Fearing her words would come out broken, she nodded.

He faced her and peered into her eyes. "Don't ever feel as though you have to hide your feelings from me. You've played the brave soldier long enough."

And there it was, the essence of all she was feeling. The surge of emotions were rooted in the woman she became when she was with Grady. In his presence she was more than a title, a position, and an icon of duty. With Grady she was just a woman. The freedom was as heady as the fragrance of the flowers.

He plucked a sprig of lavender and presented it to her as the finest gift. "Drink in the aroma and let it soothe you."

"Doctor's orders?"

"Grady's orders."

She held the stem of purple petals under her nose, letting its sweet fragrance calm her. "Did you know I have never walked on this road."

"What?"

"I have occasionally ridden upon it in the carriage, but I have never walked its length."

"Did we never?"

She shook her head. "It was too public. My parents . . ."

"Ah. Yes."

She regretted bringing up the deficiencies of the past. "But we are here now. Together. Walking."

He pulled her hand back around his arm. With his mention of that fact, she balked. What if people saw them walking like this? What would they think of her? Of them?

She tried to pull her hand free, but he held it fast. "My darling Addie, This revolutionary walk is but the beginning of the new experiences we shall share."

She felt a flicker of excitement, but the decorum that had held her captive for nearly fifty years immediately tried to extinguish the feeling.

But as they reached the outskirts of the village and came into the presence of others, a sense of uneasiness crept upon her. "They're staring at us," she said.

Grady whispered for her ears alone, "Perhaps they've never seen two people so much in love."

She ignored him and pulled her arm free.

"When was the last time you came to town?" he asked.

"I do not come to town."

"Which explains why they're looking at us as if we're both strangers."

As they walked across the village square, it was obvious word was spreading that the dowager countess was in town, because more than a dozen people came out of their houses and businesses to offer her a bow or curtsy.

Their homage made her feel at ease. *This* she knew.

"The people like seeing you."

"Of course they do."

Grady slowed their walk. "Why 'of course'?"

At his tone, the brightness of the day turned cloudy. Her word choice was faulty, but she wasn't wrong. Being seen was part of her responsibilities.

But before she could attempt to explain they arrived at the blacksmith's. The man was flustered at her presence, wiping his grimy face with a cloth, running a hand through his tousled hair before offering her an awkward bow. "Lady Summerfield."

"Colonel Grady's horse needs some attention," she said. "Do you have time to tend to it?"

"Of course, my lady. Right away."

Grady stepped forward. "His left rear is bothering him."

"I'll take a look at all four, sir. I'll do it right."

Grady nodded. "Thank you, Mister . . . ?"

"Reed, sir. Arthur Reed."

"Thank you, Mr. Reed. If we come back in an hour or so, will that be enough time?"

"Should be, sir."

"Very good." Grady led Adelaide out to the road, where a small crowd had gathered.

She found it disconcerting being so close to them, out of the carriage, in their territory. It was not a formal event where she was the hostess and could control both the access and substance of their interaction. She was a foreigner here, and she didn't like it.

"Might we find a private spot to sit and wait?" she asked Grady.

He peered up the road. "We're nearly through town. Let's walk a little farther and find a place."

She let Grady lead her down the road and veer onto a path leading to a small grove of trees. He removed his coat and set it on the shady grass, then extended a hand to help her.

"You want me to sit on the ground?"

He scanned the meadow. "As I don't see any chairs . . ."

She eyed the grass, considering the logistics of getting from here to there in a ladylike fashion.

"Come on, Addie. If I remember correctly, you didn't used to shrink from sitting on the grass. Sitting or — "

"Hush." To cover her blush, she took his hand. He helped her kneel, and then sit. Her corset and bustled skirt made it awkward and uncomfortable.

"Are you having problems?"

With an *oomph* she nudged her bustle to the side. "Dresses were simpler then, with wider skirts."

"And you were younger."

She pointed a finger at him. "I am not the only one who's grown old. Older."

"You're irritated," he said.

Was she? She glanced at the grove, and for the first time fully acknowledged the setting and their position. "I am not sure how you managed to get me in the woods, sitting on the ground."

"You asked for a private place to wait." He spread his arms, presenting nature's privacy as the culmination of her request.

"I suppose I am simply accustomed to being in control."

"I noticed."

He didn't sound pleased. "Now *you* sound irritated."

"I, too, like being in control, and am accustomed to managing my own business."

She thought back. "The blacksmith?"

"Mr. Reed."

"I was merely trying to help."

"But it was my horse."

Semantics. "I am sorry you disapprove . "

He shrugged and leaned back on his forearms. "You took charge and . . ."

"And what?"

"You didn't even know the man's name."

She felt a slight stitch—but only slight. "And what else did you observe?"

He hesitated, but continued. "I've been out of the country a long time, but from what I've observed it seems that Summerfield is governed very much like the army. The men without rank give every indication they respect the officers. But whether or not they truly hold them in esteem is uncertain."

"Are you suggesting the people of Summerfield don't respect me?"

"I haven't been back long enough to know. But in my experience, an officer has to earn the respect of his soldiers. Part of that is knowing their names."

Adelaide took offense. "I have never done anything to impede their respect."

"I'm sure you haven't. And forgive me if I implied unpleasant feelings where none exist."

She was confused how one interaction with a smithy had caused this conversation. "Do you want me to go through town and say, 'Hello, Joe, how you been?'"

"Not in those words, no."

She felt a wave of frustration rise. "The people of Summerfield look up to my family for the legacy we represent."

"They offer you their deference "

Where was he taking this? "Of course they do."

"But do they care about you?"

"I assume so."

"As much as you care about them."

He was twisting her carefully ordered life into a knot. And she was done with it. She struggled to her feet, and when he stood and tried to help, she pushed his hands away. Only when she was fully stable did she respond. "Are you certain you've spent your time away in India? For you sound horribly American with your democratic, 'we're-all-created-equal' notions." He began to speak, but she stopped his words with a hand. "British society is firmly grounded in centuries of tradition. The titled rule over the title-less, who in return are given security, compassion, guidance, and . . . and. . ."

"Servitude?"

She gasped.

He let out a sigh. "I'm sorry, Addie. I went too far."

"Lady Summerfield to you."

Their anger opened a crevasse between them. Adelaide regretted her last words, regretted the entire conversation. Of all people in the world, she did not want to argue with Grady. Even though he'd only just returned, he'd already become her safe place, her respite, and her haven.

"I am sorry too, Grady."

"Colonel Cummings to you." But he said it with a smile and extended his hands. "My point was too severe and expressed too harshly. Simply put, the fact that something is *old* does not mean it's *right*. Or fair."

She kept her own hands at her side. "So you want me to change the entire structure of British society?"

"I want you to consider tearing down the wall that stands between your family title and the people of Summerfield. Tear down the wall that stands between your family title and . . . and me."

She was moved by words. "There is no wall between us."

"Isn't there?"

It was a complicated subject.

He cocked his head, studying her. "Let all of Summerfield see the extraordinary woman behind the title. Let them see a bit more of the Addie I knew."

"That woman doesn't exist anymore."

He touched her hand. "Perhaps she's been tucked away, letting Adelaide and Lady Summerfield take over, but I assure you she is alive and well."

"You assure me."

He wove his fingers through hers. "I do." He took a fresh breath. "'A man's heart deviseth his way: but the Lord directeth his steps.'"

"You insult me and now you quote scripture at me?"

"Not *at* you," he said. "I'm sharing *with* you." He sighed deeply, looking past her. "You're so accustomed to directing others and doing things the way it's always been done. Perhaps *you* could use some direction."

"By you, I suppose."

"Addie . . . I was talking about God."

As her presence was detached from the daily lives of Summerfield's villagers, so was the presence of God detached from her own life. She believed there *was* a God, and she prayed occasionally and attended weekly church services. But she had never considered asking God for direction. He'd created her to be a capable woman, and that fact directed her actions. The idea that *God* should direct those actions was a bit unsettling.

"Shall we go check on my horse now?"

She let herself be led back to town.

Mother stood at the store window, gazing upon the square.

"There she goes again."

"There who goes again?" Nana asked.

"The dowager. With that man."

Lila helped Nana string the spools of ribbon onto the stick they'd brought back from the woods. Papa had set two nails into the edge of a shelf, creating a brace from which to rest the branch. It was a very good idea. "Please, get away from the window, Mother. You saw them go to the blacksmith's earlier. They've probably come back to pick up their horse."

"Not their horse. His horse."

Why did it matter?

"I wonder where they've been for three-quarters of an hour."

"Taking a stroll. She's entitled. The village *is* part of her family's estate. Technically, it's all hers."

Mother shook her head, her eyes glued to the action outside. "She never walks. Even when she was younger she always came to town by carriage."

"It's a lovely day," Nana said, making all the ribbon-ends even. "Perhaps that's the reason for her stroll."

"I wonder when the colonel is leaving town," Mother said.

"When he's done with his business, I suppose," Papa said. "Really, Fidelia. Come away from the window."

She did turn away, but the subject wasn't closed. "What *is* his business? Every day he leaves the village and goes . . . somewhere."

"Now that *is* suspicious," Papa said.

Mother stomped her foot. "Don't make fun of me. Everyone wants to know what's going on."

"I don't," Lila said.

"Neither do I," Nana added.

As expected, their comments earned a vicious glare. "If you don't care what's what, then I won't bother you with the details when I find them out."

"That sounds agreeable," Papa said.

Mother spun toward the door and left the mercantile, her petticoat causing a stack of pots to topple with a crash.

"A fitting exit, all in all," Papa said.

They shared a laugh at Mother's expense.

It served her right.

It is a truth universally acknowledged, that a single man in possession of a good fortune must be in want of a wife.

Ruth hated starting a new book, even if the book had such a promising first line as did *Pride and Prejudice.*

And today . . . to be honest, she didn't feel like reading. There was a restlessness within her that had caused her to flit from her embroidery to the arrangement of some flowers Molly had cut for her, to the window seat to read a new novel.

She put a hand to her torso, feeling a flutter of . . . anticipation? Was something going to happen?

Movement outside drew her attention, and she quickly set

the book aside in order to see. There, walking up the drive was her mother-in-law on the arm of Colonel Cummings.

Their progress wasn't important, but the way Adelaide bumped shoulders with him, and laughed, and touched his arm . . .

"They're in love," she whispered.

And suddenly she wanted to be a part of it, a direct witness, a participant.

She glanced at the clock on the mantel. *Yes. You must do this. You must.*

She hurried to the bell-pull to call Molly. Her stomach danced in anticipation.

And fear.

A few minutes later, Molly came in. "Yes, my lady?"

"Help me dress for tea."

Molly looked confused. "I was going to bring some up for you."

Ruth shook her head. "I want to go down for tea."

Molly's eyebrows rose. "That's wonderful, my lady."

"My green bengaline, please."

She knew it brought out the hazel in her eyes. If she was going to do this, she might as well make a good impression.

Ruth hesitated at the door to her bedroom and smoothed the dress's ruching against her hips. She turned back to Molly. "How do I look?"

"You look beautiful, your ladyship." Molly said. "Your family is going to be so glad to see you."

Surprised was a better word.

"Wish me luck." She put her hand on the doorknob and felt her nerves tingle. *If I do this, there will be no turning back.*

Years ago she'd stepped into her private vessel and had cast off from the busyness and business of the shore. She lived her life perpetually floating on a serene lake. She was vaguely aware of an unseen world of day-to-day activities that whirled and swirled in the water below, holding her up, allowing her the serenity of being suspended above it all.

She'd grown content in this state of separation, and as one year had passed to another, the idea that anything *beneath* would break through the calm of the surface, or that she would dangle her hand over the side of her vessel and breach the tenuous border between them, was impossible.

Until now. Until these odd and interesting developments between her husband and Lady Carlton, and now between the dowager and a man who was making himself very, very familiar. There was now something to be lost by floating on the lake. Something to be missed. Something at stake.

"Your ladyship?" Molly asked. "Is something wrong?"

"I'm fine. It will all be fine."

Molly appeared at her side. "It *will* be fine."

Ruth nodded, then turned the doorknob to the right. She felt the door loose itself from its frame, ready to do her bidding. With a single movement she could slip into that other world without making a splash.

And so, she did.

She heard voices in the drawing room. Frederick, Clarissa, Adelaide, and the colonel.

Retreat! There's still time.

She shook her head against the inner voice that had held her captive far too long. Love was in the air, and love was at stake. She could be brave for love's sake.

Ruth walked downstairs, gripping the railing. With a fresh breath she crossed the foyer and paused only a moment before making her entrance. *Help me do this.*

"Mother!"

Clarissa's exclamation was only the first.

"Ruth!"

"My dear," Frederick said, coming to her side. "How nice of you to join us."

Adelaide called for another cup for tea.

"I am sorry to interrupt," she said.

"It is no interruption," Frederick said. There was a certain flush to his cheeks, as if he was genuinely glad to see her.

She took a seat near the fireplace.

The colonel stepped close. "I'd like to introduce myself. I'm Colonel Cummings, at your service, Lady Summerfield." He gave her a smart bow.

She felt her cheeks grow hot. Although he was the dowager's age, he was a very handsome man. His wrinkles only added to his appeal, somehow marking him as a man who had *lived*. "It is a pleasure to make your acquaintance, Colonel."

Another cup was brought and poured.

And then there was silence. The conversation and laughter she'd heard before her entrance fizzled as though her presence was a pail of water poured upon a fire.

"Well then," Clarissa said.

Ruth sipped her tea, her heart beating furiously. *Someone please say something.*

The colonel made the first attempt. "What are your best crops, Lord Summerfield?"

"Oats and barley. And the plum and apple orchards are doing well."

"We will plant alfalfa soon," Adelaide said.

"And we put an abundance of hare on the menu at this time of year," Clarissa said. "Pesky pests."

"How is the sheep market?" the colonel asked.

"Fair to middling," Frederick said. "The wool market fluctuates."

"But it is holding," Adelaide said.

They continued to talk around Ruth, as if she wasn't in the room.

I don't belong here. I know nothing about the estate; about crops, wool, or even menus.

Ruth felt tears threaten and bit her lip, willing them away. But they were persistent, and she knew the battle would be lost if she stayed.

She rose from her chair and set the cup and saucer upon the tray. "If you will excuse me." She hurried from the room, desperate to escape to her suite.

Frederick ran after her, catching her in the foyer. "Ruth. Stop." He took her arm. "What's wrong?"

She didn't know how to explain to him what she couldn't even explain to herself. And so she simply shook her head. "I'm sorry. I shouldn't have come to tea."

"Of course you should have come. I'm glad you joined us." Tears streamed down her cheeks and she wiped them away. "I'm sorry. I don't know why I'm crying."

He stopped the trail of a tear with his thumb. "Then stop," he said softly. "There is no reason to cry."

She couldn't remember the last time he'd been so tender — the last time she'd let him be tender. "I'm sorry," she said again. "It's silly."

"Yes it is," he said. "So stop apologizing."

"I'm sor—" She managed a smile.

Which he returned. "Do come back in."

She looked toward the drawing room and heard the conversation that had resumed in her absence. The idea of returning after running away . . . it was too much to bear.

"Perhaps another day."

He took her hand and squeezed it once. "I would like that."

Really? She climbed the long staircase, pausing once to look back.

Frederick stood at the bottom, watching her.

She'd come downstairs to witness the love between Adelaide and the colonel, only to witness a moment in her own love story.

Her stomach did another kind of dance.

Chapter Nine

Lila carefully lettered a sign to put in front of the new display of preserves: *Succulent Blackberry Preserves: 6d.* Once complete, she set it on a small table on which she'd draped a pretty bolt-end of sprigged cotton. Then she added a basket of fresh berries to draw the eye. The twelve jars of preserves they'd made the day before were arranged just so.

"That's so pretty," Rose said. "It makes the preserves look special."

Mother gave it a glance. "People will be snitching those berries, you know they will."

"Which will make them want more and buy the preserves," Lila said.

Mother harrumphed and went back to her work.

"Your ribbon display inspired me, Nana," Lila said. "I was also thinking about arranging something for the toothpaste pots. We now have areca nut *and* cherry flavors, *and* badger hair toothbrushes, but people aren't buying."

"Probably because they don't notice them," Nana said.

"Probably because they're too expensive," Papa said. "People are content with boar bristle. They don't want to pay more for badger."

Mother prickled. "What people want and what they can be tempted to buy are two different things. If I'd had my way, we would have ordered them with silver handles rather than bone."

Mother wanted to tempt customers but disparaged Lila's attempt to make special displays? She couldn't win.

But then the front door burst open. "Hallo, family!"

In a single motion Morgan tossed his valise to the floor and whirled his mother around.

"Put me down, you silly boy," Mother giggled.

With her cheeks flushed, she was almost pretty.

Papa and Lila were next, embracing the scholar, welcoming him home.

He winked at Rose, and said, "Glad to see you, Rosie," which made her blush.

And then he saw Nana. His eyebrows rose. "Nana? What are you doing here?"

"She lives here now," Mother said. "Came to live with us after your grandfather died."

Lila cringed at her directness.

Morgan froze in place. "Grandfather died?"

Nana nodded

Morgan gathered her in an embrace as delicate as his mother's had been exuberant. "I'm so sorry."

Lila could see Nana relax in the comfort of his arms. "He was so proud of you. As am I. You've grown taller and stronger, from a boy into a man."

"Yes, well . . ." His brow furrowed, then smoothed. He had something on his mind.

Mother pulled him away. "I say we close the store and celebrate my son's return."

"Our son," Papa said.

"Oh piddle," she snapped, and moved to lock the door. "Morgan is home. Our wonderful son is home."

"Mother, really," Morgan said, with a glance to Lila. "There's no need for that. Just let me settle in."

She made a pouty face. "If you insist." Then she drew his head down to her height and kissed him on the cheek with a loud *smack*. "Now that you're home, all is right with the world." She picked up his valise. "Come and I'll help you unpack."

Morgan took the valise from her, gave the rest of them an apologetic sigh, and followed his mother upstairs.

It took a minute for the room to stop vibrating.

"It *is* good he's home." Papa said.

Lila agreed. Though with Morgan home, everything changed. Not necessarily for the worst, but the atmosphere was decidedly different.

Nana moved close and asked Rose and Lila a question. "Does Fidelia always act like this when Morgan comes home?"

Lila wasn't sure what to say. "He doesn't encourage it."

Rose spoke softly. "In her eyes he can do no wrong."

Nana glanced at Lila. "Leaving you. . .?"

She let herself say it aloud. "Second best."

Nana's cheeks flushed. "I won't take anything away from Morgan, but you, sweet girl, remember you're a joy, a jewel. Even if your mother doesn't see it."

Will never see it. Lila forced a smile. "Enough talk of such things. Morgan is home, and it *is* a time to celebrate."

She tried to mean it.

Lila reached for the last roll on the plate.

"No, Lila." Her mother yanked the plate away and handed it across the table to Morgan. "Let Morgan have the last one."

Morgan glanced at Lila, took the roll, then tossed it to her across the table.

"Thank you, brother." She quickly tore it in half and buttered it lest Mother try to give it away again.

Papa sliced a piece of his ham. "So, son. Tell us about school. How did you do with your studies?"

"I received top marks. Pass the green beans, please."

"Top marks!" Mother clapped her hands in a flurry of enthusiasm. "I always knew you would earn great commendation."

Morgan shrugged. "The classes are too easy. It's quite a bore."

"Learning is never a bore," Papa said.

"Hmmph" Morgan said under his breath.

"What did you say?"

Morgan set his fork down. "I don't see the point of going to school and learning about Greek mythology or discussing whether or not Richard the Third killed his nephews in the Tower of London so he could be king."

"I would love to learn such things," Lila said. "King Richard killed his nephews?"

"He was never accused," Morgan said. "But once in the Tower, they were never seen again. The oldest was thirteen and was awaiting his coronation as Edward the Fifth, but—"

"They were young boys?" Lila asked.

"Ten and thirteen, I think, but the point is, what good does that kind of knowledge do me? I'm to be a shopkeeper. All I need to know is how to add two plus two. The rest is drivel."

Papa drew in a long breath and sat straighter in his chair. "There is more to shop-keeping than adding numbers."

"I don't mean to insult you, Papa. It's just that I'm tired of school. I think I'd be of best use to myself and to the family if I would stay here in Summerfield. Settle in, as an adult."

"Actually," Papa said, looking at Mother. "That *is* what I'd prefer. This fancy education is your mother's idea."

"And I stand by it," Mother said. "No son of mine is going to be ignorant."

Lila was not up to another argument. "So you want to settle down here?"

"I know what he wants," Nana said. "He wants to get married and give me great-grandchildren."

Morgan's clouded face brightened. "That's exactly what I'd like to do."

Mother shook her head. "There's plenty of time for that."

But Lila could tell this wasn't a generic plan. "Do you have someone in mind?"

"Actually, I do. I'm in love with Molly Wallace, and I intend to ask her to be my wife."

Mother's forehead furrowed. "Molly? Isn't she a housemaid at the manor?"

"That was years ago. She's not a housemaid anymore, she is lady's maid to the countess."

All eyes turned to Mother. "Absolutely not!" she said, slamming the flat of her hand on the table. "I forbid it."

"Fidelia, calm down."

"The Wallaces are far from an upstanding family. Her father is the town drunk and ends up unconscious in front of the Fox Run every other night."

"But Mrs. Wallace is a nice woman," Lila said. "She always greets me kindly when I buy eggs."

Nana rearranged the peas on her plate. "A man's behavior can't be blamed on his wife and children, nor should they suffer for it."

Mother pushed her chair back and stood. She loomed over the table, pointing a finger at Morgan. "I did not arrange your education so you could marry a maid, and especially not the maid of Ruth Weston."

Ah. There was the sticky in the pot.

To his credit, Morgan remained calm. "I will marry whomever I like. That you have some feud with the countess is not my concern."

"It is not a feud."

"Then for once and all, explain it to us," Morgan asked, leaning back in his chair. He crossed his arms, ready to listen.

Lila held in a gasp. Only Morgan could talk to Mother this way. But she was as curious as he about the feud. Would they finally hear some details?

Papa spoke up, "Morgan, this is hardly appropriate."

Did Papa know the whole of it?

Mother returned to her chair. "I do not have a feud with Ruth Weston, nor is it any of your business." She looked at each person and added, "*Any* of your business."

Morgan took his turn at rising from the table. "If you'll excuse me, I have a prior engagement." He looked directly at their mother. "Engagement."

As he left the dining room, Mother scrambled after him. "Morgan! Morgan, don't go. I'm sorry . . ."

Her pandering words were swallowed by the sound of the front door closing.

"Well then," Nana said. She turned to her son. "What dispute lies between Fidelia and the countess?"

"It's not a dispute exactly," Papa said.

He looked to the doorway, but Lila couldn't tell if he was concerned about Mother's return or wistful about the dramatic exchange that had just transpired.

Come on, Papa. Tell us.

His gaze returned to the table. "It happened before I met her."

"You met Fidelia in London," Nana said. "She was living there, as were your father and I. I remember that."

"Actually, her parents were there too. They'd left Summerfield for good and . . ."

"So Mother is originally from here?" Lila asked.

They all glanced toward the doorway and the sound of Mother's imminent return.

He quickly finished his sentence. "Yes, but it's complicated, and I suggest the subject is dropped. Permanently."

No! You can't go quiet now. Not when I'm finally getting some answers.

Mother entered the dining room and plopped down on her chair, yanking her discarded napkin onto her lap.

"Are you all right?" Papa asked.

It was clear more drama was forthcoming.

Thank God for the moon.

Today was the tenth, the day Morgan would be home. *Meet me at the arbor after dark.*

Dark had come slowly. But now, with only the moon to guide her, Molly made her way through the formal gardens of the manor to the farthest end, where a bench stood beside a clematis-covered arbor.

Memories propelled her: his strong arms holding her tight, the smell of his jacket, the feel of his hair across her cheek. She ran through the arbor and suddenly . . .

He took her in his arms, and she was happily smothered with kisses and desperate embraces. When Molly came up for air, she got to look at him. Even in the moonlight she could see his chiseled chin and strong nose. "I can't believe you're finally home."

He stroked her cheek. "I am home, with no intention of ever leaving."

Really? "Come tell me everything," she said, pulling him toward the bench.

He snuck an extra kiss. "You haven't had enough talk from my letters?"

"I want to hear it all in person."

He shook his head. "You first. How are you?"

"I'm the same. Not much has changed." But then she remembered Dottie. "Except my sister is working here now, as a tweeny."

"She's just a child."

"She's twelve. That was my age when I started here. And actually . . . she's not a child anymore."

After a moment he took her meaning correctly. "Even so, couldn't she wait a few years?"

Molly shook her head adamantly. "It's very important she gets out of the house."

"*Very* important?"

Molly had never told Morgan about her father. It was a part of her life she wished to forget. But now that they'd grown so close . . .

"My father is not an honorable man," she said. "Not like your father at all."

"I know he drinks."

"A lot of men drink." She left it at that. Maybe *that* was enough.

He studied her face, then took her hand and placed it on his knee. "What did he do to you?"

Tears begged for release. She shook her head, willing them to stay away. "Once I grew beyond childhood he . . ."

They shared a moment of silence. Then Morgan said, "He didn't . . . ?"

"He didn't. I managed to keep him at bay, but I wasn't getting any sleep and was living in fear of being alone with him. That's why I sought a job at the manor when I was so young. I *had* to get away." She glanced up at him, needing to finish it. "Just as I had to get Dottie away."

He put his arm around her, drawing her close. "Men like him should be shot. Or worse."

Actually, she'd thought about his demise many times. Wished for it.

"Why didn't your mother stop him?" he asked. "Surely she knew."

"It's unspoken between us. But yes, she knows. It was her idea I get Dottie the job."

"She should have stopped him."

"How? She can't leave him. Where would she go? Who would believe her?"

He kissed the top of her head. "I'm so sorry you've had to endure such fear and evil. I wish you would have told me about this before."

Molly closed her eyes and leaned against him. "I don't want to think about him anymore. I want to think about us."

"Good," he said, "because I love you. And no matter what happens in the world around us, you need to know you're safe with me."

She nodded, burrowing her cheek against his chest, feeling a surprising amount of relief for unburdening her past.

She *was* safe with Morgan. And even more than that, loved.

Chapter Ten

Lila reveled in the chance to take Raider for a ride. It was the first time they'd been out since she'd fallen and hurt her wrist.

But as she and Raider galloped across the meadow toward the river, she spotted Joseph Kidd standing next to his horse near a grove of trees. She pulled on the reins, knowing she shouldn't be presumptuous, but wanting to be.

Happily, he waved and beckoned her over.

"Miss Hayward," he said as she approached. "I see you're back in the saddle."

She bent her wrist forward and back. "I am completely recovered."

"I am glad to hear it." He took hold of Raider's bridle and stroked his forelock. "I hear your brother is home from school?"

"He is."

"School went well for him?"

Lila remembered her brother's opinion of his education. "Let's just say he's glad to be home. He much prefers working to studying, and Summerfield to the city."

"On the latter, I agree with him." He looked around, taking a deep breath. "There is nothing like the fresh air of the country. I find the sooty atmosphere of London oppressive."

"As do I," she said, although her experience of London was sporadic and short in duration—only when Papa invited her along to get supplies. While Mr. Kidd . . . she knew the Kidds had recently returned from months in London for the social season.

They both turned toward the sound of a horse. And there was Lady Clarissa, riding toward them.

Mr. Kidd waved, then looked to the ground, his face red. *This was arranged.* "I should go," Lila said. *Quickly.*

But then Lady Clarissa called out to her. "Miss Hayward, how nice to see you." She pulled at the reins, stopping the horse in front of Mr. Kidd. He helped her down, and she kissed his cheek. "My darling, Joseph."

Darling Joseph? Lila hadn't heard that Lady Clarissa and Mr. Kidd were courting.

Her need to leave intensified. If she didn't, she feared her emotions would explode in anger, embarrassment, and grief. If Lady Clarissa and Mr. Kidd were a couple, it put into question the significance of the time he and Lila had shared and the conversations they'd enjoyed.

You silly, silly girl. He was merely being polite. How could you ever think a man like Mr. Kidd would feel any sort of affection toward you beyond polite friendship? Your absurd, impossible daydreams must stop.

Lila pinched her earlobe, needing the pain to keep the tears at bay. When she felt she could safely use her voice, she said, "I really ought to be getting home. Mother wasn't keen on my being away from the store this morning, so I shouldn't delay in getting back."

"You needn't leave on our account," Lady Clarissa said.

The tears were winning. Time was short. "I really must."

Lady Clarissa slipped her arm through Mr. Kidd's, drawing him close to her side. "Before you go, I might as well tell you the happy news. Joseph's family and mine have decided we should marry."

Marry? Anger took care of the tears. Mr. Kidd was promised to Lady Clarissa the entire time he'd paid attention to Lila? "Congratulations," she managed.

But then Lila noticed something odd: when Mr. Kidd tried to pull his arm free of Lady Clarissa's grasp, she clung to it harder. He looked miserable, like an animal caught in a trap.

Lady Clarissa's face brightened as if she had an idea. "Lila, would you be willing to serve as our courier? With Crompton Hall so far from Summerfield Manor, it's been tedious getting word to each other. But since the village is in the center . . . If I had a note for Joseph, I could leave it with you at the store, and vice versa."

Mr. Kidd looked dumbstruck. "Clarissa, no. There's no need. Besides, it is not fair to involve Lila."

"All's fair in love. And she's our friend. I'm sure she's very willing to help us facilitate our courtship by passing a few notes back and forth."

But I don't want Mr. Kidd visiting the mercantile to give you a note.

Lady Clarissa adjusted the fingers of her riding gloves. "You *will* do this for us, Lila. Please? And also, you will remain silent about our future plans. Our fathers haven't decided when the formal announcement will be made."

What Lila wanted no longer mattered, and resignation fell over her like a smothering blanket on a hot day. "Of course," she said. "I'd be happy to help."

"Thank you," Lady Clarissa said. "I'll make it up to you." She turned toward the river. "Joseph, come. Let's walk."

Lila was dismissed. Once again she turned Raider toward home, but as he began to trot away, Joseph called out, "Miss Hayward! Wait."

He ran to her, and she quickly swiped a tear away.

He laid a hand on Raider's bridle, calming him. "I want to apologize for all of that. Clarissa exaggerates."

"So you're not betrothed?"

"We . . . our fathers have decided we should be."

Which meant it was as good as done. "It's none of my business, Mr. Kidd. I don't really care if you and Lady —"

"But I care. I care what you think."

A tear escaped, and this time she let it run its course.

His face was the essence of regret and sincerity. "I am so sorry for all this."

"Joseph?" Lady Clarissa called out. "Come now."

Joseph sighed deeply. "You needn't pass notes for us."

"Tis not a problem," she said. *At least it will give me a chance to see you.* "Let me go, Mr. Kidd. You are needed elsewhere."

He released Raider, and Lila spurred him into a gallop, leaning forward to better cut through the air.

Pain tore her heart in two. It served her right for believing in fairy tales.

"Where are we going, Grady?" Adelaide asked, as she sat beside him in the open carriage he'd let from the blacksmith.

"Tis a surprise."

"I do not like surprises. I like to know what's going to happen, and when."

"You like to be in control of what will happen, and when."

"What is wrong with that?"

"Today *I* am in control. And there's nothing you can do to stop me."

She didn't want him to stop, but she did wish he would slow down a bit. "I have never been in such a carriage," she said. "No coachman, just you and me."

"Nice, isn't it?"

"But the sides are so low, and the wheels are so large . . . and you are going too fast. Please slow down."

He slowed the horse to a trot. "Better?"

"Much."

"You didn't used to be squeamish. Don't you remember the two of us flying like the wind in a phaeton like this? That's why I chose this rig today. In honor of that excursion."

She found she *did* have memories of that ride. It had been wild and reckless, and if she remembered correctly, she'd squealed with delight through all of it.

"Do you want to take the reins, like you did that day?"

"No thank you."

Grady shook his head. "You're acting old, Addie. Where's the fiery woman I knew?"

"If you want to be correct about it, it was not a woman you

knew. It was a girl who felt invincible."

"Fighting in battle took care of *my* youthful invincibility."

With a quick glance to make sure there was no one to see she leaned her head on his shoulder. "How many battles did you endure?"

"On the field, too many to mention. Off the field, too many to ignore."

"What does that mean?"

"It's been a hard life without you, Addie. I had to fight through ordinary days as surely as if I'd had a rifle and saber."

"My life hasn't been easy either."

He snickered. "Oh, yes, it's hard being a countess, living in an enormous mansion that drips with gilt and crystal, with dozens of servants at your beck and call."

She let go of his arm. "It was not the place where I lived that was difficult, it was the place that died inside me that caused me to suffer. I loved you as much as you loved me, Grady Cummings."

"Love you," he said softly. "I love you."

She took his arm again. "And I . . ."

He looked at her. "Come now. You can say it."

She should have said it without his goading. "I love you."

He kissed her cheek, then turned the carriage from the main road onto a narrow dirt road.

"What are you doing?"

"You'll see." After a few hundred feet he surveyed the area. "This will do."

"We are in the middle of nowhere. It's a field."

He stopped the carriage and helped her down. Then he led her across the field of grass that was spotted with pink and purple wildflowers. Trees edged the horizon, but when he finally stopped walking it was as though they were standing in a sea of undulating green.

"I bet no one's ever stood right here," she said. "It smells completely and utterly fresh."

"That was my plan," he said. "To take us to a rare place,

separate from people and noise and all that is Summerfield."
He took her hands in his. "This place is ours now, Addie. I
claim it as a place that will always represent this moment in
our lives." He got down on one knee. "My dearest Addie, will
you do me the great honor of becoming my wife?"

Her practical side conjured a dozen logical reasons why
this was madness. But she closed her eyes, shutting the
reasons away. For once in her life — for the first time in her
life? — this was not a time for the Countess of Summerfield, it
was a time for just plain Addie.

She was surprised to hear her words said aloud, yet
relieved when she heard them. "I will," she said. "I will marry
you."

He took a ring from the pocket of his weskit and placed it
on her finger. "It was my grandmother's. It's the ring I
planned to give you forty-seven years ago."

It was a lovely topaz in a filigree setting. "So we do now
what we should have done then?"

"Exactly," Grady said. "We love each other until death do
us part."

Riding home from the place of their betrothal, Addie no
longer minded the tight seating of the phaeton. She couldn't
get close enough to Grady.

She was engaged. At her age? It was shocking. It *would* be
shocking to her family and all of Summerfield.

She didn't care.

"Look," Grady said. "There's Lady Clarissa riding with a
young man."

Addie looked in the direction he pointed. "That's Joseph
Kidd."

"Is he her beau?"

"Remember I told you he's to be her husband. It's been
arranged."

"Arranged? As in, arranged by others?"

"Frederick and I have spoken with his father."

"Addie. How dare you. After what we suffered, you do the same to Clarissa?"

"It is not the same," she said. "Clarissa has no one else in mind. Or rather, she has too many in mind. We're doing her a favor by choosing for her, encouraging her to settle down."

"Does she feel a favor has been done?"

Addie didn't answer.

When Clarissa saw the phaeton, she said something to Joseph that caused him to ride away while she rode toward them.

"Grandmamma. Colonel Cummings," she said, pulling her horse beside them. "Isn't it a glorious day for a ride?"

"A perfect day," Grady said.

"So what have you two been up to?" Clarissa asked.

And then, without meaning to say it, perhaps goaded by Grady's pointed questions, Addie answered. "Grady just proposed and I accepted. We are going to be married."

With that, she took the reins from Grady, chucked at the horse, and pulled away.

"My, my," Grady said. "You are the girl I fell in love with, aren't you?"

"I believe I am."

Chapter Eleven

Adelaide Styler Weston, the Dowager Countess of Summerfield, felt a ridiculous pull in her stomach as she sat in her own drawing room.

"Take a breath, Addie," Grady whispered from behind her chair. "It's not like the first time we announced our intention to marry." He laid a comforting hand on her shoulder.

She took his hand, kissed it, and kept hold of it.

He was right, of course. The first time they'd declared their love, they had been in the parlor of her childhood home, positioned just like this, with her on the settee and Grady standing behind. She remembered watching him step forward to proclaim his intentions and seeing his left leg shake the fabric of his stirrup trousers.

He'd had good cause to be nervous—as had she. For their request to marry was a long-shot, a shot that missed its mark. As a mere army private, Grady was not good enough for Adelaide. Not when she had the chance to marry the next Earl of Summerfield. *Let's be practical, Adelaide.*

Her father's words still haunted her. For her marriage to Samuel Weston was the essence of practicality. Every day of her life was pragmatic, functional, and ever so sensible. In Samuel's defense, he'd also been pushed into the marriage. And so, they had grown to respect each other, or more specifically, to *accept* each other, and one year had grown into a decade before turning into a lifetime.

On that fateful afternoon, Addie had run from the room in tears and had watched Grady ride away. It was the last time she'd seen him until he'd recently appeared at the manor, his hand extended, his eyes twinkling, saying all the things she needed and longed to hear.

Addie heard the voices of her family, answering her call to gather. "They're coming."

"And we are ready to meet them. Present arms!"

His military command made her smile, but she took his words to heart, vowing to be strong. She was not a nineteen-year-old girl; she was the matriarch of a family. She'd never been afraid to wield her authority before, and she would not be afraid to wield it today.

"Let them come," she said, mostly to herself.

She let go of his hand and sat straighter in the chair, like a queen waiting for her court to pay tribute.

Young George came into the room first and gave her a kiss on the cheek. "Hi, Grandmamma."

He smelled of fresh air and horses. He slouched in a chair nearby, with only the back of his head and his bottom touching its upholstery.

Clarissa arrived and looked at her grandmother, Grady, and her grandmother again. "Are you telling everyone?" she whispered.

"You shall see."

Frederick arrived next—with Ruth. Ruth must have come at his invitation, because Addie had not invited her. Seeing her downstairs would take some getting used to. They both looked wary.

Once they were settled, Frederick said, "So. Mother. You summoned us for a reason?"

She'd practiced what she would say in front of the mirror this morning, but suddenly the words scattered like chaff being thrown into the wind, never to be fully recovered.

"I . . . I . . ."

Grady spoke up. "I have asked this dear lady to be my wife."

Each set of eyes—save George, who was busy picking a scab on his elbow—looked from Grady to Addie, awaiting her confirmation. Even then, all she could manage was, "I accepted."

Clarissa, being a well-bred girl, was first to step forward to kiss her cheek and shake Grady's hand. "Best wishes and congratulations, Grandmamma. Colonel. I wish you every happiness."

Ruth looked to her husband as if to ask, *Do we support this?* But when he sat silent, she surprisingly stepped forward to offer her good wishes.

All eyes turned to the earl. He stood stoic, his hands clasped behind his back, his forehead wrinkled, his head slightly cocked like he hadn't heard quite right. He blinked too often, as if hoping to keep the issue from settling.

"Frederick?" Addie said. "You are to give us your blessing."

Unfortunately, for the first time in his adult life, he did not succumb to his mother's command.

"Father. . ." Clarissa said.

Apparently, her voice broke the spell that held him captive, and he looked at her. Then at his mother. "Marry?"

Addie had to laugh. After all the drama of his reaction, this was all he could muster? Yet the humor in it helped her move toward action. "Yes, marry." She stood and drew Grady out from behind the chair so she could take his arm. "The truth is, Colonel Cummings and I wanted to marry when we were Clarissa's age, but my father insisted I marry your father."

She had a sudden thought that Frederick would be hurt by this point and tried to soften it. "I did my duty to my family. I honored my parents' wishes, just as your father honored the wishes of his parents." Addie couldn't help but glance at Clarissa but didn't hold her gaze very long. "Yet just because we couldn't marry didn't mean we ever stopped loving each other." She looked at Grady, who smiled down at her. My, he was a stunning man.

"It is highly unorthodox," Frederick said. "You are the dowager countess."

"A title that is mine for life."

"But your duties . . ."

"I have lived a life of duty, always doing what was needed, meeting every obligation and every responsibility to the best of my ability." She felt her throat tighten and prayed she could finish her thought with strength. "I sacrificed for this family and this title. Now, in my later years, I am going to discharge another sort of duty — the duty I have to myself to be happy with the man I love."

Grady nodded and met her gaze. "My life's duty has been to queen and country. I put my life at risk to discharge that duty. Your mother's duty has been to her title and her family. Both of us have gone beyond what was expected of us and have served our obligations well. Now, for the remainder of our years, our first obligation will be to each other." He looked upon the family. "I promise to cherish your mother, to adore her, and to put her happiness above my own."

"Until death do us part," Addie said.

Grady smiled down at her and whispered, "Does this mean we're married?"

"Soon," she whispered. "So then, Frederick," Addie declared, feeling her usual authority return. "I assume I have your blessing?"

He took a deep breath, but nodded. "You will do what you want anyway, so yes, I suppose you do."

"Good." She stepped away from Grady and drew Frederick into an embrace. "Thank you for your support."

Then Addie nodded to Ruth, who nodded back and smiled her approval, making Addie glad she'd left her sanctum.

Clarissa hugged her grandmother, then asked, "When is the wedding?"

Addie looked to Grady. He gave her a wink, then said, "We were thinking of Saturday."

"This Saturday?" Clarissa asked.

Addie returned to Grady's side. "We want a simple wedding in the garden, with just family and the household present. Will you handle the details for us, Clarissa? If anyone knows about parties, you do."

"I would be happy to."

George showed his first interest in the proceedings by popping out of the chair. "Can Johnny and the others at the stable come?"

Addie nodded. "All the stable workers, the footmen, the grounds-workers, the entire household." She remembered another issue. "Clarissa? Would you stand up with me?"

"I would be honored."

"Can I be in the wedding too?" George asked.

"You are too old to be a page. Perhaps you can be an usher," Addie said. "And I would like Frederick to give me away."

"That's rather unusual," her son said.

"But appropriate, I think."

Grady looked to the foyer, where Dixon stood, alert. "Since Frederick and George have their duties, I was hoping that Dixon . . ." He strode to the butler. "Mr. Dixon, since you have known me longer than all others, will you stand up with me as my best man?"

Dixon looked flabbergasted, and his eyes strayed to the family. Did he want their approval or to be saved?

Frederick stepped forward. "Join the unorthodox wedding, Dixon. For I too can think of no better best man."

Dixon cleared his throat, then said, "I would be happy to stand with you, Colonel Cummings."

"There then," Grady said, returning to the drawing room. "It's settled."

"There is one more thing," Frederick said. "Will you be living in your suite, Mother?"

They hadn't talked about that. "I suppose we could. Or we could take over a few of the guest rooms and have them adapted to our use. Even with that, we would still have twenty to spare."

But Grady shook his head. "I have another idea. In fact . . ." He took her hand and stepped toward the front door. "If you will excuse us?"

"Of course," Frederick said.

Grady winked at her. "Come with me."

"Where are we going?"

"It's a surprise."

Clarissa excused herself to check out the garden as a possible wedding site, and George ran off to wherever he spent his days.

Leaving Ruth alone with her husband.

She excused herself to return to her room. Everyone had a place in the wedding party but her. Even the butler.

Frederick stopped her with a hand to her arm. "She didn't mean to slight you, Ruth."

"Yes, she did. And I deserve it. I am not a part of this family anymore, so why should I have a place in its festivities?"

"You are a part of this family. But . . . out of sight, out of mind."

Touché.

"We do like seeing you out and about."

She looked into his eyes, wanting to believe him. "I want Adelaide to be happy. I find their romance sweet, and it's changed her. Even in this short time her hard edges have been worn down—a bit."

Frederick nodded, but then his eyes grew sad. "But what she said . . . does this mean she never loved my father?"

Ruth touched his arm. "I'm sure they came to share a certain understanding. People adapt."

"I suppose. Though Father was such an autocrat, I am not sure he was capable of true love."

"Unlike his son?"

Frederick looked at her as if she'd said something shocking. She held his gaze, willing him to respond in a way she needed. *Please, Frederick, tell me you love me. Tell me you're happy that we married.*

Frederick broke the moment by letting his gaze fall into

nothingness. "I hope I'm nothing like him. Now, if you will excuse me, my dear."

Ruth stood alone in the room, the words she'd wanted to hear battling against the words said. He'd insisted she come downstairs. How hard would it have been for him to say something nice? The drastic steps she'd gone through in order to win him dogged her with doubt. Even after more than two decades the question lingered. If she had not taken those measures, would he have married her?

She left the questions in the drawing room and returned to the solace of her suite.

"Married?" Mrs. Camden said. "The dowager is getting married?"

Dixon turned to Nick, who'd spread the news around the servants' tea table. "You are not to share private news from the family among the household."

"Pardon me, Mr. Dixon," the footman said, "but it's not gossip, nor was it a private conversation. The old dowager —"

"The dowager countess, or her ladyship," Dixon corrected.

"The dowager countess gathered the family to make the announcement. Besides . . ." He looked around the table for effect. "The wedding's to be this Saturday."

Mrs. McDeer dropped her teaspoon, sending it clattering against her saucer. "This Saturday? I'm to create a feast for hundreds of guests in that short a time?"

"There's just to be the family and us. The household."

Molly liked the sound of that. "I love weddings."

Mr. Robbins pushed away from the table. "If you'll excuse me, I must check the condition of Lord Summerfield's morning coat for the wedding."

But the other servants were more concerned with whether they'd have to work the wedding or not. Dixon assured them they wouldn't. "We are to be guests," he kept saying.

"Will there be cake and sweets?" Dottie asked.

Her question received a laugh. "Your teeth are going to rot from all the sweets you want to eat," Gertie said.

"Want to eat," Dottie said. "Don't get to eat."

Sally spoke up. "But the dowager marrying at her age."

"What's wrong with her age?" Bridget asked.

All eyes turned in her direction, for Bridget rarely spoke.

"Nothing's wrong with her age," Molly said. "But it is unusual."

Bridget added milk to her tea and stirred. "Be that as it may, I think it's wonderful. True love knows no bounds or age limitation."

After a moment of silence, Mr. Dixon gave his instructions. "Finish your tea now. Attending or not attending the wedding, there is work to be done."

Molly hurried upstairs, eager to hear the countess's thoughts on the matter. She sensed happy times ahead.

Mother rushed forward to greet a customer coming into the mercantile. "Good morning, Lady Clarissa. How may we help you on this fine day?"

"You may be able to help me tremendously," Clarissa began, looking at Lila. "For I am happy to share some glorious news. My grandmother, the dowager countess, is to be married to Colonel Cummings."

Mother fluttered like a flustered chicken. "Oh, my! That is marvelous news, rather surprising, but a wedding . . ." Then suddenly — Lila saw her mother's mind working — she quickly retrieved paper and pen, ready for the orders Lady Clarissa would give them. "Mr. Hayward and I have numerous connections with the finest London shops, so we're able to supply the wedding with all manner of decoration and finery. I suppose it will be a very large event . . . will our church be large enough for the ceremony?"

"Actually, the wedding is to be a simple family affair in the gardens of Summerfield Manor."

Mother looked as if she'd been slapped. "Just the family?"

"Immediate family," Clarissa said. "And the manor staff."

"That sounds lovely," Lila said. She watched her mother's cheeks redden as the reality of lost sales sank in.

Papa nodded. "So how can we help?"

"The wedding is this Saturday —"

"Saturday!" Mother said. "That is four days from now."

"Since the timing is short . . ." Clarissa pointed at the rolls of ribbon hanging on the stick and inspected the colors. "I'll need all this ribbon except the black, navy, and brown. Happy colors. I will weave them into the garden arbor."

"Of course," Mother said, pointing at Rose to get to it.

That accomplished Clarissa said, "Since there is such short notice, I wanted to ask if Lila would be willing to help me with the arrangements."

Lila was surprised. "Of course. I'd be happy to."

"Perhaps we could go outside to discuss it?"

"Certainly."

As they sat on a bench in front of the store, Clarissa wasted no time in slipping Lila a note. "If you please."

So that's it. Lila slid it into her apron pocket.

"And?" Clarissa said. "I assume Joseph has brought a note for me?"

"I'm sorry, he hasn't."

She smoothed the skirt of her dress with a gloved hand, a twitch in her cheeks revealing her disappointment. "Very well then. If you will pass mine along?"

"Of course." Then Lila added, "Do you really need my help with the wedding?"

"Not particularly."

Lila felt like a used bit of string, tied, cut, and tossed aside.

Clarissa explained. "Since it's a small affair, the servants will take care of whatever details are needed. Though perhaps on the actual day, since they are also guests . . ." She shook her head. "I will think about that later. First things first. The ribbon and the note."

As if Lila had a choice.

Lila dropped a shaving mug to the floor, shattering it into a hundred pieces.

Mother looked over from her work, "What's wrong with you today? You've been a fumble-fingers all morning."

"Sorry," Lila said. "I'll clean it up."

"As if *I* would?"

Rose had already gathered the dustpan and broom. Lila was in the midst of sweeping up the fragments when Joseph Kidd came into the store.

She was glad she wasn't holding something else breakable.

Mother rushed to greet him. "Mr. Kidd. How lovely to see you. What can we help you with today?"

He looked toward Lila, assessing the situation with a glance. "Would you like some assistance, Miss Hayward?"

She peered down at the debris. "This is my second breakage today."

He took the dustpan and knelt beside the shards. "Then perhaps it is time for a break of another kind?"

She didn't want to smile at him, but did. And though she knew her insides shouldn't dance at the thought of spending a few minutes with him . . . they did.

Between the two of them they cleaned up the mess. Mother fussed nearby, saying that Mr. Kidd should *not* belittle himself doing cleanup, but before she could get in full-fuss mode, the chore was done and Lila was accompanying him out to the square.

They avoided the usual gaggle of old men gossiping near the water pump, and Lila pulled the note from her pocket. "Here. From Lady Clarissa."

He slipped it in his left pocket and from the other one, pulled out his own note. "An exchange, though not an even one."

She put his note away. "What do you mean, not 'even'?"

"I suspect not even in content, word count, or emotion."

She held her pleasure in check. "You don't like writing notes?"

"I don't like being told that I *must* write notes. And I . . ." He stopped walking, looked to the ground, and scuffed a pebble with his shoe. "I don't like being expected to write *love* notes when I don't feel the emotion."

Lila looked at his face, willing him to raise his eyes to hers. Which he did. "You don't feel the emotion?" she asked softly.

He shook his head. "I do not. I wouldn't think of sharing this confidence with you — with anyone — but since Lady Clarissa has drawn you into the middle of this arrangement between our families, I assure you ours is not a love match."

"Arranged marriages seldom are."

"It's financial, pure and simple. I won't go into details, but our fathers need something from each other, and Lady Clarissa and I are the means to an end."

She couldn't help but feel sorry for them.

And herself.

He shrugged. "I assure you I wouldn't have met with her yesterday if she hadn't had the hall-boy deliver a note saying she desperately needed to see me." His fingers barely touched Lila's, then withdrew.

Although she was delighted by his revelations, she wasn't sure what good they would do.

"To be more blunt than I have a right to be, I have no feelings beyond friendship for Lady Clarissa."

Lila pressed a hand to her chest. "I don't know what you want me to say."

"Do my words make you happy, Miss Hayward?"

She nodded and risked being honest. "I admit being pained by the sight of the two of you, the thought of the two of you . . ."

He pointed to her pocket, to the note. "I have tried to tell her my point of view in all this, tried not to hurt her. For she doesn't deserve to be hurt."

"I agree," Lila said.

"I don't know if there is a way for us to break this agreement between our families, but if we can, I would like us to try."

"Will your father listen?"

"I don't know. But feeling as I do I must see if there's a way."

Lila wanted to throw her arms around his neck, right there in the middle of the square. *Please, please free yourself!*

"I don't think I could ever make Lady Clarissa happy. She has such a dramatic nature and loves London and its theatres and parties far more than I."

"You prefer the quieter pursuits of country life."

"I do." He looked across the square. "The truth is, I don't play the courting game well, Miss Hayward. Unfortunately, my choice to abstain has left me without a mate, forcing my father's hand." He stood upright. "I frustrate him."

She laughed. "So you *do* play a game — your own game."

He considered this a moment. "Perhaps I do. But the constant vying for public attention during society get-togethers, the lame small talk, the pretense, the desperate need for affirmation . . ." He shook his head. "It wearies me and makes me long to be home, sitting by the fire, reading a good book."

His ideal matched her own. Lila captured a stray hair that blew across her cheeks.

He looked beyond her shoulder and she turned around and nodded toward the men watching them. "It appears we have our own public attention." She wanted to call to the men by name and tell them to mind their own business, but knew that would only make things worse.

"I must be going," he said, walking toward his horse. "I just wanted to make things clear between us."

"I appreciate that," she said. The fact he had made an effort to say all this . . . did that mean there could be a future between them?

He mounted his horse and looked down at her, tipping his hat. "Until next time, Miss Hayward — which, if I have any say, will be very, very soon."

"Next time," she said.

What glorious words!

"There it is," Grady said, stopping in front of a small cottage.

"There is what?" Addie asked.

"Our new home."

Addie could not have been more surprised if he'd just declared Windsor Castle their new home. Though this . . . dwelling . . . was far from a castle.

"It is the old caretaker's cottage," she said.

"Is it?" he asked. "No one lives here now."

"My husband built a better one, closer to the main house."

"Lucky for us." He took her hand. "Let's go inside."

She pulled her hand free. "You cannot be serious."

"I am totally serious."

"You can move into the manor, Grady. We will fix up some rooms to give us our own private space."

"*This* is our own private space. Completely ours." He faced her. "When you become my wife, you will start a new life. Yes, you will still be the dowager countess, but you will also be Mrs. Cummings. I don't want us to live your old life or my old life. I want to start a new life that's just ours, the life we should have had."

He had a way about him that calmed her, made everything seem possible, and made his way seem like the right way.

"At least take a look," he said.

That she could do.

Grass grew between the steppingstones leading to the door, and the flowers that edged the front of the house were overgrown and weedy. A portion of the thatched roof was missing.

Grady stopped at the door and looked nervous. "I wonder what we'll find inside."

"You haven't seen it?"

He shook his head. "I looked through the windows, but I wanted to explore it together."

"Our first adventure," she said, though she was wary.

"The first of many."

He opened the door. It took a few moments for her eyes to adapt to the dimness. Grady opened some curtains and the room was flooded with light. There was one large L-shaped room with an assortment of chairs and odd tables to their left, and an eating table for two and some cupboards to her right. One chair lay on its side, the victim of a broken leg. The missing part of the roof was *on* the eating table. Everything was covered with dust and age, and a mouse sped into the bedroom, which was through a small door.

Grady removed two straw hats from nails on the wall. "One for you and one for me," he said as he tried to put it on her head.

She stopped him. "That hat will never sit on this head."

He put them back on the hooks. "The place needs work, I can see that." He righted another toppled chair, then swiped a hand over the thatch on the table, brushing it into a nearby pail. "I'm sorry. I didn't think it would be this dirty." He stepped into the bedroom. "Animals have picked apart the mattress." He returned to her, shaking his head, obviously disappointed. "I should have gone inside before now. It was a silly idea. I—"

"It's perfect."

Grady's eyebrows rose in unison. "It is?"

Addie strolled to the two chairs facing the fireplace, one a rocking chair, the other an upholstered chair with padded arms. She could imagine them sitting here at night, looking into the fire, talking about their day. Or they'd read to each other. And laugh.

And be happy.

It wasn't as though she didn't see the grime to be cleaned or the repairs to be made. It was that none of those issues mattered. Being alone with Grady was everything.

She stood beside the upholstered chair and said, "Come sit

by our fire."

"There's an old bird's nest in the grate."

She ignored his words, waited for him to be seated, then sat in the oak rocking chair. "How was your day, husband?"

He laughed, then said, "Very fine now that I am home with you, wifey."

He extended his hand into the space between them.

She took it, reveling in the moment and the blessed assurance of more moments to come.

Chapter Twelve

Frederick dropped his fork against his plate of eggs and boiled tomatoes. "You are moving where?"

Addie had expected this reaction. "To the old caretaker's cottage. That's why I asked the colonel to join us for breakfast this morning. We have a lot of work to do." She turned to Dixon who stood nearby, overseeing the buffet as Clarissa helped herself to a huge helping of breakfast potatoes. "Speaking of work . . . Dixon, would you please see who can be spared? We need a man to move out the old furniture and—"

"Two would be better," Grady said, putting blackberry preserves on his scone.

"And not footmen. We need workers who won't say it's beneath their position to get their hands dirty."

"Yes, my lady."

"So let's make it two hardy men and two housemaids— because the place is crying for a top-to-bottom clean. Once it's prepared, I want the bed in the red guestroom moved into the cottage. The current bed will have to be burned. Too many animals." She turned to Grady. "What did you call them?"

"Critters."

"Too many critters have used it to cushion their nests."

"Grandmamma! Critters?" Clarissa said, taking her seat.

She enjoyed their unease. "That does appear to be the best term." She looked again at Dixon as he finished holding Clarissa's chair. "If you could arrange for the help to join us at the cottage at half-past ten."

"Yes, my lady." Dixon nodded to the first footman, giving Nick the room while he left to make arrangements.

Addie noticed that Clarissa was smiling. So was Frederick. "You find this amusing?" she asked.

Clarissa scanned the faces at the table. "Actually yes. The idea of the Dowager Countess of Summerfield living in a thatched cottage. Does it even have water?"

This *was* a sore point for Addie, but she refused to let on. "I believe there is a pump at the sink. We will have water warmed for our bath, just as it is warmed here."

"But with no servants to carry it for you." Frederick set down his fork. "Mother, this isn't necessary. Here at the manor we can designate certain rooms as yours alone. With thirty bedrooms, we have an abundance."

"I believe there are only twenty-five, Father," Clarissa said.

"Really? I was certain there were an even thirty." He shook the discrepancy away. "Either way, there is room for you here."

"You could make the morning room your parlor," Clarissa said.

Addie felt her resolve weaken. To leave Summerfield Manor where she had lived all her adult life, for some two-room cottage . . .

"And what about Albers?" Clarissa asked. "Is there room enough in the cottage for your lady's maid? Or do you expect her to traipse down and back every time you wish to change clothes?"

Addie hated the sarcasm, and she'd expected the questions—for they had been her own. Yet with each "But what about . . .?" question she'd raised, Grady had assured her all would be well. It was a matter of trust. Did she trust him to make their lives comfortable and happy?

The answer was a cautious, shocking, and courageous *yes*.

"I will be her lady's maid," Grady said. "And she will be my valet."

Everyone's eyebrows rose. Addie appreciated Grady's suggestion, but surely he knew it wasn't proper to publicly suggest a male and female saw each other in their underclothes, even though they obviously . . . did.

Addie pushed back from the table, sending Nick scrambling to help with her chair. "Grady, if you will come with me, I'd like to show you a certain dresser we might procure."

Grady offered her his arm and together they left the dining room. When the family was out of earshot, Grady said, "We don't need to do this, Addie. I want you to be comfortable."

Although her mind swam with doubts, she offered him a smile. "*You* will be my comfort."

It was something Grady would say.

It was rather amusing seeing Bridget's face when Addie entered her bedroom with Grady in tow. "Miss Albers, have you met Colonel Cummings?"

"No, my lady." Her eyes found the floor as she nodded at Grady. "Nice to meet you, Colonel."

"And you, Miss Albers. Lady Summerfield has often mentioned your good service and loyalty. How long have you been with her?"

She looked up. "Forty-three years sir. Master Frederick was just learning to walk, and Master Alexander was two and —" She put a hand over her mouth. "Forgive me, my lady. I shouldn't have mentioned him."

"You are forgiven," Addie said, though the mention of her eldest son still ignited a spark of sorrow. She glanced at Grady, and saw his eyebrow rise. He didn't know about Alexander.

Addie focused on the business at hand and moved to a walnut dresser with carved leaf pulls. "What do you think about this one?"

"It's a little large for the bedroom, but perhaps we could use it in the sitting room." He looked at her enormous canopied bed. "This isn't the one you planned to take, is it?"

"Heavens no," Addie said. "There's a smaller bed in the Red Room that should do quite nicely."

Suddenly, Albers faltered, as if her legs had gone weak. Grady ran to her aid. "Miss Albers, sit."

Addie chastised herself. Her family knew of the move to the cottage, but Albers was unaware. She moved a chair close. "I am sorry to spring this on you, Albers. It was very rude of us to barge in and begin talking about moving when you didn't know."

"You're moving?"

"Not far. Just to the old caretaker's cottage. We will still be on the grounds of the estate."

Her forehead furrowed. "I'm not aware of the place, my lady. If I could ask . . . are we bringing Sally or Prissy as housemaid? Or maybe we could take that new one, Dottie. Training her from scratch might be to our advantage."

Addie looked to Grady for support, but he only shrugged. There was no easy way to say this. "I fear it truly is a cottage. We—the colonel and I—are moving in and will have to make do without assistance." It was a bit frightening to say it so plain, but she'd already made her choice and wasn't about to back down.

Albers looked as though she'd been told the world was flat. "No assistance?"

"Actually," Grady said, "if I may offer a suggestion?"

Please do. "You may."

"Although my wife-to-be may not realize it, she may require some adjustments to her daily attire. Our new life will be less formal than it is here at the manor, and as such, perhaps some of her ensembles could be . . . simplified?"

"Really?" Addie said.

"Really?" Albers said.

"There will be no need to dress for dinner, my dear, not with only you and I in attendance."

But I always dress for dinner, dress to go on calls, dress for riding, dress for social occasions. And dinner? What are we going to do for meals?

"Perhaps we should concentrate on the furniture?" Grady asked.

Furniture. Yes.

One step at a time.

Was she seeing correctly?

Addie tiptoed closer to the alcove. Unfortunately, she was.

She rushed forward, took her grandson's arm, and yanked him back—away from the maid.

"George Alfred Weston! What are you two doing?"

"Nothing, Grandmamma."

The girl rightfully looked to the floor, her face red.

Addie wasn't in any mood to deal with such an issue today when she had a thousand problems of her own to solve. But she knew from experience that this sort of fraternization had to be nipped in the bud. Immediately. "Girl, what's your name?"

"Dottie."

"I'm sorry, Dottie, but I am letting you go."

"Go?"

It was drastic, and Addie was a bit surprised that the words had come from her mouth. But it was too late now. "You no longer have a position at the manor."

Her eyes grew large. "But . . . I didn't . . . he's the one who—"

Actually, Addie suspected as much. She turned to George. "Where's Nick? He's supposed to be looking after you until you go back to school."

George shrugged.

"Go on then," she said, shooing him away. "You have caused enough trouble for one day."

With a wink to the girl, he ran down the hall. *Insufferable boy.*

She turned her attention back to the maid. "Please collect your things and be off."

Dottie began to cry. Obviously drawn by the sound, Ruth's lady's maid came close. "Excuse me, your ladyship. Can I be of assistance?"

Then Addie remembered. Dottie was the sister of Miss Wallace. "Your sister has been let go."

Miss Wallace gasped. "But . . . but why?"

"It doesn't matter why," Addie said. She was weary and needed to be done with it. She pointed toward the back stairs. "Go on now."

Molly followed her sister to her room. "Dottie, what did you do?"

"I didn't do anything! Master George cornered me, and pushed me back against the wall, and . . . and he kissed me. I didn't want him to, but he did and I didn't know what to do, and then the dowager saw us and pulled him off and . . ." Dottie sank onto the bed, her head shaking. "Why did she let me go? I didn't do it. He did."

Molly sat beside her. "I know it isn't fair, but when it comes down to it, the family is always right, and the servants always at fault."

"But I'm not. At fault, that is."

"I know." *But it doesn't matter.* "Get your bag and pack."

Dottie retrieved her worn carpetbag from under the bed and Molly helped fold her good uniform to put inside. She held up Dottie's doll. "Don't forget Victoria."

"You can have her."

Molly was going to argue, but nodded. "I'll keep her safe for you."

Safe. It was bad enough to get sacked, but the thought of Dottie returning home to the danger of her father . . .

Molly pulled the doll to her chest. "I have to *do* something. I can't just let you go."

Dottie looked up from packing, her eyes hopeful. "So I can stay?"

Molly touched her sister's cheek. "No, you have to leave. But I'll . . . I'll talk to the countess. She's trying to be more involved with the family. Perhaps she'll speak to the dowager for us."

The thought of the countess speaking up for anything — much less a lowly maid — was doubtful. But she had to try.

She kissed Dottie on the forehead. "Go on home and I'll see what I can do."

"Thank you, Molly. I really didn't mean to cause trouble."

"I know. But there is one thing you have to do for me."

"What's that?"

How could she word this? "Stick close to Ma and Lon, all right?"

Dottie looked confused. "All right."

"Stay away from Da. Don't let yourself be alone with him."

"He's going to be mad, isn't he?"

Mad? Molly pulled her sister close. *Please, God, keep her safe from evil.*

"Come in."

When Molly entered, Ruth could tell that something was terribly wrong.

"What happened?" she asked.

The fingers of Molly's right hand played with her lace collar. "I'm sorry to bother you, my lady, but . . ."

"Just say it, Molly."

"The dowager just sacked my sister."

"May I ask why?"

Molly looked past her, then at the floor. "Master George is about her age and . . . he . . . I think there was some kissing involved."

Ruth never thought of George as old enough to even consider such a thing. Yet he *was* thirteen.

As such she agreed with Adelaide's decision. "We cannot condone that type of behavior."

138

"I know, but . . ." Molly pressed her fingers against her forehead as though she had a headache.

"But?"

And then she began to cry.

Ruth was taken aback. Molly was the strong one who comforted Ruth when *she* was unhappy.

"Oh, my dear girl. Come sit and tell me what's troubling you."

"I'm so sorry, my lady. I shouldn't . . . you shouldn't . . ."

"Nonsense," Ruth said, sitting beside her on the window seat. "Sometimes a woman needs to cry."

Molly retrieved a handkerchief from her pocket, and dabbed at her eyes. "I'm not crying for Dottie's position as much as I'm crying at the thought of her having to return home."

"What is wrong with 'home'?"

And then, as if a floodgate had been opened, the words poured out. Ruth could hardly believe the tale of paternal cruelty and wickedness.

"So you see why it's imperative Dottie gets away from there. I can't let Da do to her what he tried to do to me."

Tears stung Ruth's eyes as she took Molly's hand. "I am so sorry for what you've had to endure."

Molly shrugged. "Thank you, my lady." She took a fresh breath. "Is there — could there be anything you might do to get her job back?"

Would Adelaide and Frederick listen to her?

"Please, your ladyship. I beg you."

And so, Ruth nodded. "I will see what I can do."

Ruth hesitated outside Frederick's study. She couldn't remember the last time she'd been in the room. And certainly she'd never interfered in any manor business.

Think of little Dottie. Think of her dreadful father.

She shuddered, took a deep breath, and knocked.

"Come in."

She tentatively opened the door. "Frederick?"

He stood up from his chair and smiled, then came around the desk to greet her. "Ruth, how nice to see you." He took her hands and kissed her cheek.

She was overwhelmed by his welcome. Perhaps she could do this after all. She took a seat, and he sat nearby. "I *am* sorry to disturb you."

"Not at all. To what do I owe this honor?"

"It is not an honor really. Not at all. I . . . I must ask a favor."

"Of course, my dear. Whatever you wish."

Really? Emboldened, she continued. "My lady's maid, Molly, has a little sister who also works here — worked here."

"Worked? Past tense?"

"Your mother let her go this afternoon."

"Why?"

"Apparently she and George were found kissing."

He sat back. "That will never do. We have both heard stories of families and their servants. It is not acceptable."

"Absolutely not," she said. "But there are extenuating circumstances."

"That make such affection acceptable?"

"I don't mean that," she said. "It has to do with Dottie's situation at home."

He looked to the air, as if gathering memories. "The Wallaces. Three children: two girls and a boy."

She was impressed. "That's right. But the father . . ."

"Has a weakness for drink."

She hesitated. "I'm afraid his weaknesses extend beyond that."

Frederick's eyebrows rose. "What are you implying?"

She stood, unable to meet his eyes. "It's unspeakable."

Silence fell between them, and Frederick bit his lip.

"There have been allegations?"

"Molly confided in me."

"And you believe her?"

"Of course I do."

"Perhaps she just wants to regain her sister's position."

"Of course she wants that, but there are serious reasons behind it."

"Private reasons. Family reasons that are none of our business."

Ruth was shocked. "But Dottie is a child. She needs protection."

"But he is a father."

"Frederick! How can you take his side?"

"I do not take his side. I simply want to let—"

"The girl suffer?"

"Ruth, this really is not our concern."

"You are the Earl of Summerfield. People look to you for guidance—and justice."

"I would be overstepping my bounds if I interfered when there is no real proof."

How could he be so callous? "What good is a title if it can't be used for good, to protect the weak?"

He stood, his hands pressing the air between them. "Ruth, calm down. You know nothing of estate business and how things are done."

"I know what's right, and how things should be done."

He blinked. "You go too far, my dear."

"And *you* do not go far enough." They stood a few feet apart, Ruth's breathing heavy. "At least get your mother to rehire her."

"I will not interfere. Mother handles the hiring and firing. And considering what this girl did to our George—"

"Can you even consider that George might have instigated the kiss?"

His jaw tightened. "Perhaps if he had a mother who was involved in his upbringing . . ."

She drew in a breath. "And why should I be involved when no one listens to me?"

"We don't listen to you because you have done nothing to prove you are worthy of being heard."

Ruth couldn't believe what she was hearing. "Is that the way it's going to be?"

He flipped a hand at her. "Go back to your room, Ruth. Leave the rest of us to do our jobs."

She strode from the room, slamming the door behind her.

Dixon peeked in from down the hall. She stormed past him, up the stairs, and into her room. It felt good to slam that door too.

Though a lot of good it did. She had no power.

And a little girl was in danger.

Ruth leaned against the back of the door and let herself sink to the floor in despair.

Ruth braced herself as she rang the bell to summon Molly. The girl entered the bedroom, her face hopeful. Expectant.

"Yes, my lady?"

"I am sorry, but I have bad news."

The hope faded from her face. "Oh."

"I talked to the earl, but he . . . "

"He wouldn't help?"

"I'm afraid not."

"Didn't he believe me?"

"I am not sure if he did or didn't. The point is, he is in charge, and I am not. I have no power here. It is my own fault, but now, after all these years, they won't listen to me."

Molly swiped a tear away. "They will listen to you."

"What do you mean?"

"With the dowager married and moved away, you'll be the lady of the manor. You'll be in charge."

I'll be in charge? Ruth had never been in charge, not even when she'd first become Countess of Summerfield. Her mother-in-law had been reluctant to relinquish her power, and Ruth had been too weak and uncertain to insist. It had soon grown easier to acquiesce and withdraw.

But now, with Adelaide moving out. . . could Ruth take

over the hiring and firing duties?

"Perhaps I'll be able to do something for your sister after the wedding."

Molly's eyes lit up. "Will you?"

Ruth made a decision. "I will do everything I can. Just be patient."

Molly looked toward the windows, toward the village. "I pray Dottie is safe until then."

Lila gave Lady Clarissa the note from Joseph Kidd. She almost pitied the way her face lit up in expectation.

Clarissa wouldn't be pleased when she read it. Joseph had said he was letting her down gently, with the point being, he *was* letting her down.

Clarissa slipped Lila a note in return. "If you don't mind, I shall step outside and take a read of it. I simply can't wait longer than that."

But I do mind.

As Lady Clarissa went outside the store and sat on the bench, Morgan came to Lila's side. "What's all that about?"

"I'm the go-between."

"Between Lady Clarissa and whom?"

She might as well tell him. "Joseph Kidd."

"Now there's a most unsuitable match."

"Why do you say that?"

"Because he's the horsey set and she's all about the theatre."

"How do you know?"

"Lady Clarissa's maid told Molly that in London she spent a great deal of time with artists and actors. She sees herself as more cosmopolitan than country. Apparently Lady Clarissa doesn't care for Mr. Kidd romantically, but is merely using him to keep her parents off her back and get herself set up in London."

Lila's mind swam with the implications. "Does Mr. Kidd

know this?"

"Obviously not if he's sending her notes."

Lila had the urge to go tell him immediately. Mr. Kidd deserved to know. It would give him an added reason to end their arrangement.

But then her attention was drawn to the window, where she saw Lady Clarissa stand, her eyes still upon the note. *Oh no. She's going to be upset.*

But instead of anger or tears, Clarissa perused the note again, moving her lips with the words, bobbing her head left, then right, and back again.

And then she put it to her chest, as if holding Mr. Kidd's words to her heart. *What?*

Clarissa must have sensed she was being watched, for she looked through the window, smiled, and gave Lila a wave before walking away.

"She looks happy," Morgan said.

"Yes, she does." Either Lady Clarissa was a very good actress, or Mr. Kidd's words had missed their mark.

Or . . . he'd misrepresented the content of the note.

"Lila?"

She shook the questions away. "We'd better get to work."

"You never answered me. Why are you acting as if you care about Lady Clarissa's love life?"

"I'm not, because I don't." The lie being plainly stated, she gave her attention to a display of buckets.

That afternoon, Morgan came in the store, nodded to Lila, and said to his father, "It's ready."

"What's ready?" Mother asked.

Lila could barely contain her excitement. But instead of answering Mother's question, Papa walked over to Nana and held out his hand, palm up. "Come with me."

"Where are you going?" Mother asked. "What's going on?"

Nana put her hand in his, and he tucked it around his arm.

"We'll be back soon," he said.

Lila removed her apron, which ignited more questions. "Lila gets to go? Why can't I?"

Morgan sacrificed himself to the cause and put his arm around her shoulders. "I'll stay here with you. It was Lila's idea. She needs to go."

"Idea? What idea? Jack?"

Papa spoke to his wife over his shoulder as they walked away. "We won't be gone long."

As they walked out of town, Nana asked, "Where are we going?"

"You'll see," Papa said.

He led them off the road, into the woods. Nana's woods. Nana kept looking at Lila, wary.

"It's all right, Nana. I promise."

And then they saw them. Three small headstones, lined up in a row: Howard, Hester, and Fanny. And around the stones, a low wooden fence with purple asters planted along its edge.

"I'm sorry I didn't know the years," Lila said.

Nana knelt before the little cemetery. "Oh, Lila."

Lila knelt beside her. "It was my idea, but Papa and Morgan did the work."

Nana traced Howard's name with her fingers. "Seeing my babies' names . . . now everyone can know they lived."

"Including me." Papa got down on his knees. "Why didn't you tell me?"

"Your father didn't like me talking about them, so I kept their memories private."

Lila let her tears join Nana's. Papa offered his handkerchief and Nana leaned toward him, ducking under his arm.

"These are partially happy tears," Nana said. "I'm happy their brother cares enough to do this even as I'm sad for the brevity of their lives." She tried to stand, and Papa helped her to her feet. "What did I ever do to deserve a son and granddaughter like the two of you?"

Nana wrapped her arms around their waists, and together they rocked gently with the breeze.

Chapter Thirteen

Addie stood with her hands on her hips, surveying the chaos that was the cottage. "I do *not* see how it can all be done in time, Grady. Our wedding is tomorrow."

Men were on the roof, repairing holes and replacing the thatching. Two maids from the manor were cleaning every corner, and the groundskeeper and his staff were taming the unruly flowers, trees, and bushes.

"Trust me, Addie. It *will* be finished." Grady wiped his forehead with his sleeve and turned over the repaired chair, testing the level on its new leg. "Voila!"

"You have hidden talents," she said.

He winked at her. "You have no idea."

Addie scanned the room, hoping no one heard. If they had, they didn't show it. In truth, she was looking forward to enjoying that part of marriage. Better late than never.

She heard a wagon approaching and they went outside. The bed from the red guestroom was being delivered.

How appropriate.

Lila wasn't surprised when Lady Clarissa walked into the store. What did surprise her was the angry look on her face.

"Lila," Clarissa said, bypassing her usual greeting to Lila's parents. "Outside, if you please?"

Something was terribly wrong. Not wanting Mother to overhear, Lila led Clarissa outside, across the square.

When they reached a private spot near the butcher shop, Clarissa stopped. "Why didn't you give Joseph my note from two days ago?"

Lila thought back. "But I did give it to him."

"The one I brought in the day I purchased the ribbon?"

"Yes, I remember it. He hasn't been in for the one you gave me yesterday, but the day of the ribbons . . . yes, I gave him that note."

Clarissa turned in a circle, her hand to her mouth. Obviously it was a very important note.

When she finished her circle, she sighed deeply then pressed a new note into Lila's hand. "See that he gets this one immediately."

"When he comes in, he usually comes during the afternoon."

Clarissa shook her head. "That's not good enough. You must ride over to Crompton Hall, hand-deliver it, and wait for an answer."

Lila had never been to the Kidd estate. She knew from others that it wasn't nearly as grand as Summerfield Manor, nor did it possess the breadth of history associated with the same. But grand or not, her sudden appearance there would be awkward.

But possible. And it would provide a way for her to tell Mr. Kidd what Morgan had told her about Clarissa's questionable motivations for pursuing the match. "I suppose I could, if it must be done."

Clarissa released a long breath. "It must be done."

"Can you tell me why you're so upset?"

"Just deliver the note, and all will be forgiven."

Forgiven?

Lady Clarissa left Lila standing alone. Lila looked down at the note. How she longed to read it, or better yet, tear it in a million pieces and scatter it to the wind.

Only the thought of seeing Mr. Kidd kept the note intact.

"You're going to Crompton Hall?" Mother asked.

"Lady Clarissa asked me to deliver a message."

"About the dowager's wedding?"

"I don't really know." And she didn't. Not really.

"Will you see Mr. Kidd?"

"I don't know."

"But you hope you will, don't you?" Mother sighed deeply. "Wouldn't it be grand to live in the Kidd mansion? I used to love playing hopscotch on the black and white tiles in the foyer."

Lila didn't understand. "You did what?"

Mother glanced at Papa, then busied herself with some pencils and erasers. "It would simply be nice to have you living in such a fine manor."

"Yes, it would," Lila said. "But it's impossible, so I wish you'd stop pressing the issue."

"As you wish."

Hopscotch?

Lila didn't get the chance to see whether the foyer at Crompton Hall had black and white tiles, for as she rode up the drive on Raider, she spotted Mr. Kidd walking in the garden.

He waved, and came to greet her. "Miss Hayward. You've made my day bright."

How sweet of him.

"I come as postmistress for Lady Clarissa." She gave him the new letter as well as the one Clarissa had brought to the store the day before.

He took the notes but seemed in no hurry to open them. "I fear she's angry with me."

"Why?"

"She asked me to meet her at the grove today, and I . . . I didn't go."

You didn't go? "Why not?"

"You know why not."

She hoped she knew, but she wanted to hear it from him. If he would voluntarily back out of his match with Clarissa, there would be no need for her to tattle about Clarissa's true motivations. Telling him he was being duped would surely hurt his pride.

"Will you stay a bit and walk in the garden with me?"

"I'd love to."

To help her dismount, he put his hands around her waist and set her gently to the ground. If only she could have lingered there.

He offered her his arm and they walked on a path among the flowers. "Again, I apologize for your awkward position as our messenger. It's not the least bit fair to you."

"At least it brought me here," she said. Her own boldness caught her by surprise. "I'm sorry, I shouldn't say that."

He patted her hand. "I'm glad to hear you say exactly that."

Lila tried to keep hope at bay. "You'd better read the notes. Lady Clarissa insists I wait for a reply."

"If I must." He led them to a bench. "Which one first?"

Lila pointed to the one from yesterday that had a smudge on the corner. He broke the seal and read it silently, then closed it again and opened the newest. This one caused him more distress, for after reading it he sighed and dropped his hand to his knee. "She invites me to her grandmother's wedding."

"But it's only for the manor staff and—"

"Family," he said. "She says it was her grandmother's request."

"Then you must go."

He rose, shaking the notes between them. "She keeps insisting we meet, but I don't want to meet. I wrote to her, saying as much."

"Perhaps she's interpreted your words her own way. When I saw her reading your last note, she . . ."

"She what?"

"She read it more than once, then held it to her heart."

His brow furrowed. "But in that note I told her I wanted to find a way *out* of the arrangement. I told her I wasn't going to meet her at the grove or anywhere. I suggested she talk to her father, and I offered to talk to mine. How could she be happy with that?"

"Perhaps she sees the words she wants to see."

He flicked the notes against his leg. "Perhaps in an attempt to be polite, I was too vague. Lady Clarissa seems to live in a world of her own creation. What she wants is her reality."

"And she obviously wants to marry you." *For her own reasons.*

Mr. Kidd looked up. "Has she ever told you as much?"

Lila bought some time by smoothing the fingers of her glove. "She's ignoring your pleas to break it off, which means . . . she does want you, Mr. Kidd. However, I'm not sure her motives—"

"Joseph. Please call me Joseph." He smiled. "If I may call you Lila?"

She gave him a nod. *You can call me whatever you'd like.*

"Lady Clarissa doesn't understand my position at all."

"Actually," Lila said softly, "neither do I."

His eyes were sad and sincere. "Truth be told, I plan to talk to my father about *you*, Lila. About my feelings for you."

It was like a dream come to life. Tears of joy and relief filled her eyes. "I shouldn't cry, but your words make me so happy." But then, a wave of reality threatened to drown her. "But . . ."

"But?"

"No matter what we want, the situation is hopeless."

He sat beside her.

"Your father will never approve."

"I will make him approve."

The odds were against them. How cruel to touch the dream, only to have the wall of reality block it from reach.

He drew her hand to his lips. "We may not know each

other very well, but I assure you my words are not said in haste. You, Lila Hayward, are the woman I love."

The dream moved back into reach.

"We are meant to be together. I knew it the moment I rushed to your side after causing you to fall off your horse."

She smiled. The memory was never far from her thoughts. "I was so concerned about preserving my modesty, I can't imagine I made a good impression."

"You want to know when I knew you were meant for me? The very moment?"

"Very much."

"When you were trying to get your skirt to cooperate, and it was all tangled, and—"

"*That* made an impression?"

He raised a finger, wanting to continue. "It was tangled, and you gave up and lay flat on the grass. You laughed at yourself and said, 'I surrender.'"

"I don't understand how that would impress you."

"Your ability to laugh at the situation rather than be upset by it, spoke volumes about your character. I can think of no other lady who would handle the moment with such genuine ease and good humor."

The compliment collided with another immovable fact. "But I'm not a lady."

"You are everything a true lady should be. And I must marry you or be half-filled for the rest of my life. You, my dearest Lila, are my other half."

He took her into his arms, and her doubts were pressed away by the warmth and strength of his nearness. Finally she let herself relax against him. They did indeed fit together, two halves to make a whole.

Too soon he pulled away. "I *will* talk to my father, but first I must have things out with Clarissa. I must make her understand that there is no *us*, and only by being united against our families can we break this agreement."

Worry stood at the door, demanding an audience. "Clarissa always gets what she wants. She has a way about her that makes it impossible to refuse her."

Joseph nodded. "I haven't wanted to be unkind, but it is clear she requires a direct approach. As soon as the dowager's wedding is out of the way, I will speak to her." He put a finger beneath Lila's chin and peered into her eyes. "I promise."

Then he kissed her, and her life's path revealed itself to be clear and straight.

When Lila returned to the store, Nana glanced up from the folding of some tea towels — and stared.

As did Rose. "Oh my," Rose said.

Oh my?

Nana crooked her finger, beckoning Lila close.

"What's wrong?" Lila asked. "Do I have something on my face?"

Her grandmother smiled. "Yes, you have something on your face. You're glowing. Isn't she glowing, Rose?"

Rose nodded. "And her smile comes from deep within."

"It's a smile that can't be erased," Nana added.

Smile? Lila hadn't realized she'd even *been* smiling.

Nana took her hand. "It's a good thing the men and your mother aren't here. Now's your chance to tell us all about it."

Could it really be so evident?

"What happened at Crompton Hall?" Rose asked.

"You saw Joseph, didn't you?" Nana asked. "More than saw him, I'd wager, by the blush to your cheeks."

Until they asked, Lila hadn't realized how much she wanted to share her joy. She drew them to a corner of the store and told her story, finishing with, "He said he loves me and wants to speak to his father about marrying me."

Rose gasped, and Nana flung her arms around Lila. "Oh, my sweet girl. I'm so happy for you."

Lila's face clouded. "But it's not happening just yet. Joseph will talk to Clarissa and make sure she understands. *Then* he will speak to his father about me." She bit her lower lip, and doubt rushed in. "But even if he does speak to him, what if his father says no? For surely he *will* say no. I'm no catch, and —"

Nana swatted her arm. "Stop that! You are a remarkable young woman who possesses character, drive, and a heart full of love. The Kidds would be lucky to have you in their family."

Lila smiled. "Whatever happens, don't tell Mother. If by some miracle it works out, she'll be ecstatic, but if it doesn't, I don't want to endure a lifetime of lectures regarding how I ruined my chance to marry well."

"Agreed," Rose said.

"Agreed," Nana said.

Lila removed her bonnet and ran a hand over the loose wisps of her hair. "By the way, do either of you know what Mother was talking about when she mentioned playing hopscotch in the foyer of Crompton Hall?"

"I have no idea," Nana said. "I only met her when she was grown and living in London with her parents — though I never met them. Perhaps when she was young, Fidelia was a maid there."

"She must have been very young to play hopscotch," Rose said. "Perhaps she was an under-housemaid or a scullery."

It wasn't in Mother's character to serve.

"If that's true, it's no wonder she wants you to marry Joseph, so you can live in the house she worked in."

"And I'd love to give her the satisfaction." Lila offered them a mischievous smile. "And attain some of my own."

They all turned toward the sound of the others returning. Lila raised a finger to her lips, and Rose and Nana nodded. It was their secret. Oh, what a secret.

Clarissa started and looked a second time when she saw Ruth coming down the front stair. "Mother, what are you doing?"

"I am coming to dinner."

"Why?"

Ruth stopped on the bottom stair. "Don't be rude."

"Sorry," Clarissa said, "but it is a logical question. I can't recall the last time you dined with the family."

"Neither can I. Which means it's been far too long." She stepped onto the marble foyer and took her daughter's arm. "Shall we?"

Ruth took advantage of their bowed heads to add a prayer of her own, *Give me the strength to stay put and endure whatever they cast my way.*

Amen.

Unlike her visit to tea, this time Ruth didn't mind when they spoke around her. With each mention of Adelaide's cottage or Clarissa's plans for the wedding, Ruth felt a door open, allowing her a glimpse into the family fold.

And it felt good—especially since yesterday, when she and Frederick had parted with harsh words. As each course was served, he seemed to be studying her.

She made every attempt to listen carefully, make suitable comments, and be supportive. Now was not the time to make waves. Now was the time to wade gently into the water.

The only awkward moment came when she asked, "Can I help with the wedding preparations in some way?"

"It's a little late now," Clarissa said.

Instead of showing how insulted she felt, Ruth simply nodded.

By the end of the meal she was exhausted. Yet when Frederick escorted her out of the dining room, and when he touched her hand before retiring to his study, she felt victorious.

But oh, was she glad when she was safely upstairs again.

After dinner, Ruth sat on the window seat, gazing across the grounds. The sun was setting, but if she looked carefully, she could spot the chimney of the caretaker's cottage.

Adelaide's cottage.

She found it laughable that the dowager would move to such a place. Two rooms and no servants. However was Adelaide going to manage? Yes, she was a capable woman, but she was used to ordering others to do *for* her, not having to do for herself.

Yet in a way it was romantic.

Memories of years gone by slipped into her thoughts. When was the last time she and Frederick spent the night together?

For more than five years, soon after she'd become the countess and moved into this suite. Since then Frederick had not entered her room in that way. In his defense, he too had been overwhelmed with his duties. They'd both let their titles slip like a wedge between them. They'd both shut the door on their romance, each from their own side.

For it had been a romance. Ruth let the window curtain fall away and turned sideways, her back against the wall of the window seat. She drew her legs onto the padded cushion, closed her eyes, and remembered waltzing in his arms, their gaze locked, her skin tingling beneath his touch.

Their actual wedding—which had been a lavish affair attended by three hundred of their closest friends—was a blur. But the memories of their wedding night and their three-month tour of Europe were as vivid as if they'd happened yesterday: walking up the winding stairs of St. Peter's in Rome to view the city from the dome, with Frederick tugging on her skirt and tickling her ankles as she walked in front of him. Sitting hand-in-hand as they attended the Paris opera, letting the strains of "Romeo and Juliet" waft over her like a heady breeze. Hiking up the mountains outside Lucerne, sitting in an alpine meadow and feeling completely alone but for the faint music from the neck-bells of grazing cows.

The monuments, the cathedrals, and the meals held small

places in her memories. The private moments with Frederick loomed large and lingered, waiting for her to visit. Why had she ignored them for so long? They were the happiest times of her life.

You can be happy again. Look at Adelaide and Grady.

The thought energized her, and she sat upright, her feet finding the floor. A plan formed.

She rang for Molly before she changed her mind.

Molly knocked gently, then entered. "Yes, my lady?"

"I would like a bath."

She looked surprised.

"I know it's rather late, but I feel the need to relax."

"The hip bath or the copper?"

"The copper, if you will. And ask the dowager if I may borrow one of her scented oils."

"Yes, my lady."

Ruth walked into her dressing room and found what she was looking for—a gorgeous pink dressing gown edged with Belgian lace. And to wear underneath, an ivory nightgown adorned with rows of tiny pin-tucks on the bodice and embellished with a myriad of pink satin bows.

So began the pulling out of her French copper bathtub and the buckets of hot water brought from below stairs. She recognized the extra work involved in filling the much larger tub rather than the hip bath, but she felt the need for the luxury.

Ruth remained in her dressing room while Molly oversaw the preparations. When the bath was ready, she emerged and let Molly help her undress. Molly lowered Ruth's skirt, and Ruth stepped out of it. Her petticoats and bustle were next. Then her corset. When Ruth was down to her camisole and drawers, Molly raised a sheet between them, allowing Ruth privacy while she removed her final undergarments and stepped into the steaming bath.

She leaned her head against its back and felt her muscles relax. This was just what she needed.

Molly picked up the clothes to put them away, but Ruth

said, "I'll be fine getting out and dressing for bed, and we can leave the water until morning. That will be all for tonight."

"Are you sure, my lady?"

"I'm sure."

Molly set a stack of towels close by, then left.

Ruth closed her eyes and let the delectable smell of lavender give her the courage to go through with her plan.

Ruth put her ear to the door of her room. The house was quiet, with both master and servant retired for the night.

She slowly turned the knob, glad when it didn't make a sound. The door creaked a little when she opened it, but she felt secure that the sound was unheard by anyone but herself.

Taking deep breaths for courage, she ventured into the hallway, checking left, then right. Then she tiptoed to Frederick's room.

Ruth started when her husband's valet exited the room. His eyes took in her attire.

"Mr. Robbins."

He recovered quickly from his surprise, nodded, and said, "Your ladyship," then walked down the hall.

She was mortified. Her attire, added to the time of night, and her destination . . . Mr. Robbins would guess her intentions.

But so what? Husbands and wives were supposed to spend time together in the bedroom. There was no reason for her to feel like a thief in the night, stalking through a darkened house so as not to be caught. Besides, she had no reason to believe Mr. Robbins was not a man of discretion.

Emboldened, Ruth readied her knuckles to knock.

But something stopped her.

First, it wasn't proper for a wife to initiate such a thing. If Frederick wished to renew their relations, he would have come to *her* room.

The fact he hadn't . . .

The image of Frederick laughing with Lady Carlton intruded. Had Mr. Robbins ever been forced to use discretion in London while serving her husband?

The possibilities ignited humiliation and pain.

Ruth pulled her hand away, stepped back, and returned to her room.

Chapter Fourteen

"But why were you and Morgan invited to attend, and not me?"

Lila secured her bonnet with a pin. "We weren't invited to the wedding, Mother. Lady Clarissa enlisted our services to help with the reception, as the household staff are all attending as guests."

"There's the other thing," Mother said. "The dowager countess is getting married and invites servants rather than the citizens of Summerfield? That's absolutely vulgar. And common."

"I think it's nice," Nana said. "If the wedding is to be small, why not keep it in the family?"

"Servants are not family."

Lila stole a look at Rose and Nana. Perhaps her mother *had* been a servant once. "I expect Lady Summerfield will have the wedding exactly the way she wants, despite how others would see it done."

Morgan adjusted the rim of his Derby hat. "I'm glad to help out. It will give me a chance to see Molly."

Only Morgan could get away with being so flagrant.

"You said that to hurt me," Mother said.

"I said that to be honest with you." He kissed her cheek. "But I am there to work, not play. I promise to have a horrible time."

"Not at all," Papa said. "I want both of you to have a very good time, even as you work. It's a momentous day when a dowager countess marries."

"A bizarre day," Mother said. "Marrying down, marrying an army man."

"From what I've heard, Colonel Cummings has served queen and country in multiple wars and in India."

"I suppose the Westons always have married whomever they wanted, even if it wasn't the best choice."

Lila had no idea what Mother meant by that. "I'll bring each of you a piece of cake if there's extra."

"Don't bother," Mother said. "I don't need the Westons' crumbs."

As soon as they left, Morgan said to Lila, "From what I know of Mother, she'd lick the Westons' crumbs from a muddy floor if we let her."

As they walked toward the manor, thoughts of Lady Clarissa's grandmother getting married made Lila think of her own grandparents. "What do you know of Mother's parents?"

"I don't remember them at all. I think they lived in London. That's where Mother and Papa met and fell in love."

"Hmm."

"All right, perhaps it wasn't love."

Lila had to correct him. "I hope it *was* love, or became love. Otherwise it cheapens our very existence."

Morgan wrapped his arm around her shoulders. "My sister, the romantic."

She shuffled his arm away. "What's wrong with romance?"

"Not a thing, I assure you." His grin gave him away.

"Do you really and truly love Molly?" she asked.

"Really and truly."

"How are you managing to see each other? The servants at the manor don't get much time off, and more than one has been sacked for romantic involvement."

"She sneaks out after the countess has gone to bed."

"Every night?"

"If she's free to meet me, she hangs a white ribbon from her window. I can see it even in the moonlight. If it's there, we meet in the garden. If not, I go home."

"Are you planning to marry her?"

"Eventually. Now that I'm working at the store, I'm saving my wages, and she's been saving hers. Once married, we'll go where we have to go to be happy."

"Mother would die if you didn't live close. And Papa is expecting you to take over the store."

"Mother will not die, and Papa will survive the disappointment. I'm not sure I'm meant for country life. I prefer the excitement of the city."

"So you're going to leave me here alone? Again?"

"You won't be alone forever, sister. One of these days a worthy man is going to come into your life and sweep you off your feet."

Wonderful memories wrapped around her.

He already had.

The Dowager Countess of Summerfield stood before the mirror in her room, readying herself to become Mrs. Grady Cummings. Never, ever, could she have imagined such a thing. The renewal of their love had been accomplished in a whirlwind courtship, and then some.

Albers fiddled with a pair of satin bows that showcased the curve of Addie's spine, Clarissa adjusted the flowers on Addie's small, flat hat that sported striped ribbons hanging down the back.

Ruth presented her with a handkerchief edged in lace. "See?" she said. "I've monogrammed your initials on it."

Addie was touched and ran her finger along a delicate blue C with a gold G and A on either side. "Thank you, Ruth. This is very special." She tucked it in her pocket.

"I wish you had given us time to have a proper wedding dress made," Clarissa said.

"And what exactly is a proper wedding dress for a sixty-six-year-old woman marrying for the second time? Certainly I shouldn't wear white."

"I think the dress is lovely," Ruth said. "A soft blue

sprinkled with mauve flowers? And the lace on the neck and shoulders is perfect for a summer garden wedding."

Addie was surprised by Ruth's opinion—and by the fact that she'd shared it. Actually, she was surprised Ruth was even in the room. She'd expected her daughter-in-law to remain confined during the preparations and would not have been surprised if Ruth had begged off the entire ceremony. Something was definitely different about her recently.

"Actually, if you want to be correct about it," Clarissa said, "You should get married in the morning, and there should *not* be a wedding dance."

"Says who?"

Clarissa seemed taken aback. "People. Rule-setters. Society."

Addie shook her head in a short burst. "I am weary of the faceless keepers of convention dictating the minutiae of my life. I refuse to succumb to them one minute longer. Today is *my* day to become a different woman."

Today was her day to become a happy woman.

God was good. All the time.

The wedding was as lovely as a wedding should be.

Ruth sat next to Frederick in the chairs set for the family as Adelaide and the colonel stood under an arbor woven with yards of ribbon. The bride looked resplendent in her dress of lace and bows, and the groom . . . Grady was striking in his red dress uniform adorned with medals and meritorious ribbons. He'd obviously distinguished himself in service. It was hard to imagine that he and the dowager would be living in a simple cottage.

The bride and groom faced each other with their hands clasped as Reverend Lyons led them through their vows.

Clarissa stood near her grandmother, looking lovely in her white batiste dress with layer upon layer of pleats around the skirt. Her blue damask jacket was appropriately adorned with pink roses parading down the front like buttons. Her curved hat was covered with pleated fabric, and pink flowers cascaded down among the ribbons.

The butler-turned-best-man, Mr. Dixon, looked as regal as he always looked in his gray morning coat and striped pants. He stood at attention, yet there was a hint of emotion in the dip of his brow.

The servants of the house — all sixty of them — stood behind the family, out of uniform, dressed in their Sunday best. Ruth glanced over her shoulder and saw Albers beaming, as though her mistress were her own blood. Some of the housemaids had their arms linked, clearly moved by the romance of the moment.

Ruth peered past George to Joseph Kidd. He stared straight ahead, his forehead creased. He looked much too stern for such a happy day. Attending a wedding when he would soon be a participant in his own . . . shouldn't that elicit happy thoughts? Theirs wouldn't be a small garden wedding but a lavish affair that would test the seams of the Summerfield church, as befitting the only daughter of the earl and countess of Summerfield.

Ruth let her attention return to the ceremony.

"Forasmuch as Adelaide Louisa Weston and Grady Roland Cummings have consented together in holy wedlock, and have witnessed the same before God and this company . . ."

The way Adelaide looked at the colonel with pure joy, and the way his gaze glowed with adoration. Their love was true love. One could just see it.

". . . I pronounce that they be man and wife together, In the Name of the Father, and of the Son, and of the Holy Ghost. Amen."

Without prodding, Colonel Cummings cupped Adelaide's face in his hands as gently as if it were porcelain. She touched his cheeks, and they shared a lingering kiss that showcased the essence of their vows.

The servants erupted in applause — which was entirely improper, but somehow fitting. Even Frederick joined in.

The colonel turned his wife toward the guests. "Let's celebrate!"

A *whoop* of approval went up from the servants, and a fiddle player began his music.

Clarissa stepped forward to kiss her grandmother's cheek. "I'm so happy for you, Grandmamma."

"You're next, child."

Ruth looked across the crowd toward Joseph, who scowled. Theirs was not true love.

One could just see it.

"Surprise."

Molly turned around. "Morgan! What are you doing here?"

"Lila and I were asked to help with the reception since the staff are guests."

She looked around for the countess and the earl and was shocked to see her mistress dancing with Mr. Robbins, and the earl with Bridget. Dancing at a wedding? And in a garden? Molly worried what the gossipmongers of Summerfield would say about it. She knew from experience that commoners often balked when those above them didn't act according to standard.

"Come, it's our turn." Morgan took Molly's hand and pulled her into the throng. The fiddler upped the tempo, testing the stamina of old and young alike.

"We can't be seen together."

"Why not? On this day all bounds have been broken." He pulled her close. "Besides, I've been dying to have you in my arms."

And she had been dying to be there. Then suddenly he kissed her on the lips.

She tried to push away, afraid someone had seen, but he held her tight. "Stop, Morgan. We'll get in trouble."

"In trouble for love. I don't care if everyone knows I love

you." He pulled her out of the crowd, near some manicured shrubs, then held her hands as a buffer between their hearts. "Marry me. Now. Today. The vicar can easily perform another ceremony."

They were words she'd longed to hear. "I can't. I mean I will. But not yet."

"Why not? Let this be our celebration too."

There was a happy shout from the dancers when the fiddler began a reel. The distraction gave her time to collect her thoughts. How she wanted to let Morgan sweep her away to a land of wedded bliss. But there were too many obstacles.

"I *will* marry you," she said, touching his cheek. "But we must wait a bit. Dottie will never be hired back if I leave, and with the dowager's marriage everything at the manor is changing. She's moving out, and my mistress is showing signs of stepping up, taking on the responsibilities of her position." Molly looked for the countess and saw her smiling like a young girl. "She's on the verge of truly being the mistress of the house. She needs me to help her through."

"I need you. You need me. What about us?"

"We can still be together. Just give it a little time."

"You don't owe her anything."

"But I do." She sought understanding in his eyes. "I'd still be a housemaid if it weren't for her."

"Lofty or low, you're still a servant."

Molly's sense of self stirred. On the one hand she was just Molly Wallace, the daughter of her parents, the sister to Dottie and Lon. But on the other, she was a survivor who'd escaped a vicious fate and had worked—and earned—a place as a lady's maid in a fine manor. The countess—*the* Countess of Summerfield—looked to her not only as a helper, but also as a friend and occasional confidante. And now, Morgan wanted her to be his wife.

She *would* be his wife.

But if she'd learned anything by working at Summerfield Manor, it was that everything had its proper time and place. There was an order to things. Molly didn't help the countess put on an evening dress in the morning, nor did she place the padded bustle on the outside of the dress.

Nor did a lady's maid abandon her mistress when she greatly needed her support. Surely in a few months, Lady Summerfield would get her footing and have enough confidence for Molly to leave with honor. For that's what it came down to. There were honorable ways to do things, ways that spoke of good character and loyalty, and there were dishonorable ways to do things that spoke of selfishness.

Molly saw the eyes of many a servant as they danced nearby, and looked in their direction. Their curiosity was evidence that both Agnes and Bridget had kept their promise not to tell about her romance with Morgan. Mrs. Camden looked especially interested.

And so, Molly took a step away from Morgan. She dropped his hand, trying desperately to hold his gaze. "I will marry you, Morgan. I love you with all my heart. But let's do this right—for everyone's sake."

He nodded toward the dancers, the Weston family, and their servants. "You choose their sake over mine? Over ours?"

He'd never been a servant. How could she make him understand the sense of pride and duty that drove her? "I choose the right way."

His jaw tightened, and his soft eyes hardened into a glare. "The right way for you. But what about me?"

With that, he turned and strode over the lawn toward the village.

I am having a good time.

Ruth surprised herself with the revelation. For this was the first public event she'd been to at the manor since becoming the countess. She'd worried the servants might stare at her or discuss among themselves why the countess had suddenly decided to be social. But their response—even if they did talk—was quite gracious. After a few curious looks, they accepted her presence.

She clapped as the fiddler played another rousing song. The bride and groom hadn't missed a dance, and the servants were exuberant in their celebration. It felt like . . . family. Clarissa danced with Mr. Dixon, and earlier she'd seen the earl dancing with Mrs. McDeer. Today was a day where love conquered all and barriers were crossed.

She spotted Frederick coming toward her, and his smile ignited her own. "You seem happy, my dear," he said.

"I am happy." That it was true only added to her happiness.

"I like seeing you out and about. I've missed you."

Her throat tightened. "I've missed me too."

Frederick gave her a look, then held out a hand. "Would you like to dance?"

She felt like a schoolgirl at her first cotillion as she offered him a curtsy and her hand. "I would love to."

Lila stood behind the punch table, wishing she could leave. Seeing Joseph and Lady Clarissa dancing and smiling at each other made her as prickly as the rose bushes nearby.

To his credit, Joseph repeatedly scanned the crowd, trying to find her.

But she also saw Clarissa's possessive hold on his arm, and the way she positioned herself so Joseph's back was to Lila — as if she knew there was something between them.

Had Joseph spoken with her yet? If so, his words had made little impact, for it was clear Clarissa was not giving him up.

The earl approached the couple and clapped Joseph on the back, saying words beyond Lila's hearing. Joseph's face looked stricken, but ne nodded, while Clarissa bounced on her toes, and kissed her father's cheek.

The earl stopped the music and strode toward the middle of the dancers. "Attention, please. During this glorious celebration, I have one other announcement. I am happy to declare that my daughter, Lady Clarissa, is now betrothed to Joseph Kidd. Soon, we will have another wedding to celebrate!"

The applause bit into Lila's being like a hundred insects finding their prey. What about Joseph's declaration of love? What about being his other half? When she'd left Crompton Hall she'd felt assured they would be together, that he would *make* it happen.

I should have told him what I know about Clarissa's motives for marriage.

But now it was too late.

It was over.

They were over.

She ran toward home.

Lila spotted her brother walking ahead. "Morgan!" He turned and waited for her, his face cloudy. "Why did you leave?" she asked.

"Why did you?"

"Things didn't work out as I planned."

He harrumphed.

"What happened to you?"

"I proposed to Molly and she said no."

"Really?"

He shrugged. "She said no — for now. She wants to wait until the countess changes the world, or some other blarney."

She ran her hand up and down his upper arm. "At least she *will* marry you."

He eyed her. "What happened to you?"

"That worthy man you told me would come into my life and sweep me off my feet?"

"Yes?"

"He's swept me up and dropped me."

Morgan looked toward the manor. Then back at her. "Joseph Kidd?"

"The earl just announced his engagement to Lady Clarissa."

"Kidd gave you hope that you two . . .?"

"False hope." She plucked a string from his sleeve. "I was stupid to believe him."

"He didn't do anything he shouldn't have, did he?"

Lila thought of the kiss. In spite of everything she would never wish it away. "He was a perfect gentleman."

"But now he's Lady Clarissa's perfect gentleman."

Her tears took her by surprise. "Don't mind me. I know it does no good to cry."

Morgan pulled her close. "Oh what of it? Cry away."

It felt good to let it out, and she thanked God for her brother's care. But she knew it wouldn't be the last time she grieved. Her heart had never ached like this, and her thoughts had never been so pulled and torn. She reminded herself to breathe.

"Come now," Morgan said. "Let's get home."

She shook her head and dried her tears. "I can't go home and have Mother ask questions."

"Want to stop by Timothy's and say hello?"

She socked him in the arm.

Yet there were worse ideas.

"Wait!" Grady said as they stood before the door of their cottage.

He opened the door wide, then returned and swept her up into his arms. He walked across the threshold, kicking the door shut with his foot.

Then he looked down at her, his eyes soft. "I love you, Mrs. Cummings."

"I love you, Mr. Cummings."

He nodded toward the bedroom. "Shall we?"

"Yes, please." Her cup runneth over.

Chapter Fifteen

Addie was awakened by birds singing and the soft snores of her husband.

Her husband.

She studied Grady while he slept. There were permanent furrows in his forehead and a delta of lines radiating from the outer corner of his eyes. His hair — once the color of wheat — was not simply gray but silver. His mustache was new to her, and she wasn't sure she liked it.

It tickled.

She sat upright and let her thoughts take over. How many times, through how many years, had she thought of him and mourned for the lack of him? Although she'd assumed Grady had married and moved on without her, a wee part of her had hoped he pined for her. It was a selfish hope, for a truly unselfish love would want him married and happy, with a family of his own.

She'd allowed herself this bit of personal selfishness because her life as Countess of Summerfield was full to overflowing with duty and responsibilities — which were the essence of self-sacrifice. It wasn't fair to say her life was spent grudgingly. Not all the time. For the perks of being who she was were numerous. But material.

It was very enjoyable living in a grand manor, wearing sparkling jewels and the latest Worth designs from Paris, eating *foie gras, cod à la béchamel*, and Charlotte Russe cake served on gilt-edged china.

What would her life have been like without any of that?

What would her life *be* like without any of that, as she lived in this simple cottage with Grady?

She had no idea what time it was. Back at the house she trusted Albers to be her clock and come in with a cup of tea at precisely half-past seven. Her maid would draw open the heavy drapes and gently rouse Addie from sleep. Then she would help her wash and dress and arrange her hair. Just in time for breakfast, which was cooked and served by more servants.

I do nothing for myself.

The truth of it was sobering. The dowager countess, a capable, smart, independent woman, was not independent at all. Living on her own, apart from all those who took care —

"Good morning, wifey." Grady ran his fingers across her back.

"Did I wake you?"

"Your thoughts did." He reached up and ran a thumb across her forehead. "What's got you so worried? I can practically hear your brain buzzing."

She didn't want to admit how vulnerable and uncertain she felt.

"Addie . . . tell me."

She pulled a pillow to her lap. "I am totally helpless. I don't know how to do anything."

"That's obviously not true."

She pointed out to the small kitchen. "I don't know how to pump water, stoke a stove, or even how to make a cup of tea."

"It's not difficult."

"But it is knowledge I don't possess. Even the simple act of getting dressed had Albers helping me. My corset laces in the back, my petticoats and bustle tie in the back, my dresses fasten in the back. I can't even get dressed by myself."

He ran a finger along her arm. "I'll be your lady's maid."

"Can you do up my hair?"

He tugged at a strand that hung across her chest. "I like your hair down."

"Don't be silly, Grady. Only young girls can wear their hair down."

He kept his hands to himself. "In the service I had a valet, so I know the advantages you're giving up." He got out of bed and stood before her in his nightshirt, his jaw tight. "Are you saying the sacrifice of being my wife is too much?"

Their first argument. She scrambled across the bed to stand beside him. "No, Grady, never think that." She wrapped her arms around his waist and leaned her head against his chest. "I am thrilled to be your wife. These last twenty-four hours have been—"

"Nineteen hours."

"Nineteen hours, have been the happiest in my life. Forgive me for being so practical, so pragmatic, so . . ."

"Annoying?"

She nodded against his chest. With his arms around her, her worries fell away.

But then her stomach growled. "I'm hungry."

He gently nudged her back to the bed. "So am I."

"You place the wood in here, crumple a little straw beneath it, and light a match." A flame sparked to life. "You shouldn't pack the area too tightly, because fire needs air." Grady looked skeptically at her blue dressing gown. "Watch your flowy sleeves. I don't want *you* catching fire."

A good point. Actually, the fact they were making breakfast while they were dressed in their nightclothes and robes was rather shocking. And freeing. How much better to move around without the constraints of a corset, petticoats, and an infernal bustle.

Grady closed the grate of the stove, then moved to the sink where he cranked the pump until water flowed. "Now we fill the kettle and put it on the stovetop." When this was done he said, "Voila!"

Addie *thought* she could do it. "Tea is fine, but what about some food?"

He plucked a black pan off of a nail on the wall. "Griddle cakes, my lady?"

"I haven't had those since I was a child."

"Then it's high time." He proceeded to stir together flour, water, some other white powder, and lard.

"Where did you get the ingredients?"

"The mercantile."

"You could have asked Mrs. McDeer."

"I could have, but I prefer to purchase my own food stuffs." He handed her the pan, which was enormously heavy. "Put it on the other burner, and add a little grease to it."

Addie dipped a spoon into the grease, then tried to get it to drop into the pan. She shook the spoon over and over.

Grady saw her dilemma. "Tap it hard on the side of the pan—or run your finger through the spoon to make it drop."

"I prefer the tapping method, thank you." She did as she was told and was relieved the lard fell into the pan. It immediately began to liquefy. Fascinating.

Grady stirred the flour mixture. "To test if the pan is hot enough, drop a bit of water on it. The droplets should dance."

"Dance. Water dance."

"You'll see."

A few minutes later Addie jumped when the teakettle began to whistle. She could hear the water rumbling inside, and steam escaped the spout. "What should I do?"

"Let me pour it in the pretty teapot." He took the hot water and poured a little in a Delft teapot, swirled it around, then emptied it and poured in more.

"Why did you waste the water?"

"I did not waste it, I tempered the pot to the right temperature. Now, to the water we add one teaspoon of tea for each of us, and one more for the pot." That done he turned his attention to the black pan. He dropped a bead of water onto the griddle—making the droplets dance as promised. Then he ladled the batter into the pan, and soon the smell of the cakes wafted through the cottage. Addie found the jar of blackberry preserves to put on top.

"Set the table," he said, which sent her into the task of retrieving the plates, forks, teacups, and teaspoons — which *she* had set on shelves when they were refurbishing the cottage.

Within minutes they were seated for breakfast.

Addie took a deep breath. "My, my. What a production this is."

"It's what goes on below stairs every day of your life, Addie. And this is very simple fare."

It was all so different, as if she were visiting a foreign country.

He took her hand to his lips and kissed it. Then he said, "Let us thank God for His many blessings."

Many many blessings.

Addie held the front of her corset in place while Grady worked at lacing the back. "Like an X, Grady. Back and forth, like you're lacing your boots."

"I'll get it," he said, "I'm not totally inept, you know."

"Never said you were." She felt him pulling the corset tight. "Tighter."

"Don't be ridiculous."

"A small waist is indicative of a woman's status."

"Ridiculous," he repeated, though he tugged tighter before tying the laces at the bottom. "Now what?"

"Now the Princess of Wales."

"What?"

She pointed to the bustle. "That thing. It fastens around my waist."

"More ridiculousness."

"You didn't think they were so ridiculous when you helped me out of them last night."

He whispered in her ear. "Oh yes I did." He helped her center the bustle over her lower back. "Why would the next queen of England want a bustle named after her?"

"I doubt it was her choice. Yet she *has* influenced many fashions. You've perhaps seen the multi-strand chokers some women wear?"

"Perhaps seen, but not noticed."

"The princess started that trend. Word is, she has some scar from a childhood surgery on her neck, and the chokers cover it."

"Pride goeth before the fall. Or is it vanity?"

"Call it vanity, if you will. Jane Austen wrote that pride relates more to our opinion of ourselves, while vanity relates to what we would have others think of us."

He kissed her shoulder. "Then vanity it is."

Somehow she'd won the debate while losing it.

Next, the petticoat. "Help me. Over my head."

The petticoat was fastened, an ivory underskirt was set in place, and an overdress of striped red and white silk was slipped over her head. "Luckily, this one fastens in front."

"Luckily," Grady said, shaking his head. "You look beautiful, my love, but I warn you you'll be overdressed for fishing."

"Fishing? We're going to church."

"Yes, but this afternoon I will teach you the intricacies of bait and tackle."

"But I already learned how to make a fire, tea, and cakes."

"And later, if we're lucky, I'll teach you how to bone a fish."

Lovely.

"Nana, are you sure you don't want to come to church with us?" Lila asked. "When you met Reverend Lyons you seemed to like him."

"I did."

"Then why won't you ever come with us?"

"I don't like being out in public that long."

Mother waved the discussion away, then tied her bonnet

beneath her chin. "There's no arguing with her. If she wants to be damned to hell for not going to church then so be it."

"Fidelia!" Papa said. "You know that's not true."

Mother shrugged. "Actually, if anyone shouldn't want to go, it's Lila now that the turncoat Joseph has become engaged to Lady Clarissa."

Lila was shocked. "How did you find out?"

Mother adjusted her bow in a mirror. "There's no way I wouldn't find out. Those Westons, always getting what they want."

"What do you mean by that?" Lila asked.

"Never mind." She strode out the door.

As they left, Lila touched Nana's arm. "Are you sure you're all right?"

Nana smiled. "Perfectly. Go on now. I'll do my praying from here."

Then Lila had an idea. "What if I stay here with you?" It *would* be a way to avoid seeing Clarissa and Joseph together.

Nana flicked the tip of her nose. "Meet him head on," she said. "Show Joseph he can't hurt you."

"But he did."

"I know."

"It's not fair."

"Life seldom is. Now hurry along and catch up with the others. I'll pray it goes smoothly."

Amen to that.

I hope Joseph is completely miserable.

Lila allowed herself this malicious thought but immediately asked forgiveness for it. If she truly cared for Joseph, she should wish him happiness.

Easier said than done.

There was no way Lady Clarissa would make him happy. She would use him, then discard him when she grew tired of him and got her way. Her way involved spending a generous amount of time in London.

Perhaps that was best. The thought of seeing Joseph around Summerfield, married, caused Lila pain.

She was already seated with her family when the Westons arrived at church. She wondered if their last-minute arrival was planned so they could gain the most attention. Planned or not, it worked.

First in were the dowager and the colonel, the new bride and groom. The entire congregation applauded and offered the congratulations and best wishes they'd not been allowed to offer in person.

"Applauding in church?" Mother said. "Highly improper."

It probably was, but Lila couldn't help but notice how the couple beamed. If the dowager could glow with bridal happiness at her age, surely Lila would have a chance.

Next came the earl—and surprisingly, the countess. Lila couldn't remember seeing her in church in years. Then George, and finally, Joseph. Unfortunately, he had Clarissa on his arm. He met Lila's gaze for but an instant, and in that instant she read a myriad of emotions: regret, pain, panic, and . . . resignation? For in spite of his wishes, it was all too late. A betrothal between the son of a viscount and the daughter of an earl was a pact not easily broken.

Lila's heart was scraped raw. She put a fist to her chest, pressing to relieve the pain.

The Westons took their place at the front pew, and Lila felt Rose's hand upon hers. "Are you all right?"

She nodded. Though she wasn't all right, she had to be. She had no choice.

Ruth couldn't stop smiling. It felt wonderful to be in church again, sitting with her family, being out in public. Frederick sat close, and she linked her hand snuggly around his arm. He smelled of musky cologne. He smelled like a man.

She was totally content. Her daughter was engaged to a

wonderful man. Her mother-in-law was married to the love of her life. George was full of youthful exuberance and was on the road to becoming the next Earl of Summerfield. And herself?

She was on the road to becoming . . .

To becoming.

To *being.*

To living the life she was supposed to live.

Ruth thought back to the strides she'd made since the family had returned from London. She'd come down for tea and dinner, she'd bravely taken up the cause of young Dottie, and even though her plea had been unsuccessful, Ruth felt stronger for the effort. And yesterday, she'd fully participated in a wedding.

Yes, indeed. She was back. Only more than *back,* for in truth she'd never assumed her proper position or the role life had given her.

The role you stole.

She shook the thought away. Not today. Today she was happy, and life was full of promise.

As the vicar quoted a verse, she knew the words were true. "'I can do all things through Christ which strengtheneth me.' Jesus is there for us, to give us the strength we lack."

Yes indeed, He was just what she needed.

From her place at the back of the church, Molly scanned the congregation. She was glad Morgan had given her a smile. She hoped it meant he'd forgiven her for accepting his proposal with stipulations. After the service, she'd do her best to make amends.

But her main concern involved who *wasn't* there.

Her family was missing. Even though Da only believed in crossing the threshold of a church for marrying and burying, Ma, Dottie, and Lon never missed a Sunday

Molly's stomach churned with nervous dread.

A dozen scenarios vied for attention, but soon the worst of them loomed dark and ominous like a storm cloud covering the sun. She rose from the pew and shuffled past Bridget and Agnes to the aisle.

"Where are you going?"

She didn't give an explanation, but hurried out of the church and turned toward home.

Ran toward home.

Stupid corset.

Since corsets and running were not compatible, Molly was forced to stop and catch her breath three times on the way to her family's cottage. Each time she added a new prayer to the previous. *Please help everyone be all right.*

She took another deep breath, then hurried over the last leg. *Just around the corner . . .*

She saw Lon and waved, but he didn't wave back.

And then she saw Dottie, sitting on the ground, her back against the house. "Dottie!"

The girl glanced up, then down, raising her knees to her chest, lowering her head onto her arms.

Da hurt her!

Molly stumbled the last few yards, falling to her sister's side. "What's wrong? Please tell me."

And then Molly saw that the sleeve of Dottie's dress was torn out of its seam. There were scratches on her bare arm. Molly pulled her close. "Oh, little polka dot. I'm so sorry. What did he do to you?"

Lon spoke for her. "He didn't do nothing."

"He most certainly did," Molly said. "Look at her."

Lon shook his head. "He didn't have a chance."

It was the first time Molly wondered after her mother. "Where is she?"

"Inside. With 'im."

Molly held Dottie's face in hers. "Will you be all right?"

Dottie nodded, then said, "Ma saved me."

As she moved toward the door, Molly's heart beat in her throat. There was no sound coming from inside, no arguing. Just an awful silence.

She opened the latch and pushed the door open. She saw furniture upended and food strewn across the floor. "Ma?"

A faint voice came from her left. "In here."

Molly entered the cottage she'd called home. She walked past Lon's cot in an alcove, toward Dottie's bedroom. The happy sun streaming through the window revealed an unhappy scene.

Ma sat on a chair, a cast-iron fry pan at her feet. Da lay sprawled on the bed, facedown. The hair on the back of his head was wet with blood.

Molly rushed toward her mother, but Ma held up a hand, keeping her at a distance. She stared into space. "Dottie was getting dressed for church. Lon and me were out in the shed, getting eggs for breakfast. Then I hears Dottie yelling and runs in and seen him and . . ." Her eyes looked down at the pan. "I was gonna make eggs for breakfast. Your da liked eggs on Sunday."

Molly helped her to standing and led her outside. "Everything will be all right, Ma."

And it would. For the evil in their life was gone.

Finally, horribly gone.

Chapter Sixteen

The congregation exited the church, shaking the vicar's hand, mingling in small groups in the Sabbath sunshine.

But then Ruth saw something odd. Coming down the road was Molly, an older woman, Dottie, and a young boy. The woman was leaning heavily on Molly.

"Frederick," Ruth said, pointing. "Something's wrong."

As her husband hurried to help, others saw too. Morgan Hayward got there first, taking over for Molly in supporting the woman until they reached the church.

"What happened?" Frederick asked.

Molly looked at her mother, then Dottie, then the earl. "I regret that we must report a death."

Morgan asked the next question. "Your father?"

Mrs. Wallace nodded. "I kilt 'im."

The crowd gasped and started talking amongst themselves. "He was going after Dottie."

Which of course caused more talking and speculating.

"You goin' to have her arrested, your lordship?" someone asked.

Ruth was indignant. She had warned Frederick about Mr. Wallace. That it had come to this . . .

"He most certainly is not," she said. Ruth strode over to the group and wrapped her arm around Mrs. Wallace's shoulders. "This woman defended her child against her vicious father. That he died is an outcome, but not a tragedy." She saw Dottie cowering under Molly's arm. The sleeve of her dress was torn free. Ruth moved toward her, cupped the girl's chin in her hand, then gently urged her to step forward. "You need evidence? Look at Dottie's injuries. Feel her pain."

"Carl always was a mean cuss," a man said.

"'Specially when he were drunk."

"Which was pretty much always."

Ruth was relieved that the villagers had turned their attention from blaming the abused to the abuser. But then the boldness of her actions caught up with her. She tried to keep her head strong and steady, but her legs felt like butter.

Luckily, Frederick took over. "I believe my wife has rightly assessed the situation. Men? Some of you come with me, and let's attend to it." He turned to the family and tipped his hat. "Mrs. Wallace, Molly, Dottie, Lon . . . my deepest condolences for your loss."

"Their loss? She's the one who killed him."

Ruth knew the voice. Although she hadn't seen Fidelia face-to-face in years, the attitude was not unexpected. But the nerve. Was she really so heartless?

Emboldened, Ruth strode toward her nemesis. A thousand comebacks and disparaging remarks filtered through her mind. But when they finally faced each other, Ruth repeated the verse that had spoken to her that morning, "'I can do all things through Christ which strengtheneth me.'"

"What's that supposed to mean?" Fidelia asked.

Fidelia's husband pulled her back. "I apologize, Lady Summerfield."

"Don't apologize to her!" Fidelia said as he led her away.

Ruth felt all eyes upon her. *I need that strength now, Lord.* And she received it.

She walked back to the Wallaces, giving them the kind attention they deserved. "Come with me to the manor. The men will take care of things."

Molly's face was heavy with appreciation and relief. "Thank you, your ladyship."

Ruth motioned their coachman to pull the carriage close. It would be a tight fit with the four Wallaces but—

"I'll run home," George said.

"And I shall be home later," Lady Clarissa said, pulling Joseph's arm close.

The problem solved, the coachman helped the Wallaces into the carriage, and Ruth entered last. Mrs. Wallace began to cry. "I didna mean to hurt 'im. I just wanted 'im to stop."

"Shh, Ma. We all wanted him to stop."

As they headed toward Summerfield Manor, Molly looked at Ruth and mouthed, *Thank you.*

They were very welcome.

Mother burst into the store and threw her hat across the room. "How dare you pull me away like that, Jack. You humiliated me."

"No, my dear. You did that well enough yourself."

She froze and stared at him. "You're taking Ruth's side over mine?"

"I'm taking the side of common sense and empathy. Don't you feel something for Mrs. Wallace? Don't you feel something for their awful situation?"

"As if I haven't been in awful situations? I didn't kill anyone, and I certainly had a right to."

What did Mother mean by that?

"That's enough, Fidelia," Papa said.

"No, it's not enough." She glared at everyone, pointing down the line, one at a time. "You want to know what's wrong? You want to know why I'm so angry I could spit nails?"

Lila held her breath. Were they finally going to hear why her mother hated the countess?

"Fidelia . . ." Papa said.

No! Don't stop her. "Let her speak, Papa."

He looked surprised, but with a flick of his hand, gave Mother the floor. "Tell them. Tell them everything," he said. "I dare you."

With his final three words, Lila knew it wasn't going to

happen.

With a groan, Mother retrieved her hat and stormed into the living quarters. The rest of them stood mute, until Lila said, "Why didn't you let her talk, Papa? We want to know this secret she carries around like hot coals on her back."

"She's in no state to explain anything."

"Then you explain it," Morgan said. "Lila and I are adults now. We have a right to know."

He looked toward the back of the house. "I really should go check on her."

Nana shook her head. "Leave her alone and tell us."

He took a deep breath and let it out fully before taking another. "Your mother's family was wealthy. They used to own the Kidd estate."

Lila felt as if she'd been hit with a brick. "Mother was rich?"

"Very."

Nana hung her bonnet on a hook. "So that's why she mentioned playing hopscotch on the black and white tiles at Crompton Hall."

"We thought she was a maid there," Lila said.

Papa let out a sarcastic laugh. "She'd die if you thought that."

"Why did her family leave?" Rose asked.

"There was a scandal."

"Regarding . . .?" Morgan prodded.

The words came out in a torrent. "Your mother and the countess competed for the earl's affections."

Lila couldn't imagine her mother wearing fine dresses and socializing with the earl's set. She wanted to ask why the earl chose the countess for his bride, but if Mother had the same personality then as she had now . . .

"All was ruined when your mother was found in a compromising situation with a coachman. Found by the earl."

Morgan let out a whistle. "That would do it."

But Lila couldn't imagine her mother being free with herself or ever considering such a temptation. Actually, she couldn't imagine her mother as a young woman the earl would ever consider marrying.

"That's why she's so angry all the time?" Nana asked.

"That one indiscretion cost her dearly," Papa said. "You know how fast rumors fly in Summerfield. Soon the entire county knew she'd lost the earl's affection—and why."

Lila surprised herself by saying, "I feel sorry for her."

"You should. She didn't deserve the consequences she was forced to endure."

"Which were?" Nana asked.

"Her parents couldn't live with the shame. They'd counted on Fidelia marrying his lordship, and after the scandal—which was worsened by the coachman's embellishments—her chance of marrying any man of position was gone. Add to that the financial ruin caused by her father's mismanagement of other people's money. They packed up and moved to London—where things became more dire, and all their money was lost."

"That's where you met her," Morgan said.

"It is." He rubbed a hand across his brow. "She was so broken and desperate for someone to love her. She was very different then."

Mother broken and desperate? Lila couldn't imagine.

"Did you know about her past?" Rose asked.

"Not until after we were married. It came out years later, after I found a man who wanted to sell this mercantile in Summerfield. I had experience running a store in London, so I thought it would be a wonderful new beginning for us. Fidelia had mentioned being from Summerfield. I thought I'd surprise her. I thought she'd be pleased."

Lila started putting the pieces together. "But she didn't want to come back here."

Papa let a weary laugh escape. "When I didn't understand, she finally told me her reasons. By then it was too late, because I'd already invested all our money in the store. We had to come, past or no past."

"How hard for her," Rose said.

"And humiliating," Nana said.

Morgan shook his head, letting it sink in. "For her to return here as a villager, to the place where she'd once been a titled lady . . ."

"No wonder she's resentful," Lila said.

Papa nodded. "For her to have to watch the countess, to see what could have been hers, makes her bitterness understandable."

Lila didn't want him to feel badly. "You've done well for her. You've loved her and provided a very comfortable life."

"It hasn't been enough."

"You can't *make* someone be happy," Nana said.

Papa's face sagged. "If you'll excuse me, I should go check on her."

The four of them stood in silence a moment, trying to take it all in. "No wonder she wanted you to marry Joseph Kidd," Rose said. "You'd get to live in her family's home."

It made an odd sort of sense. "How I wish I could have given her that satisfaction."

"It's not your fault," Nana said. "The Westons and the Kidds obviously had plans that not even true love could change."

Morgan went to the door, adjusting his hat. "I'm sorry for Mother's past, but right now I must think about Molly and her family's crisis. I'm going to the manor to see how they are."

"Tell her we're sorry for her loss, and for . . . everything," Lila said.

"You're sorry, we're sorry. But Mother?" He looked toward the living quarters where they could hear Mother's strident voice rising like the shriek of a mother fox. "I may understand her right to be bitter, but she has no right to make others suffer for it."

Lila couldn't argue with him.

Both of her parents had a right to be bitter.

Ma sat on the edge of a mahogany chair as if she didn't dare sit *on* it.

"Sit back, Ma," Molly said. "This is your room tonight."

"Can I sleep in here too?" Lon asked. He lay on the damask bedspread, his arms and legs stretched to the four corners. "The bed's big enough."

"If it's okay with Ma."

Ma got up. "Get offa there with yer shoes on. Don' you know any manners?"

He climbed down then moved to a set of Moser gilded cordial glasses and two decanters. Molly rushed forward to intercept him, stopping his hands.

"I wasn't gonna hurt 'em."

"You can't touch. They're worth a lot of money."

"They're not worth nothing if you can't use 'em."

Molly didn't want to explain that others *could* use the set. "Maybe this isn't a good idea," she said.

Ma nodded and headed toward the door. "We don' belong here. It were nice of the countess to offer, but . . ." She looked around the room. "I never seen such fancy things."

"I get to dust all of 'em," Dottie said. She amended her statement. "I got to dust things, before I was dismissed."

Molly had an idea. "Ma, you can't go home tonight, so why don't you stay in this room by yourself, and I'll have Dottie and Lon stay in my room. It's not near so fancy." *Or full of breakable things.* She stroked Ma's back, up and down. "I want you to have a good rest, in a place where you can be pampered. At least one night."

"I don' need no pampering."

"You may not need it, but I want you to have it just the same."

"I don' even have a night dress, and neither does Lon and Dottie."

"I have extra ones, and I'll borrow one from Master George for Lon."

Ma shook her head. "But he's the heir."

"Eventually. For now he's just a boy."

"A boy that made me lose my job," Dottie said.

There was a knock on the door, and Gertie entered, followed by Prissy and Sally. They carried trays of food.

"Oh my goodness," Ma said. "What's all this?"

"Beef!" Lon said.

Molly looked to Gertie. "What *is* all this?"

"Her ladyship ordered it," Gertie said. "Thought your family would like a nice meal together." She nodded toward a round table near the window. "Put it down there, girls. One can use the window seat, and there's a chair . . . now go fetch the two chairs from the Blue Room."

Lon climbed onto the window seat, eyeing the bread, meat, and fruit. "This is all for us?"

"Yes, little man, it is." They all turned toward the door to see the countess. "If there's anything any of you need, just ask."

Ma stepped toward her and was going to shake her hand, then thought better of it, and ended in an awkward curtsy. "Thank you, milady. You're very kind."

"And you are very brave."

Prissy and Sally came back with the chairs, and the dishes and food were distributed. The servants carried the trays away, and upon leaving, Gertie said, "We're sorry for the whole thing, Miss Wallace, but we're also glad Dottie's safe."

"Thank you, Gertie," Molly said. "That means a lot."

The countess looked over the meal and touched Dottie's shoulder. "*Bon Appétit*," she said.

"What?" Lon asked.

"Good appetite," the countess said with a smile. Then she left them.

But before they took their first bite, Ma extended her hands. The four remaining Wallaces held hands and Ma prayed, "Thank you for this meal and our time together. And forgive me for what I had to do. He's yours now, Father. Don' be too hard on 'im."

It was an odd prayer, yet what else could be said?

"Can we eat now?" Lon asked.

"Absolutely."

They made good work of it. It was the best meal of Molly's entire life.

***

Ruth knocked on the door of the study.

"Come in." Frederick rose when she entered. "Are they all settled?"

"I believe so. I had a meal brought up to them."

"That was very kind of you."

"It was the least we could do." They both sat. "Is everything at the Wallace residence taken care of?" she asked.

"It is. Nasty business, that."

"It was nasty business before too."

Frederick hesitated just a moment, then said, "I'm sorry I didn't listen to you, Ruth. I simply didn't wish to get involved. You must admit it was an awkward situation. And a very private one."

"Which demanded a very awkward and private solution. One that might have circumvented this final result."

"Are you saying Mr. Wallace's death is my fault?"

She shook her head. "No one could have predicted this would happen. To be honest, my greatest fear was that Dottie might be injured or even killed by her father."

He shook his head again. "At least she's safe."

"At the *very* least." She sat forward, ready to get to the point of her visit. "I want her hired back. Her mother needs the income."

"A tweeny's income isn't going to be of much help to her mother and brother."

Ruth had thought of this. "Then let's hire Mrs. Wallace to work in the kitchen. I've heard Mrs. McDeer has been complaining about the lack of help. And the boy can work here too."

"Doing what?"

"Perhaps he can work in the garden, or perhaps Nick can teach him how to polish shoes, or feed the chickens, or muck out the horse stalls. I'm sure there is something we can find for him."

Frederick smiled. "You have made this family your cause."

She was going to deny it, but couldn't. "I have."

"There is a fire in your belly about this."

"Burning hot and bright."

He laughed. "Go talk to Mrs. Camden and Dixon and arrange it all with my blessings."

She raced around the desk and kissed his forehead. "Thank you, Frederick."

At the kiss, his eyes opened in surprise "You are welcome," he said. "But no more family projects, all right?"

"I'm not promising a thing." She headed for the door.

"Ruth?"

She turned back to him. "Yes?"

"I like you like this."

She felt warm and complete. "I like me like this too."

Lila knocked on the door of her parents' room.

"Who is it?"

"It's Lila. May I come in?"

"If you must."

Lila braced herself, then opened the door. Her mother was lying on the bed, an arm raised to cover her eyes.

"You've been in here a long time. We're worried about you."

"Humph. That would be a change."

Lila sat in the chair near the bed. "I'm sorry you got so upset."

"Well. I'm fine. Leave me alone."

Lila looked at the door, tempted. "Father told us about your past."

She sat bolt upright. "What did he say?"

Lila chose her words carefully. It would do no good to mention her mother's indiscretion or the scandal that followed. "He told us you nearly married the earl but then had to leave Summerfield."

"We chose to leave. And it wasn't just because of *that*."

"Whatever the reason, it must have been difficult."

Mother hung her legs over the side of the bed, her toes skimming the floor. "We used to live in Crompton Hall." She pointed a finger at herself. "That was my house. We were richer than the Kidds by ten."

"What did your father—what did grandfather do?"

"He was a banker. All of London would come to him, longing to hear his opinion about investments. Crompton Hall was our country home."

"That's impressive."

"You bet it was—until he and mother decided to give up. I wanted to stay here and fight, to force the mealy-mouthed rumor mongers to eat their words."

So you became *a mealy-mouthed rumor monger?* Lila kept the thought to herself. "They didn't want to fight?"

"They were embarrassed. 'Shamed,' they said. But in truth, Father's bank was having troubles, and he pretended it was my fault we had to sell and move to London. I was the excuse. They couldn't blame me for his bank's failure."

"I'm sure they didn't."

"I'm sure they did! They were the ones who wanted me to marry the earl—for his money." Mother hopped to the floor and began pacing. "A bank cannot have liabilities of four million pounds and assets of only one million. There was hell to pay. We were going to lose Crompton Hall long before anything I did."

Lila was taken aback by talk of such numbers. "So they lost everything?"

Mother made a *pffttt* sound and flipped her hands. "So there I was, out of society and out of money, with dishonor hanging over my family name."

"Is that when you met Papa?"

Mother stopped pacing. For the first time, her face softened. "Jack was such a good man."

"He still is."

Mother nodded, and her shoulders dropped. "I don't mean to say the things I do, the way I do. It just comes out."

To Lila's surprise, Mother began to cry. And when Lila stood, she fell into her arms. "I'm very sorry. I'll try to be better."

Lila held her and marveled at the moment. She'd never seen her mother weakened and defenseless. "It will be all right now."

It might even be better than it had ever been.

What a wonderful thought.

"I got one!"

Addie yanked the pole higher and the fish flapped furiously, trying to free itself of the hook.

Grady ran to her aid. "That's a good one. Careful now. You don't want him to drop off."

Grady helped get the fish to the shore and off the hook. Addie hated the way it flapped around, wanting to be back where it belonged.

He put it in their basket. "We have three. Plenty for dinner. Shall we call it a day?"

"I want to get one more," she said. "Let me put the worm on this time." She picked up the bowl of dirt and worms they'd dug from the shore.

Grady laughed. "My wife, the fisherman."

Addie liked the sounds of that. And yet . . . She handed him the bowl. "Perhaps we *should* stop. I really ought to go up to the manor and see what I can do to help with the Wallace affair."

Grady shook his head. "It's been handled."

"Perhaps, but I—"

"But Ruth. And Frederick. They handled it—and quite

well, from what I saw."

Maybe.

"Does it bother you that they handled it, and handled it well?"

"Why would it bother me?"

"Because you were the mistress of the manor and now you're not."

He'd caught her as sure as he'd put a hook in her craw. "Stop that," she said.

"What did I do?"

"Stop acting as if you know my motivations and what I'm thinking."

"Because . . .?"

"It's annoying."

"Even if I'm right?"

She grabbed the bowl of worms and pressed one onto her hook.

Molly tucked a blanket around Lon as he lay on a cot beside her bed. She kissed his forehead. "Good night, sweet boy."

"Do I really get to work here?"

"Isn't that marvelous?"

He nodded. "And Ma and Dottie get to work here too?"

"The entire family."

"I like that countess lady. She's nice."

"You must call her 'Lady Summerfield' or 'my lady' or 'your ladyship.' And yes, she *is* nice."

"Not 'milady' because that's common."

Molly smiled. "You listened."

"I can do that, if I want to."

Molly opened a dresser drawer and removed something, holding it behind her back. "I have something for you," she told Dottie. She drew Victoria front and center.

Dottie hugged the doll tightly.

"I told you I'd keep her safe."

"And now *we're* safe."

Molly turned down the lamp, helped Dottie into bed, and got in after her. "Are you happy to be back at the manor?"

"I am, but I hate that Da had to die for me to get here."

Molly took her hand. "Enough of that. We should all get some—"

There was a knock on the door. "Molly?"

"Ma?"

The door opened, and Ma stood in the doorway. "That room's too grand for me, and the bed's much too big. And . . . and I don' wanna be alone."

"Climb in." Molly moved to the edge of the bed, and Dottie moved to the middle so Ma could get in the other side. It was a very tight fit.

Lon sat up. "What about me?"

Ma opened the covers and Lon climbed in next to Dottie. Then Ma turned on her side and Molly on hers. Ma took Molly's hand, drawing it across her siblings. "This is better," Ma said. "My dear, sweet children, all safe and sound."

"And together," Dottie added.

Thank you, God.

Chapter Seventeen

Mrs. Keening stepped out of her shop, fanning herself with her apron. The smell of freshly baked bread accompanied her. "Lila. Mrs. Hayward," she said. "Pumpernickel bread, fresh out of the oven."

The thought of the bread, oozing with soft butter, was enticing. "Nana and I will stop by on the way back," Lila said. "Save us a loaf."

"Where you going?" she asked.

"For a walk," Lila answered.

Mrs. Keening nodded toward the woods. "I seen you two walking thataways now and again. Me? I've not been in them woods since I was wee enough to play hide and seek."

"I like the woods," Nana said. "They're cool and quiet."

Mrs. Keening laughed. "I imagine you need a bit of quiet."

Names need not be named. Lila hated that people's opinions of her mother were so freely given. They disparaged Mother's complaining nature even as they went to her for the latest in Summerfield gossip. Hypocrites.

They all turned when they heard a horse on the road. Mrs. Keening squinted. "Looks like a stranger. Wonder what business 'e has in Summerfield."

Nana gripped Lila's arm until it hurt. "Let's go home," she whispered. "Now, please."

At her urging they hurried back toward the store. "Why did you change your mind?" Lila asked as Nana pulled on her arm. "It's the perfect day to put flowers on the babies' graves."

But as they neared the mercantile, they heard a voice behind them.

"Ma'am?"

Lila turned to see who was accosting them, but Nana pulled her faster toward the store.

"Ma'am!" It wasn't a question.

The man on the horse rode in front of them, forcing them to stop. Lila saw Mrs. Keening watching everything. And hers weren't the only eyes, as a dozen people stopped what they were doing in the square.

"May I help you, sir?" Lila asked.

"I'm looking for Mrs. Mary Hayward." He eyed Nana.

Lila's stomach clenched. Judging by his tone, this was not a social call.

"Are you she?" he asked Nana.

Nana's face went white, and she looked to the ground. Seeing her reaction, Lila knew the first order of business was to move away from prying eyes. "Perhaps you'd like to come into the mercantile to talk, sir?"

"As you wish, miss."

He dismounted, tied his horse to a post, and followed them into the store.

Lila made a beeline for Papa. "Someone's here. A man who knows Nana."

"What does he—?"

But the man was already there. Nana scurried behind her son.

Why was she so frightened?

"May I help you?" Papa asked.

The man removed his hat. "Mr. Wilson. Sir."

"May I help you, Mr. Wilson?"

"I came to see Mrs. Hayward."

Mother stepped forward. "I'm Mrs. Hayward." She pointed to a display. "Perhaps I could interest you in a piece of fresh honeycomb?"

He pointed at Nana. "No, thank you, ma'am. My business is with the other Mrs. Hayward."

Jack turned to his mother. "What's this about?"

Her face crackled with a dozen emotions. "I . . . I . . ."

The man drew in a long breath, making his cravat rise. "It's about debt, sir. Unpaid debt."

"What is he talking about, Mama?"

Nana slumped like a sail losing its wind. "Ah, me. Your father wasn't good with money, Jack. Whatever he earned, he drank or gambled away. I tried to make ends meet by watching other people's children or doing sewing work, but it wasn't enough. And when he died, his debt . . ."

"Remained, sir." Mr. Wilson removed a stack of papers from his pocket. "It comes to eight pounds, nine—"

"Shillings and twelve pence," Nana said.

"Plus interest."

Jack turned to Nana. "Why didn't you tell me you needed money?"

"I didn't want you to think badly of your father. And I truly tried to pay it off. I sold most everything we had."

"I thought Pa had changed. Last I knew he had a job at the docks."

"None of his jobs lasted long."

Mother chimed in. "No wonder you came to live with us. You were running from the bill collectors; a wanted woman."

"Fidelia!" Papa snapped.

Lila came to Nana's side. "I didn't know Grandfather well, but he seemed like a nice man."

"He was a nice man."

"Actually, he was a drunk, a gambler, and a thief," Mr. Wilson said, "and he was on his way back to jail."

"Jail?" Mother wailed. "*Back* to jail? He was a criminal?"

"Please, Fidelia," Papa said, looking at both his wife and Mr. Wilson. "We do not speak ill of the dead here, sir."

"Pay his debts and I'll leave."

Mother shook her head. "We won't do it. Eight pounds is a ridiculous sum."

Papa's jaw tightened. "We *will* do it. My father gave me life. It's my duty to see his name cleared."

"I wouldn't go that far, sir," Wilson said.

"If you'll excuse me a moment, Mr. Wilson. I'll get you the money."

Mr. Wilson looked a bit wary of Papa disappearing from sight—which Lila guessed was exactly what Nana wished *she* could do. The glare coming from Mother's eyes blazed like a bolt of lightning, and Nana looked away rather than be seared by it. She took solace under Lila's arm, and Rose offered compassionate looks. Morgan seemed prepared to have fisticuffs with Mr. Wilson.

Papa returned with a pouch of money. "Here you are, sir. The debt, plus some extra for your trouble."

Mr. Wilson emptied the pouch onto his palm and counted it. He shrugged.

"Shall we consider the debt paid in full?" Papa asked.

The man put the money back in the pouch and pulled the ties tight. "We shall."

"Might I have it in writing, sir?"

The way Mr. Wilson's eyes shuffled from Papa to Nana, to the others, then back again, made Lila wonder if he'd be completely honorable regarding the payment. "I suppose I could do that. If you insist."

"I insist." Papa wrote out a note, signed it, then handed it to Mr. Wilson to sign as well. "It's finished then, and you'll be on your way."

"I was looking for a bite to eat."

The last thing Lila wanted to do was feed the man, but Papa nodded toward the back. "Rose, please make Mr. Wilson a sandwich to take on his journey."

"And perhaps a piece of that honeycomb for my trouble."

Mother's mouth gaped, but Papa nodded. "Get it for him, Fidelia."

She removed the smallest comb with tongs and placed it in a waxed paper sack.

In quick time Rose returned with a sandwich.

"You'll have no other stops in Summerfield, then?" Papa asked.

"I have no other business here."

Good. Then perhaps the entire village wouldn't have to know.

Mr. Wilson offered a bow and left.

Mother pounced. "How dare you bring such shame to this house — not to mention the expense."

Nana fell into Papa's arms. "I'm so sorry."

"Sorry? That's it? Eight pounds and . . . how much did you give him, Jack?"

"It doesn't matter. I should have been more attuned to my parents' situation." He pulled away to see his mother's face. "I should have brought you here long ago."

"It wasn't your fault, Jack. And even if you'd offered, I wouldn't have come. Bad man or good, I loved your father and would never have left him."

"It would have done us all better if you had," Mother muttered.

"Is this why you seemed hesitant to go out in public very often?" Lila asked.

Nana nodded. "I've been afraid for so long. Afraid of the poorhouse — or worse. But now I can breathe." She looked at Papa. "I thank you with my whole heart. And I'll work hard to make it up to you."

"Your being here with the family makes it up to me."

Nana pointed toward the living quarters. "I'll go sweep out the house. I'll blacken everyone's shoes. I want to feel useful."

He took hold of her shoulders and turned her toward the door. "You do not need to earn our love, Mama. You have it without condition."

She reached up and touched one of his hands. "Oh, Jack. God is so very good to give me a son like you."

"Now now, you go do what you and Lila were going to do: bring some flowers to your babies."

As they went out into the warm summer air, Nana took a deep breath. "The air smells different now."

"How so?"

Nana smiled. "It smells of freedom."

Ruth stood at the top of the grand stairway. For years the upper floor had been the extent of her domain. But since she'd first had the notion to fully assume the role of Countess of Summerfield, she'd worn the part a little at a time, as though breaking in a new pair of shoes.

But today, with the dowager firmly ensconced in the cottage, Ruth felt the coast was clear.

Today was different because she was different.

She ran a finger under the lace stand-up collar around her neck, then pressed the fabric bow against her chest. She'd chosen her dress carefully: a moss green gabardine with pleated skirt, bustle, and cuffs. She'd been careful not to be too extravagant, for appropriateness was always the top priority. But this day-dress implied confidence and standing, and if green could ever be considered a color of authority, this dress would do its job.

Ruth took as deep a breath as her corset would allow, held the railing, and descended the stairs into her new life.

She reached the grand foyer and was a little disappointed there was no one to witness her arrival. A brass band would have been nice. But that thought vanished as George burst through the front door with another boy in chase. At the sight of Ruth, both stopped short. The other boy stepped backward, creating distance between himself and George.

"Morning, Mamma."

She couldn't help but remember the same situation a few weeks ago, when he'd asked her why she was *out*. "Hello, George. What are you up to today?"

George nodded to the stable boy, who looked like a prisoner wanting to escape an inquisition. "Johnny and I had a race, and I won."

"Good for you."

"We're going to get some sandwiches from Mrs. McDeer, then we're going riding."

Riding. Horses. Ruth jumped at the connection. "I love riding." *Loved riding.*

"You do?"

"I do." She leaned close, as if in confidence. "And I used to be rather good at it."

"Really?"

He sounded as doubtful as he should have been. For Ruth couldn't remember the last time she'd been on a horse — it was far too deep into her past for her thirteen-year-old son to have memory of it.

"Would you like to go riding with me tomorrow, George?"

His eyes grew large, as if she'd asked if he wanted to go with her to the moon. But then he nodded. Vigorously.

"Good. Tomorrow after breakfast. Just you and me."

When he smiled, she remembered his first smile as a baby. She'd been holding him close and had started singing to him, when he'd looked up at her and smiled. She'd gasped at the utter joy of it.

Then, and now.

Ruth spotted Dixon coming down the passageway that connected the front of the house to the back. He stopped and nodded. "Good morning, your ladyship."

"Good morning, Dixon. I wonder if you might know the location of my husband."

"I believe he's in his study, my lady."

"Thank you. I think I'll join him."

It was quite pleasurable surprising people.

At the study, the door opened, and a footman — Nick, she believed — was coming out. His eyebrows rose at the sight of her, but he recovered quickly and made room for her in the doorway. "Lady Summerfield."

She spotted a tea tray on her husband's desk. "Nick, is it?"

"Yes, my lady."

"Would you bring another cup please?"

"Yes, my lady."

Now for the best part: she entered the room and enjoyed Frederick's look of surprise. He was seated at his desk. "I do hope it's all right for me to join you for your morning business."

Frederick rose. "Of course, my dear. I am happy for your company." He greeted her with a kiss to her cheek, then led her to a facing chair.

"So," Ruth said, praying for the proper words to break through her years of silence. "My poor dear, being left to fend without the dowager. How can I help?"

His brow dipped.

"I know you think the notion is absurd because I have shown no interest before, but I am determined to change all that. With one less set of hands, it is time I do my part." She pointed to the open ledger on the desk. "What are you working on?"

After a moment's hesitation, Frederick sat down. "Mother took care of checking the books, paying the bills, and settling the accounts."

"I was always good at sums."

"You were?" he asked.

"Although it's been ages, I used to add rings around my two brothers, making their tutor declare me a . . . a . . ." She tried to think of the word that had made her so proud when she was George's age. "Prodigy. That's it. He called me a math prodigy."

"Really," Frederick said, with a good bit of doubt.

"Really," Ruth said. "I am sure you never knew about it. Being born a female, I had little use for arithmetic." She extended her hand over the desk. "Let me see the ledger."

Although he hesitated, Frederick held it out to her, open face. She took it and recognized Adelaide's elegant cursive. There were columns for *Money In* and *Money Out*. She turned back the pages and saw a page for each merchant, and other pages with surnames at the top. "These are our tenants?"

"They are," Frederick said. There was a hint of excitement

in his voice, as if her simple recognition of this fact was the answer to some difficult equation.

She saw columns for rent, and checked three pages before saying, "The Daughtrys are behind two months?"

"Mrs. Daughtry contracted child-bed fever after the birth of their son a few months ago. Although she survived, Mr. Daughtry has been preoccupied taking care of her. They have five other children."

"Oh, dear," Ruth said. "Is there some way we can help take care of Mrs. Daughtry so her husband can work, and we can be paid?"

"I believe Mother had plans to have supplies brought to them, but we've been so terribly busy. And now that she has gone off and gotten herself married . . ."

Ruth shook her head. "She didn't *get* herself married, Frederick. You act as if she's done something wrong or something to spite you. We must be happy for her happiness."

She accepted his stare with pleasure.

But enough of that. Ruth closed the ledger with a snap and held it like a piece of evidence. "I will take care of this from now on."

"No, Ruth, certainly you shouldn't."

"Yes, I certainly *should* take on some duties. If numbers are my forte, then I should work with numbers. Your mother's gift is overseeing a myriad of details."

"And my gift?" Frederick asked.

Although distanced, Ruth knew her husband well. Unfortunately, his talents were less tangible than a head for figures or skill with organization.

He was waiting for an answer, and she saw his shoulders drop as if resigned to some inner mediocrity.

"Your talent is being the eleventh Earl of Summerfield, a man who oversees a grand estate with wisdom, compassion, and honor." She smiled at him and realized the simple gesture had been long dormant. "You wear so many hats, Frederick. Husband, father, master, and earl. I know the enormous responsibility that weighs on you. I apologize for abandoning you for far too long." Before Frederick could respond, she wanted him to know how special he was. "People look up to you, Frederick, and they recognize the legacy and heritage you represent. Just be the good man you are, for there is none better."

Were there tears in his eyes? She could see he was about to thank her when Nick came in with another teacup. "Ah, the tea. And just in time to fortify us in our work."

Our work. What a wonderful phrase.

Grady positioned the fish just so. "You must hold the knife sideways so you can cut under the skin and just above the bones."

He did it with such ease. Addie had badly butchered the last two fish she'd tried to fillet.

He handed her the knife. "Try again."

She adjusted her straw hat to block the sun and was just about to give it a go, when she heard a sound. A pony cart.

Addie looked up and waited for the cart to round the bend near their cottage. "Clarissa!"

Grady walked over to help the girl down from the cart. "Lady Clarissa, how wonderful to see you."

"I hope I'm not intruding," she said. "I was instructed by Father to bring some supplies and one of the kitchen maids over to the Daughtrys' house."

"Ah, yes." Addie said. "Mrs. Daughtry recently had a baby."

"She's recovering from number six, and from some fever-thing." Clarissa shuddered. "Six. Can you imagine?"

"Children are a blessing, my dear."

"One perhaps, but six?" She shook the thought away. "At any rate, Father hopes the extra pair of hands will help until she can get on her feet again."

"Very wise and good." Addie felt guilty, for she had

spoken with Frederick about helping the Daughtrys but had never followed through to see it accomplished. "Enough of that. Come give me a proper hug." She approached with her forearms upraised as her hands were dirty. She kissed Clarissa's cheeks without touching her.

Clarissa gave her a good looking-at. "I can honestly say I have never seen you with the sleeves of your dress rolled up above your elbows, and your skirt covered with an apron. And do I smell . . . fish?"

"Grady's taught me how to fend in the wild by deboning and filleting. Today I caught three."

"You caught fish?"

"She's becoming an expert angler," Grady said.

"Come in and I shall make us some tea," Addie said.

Clarissa's look of surprise made Addie laugh. "Yes, I will make the tea. I am getting quite good at that too."

Once inside, Grady cranked the pump so she could wash her hands. That done, he left to gather the fish before some animal snatched them for a free lunch.

While he was gone, Addie filled a kettle and put more wood in the stove, blowing the fire to life. "There now," she said.

Clarissa laughed. "I find you filleting a fish—which you caught—and making tea on a stove, and all you can say is 'there now'?"

Addie nodded toward the small dining table, wanting her granddaughter to sit. "Tis a miracle, that's what it is. All these things I am able to do that I didn't know how to do."

"You seem to be enjoying yourself."

"Blessed be, I am. Who would have thought the accomplishment of simple tasks could bring such joy?"

"You're truly happy then?"

Addie glanced out the window where Grady was finishing with the fish. "I am more than happy, child, I am jubilant."

"Jubilant?" Clarissa sighed and sat at the table. Her face showed the opposite emotion.

Addie reached across the table and touched her hand. "A

newly engaged girl should be the essence of jubilance."

"You would think so."

"What's wrong? Is Joseph treating you badly?"

"Not really. And I am trying my best to have proper feelings for him." Clarissa shrugged. "But I fear he doesn't like me much at all."

This would never do. "Is he not . . . attentive?"

"Reluctantly. I have had to ask him out for an evening with friends, and when I leave notes for him, he doesn't always respond in a timely manner."

"You leave notes? Where?"

"At the mercantile. Lila Hayward acts as our go-between. Crompton Hall is such a distance from the manor."

"Send a hall boy back and forth. They are usually glad to get out of the house."

She shrugged. "I probably should have, but when all three of us were together, I had the notion to ask Lila to do it. And so it is."

Addie knew of Lila. She was a sweet girl. Pretty too. And she was about the same age as Clarissa.

Suddenly a thought came front and center. Could Lila and Joseph . . .? "Is it wise sending a pretty young woman as your go-between?"

"The shopkeeper's daughter? Grandmamma, be serious. As though I have anything to worry about from that corner."

"Love does not always abide by the limits of social status."

Clarissa flipped the thought away. "I am confident in my ability to . . ." she smiled a wicked smile, "keep the attention of any man I choose."

Addie did not like seeing this side of her granddaughter. "Love need not be so calculated."

"Since when is it not?"

Addie thought of her first husband. Samuel was the essence of calculation. But then Grady came back, reminding her that love could occur differently. "Love is not calculated when it is sincere."

Grady kissed her cheek. "If you are implying I sincerely

love you, I return the sentiment. "

"You two are special."

"I'm glad you see that." He washed his hands

Clarissa smoothed her dress across her lap. "Although it may appear that I am not keen on marriage, and place amusement above responsibility —"

"True assertions on both accounts," Addie said.

Clarissa gave her a look of disgust. "You think so little of me, Grandmamma?"

"I simply know your personality, my dear."

Clarissa's chin rose higher. "I am not single-sided, you know. Although I enjoy a lark as much as the next girl, I can be serious."

"Glad to hear it," Grady said.

Clarissa's face pulled in full frustration. She stood and faced them. "What I am trying to say is that I want what you have. I want this easy banter and feeling of . . . of . . ."

"Inevitability?" Addie asked.

"Fate," Clarissa said. "It would be nice to know that Joseph and I are fated to be together — even if our match was arranged."

It is rare to have the best of both worlds.

"Give it time," Grady said, drying his hands. He came over and kissed Addie on the cheek. "True love will wait and often takes time."

"I am not good at waiting."

No, she wasn't. Addie changed the subject. "How was it having the Wallace family visit?"

"They are no longer visiting. Mother's given all of them positions."

"All of them?"

"All of them."

"That was kind of her," Grady said. "Mrs. Wallace will need some form of income."

"Mother also gave Molly the day off to help her family pack and move."

"Well, well," Addie said. "Ruth is certainly making

waves."

"She's taking over the ledger too," Clarissa said. "Your ledger."

Addie stood, nearly toppling her chair. "She's what?"

"Down girl," Grady said, pressing her back in her chair. "It's the proper order of things. You know it is."

"But she doesn't know anything about how to keep books or pay vendors."

"Apparently she told Father she is a math prodigy."

Addie laughed. "Really."

Clarissa shrugged, then ran a finger along the edge of the saucer. "Actually she and Father seem to be getting along rather well. They are speaking to each other."

Now *that* was a revelation.

"Good for her, and good for them," Grady said.

Addie didn't share his optimism.

"Are you sure it's all right if I leave you to tackle the stack of bills?" Frederick asked.

"Of course," Ruth said, taking a seat behind Frederick's desk. "You check on that fallen fence in the north field. I am perfectly capable of writing a few cheques to pay for supplies."

He kissed her on the top of her head. "I shan't be gone long."

When he left the study, Ruth was assailed with the silence, the smell of leather and books, and the fact she had never ever been alone in this room. This was Frederick's domain. That he had let her in, and had invited her to stay, was a coup.

Her heart beat double-time at the responsibility she'd been given. She had mighty shoes to fill.

What if I am not capable?

She shook her head against her own mutinous thought, then said aloud. "Don't make a mistake, and *be* capable."

She moved the stack of household bills front and center.

The first was for the butcher. She did her due diligence and checked the arithmetic, rather surprised at the cost of meat since they raised their own mutton and pork on the estate. It would behoove her to help Mrs. McDeer select menus that relied on foods they could supply themselves.

Her hand shook as she wrote her first cheque. She was not authorized to sign them, which was just as well at this point. She wouldn't mind if Frederick checked her work.

Within a half hour she was finished with the task. "That wasn't hard," she told the room. "I could do more than just this."

She spotted another ledger on the corner of the desk. Perhaps if she learned about crop prices and other details regarding the running of the estate, she could be of even more help.

Ruth pulled the ledger close and opened it. Her mother-in-law's neat script adorned page after page of entries. There was a page for the sale of the crops and livestock. Money in, money out.

Money in. Money out.

Not enough money in. Too much money out.

She looked at the figures again. There was definitely a shortfall.

But that couldn't be.

At that moment Frederick entered the study, surprising her. "I am sorry, dear, but I was delayed speaking with Dixon and forgot—"

Ruth shut the ledger and pushed it aside, then saw that he saw.

His smile was strained, and he removed the ledger from the desk. "No need to bother with that, dearest. Perhaps I wasn't clear in that I wanted you to pay."

She pressed the stack of payments toward him. "I did all that."

"Good for you. You completed your job in swift fashion."

"I did, which made me think I could do more. That's why I looked in the other ledger."

"It is much too complicated for you to bother with."

"Not too complicated," she said. "But I did notice there were a few shortfalls between the income and the expenses."

He offered a nervous laugh. "My, my, you *are* taking this task seriously. But talking of shortfalls and income means you've learned the business of the entire estate in the span of a few minutes?"

"Of course not. I still have much to learn, but—"

"Yes, you do." He opened a drawer in his desk, inserted the ledger, and locked it with a key that lived in the pocket of his vest. He helped her to her feet. "Thank you for your assistance, but I really must attend to some other business."

She was dismissed. "As you wish," she said, walking out to the corridor.

"Close the door, my dear?"

She closed it with a subtle click.

Something was definitely amiss.

Molly ran the back of her sleeve across her forehead. She stood up from the packing, arching her back against the ache. "That's the last of it," she said.

Lon jumped off their mother's small trunk. "It didn't take long."

"Because we don't have much," Dottie said.

Molly was afraid Ma would be offended, but she was preoccupied. She walked about the room, clearly caught up in memories. She paused at the door to Dottie's bedroom. Was she remembering what she saw the day she caught Da assaulting Dottie? Or did she imagine his dead body lying sprawled on the bed? Did she still hear the sound of the frying pan against his skull? Did she still feel the reverberation of the impact rushing up her arms?

As Molly moved closer to comfort her, Ma turned around. "Let's go, family. Onward and upward to a better life."

Good for her. Good for all of them.

Chapter Eighteen

"Ruth."

With that single word from her husband, Ruth was drawn into the dining room for breakfast. "Good morning, everyone."

She saw Dixon nod to the serving footman, who scrambled to pull out a chair for her. Within a minute, her place was set with china, crystal, and sterling.

Dixon unfurled a napkin. "Would you like tea or coffee this morning, my lady?" he asked, as if she always breakfasted with the family.

"Coffee, please. With sugar. And if you could, just bring me a plate of whatever is being served."

The coffee came immediately. As she stirred in sugar she noticed that neither Frederick, Clarissa, or George had taken a bite since her entrance. "Please eat."

"To what do we owe this honor, my dear?" Frederick asked.

Ruth sat back while the footman served her a plate of sheep kidneys, broiled tomatoes, and a poached egg on toast. "Thank you," she told him before addressing her husband. "It should not be an honor to have me at breakfast, but an everyday occurrence, which it will be from now on."

"We are glad for your company," Frederick said. "As I was glad for your assistance yesterday with the bookkeeping."

"I am glad to help."

"Are you planning to . . . help me more today?"

The slight hesitation in his words made her wonder

whether or not he wanted her help. But before Ruth could answer, George spoke up. "But aren't you and I still . . . you know . . ."

"It is not a secret, George." She smiled. "And yes, we are."

"Really?"

"Really."

"What's this about?" Frederick asked.

George answered for them both. "Mamma and I are going riding."

"On horses?" Frederick asked.

"Yes, on horses," Ruth said with a laugh. "As you might remember, you and I used to enjoy a good ride."

Frederick blushed as if she'd said something suggestive, but before she could dissect her own words, George said, "Hurry up and eat please. I want to introduce you to all the horses."

"I look forward to it."

"Robin Hood is my favorite."

"That is an interesting name for a horse."

"I named them after the book Father gave me for Christmas. I have Little John, Friar Tuck, Maid Marian, Alan-a-dale, and King Richard."

"I am surprised your favorite isn't King Richard," Frederick said.

George shook his head. "I like Robin Hood best." He turned to Ruth. "But you can ride him if you want to."

"I shall let you choose for me," Ruth said.

George tapped his fork against his chin. "I think Maid Marian. She has bright eyes just like Maid Marian in the book."

"I am glad you've been reading," Frederick said.

"I like books." He dug his fork into his food. "But I like horses better. Can we hurry? The horses are waiting."

"Yes, sir." Ruth cut into her egg, making the yoke run onto the toast.

It took Ruth a good half-hour to get her body positioned comfortably on the sidesaddle. *My spine over the horse's spine, right heel down, toe up, use the crop in my right hand to cue the horse in place of my missing leg.*

George was patient with her, hanging back on Robin Hood, giving her pointers. "Maid Marian doesn't need the crop much. Just touch her side with it, and she'll do what you want."

Ruth touched the horse's right flank. The horse responded by walking sideways.

"Very good, Mamma."

"Very good, Maid Marian."

"Are you ready to try a gallop?" George asked.

Her heart beat faster at the very thought of it. "I think so."

"You go first," George said. "I'll follow."

Ruth used her left heel and the crop to spur the mare forward. She nearly panicked as the horse took off, but she held on and tried to keep her balance.

"Tally ho!" George yelled.

The two of them galloped away from the stable, past the grassy grounds, and over green hills. It was exhilarating and liberating, and she felt like a princess—a countess—escaping a castle.

George said it best. "Isn't this fun?"

"Indeed it is. How remarkable."

George's grin made the sun shine brighter.

Ruth had no idea how many miles they'd ridden, but she was happy for the slower pace on the way back to the manor. George led them overland to a road, and the two walked side by side. Her cheeks felt flush, and strands of hair were blown wild about her riding hat. She felt renewed and exhilarated.

As was her son. He seemed pleased with the ride, their time together, and with the people they saw along the way.

For he knew them all. Whether it was Joseph Kidd or a traveling tinker with his cart, George called each person by name, and each returned his greeting.

"You seem to know everyone, Georgie-boy."

"They're there to know, aren't they?"

I suppose they are. "You shall make a fine earl someday."

He shook his head. "I don't want to be the earl. I want to raise horses and race them."

"Perhaps you could do both."

They rode round a corner and saw a cottage in need of a roof patch and a front window. A middle-aged woman was spreading feed to a dozen chickens.

"Hello, Miss Sadie," George said.

She emptied the rest of the feed from her apron in order to greet hm. "Good day, Master George." She looked at Ruth, clearly not knowing who she was.

George did the honors. "This is my mother."

The woman's eyes widened, then she held the corners of her skirt and curtsied. "Lady Summerfield. Tis an honor, milady. I—" She stopped when a fit of coughing came from inside the cottage. "Sorry. Me mother ain't well."

Without a second thought Ruth said, "May I see her?"

"I . . . of course. Yes, milady. I'll go tell her."

To the accompaniment of clanking pans and a general commotion inside the cottage, George helped his mother dismount. "Perhaps I shouldn't have offered?" she whispered to him.

"I think it's nice," George said. "I've brought the Widow Schoonover tea cakes once in a while. She likes sweets."

There was something terribly wrong with the fact her son had been visiting the people around Summerfield yet Ruth had never met them.

The younger Schoonover came out and welcomed Ruth and George inside. "Excuse the mess," she said. "We weren't 'specting company."

It took a moment for Ruth's eyes to adjust to the dim light. But then she saw a very old woman, propped up in bed, a patched quilt as her cover. As Ruth approached, Sadie moved a chair close. "'Ere. Sit, milady."

Ruth sat beside the bed. "I'm sorry for your illness, Mrs. Schoonover," she said. "Is there anything we can do to help?"

The widow tried to stifle a cough behind her fist. She shook her head, then when the coughing had eased said, "There's nothing to help it, milady. I know it's just because o' my husband passing. Tis made me weak."

"I am sorry for your loss," Ruth said.

"He died last Christmas," George said.

Then Ruth thought of something she *could* do. "I too have been susceptible to coughs, and Dr. Evers prescribed a syrup of marshmallow root, elderberry, and liquorice. I find it quite effective. Would you like me to have some made for you?"

"That would be very kind, milady. Thank you."

With that accomplished, she said her good byes.

Riding back to the manor, she told George, "You let me know when you find people in need, and I shall pay them a visit."

"They'd like that. I know they would."

As would she.

⁂

Addie pulled dress after dress off the rack. "No, no. This one will not do either."

Albers stood by, her arms loaded with castoffs. "Do for what, my lady?"

"Do for fishing, gardening, and walking."

Albers didn't respond, forcing Addie to look at her. "Don't look so horrified. As my husband predicted, I no longer have need for these, these . . ." She waved a hand to encompass the dozens of gowns in the dressing room. "These frou-frou frillies."

"But they're the latest fashion, my lady. And you have a shipment coming from Worth any day now."

"Cancel it."

Albers held a hand to her chest. "We can't cancel it, my lady. They've made the clothes especially for you. They're all one-of-a-kind. Together we chose each fabric, each design, and each trim."

Addie chastised herself. Albers had spent her entire life serving as a lady's maid, and she'd been a good one, having a keen eye for fashion.

"I am sorry for shocking you so. But the truth of it is that I live in a cottage that's not much larger than this dressing room. A kitchen, bedroom, and a sitting area."

"That's all the space you have?"

"Actually, we have plenty of space—out of doors. I never realized how functional outdoor space could be. A garden doesn't have to be merely a space to stroll *through*, but a space to work *in*. I enjoy making things grow and will enjoy the eating all the more because of my own work."

Albers pressed a hand to her head. "I must sit down."

Addie helped her to the tufted ottoman that centered the room. "As my husband intimated last week, what I need are functional clothes with sleeves that allow me to raise my arms, and skirts with fewer petticoats, no bustles, and—"

Albers's eyes grew wide. "No bustles?"

Now she was being ridiculous. "Don't act as if I am saying no underwear—though that might be rather freeing."

Albers fanned herself with her hand, so Addie gave her a proper fan made of ostrich feathers. Addie stifled a laugh at the sight of her maid sitting there in a simple navy dress, gray hair pulled tightly back in a bun, furiously waving a pink feathered fan.

But back to business. "I ask that you either adapt some of my current clothing to my needs, or make me some skirts, blouses, and day dresses from scratch. Your preference."

Albers pulled at her high-necked collar, her head back, her eyes closed.

"Do you understand what I want? And that I want it sooner rather than later?"

The maid stopped her fanning. "I understand. I don't like

it, but I understand."

Addie touched her arm. "There's the Albers I know."

Now then. Back to the cottage. Back to her home.

"Second verse!" Grady called out, leaning on his hoe.

"Only if you sing harmony," Addie said.

"Why can't you sing harmony?"

"Because I am a soprano, and sopranos always sing the melody."

"Because they can't sing anything else."

Although he was right, she threw a clod of dirt at him. Knowing the lyrics that would come next, Addie acted it out as she sang. "'Early one morning, just as the sun was rising, I heard a young maid sing, in the valley below.'"

Grady took her hand and kissed it. "'Oh, don't deceive me, oh, never leave me. How could you use—'"

They both stopped singing when another voice joined in.

"'. . . a poor maiden so?'"

Addie looked over the hedge and saw a woman of her own age standing on the road.

"I'm sorry," the woman said. "I didn't mean to interrupt your song."

"Then let's continue with the next verse," Grady said. He directed them like a maestro, and the three of them sang a verse together. "'Remember the vows, that you made to your Mary, remember the bow'r, where you vowed to be true.'"

The woman stood at the hedge and added the alto part for the chorus. "'Oh, don't deceive me, oh, never leave me. How could you use a poor maiden so?'"

They all held the final note much longer than necessary, and ended in laughter. "That was wonderful," Addie said. "I haven't sang that song since I was a girl."

"Neither have I," the woman said. "By the way, I'm Mary Hayward."

"Nice to meet you, Mrs. Hayward," Grady said.

"Mary. Just call me Mary. Like in the song."

"Your son owns the mercantile, I believe?"

"Yes, he does. I've recently moved in with the family."

"How nice for you," Addie said. And how nice to meet someone who didn't seem to know who she was. To ensure her anonymity, she said, "My name is Addie and this is my husband, Grady."

Mary nodded a greeting. "'Tis very nice to meet you." She eyed Grady a moment. "You look a bit familiar, sir."

"I've been in the mercantile a time or two."

Mary nodded, and Addie was glad there wasn't more to her recognition.

Grady pointed to her basket and pail. "Did we interrupt some errand?"

"Oh no," Mary said. "I've finished with it. I just brought Widow Schoonover some chicken soup and bread. She seems to be feeling a little better for it."

"I'm sure she is."

"Would you like to come in for tea?" Addie said. "We have some scones from breakfast."

Addie made the tea, expertly stoking the fire and filling the pot with just the right amount. She poured three cups full and received a wink from Grady for her accomplishment.

During the initial chitchat it became clear that Mary truly had no idea who they were, and by that very fact, the meeting was free of the usual encumbrances of title. With a few pointed looks at Grady, Addie made sure their true identities remained hidden.

Mary seemed eager to talk about her life — which had been difficult. They had widowhood in common, though Mary's grief was fresh while Addie's had faded with time and through her happiness with Grady.

"Actually, my husband and I once lived in these woods," Mary said. "We scraped by on virtually nothing." Mary took a bite of scone, then dabbed her lips with a napkin. "It wasn't a true sorrow, merely a problem to be overcome."

"That's a commendable attitude," Grady said.

Yet in spite of her brave words, Mary's face grew solemn and sad.

"Is there something else?" Addie asked. "Some other sorrow?"

Mary nodded. "More than anything, I wanted to be a mother."

"You have a fine son in Jack," Grady said.

She shook her head, then nodded. "He is the best of sons. But before and even after Jack there were many others who died. Over and over my babies were lost to me." She nodded toward the woods. "Three are buried in the forest."

Addie lifted a hand to her chest, feeling her heart swell with compassion.

"I'm sorry," Mary said, plucking a handkerchief from her pocket. "I oughtn't cry like this. After all, it's been years and years."

Addie felt her own tears sneak to the surface. Tears not for Mary's losses, but for her own. "I know something of what you're feeling," Addie said. "For I lost a child too."

Mary laid her hand on top of Addie's. "I'm so sorry."

Addie sought her own handkerchief and pressed it to the corners of her eyes. "Alexander was just a little boy. Not even four." She took a moment to deliberately take air into her lungs, fighting the ache that gnawed with fresh teeth. "He fell into the river and was swept away."

Mary gasped. "Oh my. The poor boy. The horror of it. I'm so sorry."

Addie suffered a shudder. "Accidents happen. Tis a fact of life. But I still have thoughts about what I could have done to prevent it, if-onlys that are never resolved." *If only I'd been with him.*

Mary took her hand and squeezed it. Addie was shocked by the comfort she received from such a simple act. Then another sadness assailed her, as she realized how seldom propriety had allowed her to touch and be touched. Being the Countess of Summerfield created an unbreakable barrier that kept people away. Grady had been the first to breach the wall, and now Mary had conquered it as well—without even knowing it was there.

The women held hands and shared tears for their babies.

It felt wonderful to have a friend.

"Why didn't you tell Mary who you were?" Grady asked when she was gone.

"She is probably the only person in all of Summerfield who doesn't know of me. It was refreshing."

"She'll find out."

"Perhaps. But until then, I cherish the genuine, heart-felt talk I had with another woman my own age. Do you know how rare that is for me? I have been a countess for nearly fifty years, and in all that time I have not had a single close friend."

"That can't be true. You told me your parties and soirees were legendary."

"Parties attended by acquaintances, other titled women of society who also found themselves prisoners of their status."

"Being rich is the dregs, isn't it?"

She swatted his arm. "It *can* be. For with wealth comes the barricades of duty and decorum. Society has built itself very tall walls that can't easily be scaled—from either side."

"You scaled them today."

"Yes, I did. And it was quite enjoyable."

"So the simple life in a simple cottage with a simple husband agrees with you?"

She pulled him close and gave him her answer.

"How was your errand?" Lila asked upon Nana's return.

But before she could answer, Mother rushed forward.

"Where have you been? There's work to do."

Lila came to her rescue. "I told you where she was. She took the Widow Schoonover some soup and honeycomb and—"

"That was hours ago. How long does it take to drop off some food?"

"I sat and chatted awhile. She seemed happy for the company."

Mother put her hands on her hips, her head bobbing back and forth. "So you think you can come and go as you wish? After we just paid off your debt, you'd think you would have the manners to work more than before, not less."

"I'm sorry."

Mother pointed to crates sitting near the door. "While you were gone, a shipment came in. Have you time enough to stock the shelves?"

"Of course," Nana said, setting the basket and pail aside. "Right away."

Lila went to her side. "She's in a foul mood today."

"Every day," Nana said.

***

Molly removed the last of the hairpins and brushed out Ruth's hair. The countess closed her eyes and let the tug of the brush gently move her head forward and back. Molly enjoyed seeing her pleasure.

"So was the move accomplished?" she finally asked Molly. "Your family is settled in?"

"Very much so, my lady. Again, we can't thank you enough."

"I am glad to do it," the countess said, fingering the ruby necklace she'd worn to dinner.

Molly hesitated with the next, but only for a moment. Surely it would make the countess feel even better about her decision. "You'll never believe what Ma said."

"Tell me."

"She said for the first time in her life, she feels free."

The countess looked at Molly in the mirror. "That's wonderful."

"Actually Dottie said the same thing, and even me . . . the threat of our father has hung over us our entire lives. But now we're free of him and free of every care."

"I'm glad." They shared a moment in the mirror. Then Molly resumed her brushing. "Actually," the countess said. "Helping your family has helped *me* feel free. And stronger."

"That makes *me* glad," Molly said.

"It has been such a good day."

"You enjoyed riding with Master George?"

"Immensely. In fact, my day was so filled with joy that I feel the need to share the blessing. And so . . . there is one more thing I would like to do for you."

Molly couldn't imagine.

"I want you to have time with your beau."

Molly dropped the brush. "Beau?"

"Morgan Hayward. I saw the two of you together at the wedding."

She'd feared Morgan had been too bold. "I'm sorry, my lady. I won't let it interfere with my duties here."

"Do you love him?"

Molly's throat was dry. She wasn't sure how to answer.

"Be honest. Please."

"Then, yes. I do."

"Does he love you?"

"He does."

"True love should never be an 'interference.' I am not so dependent anymore, Molly. As long as you get your duties done, you can see him. Perhaps around nine o'clock each evening?"

Molly couldn't believe what she was hearing. "You don't mind? I mean, he's Mrs. Hayward's son."

The countess shook her head. "Life is too short and I am weary of old battles. As far as I'm concerned, the war is over. I am calling a truce."

"Oh, my lady. Morgan will be so happy."

"Then don't you think you ought to go tell him?"

Molly stopped brushing. "Now?"

"You are through here. Run on now. Go tell him the happy news."

Although she knew it wasn't proper, Molly kissed her ladyship's cheek.

Lila heard a knock on the back door. She was putting away the dinner dishes, but everyone else had retired for the night. Who would be coming at this late hour?

She opened the door a crack, then fully. "Molly?"

"Evening, Lila. Is Morgan here?"

"Yes, but . . ."

"Can you get him for me?" Molly was practically glowing, her eyes bright.

"Why don't you wait in the garden."

Lila tiptoed up the stairs, not wanting to disturb her parents or Nana. She tapped on Morgan's door with a fingernail, then went in without invitation. He was polishing his boots.

"What?" he asked.

"You have a visitor. It's Molly."

Morgan raced downstairs in his stocking feet.

Lila moved to his bedroom window and saw Molly tell him something. Then they fell into each other's arms and shared happy kisses.

Whatever the news, Lila shared their joy. Yet their happiness underscored her own loneliness.

Joseph. Dear Joseph.

If only Lila could rid her mind of the image of Clarissa at the wedding, possessively pulling Joseph close, beaming at her father's announcement of their engagement.

Joseph had not beamed, had not even smiled. He'd looked like a caged animal.

But what did that matter? The deed was done, the commitment was made.

Clarissa had won.

And Lila had lost.

Chapter Nineteen

Lila looked up from organizing the buttons and saw Timothy Billings.

"Good afternoon, Lila," he said, removing his cap.

She looked down to the buttons. There were two shades of navy, and it was hard to distinguish the difference. "What can I help you with today, Timothy?"

"I . . . well . . ."

Lila didn't need to look up to know that he had not come to shop. *Please go away. Please don't say what you're going to say.*

But the words came. "Would you like to come for a walk with me this evening?"

No.

Lila was glad her mother wasn't in the store. Last time, Mother had called him stupid for giving his work to the dowager as a gift. And she'd also told him he was on the verge of losing Lila to "bigger fish."

Joseph. Definitely a bigger fish. But now that Joseph was engaged to Clarissa, he and Lila weren't even swimming in the same ocean.

Timothy was waiting. "It's just a walk, Lila. The evenings have been fine."

He was right. "Of course. I'd be happy to walk with you."

He smiled as if she'd given him a knighthood. "I'll come by about seven?"

What have you done? Tell him you've changed your mind!
"That would be fine."

As soon as he left, Nana and Rose came close. "Timothy

seems happy," Rose said.

Lila closed her eyes and pressed a hand to her forehead. "Why did I say yes? I shouldn't have said yes."

"It *is* just a walk," Nana said.

Lila started to nod, then said, "Not to him." She stepped toward the door, then returned to her spot. "I shouldn't encourage him. He'll take it wrongly."

"So you're not interested in him?" Rose asked.

"Not like that."

"But he's a nice man. And since your Joseph . . ."

There it was again. The truth in all its hurtful glory.

Nana tucked a stray hair behind Lila's ear. "Perhaps you *should* consider Timothy as a match. Or some other local man. I don't want you to be alone."

"And I don't want to be alone!" She hadn't meant to say it so loudly, and when Papa and Morgan entered carrying sacks of flour, she took a moment to calm herself.

She waited until they left to continue. "The truth of it is, I feel a check, a hitch, a stop in my stomach whenever I think about Timothy wanting to marry me."

"Mmm," Nana said. "Maybe it *is* a stop. A sign you *should* stop."

"Maybe God is telling you He has another man on the horizon for you."

Lila pounced on that idea. "Do you really think there's someone out there for me?"

She must have looked as pitiful as she felt, for Nana pulled her into her arms. "Of course there is."

Lila accepted her comfort, then pushed away. "But what if I'm meant to be alone?"

Rose bit her lower lip. "I think being alone would be better than marrying just to marry."

"I agree," Nana said. "Sometimes I think the *stops* we feel are as important as the *starts*." She took Lila's face in her hands. Nana's pale eyes were intense as she said, "Remember that you are a sparkling gem. And *if* you find a man, he must be someone who will help you fully glisten and shine."

Lila's throat grew tight, and she nodded. "I love you."

Nana kissed her forehead. "And I love you."

Papa and Morgan came in with another load. "Is everything all right?" Papa asked.

"Just a little talk between a grandmother and her favorite granddaughter," Nana said.

"Then we'd best stay out of it." Morgan winked at Lila.

With or without a husband, she was incredibly blessed.

Nana moved forward to greet the dowager countess and Colonel Cummings as they entered the store. "How nice to see you again," Nana said.

Lila was surprised, and Mother made an odd face, then pushed in front of Nana and gave a little bob. "Lady Summerfield, Colonel Cummings."

Nana looked confused. "Lady Summerfield?"

The dowager touched her arm and said, "It is still Addie to you."

"You're the Lady Summerfield who just got married to . . ."

"Me," the colonel said, wrapping his arm around his wife.

"Why didn't you tell me?"

"We had a nice chat, did we not?" the dowager said.

Lila looked from one to the other. "You've met?"

"Indeed we have," the countess said. "I even managed to make us some tea."

Papa stepped forward. "How may we help you today, your ladyship?"

She looked directly at Nana. "I would like Mary to help me find some chintz for curtains. Could you show me what you have?"

"Of course," Nana said. "Right over here."

As soon as the dowager and the colonel moved to the far side of the store, Mother rushed towards Papa and Lila. The crazed look in her eyes made Lila take a step back. It was too bad a rise of shelves stopped her from stepping back even farther.

"How does she know them? How did this happen?"

"Calm yourself," Papa said, with an eye toward their customers.

"But she had tea — she doesn't deserve to have tea with them."

Lila had to step in. "I think the dowager and the colonel can invite anyone they want to tea. I'm happy for her."

They watched as Nana showed the countess the bolts of chintz they had in stock, laying a few that would be appropriate for curtains on a counter. "If you have a particular color or pattern in mind, we can order it in," Nana said.

"If you don't mind, ladies," the colonel said, "I'm going to leave you to your curtains." He came over to talk to Papa. "I'm in need of a good spade and hoe, Mr. Hayward."

Mother moved closer to the dowager, pretending to stock an already stocked shelf of thread and bobbins. Afraid Mother would ruin things for Nana, Lila moved closer too.

"Hmm," the dowager said, smoothing three choices against the counter. "I do like this floral. But this star pattern . . ." She looked at Nana with a nod. "Did you know my dear little son who died had a star birthmark on his forearm? I used to call him my little star."

"A . . . a star?" Nana said.

Mother froze in place with a spool in her hand.

Lila didn't understand her reaction and didn't have time to ponder it further, as Mrs. Keening came in, wanting twenty pounds of flour.

Lila tried to hear what was going on, but by all accounts, whatever had been said had been passed over and the rest was a normal transaction. Nana cut the proper length of a floral piece, took money from the colonel, and they all said their goodbyes.

She wouldn't have thought a thing about it if it weren't for her mother's reaction. As soon as the dowager and colonel were gone, Mother rushed to Nana's side like a magnet finding its mate.

Unfortunately for Lila, Mother kept her voice low. Nana tried to turn away from her, but Mother spun her around.

"What's going on?" Papa asked.

"Plenty," Fidelia said over her shoulder.

"Nothing," Nana said. Her face looked stricken and aged a good ten years.

"Plenty and nothing. It can't be both," Lila said.

Mother's chest heaved, but she seemed to make an attempt to calm herself. She actually smiled at Nana. "If I might speak with you a few minutes, outside?"

It was clear Nana did *not* want to go, yet she nodded.

"What's this about?" Papa asked.

Mother took Nana's arm and led her outside. "Think nothing of it, son," Nana said. "It's just a little talk."

He eyed them warily. "What are you up to?"

"Never you mind," Fidelia said.

The two of them exited the store.

"I do get tired of the drama," he said.

Lila watched them stroll into the square. "Nana doesn't look happy. Should I save her?"

Papa shook his head. "I think it will pass. Fidelia didn't like that she knew the dowager."

"And that she had tea with them."

"And called them by their first names." He smiled. "That *is* rather astonishing. I can't imagine my mother having tea with a countess."

"I wonder why she didn't tell us?"

"She didn't know who they were. To her they were Addie and Grady."

"Addie," Lila said. "*I* can't imagine a countess called Addie." They both looked toward the square. "Do you think Nana's all right?"

"I haven't seen any explosions, and the sun hasn't fallen from the sky."

"Yet," Lila laughed. "Yet."

It was fifteen minutes before Nana returned. Lila ran to her side. "You look like you've been run over by a wagon."

"I have been."

Lila helped her to a chair.

"Where's Fidelia?" Papa asked.

"You don't want to know."

Lila sighed. What pot was Mother stirring now?

"Tell me where she is," Papa said. "I'll bring her back where she belongs. She needs to calm down."

Nana shook her head. "It's too late. She's on the way to the manor."

"Why would she go there?" Lila asked.

"She said she was going for justice," Nana said.

"What in the name of Summerfield does that mean?"

Nana stood — or tried to, as her legs gave out beneath her.

Papa rushed to her side. "What did she say to you?" he asked. "Fidelia must learn to hold her tongue."

Nana kept shaking her head. "This won't end well. Not well at all."

"What won't end well?" Lila asked.

"I need to lie down." She let Papa lead her upstairs.

Lila ran outside and looked in the direction of the manor. She felt another hitch in her stomach. A stop.

But *she* wasn't the one who needed stopping.

"Thank you, Dixon."

Ruth put on her riding gloves then retrieved her riding crop from the butler. She was meeting George at the stables and planned to impress him by remembering the names of each and every horse.

But as Dixon opened the front door, Ruth spotted Fidelia Hayward marching up the front steps towards them. Ruth stepped back. She hadn't spoken to the woman in years. There was a wild look in her eyes, and a determination in her stride that implied she would not be deterred.

"Fidelia," Ruth said, meeting her at the door. "What a nice surprise."

"A surprise yes, but nice? You can determine that after I leave."

Ruth's stomach tightened. "I was just going out to ride."

"It will have to wait."

Ruth had no idea what this was about, but she had the distinct feeling it would have been better if she'd remained in her room today.

"Would you like to come in?" she asked, stepping aside. A nervous knot formed in her stomach.

"Don't mind if I do." Fidelia brushed past her into the foyer.

Dixon eyed her suspiciously, and Ruth knew he would come to her aid if she asked. But surely whatever petty grievance was driving Fidelia could be addressed in short order.

Ruth gave Dixon her crop, her gloves, and her veiled hat and walked into the drawing room. "Please, have a seat. Would you like some tea?"

"No thank you," Fidelia said, sitting squarely in the middle of a brocade settee meant for two.

"Will there be anything else, my lady?" Dixon said.

"No thank you, Dixon. That will be all."

"Actually, you might shut the doors on your way out," Fidelia said.

Dixon looked to Ruth, who nodded. He pulled the double doors shut.

Ruth's mouth was dry and she longed for tea on her own account. "So, Fidelia. What has brought you here?"

"Justice."

Ruth felt her eyebrows rise, but tried not to look as shocked as she felt. Surely this couldn't still have to do with Frederick. "I'm afraid I don't understand."

Fidelia smoothed the skirt of her dress. "You wouldn't."

Ruth sat in a chair close by, feeling strengthened by her reliance on its four legs rather than just her two. "Perhaps you could explain?"

An evil smile took Fidelia's face captive and made Ruth long to flee.

"I have a secret."

"Oh?" she managed.

"One that involves you. And Frederick. And Jack. And everyone in Summerfield."

Jack? This was getting ridiculous. "Sounds interesting."

"Oh, it's beyond interesting. It's life-changing."

Fidelia's glee was Ruth's misery. She stood, wanting reinforcement. "Perhaps if it's as serious as all that, I should get my . . . I should get Lord Summerfield."

Fidelia pressed a hand in the air. "Not yet. He'll know soon enough."

Ruth could feel the pulsing of her heart. With the tension came the inability to be polite. "Enough, Fidelia. Tell me whatever it is you're bursting to tell me."

"Very well, I will." She took a deep breath. "You are not the legitimate Countess of Summerfield."

A laugh escaped. "Then who is?"

"Me."

Ruth felt the tension ease. This *was* about Frederick. "If you want me to say I'm sorry Frederick chose me over you, you'll be disappointed."

There was a flicker on Fidelia's face, as if Ruth's words had forced her out of her focus and into another place. "So you want to rehash *that*?" she asked.

Aren't you rehashing that? "You are the one who declared that I am not the legitimate countess."

Fidelia's malicious smile vanished and was replaced with anger. "You set me up to be humiliated."

So she is talking about winning Frederick's hand. "You managed your own humiliation."

"That coachman was your henchman. He lured me into the barn and into a compromising position."

"You didn't have to say yes."

"And you didn't have to stroll in with Frederick."

And there it was. Her shame. The guilt made her look to the floor.

Fidelia noticed. "You don't deny setting me up, ruining my reputation, and destroying my family name so we had to move to London?"

"I may have supplied the kindling, but you lit your own fire. You need to own some of the responsibility. And it was your father's financial dealings that caused you to lose Crompton Hall."

Fidelia's chest rose and fell. There was a certain twitchiness in her body that made Ruth fear she would spring across the room and attack.

"Fidelia. I *am* truly sorry for my part in that . . . barn situation."

"I bet you are."

"It brings me great shame to remember how far I went. The fact Frederick didn't get to choose between us without my tampering has haunted me."

"Good. For he would have chosen me."

"Perhaps."

Fidelia seemed surprised by her answer, but all that being said, and her apology given, Ruth wanted this meeting to be over. She rose. "Again, I am truly sorry and—"

Fidelia shook her head until her earrings swayed violently. "This is not what I meant when I said you were not the legitimate countess."

Ruth took a moment to reset. "I don't understand."

Fidelia smoothed her skirt. "You are not the legitimate countess because Frederick is not the legitimate heir."

She made no sense. "Then who is?"

"My husband, Jack."

A laugh escaped. "Really, Fidelia, you must—"

"The dowager's son who drowned? He didn't drown."

What?

"It's true. He—"

Ruth heard noise beyond the drawing room doors. It sounded like George coming to look for her. Whatever else Fidelia had to say, it had to be said in complete privacy.

"Let's go out to the terrace to continue this discussion."

With a nod, Fidelia accepted the invitation, and they moved onto the raised terrace overlooking the garden. Ruth closed the French doors. "Now then, continue this amazing fairy tale."

"It's not a fairy tale. Jack's mother—who you may or may not know has come to live with us—well, forty years ago, she and her husband lived in the woods around Summerfield. They were destitute. Mary had lost many babies and desperately wanted a child. One day Jack's father brought her a little boy of about four. He told her the boy was an orphan and needed a home." Fidelia stopped the story and lay her hands open. "The boy was the dowager's firstborn, Alexander."

"But he drowned. He was swept down the river."

"Did they ever recover a body?"

Ruth didn't know, but there *was* a tombstone in the family cemetery. The entire thing was too fantastic. "You have no proof. Any man of the proper age could step forward and say he was Alexander."

"But not any man has a star-shaped birthmark on his right forearm."

Birthmark? "I know nothing of such a birthmark."

"You might not, but the dowager does. She was in the store just this morning and mentioned it."

Ruth's heart skipped a beat. "So she has heard this tall tale?"

Fidelia shook her head. "She saw some fabric with a star and mentioned its likeness to her son's birthmark to my mother-in-law. I overheard. Jack has such a birthmark. Jack is Alexander."

"Does he know of your absurd assumption?"

The wicked smile returned. "Not yet. So far it's just between you, me, and my mother-in-law, and she's not keen to admit she was part of a kidnapping. I decided such a tasty bit of knowledge ought not be blurted outright but deserves to be savored. First you, then Jack, then the dowager. Then the rest of both families." She strolled toward Ruth, her eyes flashing. "I can hardly wait to inform my Morgan that *he* is the heir. He will be the next Earl of Summerfield."

Suddenly, George came running around the corner from the front of the house. Fidelia stepped to the top of the steep stairs leading to the garden and called down to him, "Master George! Would you like to hear something interesting?" She stepped forward to make her descent.

"Stop it!" Ruth grabbed her arm.

But Fidelia wouldn't be stopped. There was a pull and tug between them, and then . . .

Fidelia yanked her arm free.

And lost her footing.

She tumbled down the stone stairs.

And landed at the bottom, her body twisted.

Ruth froze. *No. No.*

"Mamma?"

Ruth forced herself into action. "Go get Dixon! Go get your father. Hurry!"

George ran to get help while Ruth rushed down the stairs. She knelt beside Fidelia, not knowing where to touch. Ruth stroked her hair, then felt a wetness . . . A pool of blood began to form a halo around Fidelia's head. "Oh no, please no. Fidelia, wake up. God, please. Help her wake up."

Dixon and Frederick came running, along with two of the footmen and George.

"She fell down the stairs," Ruth said. She moved aside so Frederick could get close.

"Shall I send for Dr. Evers?" Dixon asked.

Frederick felt for a pulse at Fidelia's wrist, then behind her ears. He shook his head. "Unfortunately, there is no need. Fidelia is dead."

Ruth fainted.

Chapter Twenty

Ruth awakened on the chesterfield in the drawing room, with Frederick sitting beside her. "My dear. Are you all right?" he asked.

Reality swept over her like a cloud of locusts. "Fidelia is . . . dead?"

Frederick glanced at Clarissa, who was standing close by. "Regrettably, she is. What happened?"

"Why was she here in the first place?" Clarissa asked.

The details of Fidelia's secret stood at attention, begging to be recognized. If Jack was Alexander and the legitimate earl, then . . .

But Fidelia's dead. The only other person who knows the truth is Mary Hayward.

Perhaps the secret could die with Fidelia.

Perhaps Fidelia's death was a blessing.

Ruth shuddered at the horrid thought, which Frederick took to mean she was cold. "Fetch a throw for me, Clarissa. You mother's suffered a horrible shock."

That, she had.

Lila was surprised to see the Earl of Summerfield walk in the mercantile.

Her father stepped forward and paid his respects. "Lord Summerfield. How nice to see you."

"Mr. Hayward." He nodded at Lila and Rose.

Lila wished Nana were downstairs for all the excitement. It wasn't every day they had such a visitor. Especially after the dowager and the colonel had visited just that morning. Yet with his sudden presence, and the fact her mother had gone to the manor in a tizzy about something . . .

A breeze of dread blew in through the door.

When the earl removed his hat and twisted its brim between his hands, she knew it wasn't a pleasure call. "I come with very bad news. Awful news."

They all exchanged glances. What had mother done now?

"Your wife," he said to Papa. "Your mother," he said to Lila.

"What's happened?" Papa asked.

"She had an accident. I . . . I am sorrowed to tell you she is dead."

As the conversation continued, a fog swept over Lila, and all she heard were disjointed words. *Sorry. Fall. Stairs.*

Dead. No. Couldn't be.

Dead?

Rose helped her remain erect.

Nana came down from her bedroom. Seeing the scene, she rushed to Lila. "What's wrong?"

"Mother is dead," Lila said, shivering at the sound of the words. "She was at the manor and fell down some stairs."

Nana turned white and shook her head back and forth. "It's all my fault."

Her fault?

Nana's words were set aside as the earl offered his condolences and said goodbye.

Papa stood alone, his arms wrapped around his torso. And then he began to sob.

Lila rushed to offer him what little comfort she could. Her own grief was riddled with questions, and her initial shock ran head on with . . . with . . .

She tried not to identify the emotion, but it burst front and center, demanding recognition.

For above all other feelings was . . .

Relief.

She was a wicked, wicked daughter.

Ruth retired to her room and sat by the fire. She was cold. So very cold.

If only she'd remained a recluse, she never would have met with Fidelia, nor heard the awful secret. And Fidelia would still be alive.

She shut her eyes, trying unsuccessfully to remove the image of Fidelia's broken body. But more than removing the image, Ruth wished she could remove the nagging fear that she had somehow caused Fidelia's death. She hadn't pushed her. No, it wasn't so blatant as that. But in her attempt to prevent Fidelia from talking to George, she *had* grabbed her arm.

She still remembered the wild look in Fidelia's eyes as she pulled away. And the brief flash of surprise when she knew she was falling.

Ruth pressed her hands against her face. "Oh God, I am so sorry. If only it hadn't happened. Please forgive me."

There was a knock on the door and Frederick entered, carrying a tray of food. "You didn't come to luncheon. You must eat something."

"Why?"

He seemed confused by her answer, and set the tray on a table nearby. Then he sat in the other chair by the hearth. "It is not your fault, Ruth."

"Isn't it?"

"You . . . you didn't push her. Did you?"

"No." Although she was surprised by the blatant question, she was glad she could honestly answer in the negative.

His shoulders relaxed. "Accidents happen."

"Do they?"

They gazed at the fire until the only sound was its flicker and snap.

"Why did Fidelia come here?" Frederick asked. "Dixon said she was agitated."

And there it was. Her chance to share the secret. But she still hadn't figured out whether the secret *should* be shared.

When she didn't answer, Frederick asked, "It was about your silly feud, wasn't it?"

The subject *had* been discussed. "Yes, it was," Ruth said.

"It is utterly ridiculous that Fidelia has harbored resentment against us all these years. Doesn't a person have a right to marry whom they choose?"

Clarissa's marriage arrangement came to mind, but an inner nudging brought Ruth back to Frederick. *Tell him your part in it.*

And just like that, she knew it was time. "I have a confession to make," she said, straightening her back. "Remember that night, when you and I walked into the barn and caught Fidelia—"

"Yes, yes," he said. "An awful moment."

Ruth nodded. "A moment I orchestrated."

He cocked his head. "In what way?"

She set the words free in a torrent. "I knew she was a flirtatious woman who didn't truly care for you—nor did she deserve you. I had no proof, but she seemed to have an ulterior motive for wanting to marry you."

"I was not aware of anything like that."

That did not surprise her. Frederick had never owned a keen intuition about people, he saw only what was on the surface. "Perhaps I was too desperate, perhaps I should have left things alone, but . . . ." She took a fresh breath to fuel the rest of her confession. "I set her up. I bribed your coachmen to take Fidelia up on her flirtation and place her in a compromising situation. And then I arranged for you and I to walk in on her. On them."

His face was clothed in disappointment. "Oh, Ruth, why?"

"Because I feared she would win you over. I thought you might end up loving her best, and I loved you, and . . . and I couldn't risk losing you."

He left his chair and knelt beside her, taking her hands in his. "Oh, my dear. I didn't love Fidelia. I knew what kind of woman she was. I loved you, Ruth. I have always loved you, and only you."

The tension of the day burst open like a floodgate. Ruth expelled a breath as if she'd been saving it for more than twenty years. "You loved me?"

He pulled her face forward. "I love you still."

Before happiness took hold, there was one more issue to be brought forward. "And what of . . . Lady Carlton?"

Frederick shook his head. "Ruth, it was nothing. I guarantee you. I swear."

"I don't need you to swear."

"I will." He ran a finger along her cheek. "We have both let other things keep us apart. No more."

No more. No more. No more. She couldn't believe it was finally over. Years of pent-up guilt and fear evaporated like fog on a sunny day.

Ruth finally released the joy and cried happy tears.

They kissed and folded into each other's arms as if they had never been apart.

"A murder in the house," Gertie said. "I never thought I'd be working in a house where there was a murder."

"Mrs. Hayward wasn't the easiest woman to get along with," Mrs. McDeer said as she passed the carrots around the servants' dinner table.

Molly had to intervene on Morgan's behalf. "If you'll excuse me, difficult or no, she deserves a little respect."

"Good point, Miss Wallace," Mrs. Camden said. "We must not speak ill of the dead."

"Lord Summerfield would agree," Mr. Robbins said.

Nick shrugged. "It's just that knowing how testy Mrs. Hayward was, I wouldn't blame the countess for—"

Mr. Dixon slapped his hand against the table. "Enough! I

have heard titterings all day regarding the regrettable death of Mrs. Hayward, but I am ashamed to hear even the hint of talk that it was intentional, and that Lady Summerfield was involved."

"They *were* arguing," Nick said. "Sir."

Mr. Dixon's eyebrows rose, and he glared at the footman. Nick looked at his plate.

"We must support the family during this unprecedented time." Mr. Dixon pointed at their food. "Now eat."

Suddenly Dottie began to cry.

Ma, sitting beside her, touched her arm. "Ah, Dot, I know it's a lot to take in so soon after your da died. But it'll be all right."

Dottie shook her head and used her napkin to blow her nose. Mrs. Camden nodded at Molly. "Take your sister out, Miss Wallace. Get her calmed down."

Molly led Dottie into the passageway. As soon as they were alone, Dottie flung her arms around Molly's waist.

"I seen it. I seen it all."

Molly pushed her back. "You saw what?"

"I saw the lady fall."

For a moment Molly couldn't breathe. Although she believed the countess's account of the accident, she was suddenly filled with an inkling of doubt. Now that there was a witness . . .

Voices from the servants' hall reminded her that there were too many ears close by. She led Dottie to the still-room where cakes were made, and closed the door. "What did you see, and how did you see it?"

"I was dusting the Green Bedroom when I heard voices outside and went to the window. I saw the countess and Mrs. Hayward on the terrace." Dottie covered her face with her hands, shaking her head. "It was awful."

Molly had to ask. "Did the countess push Mrs. Hayward?"

Dottie dropped her hands and shook her head. "Mrs. Hayward was standing on the steps, calling after Master George, and lost her balance. It weren't the countess's fault."

Molly took a long cleansing breath. "I'm so glad. I mean, I never really thought, but to know—"

"That's not why I'm upset," Dottie said. "It's not what I saw, it's what I heard." Her head shook back and forth like a pendulum. "It's bad, Molly. Real bad."

"They were arguing. People say bad things when they argue."

"This weren't no argument. Mrs. Hayward was the one doing the talking."

That wasn't surprising. Morgan's mother was known to be a chatterbox and a gossip. "What did she say?"

Dottie sat on a stool and fingered the cambric of her skirt. "It was a long story, and I didn't understand a lot of it, but it comes down to the earl not being the real earl, and the countess not being the real countess."

Molly laughed. "Don't be daft. And don't you dare go spreading such rumors."

"It didn't sound like no rumor." Dottie looked to the ceiling, then back at Molly. "The dowager had some boy who drowned, only he didn't drown. He was stolen by some people in the woods, and—"

Molly remembered the story of the earl's brother. "Alexander. His name was Alexander."

"Not anymore. His name is Jack now. Jack Hayward."

Molly backed up and found her own stool for support. "Jack Hayward is Alexander Weston?"

"That's what the dead lady said."

"What did the countess say?"

"Not much. Except to ask who knew."

Which meant she believed it.

In spite of her shock, Molly's mind sped ahead to the repercussions. If Jack Hayward was the real earl, then Frederick, Ruth, Clarissa, and George moved down the ladder of title and status. And . . .

And Jack, Lila, and Morgan moved up.

She gasped.

"What's wrong?" Dottie asked.

Everything. With Morgan as the heir . . . she couldn't marry him. Molly rose and pointed a finger at her face. "You can't tell anybody. No one."

Dottie nodded, her eyes big. "It really messes things up, don't it?"

That was an understatement.

With another warning to keep the secret to herself, Molly took Dottie back to the servants' hall to finish their meal.

"All better now?" Ma asked Dottie.

With a glance toward Molly, Dottie nodded.

"Well then," Mr. Dixon said. "You two need to hurry and eat. There are things to do."

Dottie dug in, but Molly had trouble getting down even one bite.

Yes indeed, there were things to do.

And hard choices to be made.

Ruth sat at her dressing table, staring at her reflection.

"You are not the Countess of Summerfield."

Fidelia is.

Fidelia was.

Fidelia was dead.

"What am I going to do?"

Her reflection asked the same question, but neither one of them had the answer.

She leaned forward, resting her head on her hands.

What an awful mess.

The countess summoned Molly to help her dress for dinner.

Before getting Dottie's account of the day's drama, Molly had expected the countess might need extra attention in an effort to find some peace from her horrible day. She'd never expected her to go down to dinner.

243

And yet, that *was* the traditional Weston way. Staying the course, abiding the schedule, keeping a stiff upper lip . . . except for the countess, they were a pragmatic lot.

But now, standing before the door to her mistress's suite, Molly's simple plan to offer comfort evaporated as the truth demanded attention.

She's not the real countess.

And she knows it.

And I know it.

So what now?

Having no plan and no idea of what she would or even *should* do, Molly knocked and entered the room.

The countess sat at her dressing table, her head in her hands.

Molly rushed toward her. "Oh, my lady. Are you all right?"

She sat upright, her face pained, her eyes sad. "Not really," she said. "Fidelia is dead. If only I could turn back time."

Molly would second that wish. "Sometimes knowledge can be a bad thing."

The countess's brows dipped. "Knowledge?"

Molly hesitated. She was being offered a chance to confess what she knew.

But then she remembered one of Ma's sayings: *You can't unring a bell.*

Once the words were said, they couldn't be unsaid.

"Molly?"

"Sorry, your ladyship. Knowing life can end in a moment can be a burden."

The countess nodded and touched Molly's hand. "You're thinking of your father, aren't you?"

She wasn't, but it applied. "Yes, my lady. Two deaths in such a short time. I hope death is satisfied and will leave Summerfield alone for a long, long while."

"There has been enough turmoil and tragedy. It is time to recoup and find peace again."

Molly accepted her cue. "Have you chosen a dress you'd like to wear to dinner?"

"You choose for me. I trust you."

Trust *was* the issue. Being trustworthy *and* trusting others. It would be difficult to do both.

The Haywards' dinner remained untouched on the table nearby.

The family and Rose sat around the fireplace, each staring into the flames, mesmerized by the flickering and the crackle and pop of the wood.

Mother was dead. How could that be?

Papa stood to poke at the fire, then broke the silence when he fell back in his chair with an expulsion of air. "I don't know what to do, what to feel."

"I can't believe she's gone," Lila said.

"Why was she at the manor again?" Rose asked.

The question had loomed over dinner. Lila looked at Nana. "When we first heard, you said it was all your fault. What did you mean by that? You must tell us."

Nana's head shook in short bursts.

"You were talking to Fidelia before she rushed away," Papa asked. "What were you talking about? What got her so agitated?"

"Did it have something to do with her feud with the countess?" Morgan asked.

Papa hung his head, as if the weight of his thoughts was too heavy to bear. "I tried to be enough for her. I tried to give her a good life and make her happy."

Papa's pain spurred Nana to speak. "You were the best of husbands."

Rose nodded. "That *she* didn't appreciate you . . ." Even by the firelight Lila could see a blush in her cheeks. "I'm sorry. That wasn't respectful."

"But it's true," Lila said. "We all loved Mother the best we could."

Papa offered a mournful nod. "If only she could have

loved us."

"Perhaps she did," Nana said. "Perhaps she loved us the best *she* could."

It was little consolation.

Lila didn't like the idea that love had limits or could be deemed insufficient.

But apparently it did and it was.

Chapter Twenty-One

"Ashes to ashes, dust to dust."

Lila stared at her mother's grave, at the coffin that contained her body, at the dirt that would soon cover her.

This couldn't be real. Surely Mother would storm around the corner of the church, put her hands on her hips, and call out, "What *are* you all doing? How dare you not invite me."

She was invited all right. She was here, but not here. Gone from this world to the next.

The finality of her absence shredded Lila's heart. Mother would never see her marry or have children of her own. She would never grow old at Papa's side. She would never truly be—

Lila's tears increased at the knowledge that her mother had doggedly kept happiness at arm's length. How dare God take her before she'd ever felt pure joy.

Yet even if she'd lived to be a hundred, there was a good chance joy would still be a stranger. Joy and Fidelia Hayward seemed as incompatible as a spring breeze during a blizzard.

To be truthful, intertwined with the grief was an awkward release. For now the family could finally find a moment of tranquility that was void of bitter complaints, petty arguments, and unrelenting envy. These thoughts were harsh, but also deserved recognition.

Reverend Lyons came over to offer his condolences. "Take heart in knowing she is at peace."

The notion made Lila blink. Her mother at peace? Lila's mental image of heaven was a place where loved ones could reunite and fully worship God, free of the earthly restrictions of pain, troubles, and doubt. It was a place where faith was fulfilled, and everything was overflowing with perfect harmony.

But her mother *at* peace? That was harder to imagine.

Yet Mother *was* there. Although Fidelia Hayward had not led a perfect life, or even a particularly godly one, she had believed Jesus was who He said He was: the Son of God who had died to take the punishment for her sins. Fidelia believed that Jesus was the Way, the Truth, and the Light. Lila had to take comfort in knowing God had her now. Hopefully, her mother had no complaints about the place.

The thought of her giving the Almighty an earful for some perceived heavenly deficiency made Lila smile, which caused the brow of Reverend Lyons to wrinkle.

She erased the smile from her lips, but kept the humorous image to herself.

Somehow, it brought her comfort.

Ruth shed a tear for Fidelia. Feud or no feud, the woman did not deserve to die. Yet Ruth couldn't help but feel relieved.

Their dispute was over. She and Frederick were close again and the guilt Ruth had carried throughout their entire marriage had been shared and set aside. It was over. Washed clean. For the first time in her adult life, Ruth could breathe freely.

Almost. For Fidelia's new secret lingered.

Only two people knew of its existence: herself and Mary Hayward. Her own decision about whether to tell the secret was simple. No. Ruth saw no good emerging from the total disruption of two families. Yet she would find a way to give the Haywards some of the prosperity they deserved.

Which left only one break in the chain: Mary Hayward. The elder — now the only — Mrs. Hayward must not tell. Although it obviously would give the old woman great pleasure to elevate her son and his family to a higher station, she *would* remain silent. Ruth would see to it.

Toward that end, she had to speak with her as soon as possible.

With the service over, the mourners began to disperse. Lila walked with her father, while Morgan walked behind with his grandmother.

"Are you ready to go home, my lady?" Molly asked Ruth.

Suddenly, Molly's presence became a means to an end. "Not yet. Would you like to accompany me and give the Haywards our personal condolences?"

"I'd like that, your ladyship."

And so they walked toward the Haywards. They spoke to Jack and Lila first. When Molly turned her attention to Morgan, the two lovebirds stepped away, finding a few moments together.

Leaving Mary Hayward alone.

"Mrs. Hayward." Ruth waited to say more until Jack and Lila had moved on. "I am very sorry for your loss."

"Thank you, Lady Summerfield," the woman said with a bob. She plucked at the sleeve of her dress and looked toward her family who were waiting for her down the road.

Ruth scanned the area, making sure they had some semblance of privacy. "I had a very interesting discussion with your daughter-in-law before her awful accident."

Mrs. Hayward's eyes widened. "You did?"

"I barely have words for the despicable deed she divulged. It was a crime that long ago caused extreme sorrow for my husband's family." She leaned forward and whispered. "Kidnapping is a capital offense."

Mrs. Hayward's eyes welled with tears. "I didn't do it," she whispered back, looking left and right to see that no one else was listening. "My husband did. I didn't know who the boy was. Until yesterday I didn't know that Jack was Alexander. Stanley said the child was an orphan. Since I couldn't have children, he just wanted to make me happy."

Ruth took interest in the details and actually felt

compassion for the woman. But she couldn't reveal her empathy just yet. "The court shan't believe you didn't know. And . . . your husband is deceased, is he not?"

"Yes."

"Leaving you to take the blame."

Mrs. Hayward grabbed Ruth's hand. "Please, milady. Have mercy on me."

Ruth did feel merciful. She hated doing this, but there was no other way to save her own family. She patted the woman's hand and hoped her distress would be taken as a symptom of her grief. "I do have mercy for you, Mrs. Hayward. We both love our families deeply. I have no wish to disrupt anyone's life, especially that of your family, which is still reeling from the loss of Fidelia."

"I don't want to upset them anymore either."

"I would love for you to be able to remain with them here in Summerfield—not sent away to London and locked away in some . . ." She let the last word remain unspoken.

Mrs. Hayward nodded fervently. "I agree, milady. Let things remain as they are."

Ruth stifled a sigh. "You are right. That is the best course. I shall remain silent."

"You will?"

"I will if you will."

Mrs. Hayward nodded vigorously. "I will. I promise."

Relief refreshed Ruth like a spring rain. "Very good then," she said. "Again, I extend my sympathy to you and your family."

Mrs. Hayward curtsied then hurried off to join her clan.

Ruth saw Frederick and the children gathering near the carriage and went to join them.

The deed was done, the crisis averted. Nothing would change.

Life could go on in a normal fashion.

"I'm so sorry, Morgan," Molly said. "How is your family faring?"

"Better than expected," he said, offering her his arm and taking a few steps away from the rest of his family. "We still don't understand exactly why she rushed over to the manor like that."

Molly needed to find out more. "She didn't say anything about her reasons?"

"She and Nana were helping the dowager with a purchase. When Lady Summerfield left, Mother pulled Nana outside, and next we knew, she was off to the manor." Morgan nodded toward his grandmother, who was standing with the countess. "Nana looks upset. Perhaps I should go to her."

Molly held onto his arm. "Let them have a moment together."

He relaxed. "I suppose you're right. They've both suffered in this."

Molly prayed the suffering would end right here and right now.

"Miss Hayward?"

"Mr. Kidd."

An awful formality fell between them, a crevice that kept them apart. Joseph stepped to its edge, his hat in his hands.

Their gaze met, and in spite of their estrangement, Lila felt a bond that moved far beyond simple recognition. Joseph must have felt it too, for he nervously turned his attention to the trees on his right.

Look at me again! Tell me we're meant for each other.

"I am very sorry for your loss," he said, glancing back at her.

She suffered a surge of annoyance. "I've heard those words a hundred times today. I was hoping for more from you, *Mister* Kidd."

His face grew red, as if her words had slapped him. This

time he held her gaze. "I am very sorry for what we have lost too."

The dam of her anger was breached, and it flowed away. She wanted to touch his face and run a finger over the worry lines that spanned his forehead. She wanted to embrace him, to let his strong arms pull her close until she could hear the beating of his heart. All that done, she wanted to close her eyes and know that when she opened them, he would still be there.

"Joseph?"

Her dream was swept away at the sound of Lady Clarissa's voice. Yet Joseph didn't turn toward his fiancée, but kept his eyes on Lila. "I must go."

"I know."

He set his hat upon his head. "There are many losses to mourn this day, some deeper than others."

Then he left her.

Lila had never felt so alone, and her heart called out to God to fill the terrible void.

And then . . . Timothy approached. "I'm very sorry for your loss."

"Thank you, Timothy."

"When my own mother lay dying, your mother brought her flowers and soup. I've always remembered her kindness."

Lila was taken aback. Her mother, kind? "Thank you for telling me that. It means a great deal."

"When you feel up to it . . . we missed our walk because of . . . well, anyway, would you like to go riding sometime? Your Raider is such a fine horse, but I have a new stallion that might give him a run."

She couldn't help but smile. "You think so, do you?"

"I'd like a chance to find out."

She was surprised to find pleasure at the thought. Timothy was a caring man, with a gentle heart, who made her smile. Weren't those high among the qualifications of a good husband?

If her mother's death had taught her anything, it was that

life was fleeting. Nana called her a gem. But what good did it do to be a gem with no one to admire her sparkle?

"I'd be happy to go riding with you, Timothy."

Addie yanked off her black hat, ignoring the hairpins that came with it. "Grady, help me out of this monstrosity before I melt into a puddle."

He made a turn-around motion, and she showed him her back. He started working on the buttons that paraded up her spine. "So much for mourning," he said.

"I am not in mourning. Not for Fidelia Hayward. She was a testy, stubborn woman who always wanted her own way."

He stopped unbuttoning. "What was her name again? Adelaide . . . ?"

"Stop it," she said, though she *was* rather shocked that Fidelia's traits matched her own. "You cannot compare me with Fidelia."

"I wouldn't dare."

"She was annoying and obstinate and . . ." Addie didn't like where this was going. Yet how could she deny it? She sat on the edge of the bed. "Am I annoying and obstinate and all those others things?"

He sat beside her. "You can be."

"But people didn't like Fidelia. They like me."

"Yes, I think they do."

It was not a strong bit of support. "Or do they pretend to like me because of my title?"

Grady cocked his head. "That is a risk."

"But how do I know if they are sincere?"

He took her hand in his and rested them both on his knee. "You don't."

"You're supposed to tell me what I want to hear."

"I am?"

"That's your job as my husband."

"I thought my job was to tell you the truth."

She bumped her shoulder into his. "I do want to be liked. When I die I want people to truly mourn my passing."

He pulled his hand from hers and wrapped it around her shoulders. "They will, dear wifey. They will."

She looked up at him. "Are you telling me what I want to hear?"

"I'm telling you the truth."

What would she do without him?

Chapter Twenty-Two

Life moved on.

And Lila felt guilty for it.

Her ability to carry on after the death of her mother made her question love. It was too easy to move forward, day to day, and rarely think of her—other than to have the traitorous thought that things were better without her.

How dare she think such a thing? What kind of daughter felt relief at her mother's death, and worse than that, found happiness in the vacancy?

Of the family, Nana seemed the most upset. She wasn't herself, and today she'd announced she was going to talk to Reverend Lyons. Although Lila was surprised, she was hopeful that speaking with a man of God would give her some comfort.

Lila didn't even notice Papa coming close until he nudged her arm with his own. "You're not *here*," he said.

Lila adjusted the truth to save her father pain. "I'm just thinking about Mother."

He nodded and began to sort through some nails. "It is rather peaceful around here, don't you think?"

He'd noticed it too? "It makes me feel guilty," she said, "I mean, I enjoy the peace but—"

"Your mother was a difficult woman. She was like a wasp trying to find someone to sting."

Lila couldn't believe what she was hearing. "I always wondered what I could do to make her happy. If I worked harder, or was sweeter, or truly listened to her every word, or sold more goods . . . but nothing worked."

"Your mother has finally found her happiness." Papa pointed toward heaven. "And she wasn't always so bristly. When I met her she was very unassuming and almost sweet. Vulnerable.. She needed me, and I longed to save her."

"You did save her," Lila said. "She was the one who lost herself to bitterness."

Papa nodded, then looked toward the open door of the store. "Whenever one of the ladies of Summerfield strolls by, I expect Fidelia to race outside to catch up on the latest news."

"She did enjoy her gossip."

"She never forgot a single detail."

"Nor forgave it," Lila said. It was time to mention the countess. "Do you really think Mother's bitterness toward the countess led to her death?"

Papa shrugged. "I don't know what spurred her to run to the manor on that particular day, but yes, the discord between them was always present." He lowered his gaze. "Always."

Although Lila didn't make a habit of talking about intimate subjects with her father, this was an exception. "I'm sorry she never gave you the love you deserve."

She expected him to argue against her words. Instead he said, "As you tried to make her happy, I tried to make her love me." His eyes were sad. "But there are only so many times a man can be rejected and made to feel like a muddy shoe before he has to choose between succumbing to the mud — or putting on new shoes."

Was he talking about Rose? Lila had seen a pleasant connection between Papa and Rose but had never allowed herself to think much of it.

He waved a hand in front of her face. "No, Lila. It's not what you're thinking. I was faithful to your mother — more so than she was to me. She always made it quite clear I was *not* Frederick Weston, whereas I simply learned to find happiness in those who accepted my love. In you and Morgan, and in my mother."

"And Rose."

He nodded. "And Rose. She's a fine woman who endured much at Fidelia's hand."

"Mother treated her like a servant."

"Or worse."

Since the door was open, she stepped through. "Are you and Rose . . .?" She'd let her father fill in the blank.

"Perhaps. With time." He studied her face. "Would you approve?"

"I would," she said. "I want you—I want all of us—to find happiness."

"That's my wish too." With a clatter he dropped the divided nails into separate tins. "Timothy Billings has spoken to me, asking permission to court you."

"What did you say?"

"I said I was amenable to it, but that it was totally your choice. Do you like the man?"

"I don't dislike him."

"That's not the same, and it's certainly not love."

"Perhaps I could grow to love him. He wants to take me riding when I'm up to it." She added, "And when it's proper. It's only been two weeks."

"I'm no expert on mourning protocol, but I see nothing wrong with you and Raider getting some air. If Timothy happens to ride along . . ."

Lila was stunned. "I can go?"

"With one condition."

"What's that?"

"You don't settle. Just because Timothy is willing and available, don't marry just to marry."

She was moved by his words, and yet . . . "Thank you for giving me the freedom to choose, but we must be practical. There simply aren't that many marriageable men around Summerfield."

"Then perhaps you ought to go to London."

"I am *not* a city girl."

"Then what are your choices?"

The image of Joseph flew through her mind and out again.

She shrugged.

He squeezed her hand. "As I wanted your mother to be happy, so I wish the same for you. Hopefully I'll do a better job in your regard."

"It's not up to you to make me happy, Papa. It's up to me."

He raised an eyebrow. "My, my. Aren't you the modern woman?"

Modern? She'd never thought of herself in that way, but she liked the sound of it. "Modern or not, married or not, I *will* be happy."

He kissed her on the forehead. "I believe it."

"You do?"

He laughed. "I do. And more importantly, so do you."

"Mr. Kidd," Papa said.

Lila hated that at the sight of Joseph she immediately put a hand to her hair. *He isn't here for me. He must have a note for Lady Clarissa.*

Joseph nodded at Lila but strode to her father. "My condolences, Mr. Hayward. I am so sorry for the loss of your wife."

"Thank you, Mr. Kidd. We appreciate your kind words."

Only then did he go to Lila. "As I expressed before, I am sorry, Miss Hayward. My mother died when I was born, so I cannot imagine the loss of a parent you knew and loved. Especially a mother. I cannot envision the distress it must cause."

Or should cause.

"How can I help you?" she said.

He handed her a note. "If you would? I know the notes may seem unnecessary now that we are engaged, but Clarissa insists."

She slipped it in her pocket. "Of course. If Clarissa insists."

His eyebrows dipped. She'd hurt him. Yet despite knowing she should apologize, she couldn't bring herself to do it. She stood before him, the words she wanted and needed to say, locked tightly away.

She watched him swallow.

"Good day, Lila. Again, my condolences on your loss."

Although she'd passed a dozen notes between the couple, today the entire arrangement made her bristle. There was a pointed undertone in Clarissa's insistence that the notes continue. It was as if she knew of Lila's feelings for Joseph — or his for her — and wanted the notes to reinforce that *she* was in control. Had Clarissa's motive changed from using Joseph to get herself to London, to a simple need to conquer and win?

Suddenly outrage overshadowed all else. How dare they ask her to continue to be their messenger?

"Papa, I'll be right back. Mr. Kidd forgot something."

Lila ran outside, and was glad to see Joseph still in the square. Ironically, he was talking to Timothy and his father.

She nearly turned back, then stayed the course. Why not deal with both men at the same time.

As she approached, she heard them talking about shelves. They stopped their discussion when she came close.

"Miss Hayward," Joseph said. "Did I forget something?"

"Actually, I believe you did." She retrieved the note from her pocket and gave it to him.

He looked confused.

Let him be.

Then Lila smiled at Timothy. "Would you like to accompany me on a ride, Timothy?"

"I would love to. Name the day."

She wanted to say, *Right now,* but felt her resolve wavering. "Day after tomorrow. Good day, gentlemen."

My, but that felt good.

"They're growing!" Addie called out. "My carrots are actually growing!"

Grady rushed over from the other end of their garden. "Well, look at that. My wife, the farmer."

Addie knelt beside the plants, so thankful for the simple skirts and blouses Albers had made for her. "How long will it take until we have carrots to eat?"

"A few months."

"Months?" She willed them to grow faster.

"Be careful, or they'll wilt from the heat of your gaze," Grady said.

"Very funny."

He helped her to her feet. "So, wifey. After we're done here, how would you like to spend our day?"

Addie was a bit hesitant. They'd created such a peaceful life at the cottage, and she hated to disturb it, but . . . "I really ought to visit the main house and talk to Frederick. See how things are going in my absence."

"What are you hoping to find? Success or distress?"

"Grady, I am surprised at you."

"I am not surprised at you."

She sighed. "Am I a horrible person if I hope they still need me?"

"Just a little horrible."

Sometimes she wished he wouldn't be so generous with the truth.

Chapter Twenty-Three

Lila and Nana were busy creating a display of handkerchiefs when Mrs. Keening came in the store, followed by Mrs. Ferguson, who ran the Fox Run with her husband. Lila hadn't seen them much since her mother's funeral.

"Good morning, ladies," she said. "How can we help you this morning?"

They stopped a few steps inside the door, shoulder to shoulder, like a mighty fortress.

"We simply had to come see what you thought of the news," Mrs. Keening said.

Papa ignored them, but Lila took the bait and came closer. "What news?" She braced herself for some bit of gossip. The ladies were probably at their wits' end with the loss of the third member of their chatter group.

"Our Fidelia," Mrs. Ferguson began, "your Fidelia, was murdered."

Papa spun round to face them. "What?"

"We have it on good authority that the Countess of Summerfield *pushed* Fidelia down the stairs to her death."

"That's ridiculous," Morgan said.

"It is not ridiculous," Mrs. Keening said.

"It is, because the countess is a good woman," Lila said. "She's a woman of bearing and elegance."

"Which means she can't push someone?"

"Fidelia always hated the countess for what was done to her," Mrs. Ferguson said. Then, obviously remembering she was talking to Fidelia's family, she reddened. "Of course you know all that."

"I would appreciate it if you ladies would keep our family's private business private," Papa said. "Who started this ludicrous rumor?"

Mrs. Keening lifted her chin defiantly. "If you wish to know the source, I can't tell you. The town talks."

"The town talks too much," Papa said.

The ladies shrugged.

Papa herded them out the door. "As the husband of the deceased, I insist you ladies stop spreading the rumor, and if approached with it, set the speaker straight."

"But you don't know she didn't," Mrs. Ferguson said.

"Enough, I say. Heaven forbid what will happen if this atrocious slander gets back to the earl."

The two women looked at each other, and Mrs. Keening whispered, "To find out his wife is a murderer. Oh my."

Papa pushed them on, none too gently. Then he closed the door of the shop and turned the key in the lock. "We are closed for the day."

"I'm sure the entire county has heard the rumor," Morgan said.

"Which is why I'm going to the manor to speak to his lordship."

"What are you going to say?" Nana asked.

"I'm going to speak plainly and assure him that I believe none of it."

"But . . . what if it's true?" Lila asked.

He took his hat off the peg and placed it on his head. "I pray to God it isn't."

"Can I go with you?" Nana asked.

Both Lila and Papa were surprised by the offer. "Why would you want to do that?" he asked.

"I'd just like to give you support, to show a family united."

"As you wish."

Then Lila wondered, "Should I go too?"

"Or I?" Morgan asked.

"No," Papa said with a finality to his voice. "I don't want it to seem like we're ganging up on them. Mother and I can represent us all."

Lila helped Nana with her bonnet. As they were leaving Nana leaned close. "Pray for us."

She would do that.

***

"Excuse me," Dixon said at the door to the study, "but Mr. Hayward is here with Mrs. Hayward."

Ruth's stomach turned. Fidelia?

But then she realized Dixon meant the other Mrs. Hayward. Mary.

She'd rather have it be Fidelia.

"What do they want?" Adelaide asked.

"Mr. Hayward says it's quite urgent," Dixon said.

Ruth's mind swam with awful questions. Had the elder Mrs. Hayward told the secret? Were they here to claim Jack's title? Was this the beginning of the end?

Frederick stood. "I suppose I will see them. Seat them in the drawing room, and I will meet with them shortly."

"They specifically mentioned speaking with the countess too, my lord."

Ruth's head spun and her stomach rolled. This *was* it.

Frederick stood by her chair and offered her his hand. "Well, my dear. Shall we go see what they want?"

She looked up at him, imploring him to let her remain behind. "Actually, I am not feeling very well."

Adelaide rose. "Nonsense. You have rejoined the world, which means you must deal with the people in it." She looked at her husband. "Come, Grady. Let's tag along." She gazed at every face. "If no one objects."

"No, of course not, Mother. You are always welcome."

Adelaide strode out of the room, leading the way.

Was this how it felt to be led to the guillotine?

***

Jack and his mother refused the offer of refreshment, only adding to Ruth's feelings of doom. This was not a social call.

She tried to capture Mary's gaze, but the woman looked everywhere, at everyone else, besides Ruth.

Which also added to Ruth's unease.

And seeing Jack Hayward sitting just feet away from Frederick was disconcerting. They were brothers. It was difficult to comprehend, yet there *was* a similarity around the eyes—which were dark and rather small, crowned by bushy brows. And their chins were strong. But Jack looked far older than her Frederick, though there were fewer than two years between them. Could it be attributed to a life of struggle versus a life of ease?

"So, Mr. Hayward," the earl began. "To what do we owe this visit?"

"Rumors, my lord. Awful, destructive rumors."

Ruth's mind relaxed a little. At least he hadn't proclaimed, "I am your brother."

"What sort of rumors?" Frederick asked.

"There's no way to say this gently. There are rumors around Summerfield that your wife," he nodded to Ruth, "that the countess pushed my wife down the stairs. Of course we—"

The dowager interrupted. "You are accusing the countess of causing—"

The colonel put a hand on her knee. "Let's listen to all of it, Addie. Mr. Hayward?"

Jack continued. "We, of course, believe none of it, but seeing as the rumor disparages your family, I thought you deserved to have it brought to your attention."

"I appreciate that," Frederick said. He extended his hand to Ruth, who gladly took it for support. "Of course the rumor is unfounded."

"Of course it is," Jack said.

Suddenly, Ruth felt the need to elaborate. "I do think you deserve some explanation. When Fidelia arrived, she was agitated about . . . about our silly feud. The discussion that followed was heated, and I did take your wife's arm to calm her. But as she pulled away, she fell. It was a horrible accident, and I cannot express how badly I feel. If I could take back that meeting and that moment, I surely would."

Frederick stood. "We really do wish to express our sympathies, Mr. Hayward, Mrs. Hayward. If there is anything we can do . . ."

Jack also stood, and his mother followed suit. "We appreciate your thoughts and prayers. And we will do everything we can to see that this rumor dies away as quickly as it spread."

"We appreciate that," Frederick said. "Come, I will see you out."

Only then did Mrs. Hayward looked at Ruth, her eyes a bit panicked. Ruth simply nodded. "It was good of you to come, Mrs. Hayward. I am glad everything is resolved."

Only it wasn't. And would never be.

"Don't be so glum," Grady said as they walked back to the cottage.

"I have a right to be glum," Addie said. "They have gone on without me. I feel like an afterthought. And Ruth? She finally emerges from her room, and I miss it? Then it turns out she is skilled at keeping the books? Why didn't she assume her responsibilities earlier?"

"Perhaps because *you* were there, assuming *her* responsibilities."

Addie stopped walking and faced him. "So she hid away in her room because of me?"

"Probably."

She swatted his arm. "Probably?"

"You are a whirlwind, wifey. Taking charge is second nature."

"Whatever is wrong with that?"

"Not a thing, unless by doing so you prevent other people from learning how to fulfill their own calling." He moved a strand of hair away from her eyes. "You are the most capable person I know. But sometimes you need to step back and give others a chance to excel."

He made sense, which was maddening. "If Ruth wanted to participate why didn't she just say so?"

"Would you have listened?"

She sighed. "It does not seem right that my strength is a liability."

"Your strength is an asset. You simply need to allow your family to gain their own strength."

She linked her arm in his and started walking again. "How did you get to be so smart?"

"Years of supervising reluctant soldiers."

"I bet you were good at it."

"I was."

Her mind flitted to the other subject at hand. "Do you think this rumor about Ruth will die?"

"No."

"Neither do I."

Molly fell back upon her pillow with a sigh. It had been a long day. She'd heard snippets of what was said when Morgan's father and grandmother had come to call. Supposedly they didn't believe a word of the rumors.

Which was good.

But just because all parties agreed on the truth, wouldn't stop the gossipmongers from continuing to spread their version. It was like trying to prevent a waterfall from flowing over a cliff.

The countess put up a good front, but that night as Molly helped her get ready for bed, her small talk was too small and her laughter too forced. She was definitely worried. Worried about the murder rumors, and no doubt doubly worried about the much larger issue: the truth.

Molly closed her eyes but immediately realized it was too warm in her bedroom, so she got up to fully open the window. The white ribbon she often displayed to alert Morgan that she'd meet him remained on the dresser. *Not tonight, my love.*

While she was up, she heard a tap on her door.

"Molly?" came a whisper.

Molly let Dottie in. "What are you doing up?"

"I can't sleep."

"Why?" though she could guess.

Dottie climbed onto Molly's bed. "I'm hearing the rumors about the countess pushing Mrs. Hayward. She didn't do it. I could clear her name."

Molly was taken aback. Dottie *was* the only true witness. And yet . . . "You can't say anything."

"Why not? The countess is nice. She hired me back and took in Ma and Lon."

"I agree, and your loyalty is commendable. But if you start telling the story about what you saw, you just might let slip about what you *heard.*"

"Oh that."

"Yes, 'oh that.' If you care about the countess, then *that* can't come out. Ever."

Dottie nodded.

Molly ran a hand along her sister's upper arm. "You're a good girl to want to set things right, but in the long run, it would make things worse. The family we love would be destroyed. Understand?" She decided to up the ante. "And it would destroy *our* family. We're all happily together. We have a future here at the manor. If you destroy the lives of the earl and countess, we're gone. We're out of our jobs and will have to fend for ourselves back home."

"I do like it here," Dottie said. "I even like my dark little room, because it's *my* room. And the food's much better than at home. The work's hard, but—"

"If we were all back home, we'd have to work just as hard

doing who knows what."

Dottie shook her head, making her curls bob. "I don't ever, never want to go back to that house."

"Neither do I. Which is why we need to keep the secret a secret."

"But will the rumors stop?"

"I hope so. Maybe something will happen to divert people's attention elsewhere."

"Like what?"

Too many questions. "Off to bed now. Everything will seem better in the morning."

The chance of that was slim to none.

Chapter Twenty-Four

"Race you to the fencepost," Lila told Timothy. She firmed her grip on the reins. "Ready, set—"

"Wait, I'm not—"

"Go!"

She bolted ahead, urging Raider ever faster. She heard Timothy yelling at his horse and looked over her shoulder. He was coming up fast, leaning forward, his muscles taut, his blond hair blown straight back from his face.

He's a beautiful man.

She had to let the thought go as there was a race to be won. But once she edged him out by a nose and they pulled up on the reins, she let herself have the thought a second time. *He's a beautiful man.*

The fact that she'd twice thought him beautiful instead of handsome puzzled her. For didn't "beautiful" imply feminine? Timothy was all male. He had the massive arms of a man who made his living using tools. His shoulders were broad, and beneath his shirt his chest rose and fell with a distinctive strength. Yet amid this obvious power there was beauty.

"I knew I'd win," she said.

"You caught me off guard. Next time line us up right, and I'll be the victor."

"You can only hope."

When he smiled, she knew one reason she thought him beautiful. He had a disarming smile, absent of guile.

"Shall we ride to the old stone bridge?" he asked.

"Do you want to race?"

"I'd rather take our time."

As their horses walked side-by-side down the road, Lila decided to bring up the latest gossip to find out what he knew about it. "I supposed you've heard the rumor about the countess."

"I have."

She was surprised he left it at that. "My father and grandmother went to the manor yesterday."

"To confront her?"

"To be united against the gossip."

He nodded. "I don't know the countess—"

"Very few do."

"But my father and I *have* done work for the earl and find him to be a true gentleman. I can't imagine his wife being aggressive."

"Neither can I," she said. *My mother was aggressive enough for both of them.*

They took a fork toward the bridge and let the sound of the horses' hooves accompany their thoughts.

"I'm glad you felt up to riding," he finally said.

"Me too."

The bridge came into view. No one knew its origin, for it was one of those landmarks that had always been there. It was formed by a single arch over the river and a knee-high stone edge. It was surrounded by shadowy woods on both sides of the water, and the trees, moss, and vines made the bridge their own, converting it to a creation of nature.

"Shall we walk?" Timothy asked. "We could search for berries."

Lila readily agreed and let him lift her to the ground. His hands lingered at her waist a moment longer than necessary, but she didn't mind. And standing in such close proximity . . . why hadn't she noticed that he was taller than her father by a good three inches, making him a full head taller than herself?

They walked to the crest of the bridge and looked out over the river. The flow of water made Lila hold her breath rather than disturb the stillness.

The sound of voices did that for her. They both turned to the right, listening. It was a man and a woman arguing.

"Someone's not having a happy afternoon," Timothy said.

And then Lady Clarissa appeared on the far road, riding toward them, fast.

Timothy wrapped a stabilizing arm around Lila as they made themselves slim against the stone railing.

Clarissa saw them before reaching the bridge and slowed her gallop to a trot. Lila watched her face change from angry to pleasant, as if a mask was set in place.

"Good morning, Lila. Timothy."

Timothy nodded his deference. But Lila simply said, "Lady Clarissa." Then she remembered the voices they'd heard. Female and male.

Clarissa and Joseph?

Lila hated feeling hopeful. "Is everything all right?" she asked.

Clarissa's face hardened. "Of course. Why wouldn't it be? If you'll excuse me."

And off she rode.

"That *was* her arguing," Timothy said.

They both looked to the road as they heard another horse approach. This one wasn't running wild, but was walking.

And then they saw Joseph. His face softened at the sight of her.

"Miss Hayward, Mr. Billings."

Her own pleasure was tinged with embarrassment for being seen with Timothy. The reaction left her feeling guilty and confused, for she wasn't ashamed of him.

You're ashamed of yourself for using him.

"We're gathering berries," she told Joseph.

He looked at them. "I don't see any berries."

She felt herself redden. "We haven't picked any yet."

Joseph leaned forward and stroked his horse's neck. "I apologize if I—if our disagreement—disturbed you in any way."

Lila warred with herself. They were engaged. A disagreement was a bad thing.

For them.

"Don't worry on our account, Mr. Kidd," Timothy said.

Joseph looked at Lila. "And you, Miss Hayward? Did we disturb you?"

Although his face was kind, Lila felt her insides stir. "Not in the least."

His eyebrows dipped for just a moment.

"I only meant that I'm . . . that there's plenty of fresh air for everyone, and—" She let out a sigh and tried to be compassionate. "I'm sorry you were arguing. That can't be easy for either of you."

He met her gaze, and his eyes spoke volumes of regret, conflict, and duty. Then he tipped his hat. "Good day to you."

Lila turned her attention back to the water. "We should go fishing sometime."

"How long have you been in love with Joseph Kidd?"

Lila had to remind herself to breathe. "I am not in love with Joseph Kidd."

"If you aren't, you most certainly want to be."

She turned to him, needing to be honest. "I wanted to be. But I'm not."

"So who do you love?"

She let the sound of the river trickle through her thoughts. Finally she said. "No one." But then she offered him a smile. "At least not yet."

Lila felt his hand touch hers and let their fingers intertwine.

Ruth entered the drawing room for tea and found Frederick already there. He rose to greet her. "Hello, my dear." He kissed her on the cheek then looked at her intently. "How are you faring?"

"Fine, I think, although—"

In the foyer Dixon opened the front door to Clarissa.

She stormed inside. "Where are my parents?" she demanded. Seeing them, she rushed forward.

"Clarissa," Frederick said. "What seems to be the problem?"

"You have ruined everything!" Clarissa said, pointing at Ruth. "Everything."

Father took a step toward her as though ready to protect his wife. "You should not speak to your mother that way. It is unacceptable."

"And she should not put herself in situations that ruin my future. I find that extremely unacceptable."

Frederick gestured toward the drawing room. "Let us all take a seat, and then you will tell us — in a civilized manner — what's bothering you."

Clarissa sat at the very edge of a chair as if prepared to bolt at any second. Ruth sat close by, and Frederick stood at the mantel.

"Joseph's father forbids him from marrying me."

Frederick's head pulled back. "He what? Why?"

She glared at Ruth. "Because you pushed Mrs. Hayward to her death."

"But I did no such thing!"

"And apparently you had good cause," Clarissa said.

A wave of panic swept over her. The secret was out!

"She promised not to tell," Ruth said, thinking of Mrs. Hayward.

"She didn't — and certainly can't now," Clarissa said. "But apparently it is common knowledge."

Can't now?

In spite of Ruth's confusion, it seemed clear that it was all over. Ruth looked to Frederick. "I am so sorry, Frederick. I warned Mary Hay —"

"Who is Mary?" Clarissa asked.

"Mrs. Hayward. Jack's mother."

It was Clarissa's turn to look confused. "She was there when Fidelia was humiliated with that coachman?"

Two secrets collided.

Frederick pressed his hands in the air near Clarissa, clearly wanting her to keep her voice down. "That is between your mother and me."

Clarissa adamantly shook her head. "Joseph told me what his father said about the situation. How Fidelia came from a wealthy family that lived at Crompton Hall."

Both Ruth and Frederick nodded.

"Why didn't I know that?"

"What would it matter to you?" Frederick said. "What would it matter to anyone in Summerfield? That was a lifetime ago."

"For Fidelia to plunge from gentry to shopkeeper . . . no wonder she was bitter." Clarissa picked at the lace on her cuffs. "No wonder she hated you. To be discovered with a coachman, in a compromising position?"

"Clarissa!" Frederick said.

"I could say it in cruder language."

"You will do no such thing."

Clarissa shrugged. "So beyond the fact that Joseph's father is appalled at the 'pushing' rumors, I find out about this other scandal."

"Let the past die," Frederick said. "It has been dead for decades. There is no reason for it to be brought forward now."

Ruth's mind was in pieces. The rumor, the scandal, and the secret. It was exhausting.

Frederick stroked his chin. "I do not see why Lord Newley would tell Joseph about the scandal, especially since his family benefitted from it. It is certainly no reason to break your engagement."

"I told Joseph as much. But then I heard more dirty secrets."

Now the secret would come out. Ruth's stomach threatened to relieve itself. She couldn't take any more. To have an entire lifetime dismantled by the past . . .

"*Now* what are you talking about?" Frederick asked.

Ruth stood. "I am sure it is nothing. If you will excuse me."

"You are not excused," Clarissa said. "Not when my life has been ruined."

Frederick nodded at her. "Sit down, Ruth." Then, he nodded at Clarissa. "Tell us and have it done."

Clarissa pressed a hand to her brow. "After Joseph told me about the scandal involving Fidelia, I argued with him that it was no reason to break our engagement. After all, *he* was benefitting most from this marriage. Though he will eventually be a viscount, I am the daughter of an earl, which is of higher rank and position."

"Daughter," Frederick said. "That was incredibly rude."

"I was in a rude mood. But then he informed me that it was I who needed this marriage, it was I who would benefit most from it, because—"

"That will be enough," Frederick said.

Ruth was stunned. "Let her finish. I want to know what Lord Newley said against us."

"It is none of her business."

Clarissa popped to her feet and stomped a foot upon the carpet. "None of my business when it's ruining my life?"

Now Ruth *had* to know. "Please, Clarissa. Say it."

When Clarissa answered, her eyes were on her father. "I have the most to gain because *we* need the money. The Kidds' money."

Frederick fingered a porcelain cardinal on the mantel. A memory popped into Ruth's head of the time she was looking through the accounting ledgers, and the questions she'd asked Frederick about shortfalls.

He busied himself with the mantel clock, stopping its pendulum then starting it again. "It is nothing to worry about."

"But obviously it is if Joseph broke our engagement over it. You are virtually selling me, making me his wife in exchange for money. I find that deplorable and terribly sad."

"Do you love him?" Ruth asked.

Clarissa's eyes flashed. "What has love got to do with it? I am humiliated. You wanted me to marry Joseph, and like a

275

dutiful daughter I agreed to the match."

"But you didn't agree at first," Frederick said.

"As if I had a choice?" She glared at him. "You and Grandmamma told me who to marry in no uncertain terms." She stood and walked behind a chair, tracing the carved rise of its back. "If you must know, I agreed to the match because I was bored."

"So being betrothed was something to do?" Frederick asked.

She cocked her head, as if thinking. "Pretty much."

Ruth couldn't believe what she was hearing. "Clarissa, you were betrothed to a real person. You are not an actress on a stage. You cannot play with people that way."

Clarissa shrugged.

Ruth had another question. "If you only became betrothed because you were bored, then why do you care if the arrangement is broken?"

Clarissa's face regained its testy flash. "I will not be the girl who was spurned. I will not endure the shame of it. And besides that . . ." She took a deep breath. "I never lose."

Ruth believed her and shuddered at her intensity.

Clarissa let the fervor fade and moved to her father's side, touching his arm, her eyes pleading. "Father, please tell me how you plan to fix it."

Frederick patted her hand. "I am not sure I can fix anything."

"Please . . ." Clarissa's eyes implored him.

He sighed. "I will talk to Newley." He put a finger under her chin. "Do not worry. Everything will be all right."

"Will it?"

He drew in a long breath. "I said so, didn't I?"

She bounced on her toes, then went off to live in an imaginary land where fathers had magical powers.

Oh, to be so easily appeased.

When Frederick spoke to Ruth his voice was weak, as though all the fight had left him. "It *will* work out."

"But the ledgers . . . There *was* a shortfall."

"It is temporary. Every estate suffers ups and downs. The earldom of Summerfield has endured for more than two hundred and fifty years, and will continue to do so." He studied her face. "Yet in spite of what I say, you are still worried."

About so many things.

Lila gathered the baskets of fresh eggs, blackberries, and tomatoes that were displayed outside the store and took them inside.

"Miss Hayward." She turned to see Joseph. "You are closing for the night?"

"Was there something you needed?"

"Actually, what I need is to talk with you about this afternoon at the bridge."

Although a part of her wanted to hear the details of Joseph's argument with Lady Clarissa, a larger part of her . . . didn't.

"Will you speak with me?" he asked.

"I don't know if I should."

He nodded. "I understand. But if you would. Please?"

She couldn't tell him no. "Let me finish here, then we can walk."

He helped her take the baskets inside. Papa looked up from his final work of the day. "Mr. Kidd."

"Mr. Hayward. If I may borrow your daughter for a moment?"

"Of course." Papa nodded to Lila. "I'll finish up here."

As it was nearly dinnertime, the square had emptied itself of the women getting water from the pump and the old men who congregated there. It was a relief not to endure their curious eyes.

As if on cue, Mrs. Keening made her presence known, peering through the windows of the bakery. "Would you like to go sit in our garden?" Lila asked. "It's not nearly as grand as yours at Crompton Hall, but it does smell wonderfully of herbs."

"That sounds perfect."

They walked around the exterior of the store and the Hayward living quarters, and for a brief moment, Lila feared her mother would spy on them. Then with a rush, she remembered: *Mother is dead.*

"Are you all right?" Joseph asked, touching her elbow.

"Thoughts of my mother come to me at the oddest moments."

He stopped walking. "I am so sorry. I shouldn't bother you at a time like this."

She touched his arm. "You are never a bother, and I welcome the distraction. Not that you're a distraction, but . . ." She let out a long sigh. "I'm sorry. It's been a long day."

They continued to the garden. Lila sat on the wooden bench, leaving room for Joseph to sit beside her. When his leg touched hers . . .

Stop it!

"So," he said.

"So." *Why are you here?*

"How was your ride with Mr. Billings?"

"You stopped by to ask me that?"

"I was just wondering if you, if he . . ."

"Joseph, please speak plainly. Life has grown far too confusing and complicated to speak otherwise."

He nodded, as if vowing to do just that. "I came to tell you that my father has broken our engagement. Mine and Lady Clarissa's."

Her heart jumped. "But why?"

"He believes the rumors about the countess pushing your mother to her death, and doesn't want me tied to the Westons if there are to be repercussions."

"But it's not true. None of my family believes that."

"So I suspected. But I also suspect Father has other reasons. I am not sure of the details regarding the original agreement between him and the earl, but in my father's mind, it is over. I think the rumor is an excuse."

Lila rose and tried to hide her pleasure by picking a weed at the base of a tomato plant. "And what do you think about it?"

He came to her side, removed the weed from her hand, and dropped it to the ground. Then he captured her hands against his chest. "I think it is a blessing from God, because I love you."

She looked into his eyes. "Really?" It seemed such a silly thing to say, and yet—

He smiled down at her. "Really. Which begs the question: what are your feelings toward me?"

All her daydreams rushed forward. He'd declared his love, and it was up to her to finish out the scene. "I love you too."

He gently touched her chin, raising her lips to his. And then he kissed her.

A wondrous warmth flowed through her, as though she'd come home.

He pulled her close. "This is how it should feel when a man and a woman become engaged."

She pulled back enough to see his face. "We're engaged?"

He dropped to one knee. "Lila Hayward, will you do me the honor of becoming my wife?"

Yes!

But instead of repeating her answer aloud, her practical side took over. "Of course I'm very moved by your proposal." She hated to say the next, but had to. "If your father objected to Lady Clarissa, who is from an honorable family of title and status, he will surely never agree to your marrying me."

He rose to his feet, ready to defend his proposal.

She interceded before he could say more. "You must be realistic, Joseph. You're going to be a viscount, your family has a long legacy, and you hope to gain a seat in Parliament. Your father wants his heir to marry someone who will enhance that heritage and future."

"But I have been practical, loyal, and dutiful my entire life."

She found the main point. "It's who you are."

When he looked to the ground, she wanted to smother him with kisses and tell him to forget everything she'd just said. But then a final point rose in her mind, and she knew it had to be said aloud. "You were going to marry Clarissa because of your father's wishes, so likewise you will not be able to marry me and go against them."

He took her hands captive yet again. A line formed between his eyes, and she ached to press a finger against it to smooth it away.

"I know I succumbed to what Father wanted, but it made me miserable. I want to honor him, yet I know there comes a time when a man must make his own choices. If I am old enough to make decisions for this country, then I must be old enough to make decisions regarding my own life." He traced her jawline. "Actually, the dowager and Colonel Cummings inspired me. I don't want to end up married to someone I don't love just because my father chose *for* me. I want to marry the woman I love. And that woman is you."

The tension of Lila's arguments blew away like leaves in the wind. Free of them, she leaned her head against his chest and let the strength of his embrace convince her that the impossible could be possible.

Molly paced beneath the arbor, waiting for Morgan. They'd barely seen each other since his mother's death. She wasn't angry about it. He had family obligations, and was still in mourning. But with all the awful rumors, she needed to see him.

She heard footsteps and held her breath.

And there he was. He rushed toward her, pulling her into his arms. "Dear Molly, my Molly."

Her worries fell away. Yet even as she enjoyed his fine kisses, her conscience dogged her. *He's the heir. He should be the earl one day.*

He ran his thumb along the ridge of her brow. "What's this? Worry on the face of the woman I love?"

She smiled. "I've missed you so much."

"And I you." He took her hand and pulled her to the bench, whirling her under his arm and onto the seat. Then he dropped to one knee before her. "I am tired of being apart. My mother's death should remind both of us that life is short. And so, Molly Wallace, I am asking you formally and completely, will you make me the happiest man in the world and be my wife?"

His face was so sincere, and her own feelings so strong . . .

"Yes, I'll marry you."

May God help me.

Chapter Twenty-Five

Ruth settled into the barouche with Frederick at her side, and Clarissa and George sitting across from them. She held her small book of prayers in her lap. She was eager to go to church this morning. Clarissa's broken engagement weighed heavily on her mind, and pressed down upon the weight of Fidelia's secret. Added to those were sprinklings of worry about the estate's finances, and the false "pushing" rumors that ran from correction like a naughty child running from a parent. Showing up in church as if nothing was amiss was the best offense, but Ruth expected it would not be without incident. As such, she needed a substantial dose of God's peace. *Come unto me, all ye that labour and are heavy laden, and I will give you rest.*

Yes, please.

As the short ride to church began, so did Clarissa's badgering. "Father, you *will* talk to Joseph's father after church?"

"I said I would."

While Clarissa listed the points her father should make, Ruth could feel Frederick's arm tense. "I will handle it, daughter. Let it go."

Clarissa leaned back. Although she'd always had her father at her beck and call, this matter with Joseph would test the extent of his ability to give her what she wanted.

All because of me.

Ruth stilled the bounce of George's knee with a hand. "You really must learn to sit still," she said.

His leg quieted. "Can you and me go riding later?" George asked.

"You and I," she said, then added. "We shall see."

"We shall see if you sit still in church," Frederick added.

"I have to do that too?"

It felt good to laugh.

Lila and her family walked to church. Seeing Joseph would make the cloudy day fair.

Papa glanced in her direction, then in Morgan's as he walked beside them. "My, my, both of my children seem happy this morning. Please share the joy."

Lila tried not to beam, but had to keep the reason for her happiness to herself. "I'm simply glad for any new day."

"There's more to that answer," Rose said. "Do tell."

"I have no better answer *to* tell," Lila said, and diffused the attention by looking at her brother. "Morgan? It's your turn."

He took her hand and drew it around his arm. "It just so happens that I do have joy to share. I have once again asked Molly to marry me, and this time she said yes."

They stopped walking and gave him their congratulations. "I'm so pleased," Papa said. "She seems like a very nice girl."

"She is," Morgan said, accepting Rose's embrace. Then he looked to Nana. "Nana? Aren't you happy for me?"

Nana blinked, as if she'd been off in another world. Then she kissed his cheek. "Of course I'm happy. You make a lovely couple."

Papa pointed toward church. "Come now. We're going to be late."

Lila moved to Nana's side. "Are you all right?"

Nana's smile was unconvincing. "Fine, I'm fine. Really."

There was no time to talk further. They reached the church just as the carriage from the manor pulled up. People stopped their chatter and waited. The earl exited first and helped the countess step out. Then Lady Clarissa and George. The dowager and the colonel were already there and moved to greet their family. But as the countess walked by the villagers, she received half-hearted bows, and once passed, many a hand covered a mouth in furtive conversation.

Lila tugged on Papa's sleeve. "They still believe that stupid rumor. They're treating her so poorly. Papa, do something."

With a nod he left her and walked toward the Westons, slipping between them and the church entrance. He removed his hat and gave the couple a proper bow. "My lord. Lady Summerfield. My family and I wish to thank you for all your kind support during this difficult time."

Lila wasn't sure what "kind support" he was talking about but knew they were the right words to say.

The earl nodded his thanks, and the countess took Papa's hand in hers. "How is your family faring?"

"As well as can be expected, your ladyship."

"Please let us know if there is anything you need."

Papa withdrew, and the Westons entered the church. "How was that?" he whispered to Lila.

"Perfect." She was so proud of him.

But then the Kidds' carriage approached. Joseph and his father stepped out and also made their way to the church. Lady Clarissa held back, waiting for him. But when Lord Newley saw her, he put a hand on Joseph's arm, delaying their progress.

Clarissa had no choice but to enter without him.

So they are estranged! To actually see it played out in public was reassuring.

As Joseph and his father entered the church he caught Lila's eyes, smiled, and nodded.

Lila tried — unsuccessfully — not to beam.

I wish I could sit with Morgan. But Molly knew that wasn't possible. Yet.

She hadn't told the countess about her engagement. The

right time hadn't presented itself, so Molly had to be satisfied with watching Morgan from across the sanctuary. He managed to glance at her when they stood for hymns, but other than that, they were forced to keep their eyes toward the front of the church.

The morning sun broke through the clouds and made the stained glass over the altar glow in vibrant blues, reds, and golds. Jesus, with his arms outstretched, beckoned all to accept His comfort.

Suddenly, the vicar's words caught Molly's attention. "And remember this, 'the truth will set you free.'"

Molly must have jerked because Ma whispered, "You all right?"

Molly nodded, but her breathing grew heavy. The truth would *not* set her free. The truth would ruin her life. The truth had to remain hidden.

She felt Dottie's hand seeking her own. Dottie looked up at her, her forehead tight, her eyes asking questions.

Molly gave her hand a squeeze. It was the only answer she had.

The truth shall set you free.

Ruth stopped listening to the sermon as those six words wove their way through her mind and wrapped around her heart.

Seeing the Hayward family this morning and having Jack greet them and graciously save her from further humiliation, proved what a good man he was. What a good older brother he was.

Jack has a right to know he is the earl.

Adelaide has a right to know her son is alive.

Frederick has a right to know he has a brother.

Morgan has a right to become the heir.

Lila has a right to rise to a new station where she could marry well.

Yet each of these positive outcomes was met with a negative — a consequence.

If Jack is the earl, Frederick will lose his title.

Mary Hayward might be held accountable for the kidnapping.

George will lose his status as the heir.

Clarissa will lose her station, and the scandal might hurt her chances of marrying well. There will certainly be no chance of her ever marrying Joseph Kidd.

And Molly's feelings for Morgan will remain unfulfilled.

If the truth came out, the future would drastically change for many people she cared about. Yet the burden of holding it in was almost too much to bear.

The vicar led them all in the Lord's Prayer. Ruth prayed fervently, not repeating the words by rote, but feeling them. "'. . . thy will be done, in earth as it is in heaven. Give us this day our daily bread. And forgive us our trespasses, as we forgive them that trespass against us. And lead us not into temptation; but deliver us from evil . . .'"

And secrets.

Lila hung back after church, hoping Joseph would come speak with her. Yet as soon as the church emptied, she spotted the earl taking Lord Newley and Joseph aside.

Were they settling the details regarding the end of their engagement? Had Joseph already spoken to his father about marrying *her*?

She wished Joseph would look at her. One smile would speak volumes.

But before that could happen, Nana appeared at her side. "Would you walk me home, please? I have a horrible headache."

Not now! Lila looked around for Morgan or Papa, but they were busy with others.

Nana tugged at her sleeve. "Please, Lila. I really must lie down."

Joseph would have to wait.

What Clarissa wants, Clarissa gets.

As soon as the church service ended, Ruth saw Frederick approach Lord Newley and Joseph. He led them aside and began his daughter's plea.

At first Frederick did most of the talking, with Lord Newley nodding, looking very serious. Joseph listened intently, but then his body tensed, and he leaned toward the two older men and said something. Lord Newley would have none of it and shut him off. Then he and Frederick shook hands.

Frederick left them, but Ruth noticed that the Kidds began a heated discussion. Joseph's actions were not in keeping with a happy fiancé.

As Frederick approached, Clarissa beamed with the anticipation of good news.

"Well?" she asked him.

"The engagement is resumed."

Clarissa wrapped her arms around his neck and kissed his cheek. "Thank you, Father."

Then she ran to Joseph's side, taking gleeful possession of his arm. But instead of happily accepting her contact he gently removed her hand, nodded politely, then bowed before stepping away.

Clarissa covered the slight with a wave, then began chatting with a friend.

"What did you say to him?" Ruth asked her husband.

"Does it matter?" He nodded at the couple. "Look at her. She is happy again. That is all that matters."

"Is it?"

He looked at her, aghast. "You are not in favor of this marriage?"

Yes. No. Up. Down. Black. White.

Gray. Lots and lots of gray.

Chapter Twenty-Six

Lila was surprised when Lady Clarissa entered the mercantile. And more surprised when she handed Lila a note.

"If you please," Clarissa said, handing over the small envelope. "You must take this directly to Crompton Hall as soon as possible. It's important."

If it's so important, why don't you take it?

Was Clarissa trying to mend her rift with Joseph? It was far too awkward for Lila to be a part of this final effort.

Lila returned the note to her. "I'm sorry. I can't do this anymore."

A crease formed between Lady Clarissa's brown eyes, making her look far older than her years. "But you must."

"I'm sorry, but I can't be in the middle anymore."

The crease altered as Clarissa's face changed from consternation to pain. "Please, Lila. *I* can't very well ride over there unannounced. It simply isn't proper."

"I'm sure there's someone at the manor who can deliver it for you."

"But I only trust you."

It felt like a test. Did Lila believe in the love between herself and Joseph or not? Going into church yesterday, she'd seen that he and Clarissa were estranged. The memory of Clarissa standing alone, being shunned by Joseph and his father, was completely satisfying. And yet . . .

I almost feel sorry for her.

Obviously, sensing she was wavering, Clarissa pressed the note into her hand. "Please. This one last time."

So it *was* a final effort. At least it would give her a chance to see Joseph.

Lila put the note in her pocket. "One last time."

"Lady Summerfield!"

Ruth looked out of the carriage and saw Morgan Hayward. She told the coachman to stop.

Morgan ran up to the victoria. Out of breath, he gathered himself enough to offer her a bow. "Milady. Forgive me for running after you like this, but when I saw your carriage . . . I'd like the chance to talk to you. If you please. It's important."

"I really must get back, Mr. Hayward. I have just brought the widow Schoonover some food and —" *And you're my nephew, and I have no wish to speak with you.*

"It will only take a moment. I promise."

She had two choices: to send him away and never know what this was about, or to listen and risk reigniting her worry. *The truth shall set you free.*

"Very well then. Ride with me back to the manor."

The pleasure on his face surprised her and did not seem to foretell any distressing topic. So what did he want to talk to her about? They'd never spoken one on one.

He settled into the seat beside her, and Ruth wished for the privacy of the enclosed carriage. Unfortunately, whatever was said between them would certainly be overheard by the coachman. Luckily, the sound of the horses and the wheels on the road would help to muffle their words.

"I've been wanting to speak with you a long time, your ladyship, but the opportunity never arose until today."

"Go on," she said, bracing herself for the worst.

"As you may know, Molly and I are in love."

Unfortunately.

"I want to thank you for the time you have given her away from her duties so we could spend time together most evenings."

My encouragement and leniency helped create the problem.

He was waiting for some sort of response from her. "You are welcome."

Morgan continued. "Of course I am also aware of the awkward situation between our families right now, as well as the traditional directive that romance is frowned upon for the servants of Summerfield Manor."

He only wanted to talk about their romance? Ruth let her thoughts move in that direction. Perhaps this directive would offer a way out of the situation. "With sixty servants needed to run the estate it is imperative each one focuses on the task at hand."

"I know. And I know how essential Molly is to you."

"She's an excellent lady's maid." And more than that, a friend.

"Yet it's far easier for you to find another lady's maid than it is for me to find another woman to love. And marry."

Marry?

Yet he made an excellent argument.

But then, as it always did, the secret blew in and clouded her thoughts. Morgan, the heir, marrying Molly, a maid.

Morgan plucked at the fabric of his trousers, obviously unnerved by her silence. "If it would help, after we're married, Molly could still be available to you whenever you need her."

"That would be very generous, but I am not sure it would be possible. Plus, with Molly's entire family living at the manor. . ." *Remember, it was my idea.*

A twitch in Morgan's jaw suggested he understood their obligation. "We are all grateful for the compassionate care you gave them after their time of trouble. But it comes down to this, Lady Summerfield. I am asking not only for your permission to marry Molly—but for your blessing."

The angst that tightened his face made her want to say yes. And perhaps if they were married, and the secret came out . . .

Would that make things better or worse?

He was waiting for her answer.

"Molly hasn't said anything to me about your intention to marry," she said.

"She wouldn't. She's so loyal to you, your ladyship."

"Perhaps she doesn't wish to marry you."

"Oh, she does. I've asked her." His face flashed with his desire to take the words back. "I'm sorry. I should have asked you before asking her, but I assure you, it's what we both want."

There was no right answer, and so she took the coward's way out. "I must speak to Lord Summerfield about this. It will be his decision." Whether she would mention it to Frederick was another matter.

Morgan nodded and leaned back in relief. "Thank you so much. Molly and I will be forever grateful."

"We haven't said yes."

"I know, milady. More importantly, you haven't said no."

Ruth couldn't help but smile. "You are a courageous man, Morgan Hayward."

"I thank you for the compliment, but it's not courage that drives me. It's love."

How incredibly romantic.

"I'll get off here," he said, loud enough for the coachman to hear. Once Morgan got out, he gave Ruth a full bow.

The sight of him — the heir, her nephew — made her stomach tighten.

If only *she* could be courageous.

Molly met Gertie in the upstairs hall. "Good afternoon."

"Nothing good about it."

"Why not?"

Gertie pointed toward the attic. "Not with yer sister sick."

"Sick? What's wrong?"

"You'd have to ask her."

Molly raced toward the back stairs.

"An' tell her to get down here as soon as she can. We have

no time for sickness in this house."

Molly reached the attic and tapped on her sister's door. "Dottie?"

She heard a horrible retching sound and found Dottie on the floor vomiting into a chamber pot.

Molly knelt beside her, gathering stray hair away from her face. "Ah, polka dot. I'm so sorry you're sick."

When Dottie was finished, Molly dabbed her mouth with a towel and poured her a cup of water. Dottie leaned against the bed, spent.

"When did you start getting sick?"

"First thing this morning."

Molly held a hand on her forehead. "You don't feel feverish. Was it something you ate?"

Dottie shook her head. "It's something eating *at* me."

Oh.

"The secret's too much for me to keep, Mol. The vicar talked about truth setting me free. I thought that sounded good, 'cause I'm not free at all. I'm all tied up inside, and it's making me sick. I gotta tell. I just gotta."

Molly sighed. "It's been eating at me too."

Dottie looked hopeful. "So we can tell?"

If we do, we'll risk everything.

Molly wasn't sure how to proceed. "Let me talk to the countess about it."

Dottie rose to her feet. "Good. You talk to her. And fix it. Please."

If only she could.

Ruth sat at her dressing table as Molly arranged her hair for the afternoon meal. But instead of chatting with her, Molly was quiet. "Is something wrong?" Ruth asked.

Molly's hands fell to her side, and she looked to the floor. Then a hand went to her mouth.

Ruth turned around on the bench. "Molly. What's wrong?

Tell me."

When the girl began to cry, Ruth led her to the window seat where they both could sit. She handed her a handkerchief. "My dear girl. I'm sure whatever it is it can be made better." *Only I know it can't.*

Molly shook her head. "Not really. Not for everyone."

"What do you mean?"

"I know about . . . Jack."

Ruth's mouth went dry. "Mr. Hayward?"

She nodded. "I know Jack is the real heir."

Ruth was glad to be seated. The secret poured down, drowning her. "But how?"

"Dottie was at the window when you and Mrs. Hayward were on the terrace. She heard."

"Everything?"

"Enough."

To think her fate was in the hands of a tweeny. "Who else knows?"

"Just me, my lady."

"Good."

"For now."

All breath left her. Surely this wasn't a threat. Not from Molly.

Molly must have seen the terror on her face, because she quickly said, "I only mean that the secret is eating at us. Our stomachs are in knots."

Mine too. "Since you know the truth, you must be aware of its consequences."

"Too much so. I want Morgan to be earl since it's his birthright, but I also want to marry him."

"He asked me for your hand."

"When?"

"Today. He stopped my carriage. He told me how loyal you are to me but asked me to set you free to marry him."

"How did you answer?"

"I said I would talk to Lord Summerfield about it."

Molly merely nodded. "Morgan's such a good man, and I

do love him so."

Ruth saw an opening. "Then perhaps the secret should remain a secret."

Molly's head shook back and forth as she fingered the handkerchief in her lap. "Earl of Summerfield or husband to me—which is Morgan's future? If we marry, we'll have built a life on a lie. And if the truth ever does come out—and it will—Morgan will find out I knew but didn't say anything, and he'll hate me for it."

"But you'll be married by then. He can be the earl, and you'll . . ." It was an awkward thought.

"*I* would be the Countess of Summerfield?" She angrily brushed tears from her cheeks. "I started as a tweeny in this very house. I can't be its mistress, I can't be a countess. Even if society would allow it, it's absurd. Besides, you set a diamond and a pebble next to each other, it's pretty clear what each one is worth."

Ruth couldn't argue with any of it. But she hated to hear Molly disparaging herself. "You are a better woman than most, Molly Wallace. A title does not come with merit attached, it has to be earned. In fact, you are a better woman than I. You have seen firsthand what a marginal countess I have been."

"I appreciate your kind words, my lady, but I am what I am. A servant. Always have been and always will be."

Round and round they went . . . "Then perhaps it is best we don't tell. You can have a happy life with Morgan." She had to say it bluntly. "And things at the manor can stay as they are. For beyond my own title, I don't want my son to give up his future as the Earl of Summerfield."

"But shouldn't the dowager know her son is alive?"

It would give Adelaide overwhelming joy. But then Ruth thought of Mary Hayward. "There's Morgan's grandmother to consider. She stole Alexander—or her husband did. She could go to jail for it."

"I wouldn't want that. She's a nice woman."

"We are all nice people, Molly. That's what makes it so

difficult." Ruth took her hand. "I wish I was all-wise and knew what to do."

Molly nodded. "Only God knows that."

Ruth was taken aback. "Yes, He does, but unfortunately He's not sharing His will with me right now. Every time I start thinking about it, the repercussions come rushing toward me and fear takes over."

"But the vicar said, 'the truth shall set you free.'"

There it was again.

"Let's think on it," Ruth said. "Pray on it."

Ruth's biggest prayer was that God knew what He was doing.

Lila slowed Raider to a walk as she approached Crompton Hall. She looked for Joseph, hoping to hand him the note personally so they could talk. Other than furtive glances during church, they hadn't seen each other since he'd proposed Saturday night.

Then she saw him, riding out from the stables. Coming toward the road. And upon seeing her, turning toward her.

"Lila," he said.

She expected to see the exuberant smile he seemed to save just for her. Instead, he looked worried.

"Is something wrong?" she asked.

His horse seemed as antsy as he was and turned a full circle. "Forgive me, but I have a lot on my mind."

And I don't? "Can I help?"

"If only you could."

Give him the note.

Instead of obeying the nudge she heard herself say, "Would you like to join me for a ride?"

"I would love to," he said, "But I have some business to attend to. Another time?"

He sounded so formal. "Of course."

Give him the note.

He hesitated, as though wanting to say more, then tipped his hat and rode toward the village.

She did not call after him. She did not give him Clarissa's note.

"What am I doing?" she asked aloud.

At luncheon, Frederick patted his lips with a napkin and nodded towards Ruth's plate. "You must eat, my dear."

Ruth poked at her lamb and pickled onions. "I am not hungry."

"Whyever not?" Frederick said. "It is a wonderful day. A new start. I am invigorated."

She wished she could share his view.

Clarissa set down her fork. "And I am happy too, for my wonderful father made right what was wrong." She pushed herself away from the table, fluttered to his side, and kissed his cheek.

With his blush another consequence reared its ugly head. If the truth came out, then Clarissa's betrothal to Joseph would surely be broken. Again. Understandably, Lord Newley would run out of patience with the Weston family and all of their drama and scandal.

Ruth's mouth was dry. She took a sip of soda-water, but the liquid tasted like dust.

As did their future.

But then Ruth saw Clarissa's gaze snap toward the front foyer. Clarissa asked the butler, "Dixon, will you check to see if someone's at the front door. I thought I heard something."

"Of course, my lady." He nodded to the first footmen to take charge, then left.

"I didn't hear anything," Ruth said.

"Neither did I," Frederick said. "But that's not surprising. The older I get the less I hear. But I refuse, no matter how old or deaf I become, to use one of those awful ear horns."

"What's that?" George asked.

Ruth noticed that Clarissa had stopped listening and was focused on the dining room door. But when Dixon returned he looked in her direction and said, "I am sorry, my lady. There was no one at the door."

There could only be one person Clarissa would care to see with such intensity. "Were you expecting Joseph?" Ruth asked. "If I would have known I would have told Mrs. McDeer we were having a guest."

"We could have delayed our meal for him," Frederick said.

Clarissa gave her attention to her plate. "It's nothing. He wasn't formally invited. I just thought . . ."

Hoped. It was clear Clarissa hoped he would come.

"Never mind," Clarissa said. "May I have some more bread and butter, please?"

Ruth had assumed the issues between themselves and the Kidds were resolved.

Perhaps not.

Lila called downstairs from her bedroom, "I'll be down to help with dinner in a minute."

Clarissa's note had sat heavily in her pocket all day. A dozen times she'd thought about going back to the Kidds' to deliver it. But each time she had the urge, it was suppressed by a stronger urge to let the message remain *un*delivered.

You're betraying the earl's daughter. She'll find out you didn't deliver the note. Then what?

The relation between the two families was already strained. Not delivering the note wouldn't help the situation.

Lila sat on the bed, the sealed note in her hands.

Before she fully thought it through, she carefully slipped open the wax seal and unfolded the page:

> *Joseph, my dearest, my love. I am soaring*
> *through the skies with joy that our betrothal is*
> *renewed. We shall be the happiest of couples. I can*

*hardly wait for the wedding plans to begin. Soon we
will be man and wife. Nothing can bring me more
happiness. Please come to me immediately, so our
private celebration can begin.*
    Yours forever,
    Clarissa

Lila stared at the words. They were engaged again? Since
when?

An image came to mind. Yesterday, after church — before
Nana succumbed to a headache — Lila remembered seeing the
earl and Lord Newley speaking together. Was that when their
rift was mended?

Obviously, yes.

"No wonder Joseph acted so strange toward me. He
doesn't know how to tell me."

Lila knew what she had to do.

"Where are you going?" Papa asked.

"I have an important errand."

"It will have to wait."

But it can't wait. "I really must go out."

"Not this evening, you don't." Papa pointed to the
window. It was pouring rain. She'd been so caught up in
Clarissa's note she hadn't even noticed.

Lila stood at the window, gauging the clouds. They were
the darkest gray, and a wind had come up. Rain pelted the
window.

And drowned her heart.

Chapter Twenty-Seven

Lila grasped the brass doorknocker at Crompton Hall, and with only a moment's hesitation, tapped it twice, then once more for good measure. She took a step back, fighting the urge to flee.

She'd come prepared. If Joseph wasn't home or wouldn't see her, she'd written her own note, declaring her love, asking him to come to her, imploring him to remember the intensity of their feelings for each other. It sat in her right pocket. In her left, was Clarissa's note — with much the same sentiment. She had no idea which note she would deliver. One. Both.

Or none.

The door opened, and Lila's heart jumped. A butler eyed her, then said, "Yes, miss?"

Lila removed the envelope from her right pocket. "I have a note for Mr. Kidd."

His left eyebrow rose.

" Mr. Joseph Kidd."

But then, Lord Newley appeared in the foyer. "Miss Hayward?"

In spite of her desire to melt into a puddle, she managed a small curtsy. "Your lordship."

He looked to the butler, who said, "Miss Hayward has delivered a note for Master Joseph."

"He is not here."

She turned to leave, but to her horror, Lord Newley stepped forward and took the note. "This is from you?"

She hesitated, then nodded.

"I will see it's delivered."

Lila would have rather taken her chances with the butler than Joseph's father—who'd obviously agreed to a reinstatement of Joseph's and Clarissa's betrothal. If Lord Newley read her note . . . She had no idea if Joseph had talked to him about *their* relationship. Either way, things would be worse for it.

"If there's nothing else?"

She couldn't trust her voice, so she bobbed a curtsy, rushed out of the house, and hurried down the drive. Not only did her note fall into the hands of Joseph's father, but Clarissa's note burned a hole in her pocket.

Everything that was ruined would remain ruined.

Her walk turned into a run.

Home. Just get home.

"Grady, do be careful," Addie said. "Don't hurt yourself."

Her husband let the ax fall one more time before pausing to catch his breath. "It's me against these roots, my darling. And I will never surrender."

She stood in the garden, watching him hack away at a tree stump that he'd managed to partially uproot. He'd already spent the better part of two days on the chore. All because she'd mentioned she would like more room in the garden. If Grady fell over dead because of the effort, it would be her fault.

She heard a cart on the road and looked to see who it was. Hopefully some burly man who'd take pity on her old—but still amazingly handsome—husband and offer to help.

She was thrilled to see it was Jack Hayward. "Mr. Hayward," she said, approaching the cart. "Just the man we wanted to see."

Jack assessed the situation in a glance. "Care for some help, Colonel?"

Grady drew his forearm across his sweaty brow. "I'd like

to say no, but need to say yes. If you have the time, Mr. Hayward."

"My delivery is done, so I'll make the time." Jack stepped down and approached the stump, assessing the situation. "Who's winning the battle?"

"The stump has won the skirmish, but not the war. I was thinking of attacking its flank."

Jack walked around it. "You've got the roots chopped through on three sides."

"I thought that would be enough, but apparently it requires a full encirclement and ambush."

"Then let's finish it off. Do you have another ax?"

"We do." Grady turned to Addie. "Can you fetch the other ax, wifey?"

She went to the shed and by the time she'd returned Jack had removed his jacket and was rolling up his sleeves in preparation for battle.

And then . . . her gaze fell upon a birthmark on his right forearm.

It was shaped like a star.

The men attacked the stump, the rhythm of their ax-falls punctuating the rhythm of Addie's thoughts.

My son had such a birthmark.

It's a coincidence.

My son drowned.

We never found a body.

That was more than forty years ago.

You still grieve for him.

Jack can't be Alexander.

But he's the right age.

Surely there are others who have such a birthmark.

But what if . . .?

"Don't be ridiculous."

Grady looked up from the work. "Did you say something?"

"Not a thing."

"Could you please get us some water? We're working up a

powerful thirst."

She went into the cottage and gathered the glasses of water while her thoughts swam with possibilities, denials, and hope.

Although she wanted to stop the men's work and pepper Jack with a thousand questions, she knew restraint must be the order of the day. One step at a time.

She brought the men their water. When they stopped to drink, Addie had a better chance to see the birthmark. It *was* like Alexander's, on the inner right forearm, just below the crook of his arm. Distinct and unique.

Her heartbeat quickened, but she tried to act calm. "Battling this root has made me think about family roots. Where were you born, Mr. Hayward? You haven't always lived in the village."

Jack swiped a handkerchief across the back of his neck. "Actually, my parents told me I was born in the woods around here."

"The woods?"

"We were very poor." He pointed toward the forest nearby. "My mother recently showed me our old shack in the trees, but honestly, I don't remember it."

"From shack to store owner is quite a journey," Grady said.

"We moved to London when I was very small, but it was always a struggle for us. I found work at a store there and learned the business. When an opportunity to take over the Summerfield Mercantile opened up just before Lila was born, I brought my wife and son here."

Addie remembered Jack and Fidelia moving to Summerfield, mostly because of Fidelia's return after her family's quick exit, and the tension regarding her affection for Frederick. Though Lord Newley had purchased Crompton Hall, and though Ruth and Frederick were married and Ruth was with-child, the memory of Fidelia's indiscretion was slow to leave people's memories. Fortunately, it was Fidelia's problem, for the paths of the Westons and the Haywards had little need to cross.

Even though they were inextricably intertwined.

Has my son been living here all this time?

Addie's throat tightened, and the questions she wanted to ask formed a queue. *Slow now. Go slow.* "Do you remember anything about your time living here as a child?"

He took another sip of water and looked to the sky. "I remember a sweet floral smell, and I remember playing along the river." He gazed in that direction. "And I have a few disjointed images, like sitting on the floor next to a chair, but not any chair we had in the woods. A fancy one with gilt legs." He shook his head, as though dispelling the thought. "I remember far more about London."

There were gilt chairs at the manor. Could the floral scent he remembered be the scent of the flowers in the manor garden—or her own perfume? And the river . . . The reason they'd assumed little Alexander had drowned was that he'd been down by the river with his nanny. She'd sat beneath a tree and dozed off, and when she'd awakened, he was gone. Had Jack's parents snatched him from the riverbank and claimed him as their own?

Why would they do that?

Addie thought back to the day she first met Mary Hayward. Mary had mentioned losing more than one baby, and they'd shared the pain of a mother's grief. The memory spurred her to ask Jack, "Do you have any siblings?"

He shook his head, and a bead of sweat dripped off his jaw line. "My parents lost many babies before I was born." He pointed in the same direction as before. "Three of them are buried there. I recently had some headstones made for my mother's sake."

"That's kind of you," Grady said.

"I feel the responsibility of being the only surviving child." He swallowed the last of the water then handed Addie the glass. "If you'll excuse me, your ladyship, I'd like to conquer this stump and get back to the store. They'll wonder what's happened to me."

Addie wondered the same thing.

Addie stood at the window and watched them work.

She tried to see the child-Alexander in Jack's face but couldn't age her memory into a grown man. One of her biggest regrets was that she hadn't had Alexander's portrait painted before he died.

Before he was kidnapped?

She could be forgiven the oversight, for barely a year after Alexander's birth, she'd had Frederick. She had been busy with two little boys plus her husband's ascension to the earldom following the death of her father-in-law.

And *her* rise to the role of countess. She'd been just twenty-two.

Where Ruth had floundered when her turn as countess came round, it had been just the opposite when Addie assumed the title. Her mother-in-law had been a meek woman, totally cowed by her husband, the earl. As such, Addie received little instruction. But as a result, she'd been forced to blaze a path of proper etiquette, duty, and honor. All this, with two little boys.

Of course, the boys' daily needs had been addressed by Nanny Hayley and the other nursery staff. But Addie had made it a point to spend time with her children as often as her day allowed. She knew it wasn't *done*; women of her station left the daily chores of motherhood to the help. But as she gained confidence in creating a model for what a countess should be and do, she also gained confidence to be a mother who was involved in the lives of her sons. Who better to train them to be men of keen ability and good character?

She heard a verbal roar from Grady and Jack and saw they'd won the war against the stump. It lay fallen on its side, its woody tentacles severed and exposed.

It was clear Jack *was* a man of keen ability and good character, and if he was Alexander, he'd achieved those traits without her. He had lived a life separate from the one that was due to him by birth. Exactly how he'd ended up a

Hayward was a question in need of an answer.

Mary. Addie needed to talk to Mary.

She joined the men. "Congratulations," she said with applause. "Job well done."

Jack gathered his jacket while Grady thanked him for his help. Then Addie stepped forward. "Mr. Hayward? Might I ride back with you to the store?"

"Of course, my lady."

Grady looked confused, but Addie couldn't take time to explain. Besides, she didn't want to stir this pot until she was absolutely certain it was her pot to stir.

Jack helped her up to the seat beside him. He had such a strong and capable hand. She shivered at the thought that it could be her son's hand.

When he sat beside her, their legs touched. Her mind flashed back to the last time she'd seen little Alexander. He'd only been three and a half years old, and Nanny Hayley was headed outside with him. Frederick was back in the nursery because he had a fever. Nanny and Alexander had stopped in the morning room, where Addie noticed Alexander's shoes were untied. She'd taken him upon her lap and tied them tight, then gave him a hug and a kiss before they headed off.

An hour later, Nanny came screaming back to the house. *He's gone! I can't find him! The river . . .*

The rest was a blur framed by disbelief and grief.

But if Alexander hadn't been swept away, if Jack was her son . . .

Jack began talking about the cottage and all the improvements she and Grady had achieved. Addie was glad for the distraction because her entire body trembled with excitement and nerves.

"Are you cold, my lady?"

"I am fine." Perhaps better than fine.

Please, let this be true.

"Lady Summerfield," Lila said as the dowager entered the mercantile. "How nice to see you."

Jack swept in after her. "Her ladyship needed a ride to the store, so I was glad to oblige."

"What Mr. Hayward isn't telling you," Addie said, "is that he has been working the last hour to help my husband conquer a pesky stump, so it's our fault he is late getting back."

"I was glad to be of service, milady. But if you'll excuse me, I'm going to wash up."

"Is there something particular we can help you find, your ladyship?" Lila asked.

Is Lila my granddaughter?

"Actually, I would like a chance to chat with your grandmother. Our friendship was sparked weeks ago, but I fear I've been lax in keeping it up as much as I would like." She turned to Mary — who bit her lip. "If your family can spare you, shall we get some fresh air?"

Mary looked at Lila and their clerk as if she wanted them to forbid her from going. But of course, they nodded their approval.

Mary removed her work apron and handed it to Lila, then followed Addie outside.

The square was populated by villagers, going about the business of the day, but as the dowager approached, they halted their activities and offered her bows, curtsies, greetings — and privacy, as they dispersed.

Addie sat upon a bench and patted the seat beside her. "One of the perks of a title is its ability to clear a room or a village square." She smoothed her skirt across her knees. Only then did she realize she was wearing one of the simplified dresses Albers had altered. It was far from the lavish, embellished ensembles she usually wore in public.

Her clothes were the least of it.

"I suppose you wonder why I have brought you here," she began.

"I'm very glad to see you again."

"You may not be glad by the time we are through."

Mary blinked and put a hand on the lace fichus around her neck.

Might as well just say what you have to say and catch her off-guard. "Jack is my son."

Mary gasped, then held her breath.

"Aren't you going to say something?"

She finally released the breath, then said, "I know."

The two words fell between them like a stone hurled from heaven.

Mary hurried to explain. "I didn't know until recently. Fidelia was the one to figure it out."

"Fidelia? How did she do that?"

"It was when you were in the store and mentioned the star birthmark. Of course Fidelia knew Jack had such a mark. She questioned me, and memories flooded back, and . . ."

"And?"

"We came to the conclusion that Jack must be your boy."

"As if you didn't know."

Mary's face showed its first hint of alarm. "I swear to you, milady, I had no idea."

"Surely you heard all the commotion the day he supposedly drowned. Dozens of people were out looking for him."

Mary hung her head, shaking it side to side. "The day my husband brought the boy to me, he insisted quite vehemently we go to London. We left immediately."

"And you just . . . just took him with you?"

"Stanley said he was an orphan and needed a mother. His shirt was torn, and he was dirty and —"

"My boys were never dirty."

"He was that day." Mary's hand found her mouth. "Remember how I told you I'd lost so many babies? I thought the boy was a gift from God, an answer to my prayers."

Addie pressed down the compassion that tried to rise to the surface. "He was stolen!"

The volume of her words made people look in their

direction. Addie calmed herself. "That day in the store, when you knew . . . why didn't you come tell me? As his mother I have a right to know."

"Yes, you do. But things became complicated when Fidelia ran off to the manor to tell the other Lady Summerfield."

"My daughter-in-law?"

Mary nodded. "During that meeting, Fidelia fell down the stairs."

Suddenly, the rumors gained credence. *Had* Ruth pushed her? If Fidelia blurted the news that Jack was the real earl . . . it wouldn't have taken long for Ruth to understand the repercussions. And react.

"I'm very sorry, milady. Very, very sorry."

"Though I am sorry for your family's recent loss, it does not negate your duty to tell me the truth."

"I . . . I was afraid of going to jail."

Addie's head pulled back. "So you *did* kidnap my son?"

Mary shook her head violently. "I didn't. But my husband did."

Another point revealed itself. "Did it not occur to you that a boy who wasn't yet four, dressed in nice clothing, might belong somewhere? To someone?"

Mary's head bowed low enough for her chin to skim her chest. "Stanley said he was all alone and needed a home. I needed a child, and so I . . . I overlooked the obvious questions. God forgive me, I wouldn't let myself see what could be seen."

"Jack said you lived in the woods. You took my son and had him live in a shack?"

Her eyes flashed. "No, milady. Jack never lived there — though I showed it to him recently. As I said, we left immediately, walking toward London along back roads, sleeping in the woods along the way."

"You fled like people with a guilty conscience."

Mary looked out over the square as if the memories floated nearby. "I didn't let myself think about anything but the dear boy who needed me."

"He did *not* need you. He had a mother and father, a fine home with every comfort, and many people who loved him."

Mary nodded once. "I needed *him*."

"As I've needed him all these years. Do you understand the pain I felt?"

For the first time, Mary met Addie's eyes. "I do. Many times over."

Addie tried to blend anger with empathy. Right with wrong.

"I'm very sorry, your ladyship."

Sorry . . . what good did sorry do? "Did my boy ask for me? For his mother?"

Mary's eyes filled with tears. "At first, all the time. For his mamma and for . . . Hay-hay?"

Ah. "Nanny Hayley."

"But eventually he stopped asking, and I became his mother, may God forgive me."

Addie stood and faced her. "I will leave it to God to make that decision."

"Will *you* forgive me?"

Addie hesitated. The situation was too new to even speak of it. Yet the pain went both ways. Mary's face hung with despair and fear of what would come next.

"I will forgive you, as will God," Addie said. "But with forgiveness comes disclosure."

Mary's eyes grew wide with panic. "What are you going to do?"

"I will let you know." She pointed at her. "*You* will do nothing and say nothing. Is that understood?"

"Of course, Lady Summerfield."

Addie flicked a hand at her. "Go on now. Leave me alone."

Mary scurried back to the mercantile. Aware that she was being watched, Addie turned and nodded to the villagers who had congregated on the fringes of the square.

Then, with as much regal bearing as she could muster, she walked down the road, out of town.

Grady. She needed to talk to Grady.

Nana slunk into the store, her eyes downcast.

"Why did the dowager want to talk with you?" Lila asked.

Nana took up her apron but didn't meet Lila's gaze. "She was simply being polite. We hadn't had a chance to chat since I first met her at the cottage." Then Nana looked up with a blink. "She wished to offer further condolences."

The last seemed like an afterthought, and was unconvincing. Lila couldn't imagine the dowager willingly bringing up her mother's death.

But she had other things on her mind.

Like Joseph, and the question of whether or not his father had given him her note.

And then there was Clarissa's note — which still sat in her pocket.

Lila's guilt left her with three choices: she could go back to Crompton Hall and deliver Clarissa's note to Joseph. She could go to Summerfield Manor and tell Lady Clarissa that she hadn't delivered it. Or she could leave things as they were. By far the easiest choice.

But doing the right thing was often hard.

Addie had no memory of the walk back to the cottage. Until Grady came running out to meet her, the concepts of time and distance had lost their meaning.

"Wifey, why are you walking home? Surely Jack could have given you a ride."

She stopped in the middle of the lane and felt her legs buckle. Grady caught her on the way down to her knees.

"Darling, Addie . . . what's wrong?"

She buried her face in his shoulder, and clung to him as sobs gained release.

"What happened? Oh, sweet woman, what's wrong?"

"Inside."

He swept her into his arms and carried her into the cottage, where he deposited her on the bed. He sat beside her, holding her hand, stroking it, desperately urging her toward comfort.

"Are you hurt?"

She was hurt and well at the same time, in an odd place where pain and pleasure intertwined.

"Please wifey, say something."

Although she was exhausted of body, mind, and spirit, she knew it would take only four words to explain her condition.

"Jack is my son."

Questions. Answers. More questions.

Yet one question rose above all the rest.

"What are you going to do now?"

And the truth shall set you free.

Suddenly, a decision made itself clear. Addie sat up, invigorated. "I am calling a meeting of the Haywards and the Westons at the manor. Tomorrow morning at ten sharp."

Grady shook his head. "That's going to be some meeting."

One that would change everything.

Colonel Cummings came in the store. It was quite the day for special visitors.

The colonel removed his hat and looked to each face. "Greetings."

"Greetings, Colonel," Papa said. "Do you need more help with the stump?"

"No, no," he said. "It is thoroughly conquered, thanks to you."

"Then how can we help you?" Morgan asked.

"I come with a message from my wife — the dowager countess."

The last was added with special emphasis.

"Of course," Papa said.

"She would like the entire Hayward family to come to

Summerfield Manor tomorrow morning at ten."

It was not an invitation but a command. Lila looked to her family. They all seemed perplexed—except for Nana, whose face had turned white.

"Of course, we'll come," Papa said, "but may I ask why we've been summoned?"

"I'll let my wife tell you more tomorrow." He looked to each member of the family, with an extra few seconds on Nana's face. "Shall I see all of you there?"

Nana nodded but looked nervous. Morgan assented, as did Lila.

As soon as the colonel left, Papa said, "I wonder what that's all about."

"Perhaps they'll give me permission to marry Molly," Morgan asked. "I asked the younger Lady Summerfield for permission."

"That was very presumptuous of you," Papa said.

"Perhaps. But the time seemed right."

Lila hoped this was the cause of the meeting. Or had Clarissa found out that Lila hadn't delivered the note and complained to her family? Was this a meeting where Lila would be chastised?

"Or it might be a special gathering because I helped the dowager and the colonel with the stump," Papa said. "They did seem very grateful."

Perhaps.

Lila looked to Nana, who hadn't said a word. *She* was the only one who'd spoken directly with the dowager. "What do you think it's about, Nana?"

Her head shook in short bursts, and she said, "I have no idea. If you'll excuse me, I'm going to get tea ready."

Whatever the reason for the summons, they'd know tomorrow.

Chapter Twenty-Eight

What is Adelaide's meeting about?

The question that had plagued Ruth's sleep now greeted her upon waking.

The previous evening, when the colonel appeared and issued a polite command that the entire family gather at ten, Ruth had been curious. But when he'd mentioned that the Hayward family was also summoned, her imagination sprinted ahead to all possibilities, none of them good.

Either there was still an issue regarding Ruth's part in Fidelia's death, or . . .

The secret of Jack Hayward's parentage was no longer a secret.

She knew deep in the pit of her existence that it was the latter. And when the dowager made the announcement, the life they'd known and taken for granted would be gone forever.

There was a knock on the door, and Molly entered with a cup of tea.

"Good morning, my lady." She brought the tea tray near and waited for Ruth to sit upright so it could be placed across her lap. "It looks to be a fine day."

By her expression and mood, it was obvious Molly knew nothing of the impending meeting, its subject, or its implications. Would it be kinder to warn her now, or wait until things played out?

As Ruth sipped her tea, Molly pulled open the heavy draperies. "What are your plans for the day, my lady?"

She might as well say it. "There's to be a gathering at ten."

"A gathering?"

"The dowager countess has called a meeting of the family."

Molly straightened the dressing table. "That's nice."

Ruth fueled herself with a fresh breath. "She's also invited the Haywards."

Molly whipped around, her eyes asking the question.

"I expect the worst."

Molly rushed to the bedside. "So you suspect the secret is out?" Her face was stricken.

"I cannot think of any other reason for such a gathering."

Molly's hands flew to her mouth, and her eyes darted from this to that, revealing the furtiveness of her thoughts. "I've been praying about it — about whether or not to tell."

Ruth nodded. "It seems that decision has been made for us."

Molly's hands dropped to her side. "I was hoping . . ."

"Me too."

"What are we going to do?" Molly asked.

"I don't think *we* will do anything. It is going to be played out in spite of us."

"It's not fair."

"'The truth shall set us free.' Remember?"

Molly shook her head vehemently. "No, it won't. My entire life will be determined by this awful truth, and it won't be my choice at all. All my freedom will be taken from me."

Ruth had no argument.

Addie's heart threatened to beat out of her chest. Her request had been honored, and the drawing room of Summerfield Manor was filled with a full company of Westons and Haywards. She had to restrain herself from running over to Jack and pulling him into her arms. *You are my son! My long lost son!*

But now was not the time for impulsive dramatics. It was

the time for her to play the part of the Dowager Countess of Summerfield to perfection, using her well-honed ability to be calm in every situation, emitting an aura of capable authority marked with the dignity of her title.

She glanced at Clarissa, who was seated on the settee with Ruth at her side. Clarissa, whose betrothal to Joseph was reinstated. If Lord Newley had retracted his son's engagement because of a false rumor, how would he react to the news that Clarissa was not the daughter of an earl at all?

And Ruth . . . She was the least of Addie's concerns, yet lately she had made a good effort at taking on her long-neglected duties. Ruth didn't deserve to have her title yanked away. Yet, it was likely she'd known about the secret for weeks. Fidelia would have made sure Ruth knew that *her* husband Jack was the true earl. Ruth had known but had remained silent. Addie couldn't blame her for not telling anyone. Ruth was being a good wife and mother, protecting what she considered the best interests of her family.

Which was exactly what Addie was about to do. It was time to move forward. "Will you please close the doors, Frederick?"

He pulled the double doors of the drawing room shut. By the stiffness in his jaw, Addie could tell he too was nervous about the meeting. When he looked in her direction she offered him a half-hearted smile. He was the main reason for her hesitation. He'd worked so hard to be a good earl, and though there had been some missteps along the way, and though the estate's finances were tenuous, he was a good man with good intentions. In a few moments he would be cast aside, forced to step down while Jack Hayward stepped up.

In the process he would regain his long lost brother. The boys had been very young when Alexander was thought drowned. Would either have memories of the other? Would Frederick react with bitterness or joy?

"Grandmamma?" George asked as he played with a toy, trying to catch a ball-on-a-string in a cup. "How long is this going to take? I want to go outside."

She stilled his game with a hand. "Be patient, young man. It will take however long it will take."

And soon you will no longer be the heir.

Sudden doubts fell upon her like a bucket of cold water. Nothing in either family's lives needed changing. Both sides had found their place in the world and were happy. Did she really want to dismantle everything for the sake of truth?

Could the truth do more harm than good?

Grady stepped close, saying for her ear alone, "You don't have to do this."

But then she looked past him and saw the Hayward family. Mary's face was ashen, as though she would die from the awful anticipation. Lila was the loving granddaughter, sitting beside her, patting her hand, clearly concerned. And Morgan stood with his father behind their chair, a fine-looking young man with strong shoulders, a square jaw, and kind brown eyes.

Just like his father. Her eyes strayed to her son Jack, where she saw the same strength, jaw, and eyes.

Then to Frederick—who shared the same characteristics.

And finally, to the portrait above the mantel of her husband, Samuel.

Recognizing the consistency of the physical family traits, acknowledging the blood connection, she knew what she must do—and how she would do it.

"Well then," Addie began. "Thank you for coming this morning." She took time to look at each and every face. "Two striking families."

Addie took a new breath, praying for the right words. She walked toward the mantel, giving the portrait her attention. Then she extended a hand in its direction. "This was my husband, Samuel, the tenth Earl of Summerfield." She looked at Samuel's eyes, wondering what he would think of all this. *Just do the work, Adelaide. It always comes down to doing whatever needs to be done.*

His philosophy had ruled their lives, and though "doing the work" was often tedious and devoid of joy, in the end, he'd been right. His favorite verse returned to her: *"For unto whomsoever much is given, of him shall be much required: and to whom men have committed much, of him they will ask the more."*

She had been given much — the truth. And now much was required of her.

Addie realized that she had been caught up in her own moment, and that she had a room full of people waiting for her to reveal why she'd called them together.

She smiled at her audience. "Forgive me for being diverted by memories."

"You are forgiven, Mother, but I know we are all wondering why we have been brought here."

"The answer is in the portrait." She took a deep breath. "Look at the strong shoulders of my husband. His square jaw, and his deep brown eyes."

"He was a handsome man," Clarissa said.

"Yes, he was." Addie's stomach suffered a pull as she faced those she had gathered. *Just say it.* "As are his sons."

She looked at Frederick when she spoke. He said, "Sons?"

"Frederick . . ." She took a step toward Jack. "And Alexander."

The name hung in the air between them, and she wondered where it would land first.

Addie did not expect it to land on Mary. But Mary clutched her stomach and said, "Oh, my. This is it."

"It?" Jack asked.

Frederick's brow dipped. "Mother, what are you talking about?"

All she could offer him was a smile, as she turned to her eldest. "Jack, I believe you are my son, Alexander."

There was a chorus of "What?"

Addie raised her hands, quieting them. "Let me explain — with Mary's help."

Jack's family, clearly stunned, looked at their matriarch. Mary's pale face had turned bright red — which was encouraging. At least she wouldn't faint.

Addie offered Mary a hand, and the woman rose to her feet. Together they stood at the apex of the circle. Addie pulled Mary's hand through her arm and gave it an encouraging pat. Then she offered a nod and a smile. "We two women stand before you, two unwitting pawns on life's chessboard. We are both women who love their children. I had two fine sons, and Mary . . ."

"I had none."

Addie wanted to give her more credit than that. "You bore three children but lost them."

Mary suffered a swallow and nodded. Finally, she said, "My greatest desire was to be a mother and raise a child."

Frederick interrupted. "Where is all this going?"

"Patience." But Addie saw that confusion and even fear was taking control of the room. "I think it is best to be direct, don't you agree, Mary?"

She nodded.

"When my son Alexander was four, he was playing by the river. His nanny was there, and his little brother, Frederick, was back in the manor nursery, feeling unwell. But during their outing, Nanny grew tired and fell asleep on the grass nearby. At first Alexander napped with her. But then he must have gone exploring, for when Nanny awakened, he was missing. When she couldn't find him, she came running back to the manor, raising the alarm. Within minutes we had dozens of people looking for him. But . . ." She looked to Mary.

"My husband found him and took him."

The room sank into silence. Then Jack asked, "What are you saying?"

Mary's chest rose and fell. "I'm saying that I was so desperate for a baby, for a child to love, that your father took it upon himself to get me one."

"He kidnapped one? Kidnapped . . . me?" Jack said.

Mary hesitated a moment, then said. "Yes." She hurriedly added, "I don't think he blatantly snatched you. I prefer to think he found you wandering in the woods and took you in as a way to make me happy." She thought of something else. "Who knows? Perhaps he saved you. If you'd been left to wander in the woods, perhaps you *would* have ended up drowned, attacked by animals, or dead from exposure."

Addie had never considered this, but it could be true.

Mary continued. "Your father told me you were an orphan and needed a mother. And I . . ." She looked at Addie, her face drawn with pain. "And I was so eager for a child to love, I allowed myself to believe him." She hurried to Jack. "I am so sorry. I truly didn't know who you were. I didn't know any of this until recently."

"When . . . how did you find out?" Lila asked.

Mary pointed toward Jack's arm. "Your star birthmark. If you please . . ."

Jack removed his coat and rolled up his shirtsleeve. And there it was for all to see.

Addie took over the story. "I mentioned the birthmark at the store when I saw some fabric with stars on it, and later, when Jack was at the cottage helping to remove a stump, I saw it on his arm. Mary and I talked and . . ." She spread her arms. *There it is.*

Frederick grabbed everyone's attention when he slowly crossed the room toward Jack. "You are my brother?"

Jack returned his gaze. "It seems I am."

They stood face to face, studying each other, and Addie feared what would happen next. But then Frederick pulled Jack into an embrace.

Mary gasped, and Addie put a hand to her mouth. *Thank you, God.*

"It is my turn now." She walked toward Jack—Alexander. She took his face in her hands and looked into his eyes. "My son, my little star."

"I . . . did I call you mamma?"

She nodded, letting the tears come, then pulled him close. The feel of his arms around her was disconcerting, for the last time she'd held him, he'd been a child. She wished she could stay where she was, holding him forever. But the exclamations of the others broke through the moment, and Addie had to let him go.

"Do you remember this room?" Frederick asked his brother. "I haven't thought about it in years, but I think we used to play here—we weren't supposed to, but it was our favorite place to play Hide—"

"—and Seek," Jack said. He turned around, fully taking in the room. "When I was here recently, it felt familiar, but I discounted the feeling as I knew I'd never been here before. But now . . ." He suddenly moved to a chair in the corner. "One of my few early memories is of a gilt chair." He blinked once, as if a memory had returned, then suddenly turned the chair over. "Look!"

He showed the underside. Drawn on the bottom was a crude picture of a dog. "I drew this. It's . . . Scraps? Was that our dog's name?"

Frederick nodded. "He used to eat scraps from the table."

It was the final bit of proof.

"You had a dog?" George said. He turned to Frederick. "I want a dog too."

Frederick ruffled his hair. "We will see what we can do about that."

Clarissa was the one who brought up the darker implications. "But if you are the older brother . . ."

Check.

She continued. "Then . . . you are the Earl of Summerfield."

Check mate.

Addie rushed to regain control. "Sit down everyone, and let's work this through together."

When they'd all returned to their original places, she said, "This happy bit of news changes things, and for a while there will be many more questions than answers. Although we now know the truth, it *is* complicated. She went to Jack. "Yes it is true, that you, Jack—Alexander—being the eldest son, you are the Earl of Summerfield." She moved on to Frederick, cupping his face with a hand. "And my dear son, Frederick, as the second son, you are the Honourable Frederick Weston." Frederick's brow tightened, but he managed a smile. "To have my brother back . . ."

She was moved by his selflessness and kissed him. "God gave you your generous nature for this very moment."

"And I am no longer the countess," Ruth said with a nod, stating the fact without emotion.

Addie appreciated her attitude. "You are the Honourable Mrs. Frederick Weston."

"Then who is the countess?" Clarissa asked.

Fidelia.

Addie could tell that everyone was mentally saying her name. "Regrettably there is no current Countess of Summerfield."

"Unless Papa remarries," Lila said.

Jack blushed.

"Do you have someone in mind?" Addie asked

"No, of course not. It's much too soon."

Yes, it was.

Lila looked behind her, to where Morgan stood, his brow furrowed, his eyes focused on the air. "But this means Morgan is the heir."

Addie nodded. "You are right. Morgan, you will be the next Earl of Summerfield, and as the earl's eldest son, you also gain your father's secondary title — the Viscount Weston."

Morgan shook his head no and ran his hands across the arched back of the settee. "I don't think so."

"But it's true," Addie said. "You are the heir, and more than that, you are my grandson." She moved around the settee to give him a proper embrace, but he was stiff and standoffish. She'd expected him to be thrilled about becoming the heir.

Then Addie moved to Lila and drew her to her feet. "And you, my dear girl, are my granddaughter."

Lila's warmth was a strong contrast to her brother's distance. "I now have two grandmothers?"

"Indeed you do." As Lila moved to Mary's side, Addie asked the woman, "How are you faring through all this?"

"Much better, now that it's out."

"But this means George is *not* the heir," Frederick said.

"Nor is he the Viscount Weston."

"Yes, that is also true," Addie said.

George perked up. "Does this mean I don't have to go to school anymore?"

"It most certainly does not," Ruth said.

George slouched in his chair.

Someday he'd mind his loss of status. But Addie couldn't think about that now.

Clarissa stepped forward, her face red, her brow creased. "But Grandmamma, how could you share such a secret? You have destroyed everyone's lives."

Addie had expected such drama from her. "*Destroyed* is too strong a word, my dear. I believe—"

"No, it's not! What about my engagement to Joseph? Did you ever think about that?"

Now *that* was a touchy subject.

Lila drew in a breath. Clarissa's question became *the* most important question of the morning. She felt Nana squeeze her hand but dared not look at her.

"Unfortunately, the status of your engagement is up to Lord Newley Hopefully, he will find no issue—"

Clarissa popped to her feet. "No issue? We finally settled everything, and now this?"

The dowager gave her son—Frederick—a glance. It was not a hopeful glance, but one that showed she was aware of the situation. "We will deal with that later. One step at a time, child."

"But I want it dealt with immediately. It's imperative I—"

"We will deal with it in due time."

"Due time? What does that mean?"

The dowager gave Clarissa a scathing look, ending the discussion. *That was my grandmother giving my cousin a scathing look.* It was hard for Lila to fathom.

But as the gathering broke off into smaller groups—Papa

talking to his brother and Morgan, the dowager talking to Clarissa, the countess talking to George, Lila was allowed a moment to think about Joseph.

"He may be free again," Nana whispered.

"I don't dare hope for it."

"You are now Lady Lila."

The title startled her. She, who'd always been just a shopkeeper's daughter, was now the daughter of an earl? She was no longer just Lila Hayward but Lady Lila Weston?

"You are Joseph's equal," Nana said.

A shiver coursed up and down her arms. "But he's still betrothed to Clarissa."

Nana nodded toward the heated discussion that was going on between the dowager and Clarissa. "Not much longer by the sounds of it. And we both know who Joseph would prefer, were he given the choice."

Lila did know. And her heart nearly burst with the thought of it.

"Can we go riding later?" George asked Ruth as they sat together on the settee while the others talked around them.

"Perhaps." He seemed totally unconcerned about what had recently transpired. Which was good—in a way. Yet he wasn't a child anymore; he was thirteen, on the brink of manhood. He needed to understand. "Do you realize what happened here today?"

George retrieved his ball and cup game and began to play. "Sure. Mr. Hayward is my uncle, and as Father's older brother he is the real earl, which means I don't have to be."

"Have to be?"

He stopped playing, the ball hanging like a pendulum. "I don't care about running the manor. I just want to raise horses and race them."

"You could still do that if you were the earl."

He shook his head and looked directly at Ruth, his face

serious and suddenly older than his years. "It's all right, Mamma. I am much happier spending time with stable boys and coachmen than people who have a title."

"You will still have a position. You will be the Honorable George Weston."

He rolled his eyes and smiled. "Me? Honorable?"

She flicked the tip of his nose. "You. Honorable. In all ways." She interlocked her fingers with his. "What I want most is for you to live an honorable life."

"I can do that without a fancy title."

His wisdom moved her. "I know you can."

Then he cocked his head. "But what about you, Mamma? Will you mind too much not being a countess?"

She'd had time to think of this. "Actually not at all. I wasn't very good at it."

"You were getting better every day."

She was touched. "Really?" When he nodded, Ruth pulled her son close. "What would I do without you?"

"You needn't worry about that. I'm not going anywhere."

She was stirred by his sweetness. And yet . . . technically, they all might be going *somewhere*. If her family no longer held their titles, they should move out of the manor.

It was a question for another day. For now, Ruth was happy the secret was out. Perhaps it had all turned out better than could be expected.

At the very least God had proven Himself merciful.

While the family was busy upstairs, the servants took advantage of the lull to have their morning tea. Mrs. Camden poured, and the cups were passed.

Molly nearly spilled hers.

"Careful now, Miss Wallace," the housekeeper said. "What's got you all skittish this morning?"

"Nothing that a good cup of tea won't calm," Molly said. She took a sip, then asked as nonchalantly as possible. "Does anyone know what the meeting above stairs is all about?"

"It is none of our business," Mr. Dixon said.

"It's strange that the Haywards are here," Agnes said. "You don't suppose it's more to-do about Mrs. Hayward's death?"

"There will be no talk on that subject," Mrs. Camden said. "The rumors are dead, and dead they will stay." She gave Agnes a pointed look.

"His lordship did seem nervous about the meeting when he dressed this morning." Mr. Robbins said.

Mr. Dixon took inventory around the table. "Where is Nick? Has anyone seen him?"

Suddenly, Nick burst in the room. "You'll never believe—"

Mr. Dixon pointed to his empty chair. "Tardiness to tea is unacceptable."

Nick slid into his place, his face flushed. "I think you'll forgive me when you hear what I heard."

Mr. Dixon raised a hand. "If this is another rumor, we have had more than our share."

"Tis not a rumor. I heard it with my own two ears."

"Eavesdropping is also unacceptable."

Nick looked at the butler imploringly. "Please, sir. Let me speak. It's important, and it affects all of us."

Mr. Dixon released an extravagant sigh. "I suppose. But if I hear one iota of rumor, I shall stop you."

"No rumors. I promise." Nick took a deep breath. "The dowager just informed everyone that Jack Hayward is her long-lost son, Alexander."

Silence fell upon the group.

"Don't be ridiculous," Mr. Dixon finally said.

Nick raised his right hand. "It's true." Nick went on to explain the story, giving details even Molly didn't know.

The tea was forgotten as everyone talked at once. During the hubbub, Molly saw Dottie looking worried. Molly smiled and mouthed, *It will be all right.*

But it wouldn't be. Not for Molly.

Chapter Twenty-Nine

Lila and her family said their goodbyes and walked down the long drive to the front gate of Summerfield Manor.

Nana held her son's arm. "It's been quite a day," she said.

Papa stopped walking. "I wasn't thinking straight when I rejected their offer of the carriage."

"I much prefer the walk, so I can have the chance to apologize to all of you." Nana stopped in the drive. "I truly had no idea who you were, Jack. Alexander."

He patted her hand. "I'll always be your Jack."

She pulled her hand free. "But your mother is the dowager countess. By taking you, Stanley deprived you of a privileged life."

He laid his hands on her shoulders. "Mama, the life I had *was* privileged, for I was your son."

Nana leaned her head against his chest, and Papa wrapped his arms around her. "I tried to be a good mother."

Lila stepped away, letting them have their moment. She looked to her brother, but he was staring back at the manor, his mind obviously elsewhere. "Morgan? What's wrong?"

When he looked at Lila, his eyes were tortured. "Molly is what's wrong. If I'm the heir, I can't marry a servant. I can't marry Molly."

Lila had been so consumed with her own chance to marry the man she loved that she hadn't thought about Morgan and Molly. "Perhaps exceptions can be made."

He gave her the look she deserved. "Before today *you* had a hard time imagining yourself marrying Joseph, the son of a viscount. For the same reason Molly would never imagine marrying me, Viscount Weston, the son of an earl."

He was right, yet she wanted to offer him hope. But what hope? "Perhaps if —"

He ran back toward the manor, calling over his shoulder. "I have to speak with her."

"But she might not be allowed to speak with you."

He stopped in his tracks, then slowly turned to face them. "I am a viscount and the heir to an earldom. I can speak with whomever I like."

The benefits of a title were many — but they were not all-inclusive.

When they reached the edge of the village, Papa walked faster. "Slow down," Nana pleaded. "We can't keep up with you."

"I'll meet you at home," he said, hurrying even faster.

"He wants to tell Rose," Nana said.

Rose. Lila hadn't thought of Rose or what all this would mean to her. Was it the same situation that confronted Morgan and Molly — only worse? For Papa *was* the earl.

Yet in spite of her concern, Lila's mind was consumed with her own romance. "I need to go riding," she said.

Nana yanked at her arm, stopping her. "The dowager asked that we not publically share the news until she makes a formal announcement."

"Joseph isn't the public. He's directly involved."

"But shouldn't you wait until the Westons . . . until Clarissa has a chance to talk to him?"

Lila bit her lip. "I should, but I can't. I want to be the one to tell him."

"Tell him that . . . ?"

"I love him, and that I'm free to marry him."

Nana beamed. "At least someone in this family will be allowed true love. And no one deserves it more than you.

Remember what I told you the first day I came?"

Lila thought back. "You said I was a rare gem."

"Sparkling in the sun. And the troubles you've gone through recently have cut and honed you into a many-faceted jewel. Now you only need a little polishing."

Lila nodded, remembering. "A lot of polishing."

"But the end result will be stunning. So go on now. Go to Joseph."

Lila kissed her cheek and ran to fetch Raider.

"Remember every detail so you can tell me later," Nana called after her.

That wouldn't be a problem.

Ruth was passing through the foyer on the way to her room, when she heard a knock on the front door. Dixon answered it.

"I must see Molly, if you please."

"Miss Wallace is working right now," Dixon said.

"I . . . I have a right to see her."

Ruth could imagine the predicament Dixon was in. He'd only just been told of the situation. No one knew how these new roles and titles would play out.

And so, she stepped toward the door and feigned ignorance. "Morgan. Did you forget something?"

"If you please, your ladyship. I . . . I would like . . . I must speak to Molly. Please?"

Ruth turned to the butler. "I will handle this. Thank you, Dixon." She stepped aside. "Please come into the drawing room. I will get her for you."

He shook his head. "I wouldn't feel right . . . I don't want to speak to her inside. If you'll tell her to meet me in the garden?"

"Of course." But as he was leaving she said, "You know this *is* your home, Morgan. You are welcome here."

He shook his head and walked toward the garden.

Ruth saw Dixon standing nearby. "Please find Miss

Wallace and tell her that Morgan, that Lord Weston . . ." *Oh dear, what should we call him?* "That he would like to see her in the garden."

"Of course, Lady Summerfield. Your . . . ladyship?" When he sighed, it was the first time Ruth had seen him flustered since Colonel Cummings asked him to stand at his wedding. "What should I call you, my lady?"

"I have no idea."

"Perhaps 'Mrs. Weston' would be appropriate?"

Leave it to Dixon to know what was proper.

Molly ran into the garden, lifting her skirts in order to reach Morgan as quickly as possible. She saw him standing under the curve of the arbor, his arms outstretched. She ran into their comfort. "I just heard the news. Is your father the earl? Are you the heir?"

"He is, and I am, but I don't want to be." He pulled back to look at her. "I'll denounce the title. They can't make me take a title I don't want. Oh, why didn't you marry me when I first asked?"

Why indeed.

Even though he said what Molly wanted to hear, she knew his words were wishful thinking. Molly led him to the bench, and they sat side by side as they had so many times before.

Only now, everything was different.

"None of this makes any sense," he said. "It's preposterous."

"I heard it said that your father started to remember things. There's some dog drawn on the bottom of a chair?"

"Yes, but . . ." Morgan rose and began to pace. "Let's say it is the truth. That doesn't mean all of us have to drop our lives and start new ones. What if we're happy with the way things were? I like working in my family's shop. It's a better life than living in some fancy-pants manor. What am I going to do around here all day?"

"Be a viscount. Learn how to be an earl." She felt the weight of her next words before she said them. "And then you'll marry some nice daughter of a peer and have your own son, who will carry the line into the next century."

He shook his head, his hair flipping in front of his face. "I will not marry some haughty socialite."

"You haven't even met her yet."

He sank down beside her. "I don't want to meet her. I want you."

And I want you.

Yet Molly knew she couldn't freely voice her feelings. The entire situation was larger than them both. "You can't marry me." There. She'd said it plain.

"Don't you want to marry me?"

Molly hesitated, holding her tears at bay. She loved him with her entire being. "I can't marry you." The pressure of her broken heart, which by some miracle still beat in her chest, was excruciating. And then she thought of the only way he'd let her go. She rose and faced away from him. *Help me say what needs to be said.* Then she spun around, holding her chin high. "I can't marry you because I'm a selfish woman who thinks only of herself."

He reached to take her hand, but she stepped out of reach. "Don't be ridiculous," he said. "You're the kindest, most unselfish woman I know."

Molly's throat was so tight she feared she would choke. *Just a few more words and it will be over.* "But I am not unselfish. I have known you were the earl for weeks, since the day your mother died."

"What are you talking about?"

She took a step away from him and looked at the ground. "Dottie was standing at a bedroom window and overheard what was said between the countess and your mother. Your mother knew the truth and had come to throw it in the countess's face. But then she fell, and the secret—"

"It could have died with her." He pressed a hand to his forehead. "So who knew?"

She faced him with the final blow. "Dottie, myself, the countess, and your grandmother." She could see his thoughts taking roll call.

"Why didn't you tell me? Why didn't the countess or Nana tell?"

"Everyone had her own reason, but mine was the simplest and the most selfish. I knew if the truth came out, I would lose you. And so I chose to keep you from your title and your destiny. I was ready to keep the secret forever, as long as I could have you as my husband." Tears streamed down her cheeks, and she brushed them away. "Do you see the kind of woman I am? I'm the kind who doesn't deserve to marry a man like you whether you're a shopkeeper, a viscount, or an earl."

His eyes lost their supplication and gained a hard edge. "You would have kept the truth from me? Not that I enjoy knowing it now, but . . . to have you know and never tell?"

She hated seeing him angry at her, yet she had to finish this. "That was my plan. And so, I hereby relinquish any bond we had between us. Our lives are not linked by God or man. It is over. We are done."

Before her final word settled, she ran through the arbor, back toward the house. When she heard Morgan running after her, she spun around. "Stop! Not one more step. Leave me to live my life as I leave you to live yours."

She ran again, and this time she heard no footsteps.

And he didn't call out her name.

It was truly over.

Molly knew what she had to do. She ran in a side entrance of Summerfield Manor and up the back stairway, pausing when she heard voices so as not to be seen.

She tiptoed down the corridor of the servants' quarters and slipped into her room. From under her bed, she pulled out the smallest of her two pieces of luggage and began filling it with the essentials. How odd to condense one's life to the belongings in a single bag.

When she was finished, she sat at the desk and wrote three notes. She addressed one to her family, one to Morgan, and one to the countess — whatever title she was now. Inside Morgan's she slipped the white ribbon she'd hung from her window. She sealed them all, then lined them neatly along her pillow and took one last look around the room.

To leave this life she knew so well . . .

What choice did she have? She couldn't stay and be around when Morgan and his family moved into the manor. She couldn't be a servant to them.

And she couldn't cause him any more pain as he tried to make their relationship work. For he would try.

Morgan would have enough to worry about without having to contend with the impossibility of their love.

And so she took up her bag, quietly closed her bedroom door, and backtracked through the manor and out the side door. She bypassed the garden and the drive and walked past the stables toward the far road.

Steven, the coachman, called after her. "Miss Wallace? Where are you going?"

She didn't acknowledge him, focusing on each step forward, her mind consumed with completing her task.

Once she reached the road, she hesitated, but only for a second. To the left was the village. To the right was . . . away.

She turned right.

Chapter Thirty

Ruth knocked on the door to Molly's room a second time. "Really, Molly. I saw Morgan leave. I know you're back. You must—" She entered the room.

It was empty. The door of the armoire was closed upon the end of a skirt. Ruth opened the door to nudge it inside and saw only remnants of Molly's clothes.

No, Molly. No!

She rushed to the dresser and opened drawers. A few odds and ends were all that remained.

And then she saw three notes upon the bed, titled in Molly's hand: *Morgan, Lady Summerfield,* and *My Family.*

Ruth ripped open her note:

> *Your ladyship,*
> *The years I spent in your service have been the happiest of my life. I will always be grateful to you for giving me a chance. My family is also in your debt. You saved us all and gave us a life worth living.*
>
> *I am sorry to leave so suddenly, but with the secret out . . . You know the consequences that come with Morgan's rise to the role of heir. Although he says he loves me and chooses me over the title, I cannot let him make that sacrifice. He must fulfill his destiny.*
>
> *And I must fulfill mine, wherever and whatever that may be.*
>
> *I am very proud to have served you, and you*

will always be a countess in my eyes.

I have one request: please allow my family to
stay on at Summerfield Manor, that they may have
the pleasure of serving your family.

I wish you the best and pray God will bless you
and yours.

Yours faithfully,
Molly Wallace

"No!"

Frederick appeared in the doorway, out of breath. "Ruth? Gertie said you'd come up to the servants' floor. We don't belong up here, my dear . . . . What's wrong?"

She showed him the note. "Molly didn't have to leave. There are a myriad of details to work out . . . but she was always welcome here."

"I heard about Molly and Morgan. They were in love?"

"They were engaged."

Frederick shook his head. "How unfortunate. It is an impossible complication."

Ruth took the note back. "This whole title issue is unfair."

"Such is England, my dear. You get rid of the titles, you get rid of England." He put his arm around her. "I am sorry to see Molly go, but I do understand her reasons. And I am proud of her for making the difficult choice."

It was still unfair.

"How are *you* handling Mother's revelation?" he asked.

She shrugged. "Countess or the Honourable Mrs. Frederick Weston . . . I don't much care. How about you?"

He shrugged and moved to the window, checking the view. "*I* don't much care."

"Really?"

He let the lace curtain fall into place. "No one is more surprised than I."

"Clarissa is taking it hard."

Frederick sighed. "Perhaps a little hardship will be good for her."

Ruth was shocked. "This, from her indulgent father?"

"I believe she enjoyed her position a bit too much. And I allowed it."

"You think so?"

He sighed. "I do grieve that George won't gain the earldom."

"*He* doesn't much care either."

"Interesting, isn't it?" he asked. "That the titles which have shaped our lives are so easily discarded."

"Transferred is a better word."

He nodded and took a long breath. "My brother is alive. That is still hard to comprehend."

"I will help you if you will help me," she said.

Frederick stepped toward her, his expression soft. "I will love you if you will love me."

His words were totally unexpected. She stared at him. "Really?"

He touched her cheek. "Absolutely."

"It is almost like . . ." She wasn't sure she should say it.

"Like what?"

"Like we are getting a fresh start. As simply Mr. and Mrs. Weston."

"I vow to love you and cherish you, Mrs. Weston, until death do us part."

Ruth felt tears threaten. She drew his hand to her lips. "I make the same vow. For I do love you, Mr. Weston."

He took her in his arms and leaned her back, giving her a long and passionate kiss.

Finally Ruth was allowed to come up for air. "My, my, husband."

He smiled with satisfaction. "I have always wanted to kiss a missus."

Ruth sat at her desk in the morning room. The Wallace family stood before her as they read Molly's note.

"So she's gone?" Mrs. Wallace asked.

"Yes, she is."

"Where did she go?" Dottie asked.

"I don't know."

"Will I see her again?" Lon asked.

Ruth put a hand on his arm. "I don't know."

Mrs. Wallace slipped the note in her apron pocket. "Molly's a smart one. And she's a survivor. We'll pray for her every night, won't we, children?"

They nodded.

"I shall pray too," Ruth said.

Mrs. Wallace patted her pocket. "In the note she said she was going to ask if we could stay on. Can we?"

"Do you want to stay on?"

All three of them shared a look and a nod. "Very much so," Mrs. Wallace said.

"Very much so, my lady," Dottie corrected.

"Keep that up, and you will go far," Ruth said, smiling. She dismissed them. There was one final note left to deliver.

And yet . . . Ruth held the note addressed to Morgan. If she brought it to him now, he'd go after Molly. And as much as she hated to see Molly leave, it was probably for the best.

And so, she opened the desk drawer and slipped the note inside.

Lila's thoughts took on the rhythm of Raider's stride as she raced to Crompton Hall. To Joseph.

We're free to marry, we're free to marry alternated with *I love you, I love you.*

Yet as she neared the Kidd mansion, she reined Raider in, suddenly fearful. She detoured into a meadow, directed the horse to walk in a wide circle, and spoke of her doubts out loud. "Joseph *did* say he wanted to marry me. But what if he only said that because it was impossible? Rather than hurt me, he let the details of our circumstances keep us apart."

She eased Raider to a stop in order to let her fears fully

form. "What if I rush up to him and proclaim my love, and he looks horrified? Then he'll feel sorry for me." She closed her eyes and imagined the moment when she would know she'd been a fool.

A new doubt demanded attention, and Lila let Raider walk. "Or what if he does love me, but his father won't allow us to marry even though we are of equal status? What if the entire secret is too much for Lord Newley to accept, and he deems my family too dramatic and too much trouble? He might say the truth doesn't matter at all and consider us charlatans who may have a title, but don't deserve it because of how we've lived until now."

She raised a hand to her mouth, bowing her head under the weight of the what-ifs. Then she looked toward heaven. "Please . . . what should I do?"

Then she remembered Nana's oft-repeated words. *You are a rare gem, sparkling in the sun . . . you've been cut and honed into a many-faceted jewel . . . you just need a little polishing.*

"A lot of polishing," Lila said again.

And then she received a new encouragement, coming from deep inside. *Let Me polish you. This is all a part of My plan for you* and *Joseph. You are nearly where I want you to be. Do not doubt. Be strong. Go to him and —*

She said the last words out loud. "Make each other shine."

Lila turned Raider toward the road and spurred him on.

It was odd to stand before the door of Crompton Hall two times in two days. Yet yesterday was as far away from today as the moon from the earth. For yesterday she'd come meekly, as Lila Hayward. Today she came with confidence as Lady Lila Weston.

Today she came here as a jewel, ready to be polished.

She knocked with confidence even as her insides tingled with nerves. She lifted her chin, trying to play the part. The butler answered. His countenance suggested he was not amused.

"Yes?"

"I would like to speak to Mr. Kidd. Joseph Kidd. If you please."

"And what is your business with Mr. Kidd?"

It's none of your *business.* Before she could answer, she saw Lord Newley enter the foyer. He stepped toward them. "Miss Hayward. Another visit?"

He was the last person she wanted to see. "Good day, your lordship," she said. "I have come to speak to your son."

"On what matter?"

Her heart beat so hard she was certain the two men would hear it. "On a personal matter. A very important personal matter."

"Perhaps you should leave him another note."

His tone was mocking. She wanted to ask him if he'd delivered the note she'd given him yesterday. By his manner she suspected at the very least he'd read it.

"A note is not appropriate, my lord. I must speak with him in person."

"You *must?*" His look of condescending amusement was maddening. She vowed she would never, ever let her position cause her to treat another person in this way.

She was tempted to beg but controlled herself. She must meet him on a firm — if not equal — ground. "I truly must. It is imperative."

His lordship exchanged a look with the butler. "Oh, now it's *imperative.* Tis quite a large word for one so young."

"Tis the right word, Lord Newley."

He took a moment to study her, and it took all Lila's strength not to falter and let him see her desperation. Then she thought of something to say that might gain his permission. "I don't need to see him for the reason you may suspect. It's an entirely different matter. A very important matter having to do with the Westons."

His eyebrow rose, and he stepped aside. "Since it is imperative, do come in, Miss Hayward. Take a seat in the drawing room." To the butler he said, "Please tell Joseph he has a visitor — a very persistent visitor."

Lord Newley left her with a nod, and she stepped across the black and white tiles of the foyer and entered the drawing room. It was less formal than Summerfield Manor — perhaps due to the long absence of the viscount's wife? Joseph had mentioned she'd died when he was born.

The furniture was carved walnut and oak, the fabric upholstered in the deep colors of burgundy and navy often preferred by men. A painting hung above the fireplace, that of a lovely woman wearing a wide skirt with large puffed sleeves. She had fair hair and pale blue eyes.

"That is my mother."

Lila turned toward Joseph's voice.

"She's very beautiful. You have her eyes."

He nodded.

And you have my heart. She only thought the words, but before she could stop herself, she heard them said aloud. "And you have my heart."

Joseph's eyebrows rose. His smile was sincere, but bittersweet.

He came in the room, and after a look over his shoulder, took her hands and kissed her gently on the lips. "As you have mine."

"I have something important to tell you. Something that will change everything."

He looked worried and led her to a settee. "Tell me."

She looked in the air, wishing to see a clear place to start. "This morning my family was summoned to Summerfield Manor by the dowager."

"Summoned?"

"Summoned."

"That sounds serious."

"It was." She remembered how the dowager had sprung the news: simply and to the point. "My father is the dowager's long-lost, eldest son. My father is the rightful Earl of Summerfield."

Joseph blinked, then blinked again. "But how . . . ?"

Lila told him the entire story of a little boy lost in the woods, stolen by Lila's grandfather and raised as a son. Of a star birthmark and a sudden discovery. Of two families becoming one.

"That means that you . . ."

She watched his chest rise and fall. "It means that I am the daughter of an earl."

His eyes grew wide as he realized the full implication. She had to let him take the next step alone. She needed *him* to say the words.

"That means that you and I . . . we can marry."

She nodded, holding back tears.

He pulled her into his arms.

The world became very small.

And their love, very large.

Lila clutched Joseph's arm as they stood outside his father's study.

"What if he says no?" she whispered.

"I shan't let him."

"Joseph? Is that you?"

They took a synchronized breath then entered the room. Lord Newley looked up from the work on his desk. Seeing them, he removed his half-glasses.

"I thought I heard someone in the hall." He eyed them both, first Lila, then Joseph, then Lila again. "Did you resolve your imperative matter, Miss Hayward?"

Joseph looked at her, "If I may?"

"Of course." Please.

"Actually, Father, it is not Miss Hayward anymore. I would like you to meet Lady Lila Weston, the daughter of the Earl of Summerfield."

Lord Newley blinked once, then dropped his glasses. "I don't understand. *You* are the daughter of Summerfield?"

She realized he meant Frederick Weston. "I am the daughter of Jack Hayward. He is the rightful earl. He is Summerfield."

Joseph explained. "He is the eldest son of Lady Summerfield, the dowager countess."

"But she has only one son, no eldest son."

Joseph clarified. "She had two sons, but as a child the eldest was lost and thought drowned."

To his lordship's credit, he dropped his ostentation and authority. "I didn't come to the area until twenty-some years ago. But this history obviously goes back further than that."

"Indeed it does, my lord."

"Please, sit."

When they were seated across the desk from him, Lila told the full story. Lord Newley listened with little input, offering an occasional, "I'll be," or "How extraordinary."

"So that's the gist of it," Lila said upon finishing. "My father is Alexander Weston."

"And thus, Lady Lila is the daughter of an earl," Joseph said.

"What does Summerfield — Frederick — think of all this? And the countess? And George, and . . ."

Lila filled in the final name. "Clarissa is upset. The rest are surprisingly accepting."

"After all," Joseph said, "there is cause for celebration as two brothers are reunited."

Lord Newley sat back in his chair, an elbow on the arm, his chin resting on his hand. "Frederick is a good man, a generous sort. It is not hard to imagine him being gracious."

"My father is also a good man," Lila said. "He will not let the sudden title go to his head. He too is grateful that he has found his long-lost mother and brother."

"What of his other mother? The one who raised him."

"I assure you, she was innocent of all knowledge. She feels dreadful for the situation, but my father — all of us — have forgiven her for her part in it."

The viscount nodded, then returned to a past point,

"Clarissa was upset?"

Joseph answered. "She rightly fears that our betrothal might be at risk. Since she is no longer the daughter of an earl—"

"She is simply Miss Weston now," his father finished.

"Yes, but I believe her anxiety is caused by the knowledge that I don't love her." Joseph held out his hand, and Lila placed her own in his, spanning the space between their chairs. "I love Lady Lila."

"And I love your son, my lord."

"I know."

"You know?" Joseph asked.

He opened a drawer and retrieved the note Lila had left in his care the day before. "I believe this belongs to you." He handed it to Joseph.

The flap of folded note was free. "The seal is broken," Joseph said.

"Because I read it," his father said. "I know I shouldn't have, but I could sense there was something between you, and I had to know where Miss Hayward—Lady Lila—stood." He pointed toward the note. "Read."

As Joseph read the note, his brow dipped with emotion. When finished, he carefully refolded it and leaned toward her. "You are *my* everything."

"This may be all very well and good," Lord Newley said, "but for you to suddenly want to marry Lila *after* she has gained position . . ."

Lila shook her head adamantly. "He proposed to me when I was merely a shopkeeper's daughter, before the secret was revealed."

"Actually, I have proposed twice. The only thing holding us back were the rules of rank and propriety."

"And the fact you were engaged to Lady Clarissa."

"There was that." Joseph leaned toward his father. "When you wanted me to break the engagement, I was thrilled. I never wanted to marry Clarissa. She may be a fine girl, but we are not a fine match. And she doesn't love me."

Lila had a question. "Why was the engagement suddenly repaired?"

Joseph exchanged a look with his father. "I wanted to tell you yesterday, to come to you and explain everything."

Lord Newley took over. "Summerfield cornered me after church. He assured me the rumor against his wife was false and begged me to allow the engagement to be renewed. He said his daughter's happiness depended on it. There are business reasons too. We have . . . dealings." He hesitated then added, "Summerfield has powerful connections in London, that would be helpful in Joseph gaining a seat in Parliament."

Lila looked at Joseph. "You wish to serve in the House of Lords?"

He shrugged. "That is Father's wish for me."

"Yours too, son."

"That is a discussion for another time. The point is, Clarissa implored her father to fix the engagement."

"From what I've seen, she usually gets what she wants."

Lila could imagine Clarissa begging her father to fix the problem.

"I argued against it," Joseph said. "Because by that time I had already proposed to you."

"Without my permission," his father said.

"But my next step was to speak with you, Father. To do my own begging to let me marry the woman I love."

"I would have said no," Lord Newley said.

The awful truth settled between them.

He continued "What would you have done if I had forbidden it?"

Lila hated that the viscount put Joseph in such a position. "You needn't answer that," she said. "We both knew it would take a miracle."

"It appears you have received that miracle," he said.

And there it was, like rays of Divine light shining through the clouds.

"Are you saying you approve?" Joseph asked.

"I am not the hard-hearted man you may think. I married for love. Can I want anything less for my only son?"

"But you made an agreement with the earl. If you knew I didn't love Clarissa . . ."

"It was time for you to marry, time for you to give me a grandson. You have always liked Clarissa."

"Liking is not loving."

"And the financial business of what Summerfield needed, and your seat in Parliament . . ." He sighed. "I suppose there are other avenues."

It was Lila's turn to ask a question. "What are you going to tell my uncle? And Lady Clarissa — Miss Weston?"

Lord Newley thought a minute, then said, "The truth should suffice. Since this secret revealed one rather large truth, the Weston family should be open to finding out that the two of you are in love."

"So we have your blessing?" Joseph asked.

"How can I refuse? Fate or God, or whatever force has been at work here, has set everything in place. Your love was borne of its own accord without thought to title or agreements, and apparently, it will not be denied. Yes, I give you my blessing."

Joseph leapt to his feet and shook his father's hand. He embraced Lila, and they rocked back and forth in utter joy.

Then the viscount came from behind his desk. "Come, my dear. I feel it is *imperative* I give my future daughter-in-law a proper greeting." He gave her an embrace.

Lila had never felt so blessed. Not only had she gained a future husband and father-in-law, but today she'd gained a grandmother, grandfather, uncle, aunt, and two cousins. Her heart expanded to love them all.

"I'll race you to the meadow," Lila said. "Go!"

"Wait! I wasn't ready!"

Lila exulted in her horse's speed and the feel of the wind

through her hair. Her thoughts again mirrored Raider's rhythm. *Thank you, God. Thank you, God. Thank you, God!*

She heard Joseph coming up behind and spurred Raider faster. They reached the meadow at the same time. "It's a tie," she said.

"I think I nosed you out," Joseph said.

She shook her head, "It was a tie."

He tipped his hat. "I acquiesce to my darling fiancée."

"'Twill not be the last time," she laughed. They circled each other. "I do believe this is the place I fell," she said.

"Not exactly." Joseph dismounted and lifted her from saddle to ground. Then he swept her into his arms and gently lowered her to the grass. "Actually, this is the place *I* fell — in love with you."

She nestled against the grass and looked up into his eyes, tracing his cheek with her fingers. "You saved me that day."

"As you saved me this day."

Lila pulled his face close and sealed their future with a kiss.

Chapter Thirty-One

"So how do you decide what to order, and the quantities?" Uncle Frederick asked.

Papa corrected him. "What *we* decide to order." He nodded at Nana and Rose, including them in the "we."

Watching the four of them examine the details of running the store, Lila couldn't be happier. That the brothers had decided to keep the mercantile and let Rose and Nana run it, was a marvelous choice. In turn, Papa was learning the ways of running the estate.

As for Morgan . . . . She heard the sound of his ax splitting wood out back. Morgan was the only one who hadn't adapted to the situation. He spent his days engaged in solitary chores. The news that Molly had run away had drowned his spirit and made anger his constant companion.

Uncle Frederick looked toward the noise. "I do wish he would join us. I would like to hear his opinions about the store and estate business."

"Give him time," Papa said. "A broken heart is not easily mended."

"Until Ruth told me as much, I had no idea he was so close to Miss Wallace."

Above all, Lila wanted her brother to have the time he needed. She knew the ache of lost love. In her case, what was lost was found again, but she easily empathized with his pain.

"He *is* moving to the manor, isn't he?" Uncle asked.

"Eventually. For now it's just Lila and I."

"Oh!" Uncle said, reaching into his pocket. "I have

something for him. A note from Miss Wallace. I can't believe I forgot about it."

Lila took it and saw where *Morgan* was written in a lovely cursive. "How do you come to have it?" she asked.

"It was left in her room—along with two other notes."

"But she left weeks ago."

"My wife and I thought it best to give Miss Wallace some space. We feared Morgan would run after her."

"He would have," Lila said. "He wanted to."

"Which would have made things worse," Papa said.

"That was also our opinion." Uncle pointed to the note. "Perhaps it would be best not to let him see it at all?"

Lila looked at the note, considering the suggestion. Then she shook her head. "There have been too many notes undelivered. If Molly wanted him to have it, then he must have it."

"You give it to him, Lila," Uncle said.

Papa agreed. "And stay with him."

Lila watched Morgan read Molly's note. His breathing grew heavy, his brow furrowed, and a hand covered his mouth. A length of white ribbon was curled over his finger.

"What does she say?" Lila asked softly.

Morgan let the ax fall from its place, leaning against his leg. He sat on a stump, his arms resting on his thighs, the note open. "It repeats what she told me the last time we met. That she loves me but won't keep me from my destiny." His face sagged with sorrow. "I told her I didn't care about any title, that I only wanted her."

"She knew that. But she wanted more for you."

"*She* is all I wanted. She is my *more*."

Lila rose and put a hand on his back. "I'm so sorry."

"I'll always love her."

Lila could only nod.

Lila went through her mother's dresses, helping Papa pack for the move to the manor. "What do you want to do with these?" she asked.

He looked up from the opened trunk that had always sat at the foot of their bed. "I always liked that green rosebud dress. Why don't you keep it?"

"Mother did look pretty in it."

He nodded once, then glanced at the other clothes. "Let Mother and Rose choose from the rest. They'll be too plain for you now. We'll both be needing fancier clothes. You'll like that, won't you?"

She folded the green dress and packed it in a crate to move. "I suppose I will, though I have no knowledge of fashion."

"You'll learn. Ruth and Clarissa will teach you."

Lila shook her head. "I don't think Clarissa will want much to do with me." *Nor I with her.*

"She has a right to be hurt."

"But it's going to be very awkward with both of us living in the house."

"It's a big house."

"I fear not big enough." She set the other dresses aside. "I do wish Nana were moving with us."

"She's made it very clear she wouldn't be comfortable at the manor. And she's needed here, to run the store with Rose."

Which begged the question. "How does Rose feel about all this? About your new position?"

He smiled wistfully. "Rose is Rose. She has a giving, forgiving nature."

"Do you . . . love her?"

"I think I could have."

It was sad to think that their future was also being upended. "I suppose you can't marry Rose if Morgan can't marry Molly."

Papa lifted a small box from the bottom of the trunk and

opened it. "I am ignorant of the proper protocol of such things. At the moment I must get through today before I can think about—"

When he stopped in midsentence, Lila saw him leafing through a stack of letters. "Whose are those?" she asked.

His chin hardened. "It appears they are the letters I sent to my parents in London." He opened an envelope and removed the letter—and some money. The next envelope contained the same, as did the next. "No wonder Mama said she never got the money I sent her. Fidelia never sent it."

One by one, Lila helped him open the letters as coins fell onto the bed.

Papa stared at the money. "I knew Fidelia resented the idea of helping them. She always called my father a good-for-nothing."

"Mother was always harsh in her judgment of others." But then Lila saw one last letter tucked in the corner of the truck. "We missed one."

"Open it and add the coins to the rest."

Lila began to open it, then stopped. "This one's different. It's written in Nana's hand. And it's been opened."

"Let me see." Papa read the letter, his head shaking back and forth with each line. When he was finished he paused and took a deep breath. "It's the letter in which Nana tells us of my father's death and asks to come live with us." He tossed it on the bed with the others. "Forget the rest. How dare Fidelia keep this one from me?"

Indeed. "Why would she keep any of them? And why not spend the money on herself? Why hide it away?"

Papa pressed a hand against his brow. "Add all this to the list of my wife's unexplainable eccentricities."

Lila didn't know what she could say to make it better. She needed reinforcement. When she heard her grandmother in the next room, she asked. "Shall I get Nana?"

"Please." Papa began collecting the letters in one pile, the money in another.

"You need something, Jack?" Nana asked as she entered

the room.

He swept a hand across the bed. "Look at what we found: your letter telling us of Pa's death and your arrival, plus all the letters I sent to you in London, complete with the money I placed inside."

"I don't understand."

"We never saw your letter, and Fidelia never sent any of mine. She hoarded them away."

Nana chose a letter, reading a few lines. "I knew you wouldn't purposely let us flounder."

"When you said you'd never received them . . . I had no idea."

"She truly hated us," Nana said.

"I wish I could deny it, but I can't," Papa said.

Lila sat on the bed and counted the money. "There's a little over nine pounds here."

Nana drew in a breath, and her eyes grew wide. "My debt was eight pounds, nine shillings and twelve pence." She looked at Papa. "Oh my. Oh dear."

"What?" Lila asked.

"Don't you see? If I'd had this money, I could have paid our debts, and I never would have had to come to Summerfield."

They let the fact sink in. "You never would have moved in with us," Papa said.

"And if I'd never moved in, the secret would never have come out, and . . ."

Papa sank to the bed. "Fidelia's malice set in motion a world of change — including her own death."

"Including the discovery that you are the earl," Nana said.

"And opening up my opportunity to marry Joseph."

They let the ramifications and a wave of gratitude settle between them.

Papa stared at the letters. "God brought good results out of bad intentions."

"And His timing was perfect," Lila said. As the sound of Morgan's ax filtered through the open window, she added,

"There were *some* good results, *some* of the time."

Nana shook her head. "God is good *all* the time. We just haven't seen it yet."

Lila hoped she was right.

"Thank you for letting me become your lady's maid, your ladyship—I mean, Mrs. Weston."

Ruth nodded. "You are a woman of great experience, Albers. I am sure you can teach me a thing or two."

Albers shook her head mightily, making her jowls jiggle. "No, madam. Don't ever think that you need teaching. I'm the one who's honored, and . . ." Her voice cracked. "And truly thankful. With the dowager moving to the cottage, I felt worthless. Living at Summerfield Manor is all I know. And now, for you to give me purpose again . . ." She pulled a handkerchief from her sleeve. "I won't let you down, Mrs. Weston. I promise."

Ruth fought her own emotions. Although she missed Molly terribly, she was very hopeful about building a relationship with Albers.

"Is there anything I can do for you right now, madam?"

"Not at the moment. I must meet with Mrs. Camden and Gertie about the rooms that will belong to the new earl and Lady Lila."

"Begging your pardon, but who will be Lady Lila's lady's maid?"

"Unfortunately, there is no one on staff who is qualified, so we will be looking for someone from beyond the manor to fill the position."

Albers nodded. "Until then, I'd be happy to help her in any way I can."

"You certainly have a purpose now, Albers. Between the two of us, you shall be kept busy."

"That is always my preference. Hard work keeps a body young."

"I shall remember that."

There was a knock on the bedroom door, and the dowager entered and nodded at Albers. "I heard you had found a new mistress."

"Perhaps two, Lady Summerfield," Albers said.

Ruth explained. "Lady Lila will need help until we make a new hire."

"If anyone can handle the work, it is my Albers."

Albers curtsied and left the room.

Ruth felt her nerves spring to life. She had not shared any time alone with Adelaide since the secret was revealed. "I am sure you are thrilled to have both your sons back in the fold."

Adelaide strolled to the window, fingering the edge of the velvet drapery. "They've been spending time together in the study, going over the ledgers. I find Jack to be a quick study."

"You are calling him Jack?"

"I see no reason to take his name away from him."

Ruth approved. "Is Frederick a good teacher?"

"I'm greatly impressed by his patience and ability to make the estate details understandable."

Ruth was glad to hear the praise. Her greatest fear was that Jack would usurp her husband's place in their mother's heart.

Adelaide sat on the window seat. "Beyond Frederick's business ability, I am most impressed by his generous heart. To lose his title . . . . Truly, I can't imagine being dealt such a blow. When I married Grady, I still remained the dowager countess. But Frederick, and you, my dear Ruth . . . I am in awe of both of you."

My dear Ruth? And her mother-in-law was in awe of her? The sky had turned orange, and the early autumn breeze threatened snow.

"I have shocked you, haven't I?" Adelaide asked.

"Well, yes. I never expected . . ."

"Expected me to be kind?"

Ruth didn't know what to say.

Adelaide raised a hand, negating the need for a response. "We have all been subject to enormous changes, all surprising, and all overdue." She stood and adjusted the cuffs of her blouse. "Being married to the colonel has opened my eyes to many things: how to truly love, how to catch and fillet a fish, and how to acknowledge that I am an overly domineering know-it-all."

Again, Ruth was at a loss. Yet, perhaps it was time for both of them to be candid. "I never felt good enough. You were so capable and knew so much about every aspect of the manor, and about being a proper countess, that I was overwhelmed to the point of inaction."

"Part of being a proper countess is being compassionate and sympathetic to others. Duty became my god, and I put its glory above everything else."

Ruth couldn't believe what she was hearing. Apparently she could thank the colonel for the enormous transformation. "Duty does have its place."

"But family must come before all else." Adelaide slapped her thighs. "The point of my monologue is that I am sorry for making your rise to countess difficult for you. I am here to ask for your forgiveness."

Ruth was struck dumb.

"Don't gawk," Adelaide said. "Though I do suspect a contrite dowager *is* one of the wonders of the world."

Ruth laughed. "Of course I forgive you. But . . ."

"But?"

Ruth continued on the course she had started. "I am not free of conviction."

Adelaide's left eyebrow rose. "Good. I do hate to repent alone."

Although there was no true need to clear her conscience — since her sin was safe from exposure — Ruth felt it was time to confess. "I knew of the secret before you did. The day Fidelia came to the manor, she told me of your comment about a star birthmark, and of course informed me that Jack was your son and the rightful earl."

"So I assumed."

"You suspected?"

"In retrospect it seemed logical."

"Then you understand why I now beg for your forgiveness. I should have told you right away. You deserved to know your son was alive."

"I do forgive you. But why didn't you tell me?"

"Because I didn't want Frederick and George to lose their titles."

"And you, yours?"

"Countess or not, I truly don't care. But there was another reason I kept it to myself. I wanted my lady's maid, Molly, to be able to marry the man she loved."

"Morgan Hayward."

"You know that too?"

Adelaide let her eyebrows rise. "I know everything."

Ruth laughed. "Their love is the reason Molly left Summerfield. She sacrificed her love so Morgan could live out his proper future."

"An admirable girl. Have you heard from her since she left?"

"Not a word. I pray she is safe and has found a position somewhere."

"If you do hear from her, assure her that we will give her references."

"I will do that."

Adelaide pushed herself to standing. "Well then. Our sins have been confessed, and forgiveness has been exchanged between us."

"And the Almighty."

"I lean on that assurance."

"As do I." But Ruth had one more detail that remained bothersome. "What plagues me are the years I wasted being afraid of my mistakes, assuming things I shouldn't have, and not being brave. I hid from life, and while I did, my children grew up around me, without me. That makes me sad."

Adelaide nodded once. "'I will restore to you the years that the locust hath eaten.'"

"Locusts?"

"Grady gave me that verse, for between the two of us we share a cartload of regrets covering a multitude of years. God tells us to let them go. He will make the future better."

"I like the idea of that."

"The promise of that," Adelaide said.

"Grandmamma, would you come in here a minute?"

Addie was exhausted. She longed to be home with Grady, to lay in his arms and let the drama of life fall away.

"Please, Grandmamma." Clarissa motioned her into the study. Frederick was already there.

"What's this about, Clarissa?" he asked. "We all have important things to do. My brother and Lila are moving in tomorrow and—"

"And I am moving out."

Addie sank onto a chair. "Out? Out where?"

"Away. I am moving to London."

"I suppose a visit would be understandable," Frederick said.

"Tis not a visit," Clarissa said. "I have already contacted the Duvalls, and they have agreed to let me stay with them. Mr. Duvall has contacts within the theatrical community, and he has promised to help me find a place on the stage."

Addie put a hand to her heart. "You might as well say *brothel*."

"Don't overreact, Grandmamma. You know it has always been my dream to act."

Addie could remember mention of it. But she'd never imagined Clarissa was serious. "Your life is here at Summerfield."

"Not anymore."

"It is indecent for a woman of high position to be on the stage. The life is highly immoral, what with all that pretending to be someone you're not, and kissing strangers in public."

"At the moment I would like to pretend a little. I am no longer a woman of high position, as I have been demoted and am simply Miss Weston. And I wish to use my talent. You have always encouraged me to do that."

"Here," Frederick said. "We have encouraged you to use your talents here."

Clarissa's cheeks grew red. "Then tell me. What do I have *here?* Do you honestly think I can bear staying around while my old fiancé makes wedding plans with my new cousin? You and Mother may be able to accept the changes that have taken over our lives, but I cannot. I simply must leave." She stopped for the dramatic effect. "And you can't stop me."

Unfortunately, except for the mention of the theatre, Clarissa's reasoning was sound. It *would* be difficult for her to witness Joseph and Lila's betrothal, especially with Lila living under the same roof. More than difficult, excruciating. For both of them.

"I will agree to a visit to London," Addie said. "But you must promise there will be no talk of the theatre."

"Really, Clarissa," Frederick said. "It is out of the question."

She went to her father, hugging him from behind. "But I am a good singer and actress, Father. You know I am."

He tapped her arm. "I mean it, daughter. No theatre ."

"Fine," she said.

Her quick acquiescence made Addie suspicious, but she knew further discussion was futile. Although it was Addie's duty to dislike Clarissa's rebellious nature, she also admired it. "When are you leaving?" she asked.

"Tomorrow. And I am taking Agnes with me."

Addie let Frederick take over the argument. She was done. She slipped out and hurried home to Grady.

She found him pulling radishes in the garden. "Look! We can have them for dinner."

Addie rested her head against his chest. "I don't need dinner. I just need you."

He dropped the radishes and held her close. She could hear the beating of his heart, and she breathed deeply of his scent. The sound of the birds singing nearby eased her frazzled nerves.

Grady stroked the back of her neck, that special place he'd found to calm her. "Would you like to move back to the manor? You must want to be near your sons."

"I do. But I can't."

"Why?"

She spoke into his shirt, unwilling to meet his eyes. "I know myself too well."

"Ah," he said.

"They need to find their own way there — as I have found my own way here with you."

He kissed the top of her head. "I caught a fish for dinner. I'll go fillet it."

"Let me. You know I do it better."

"Only because I taught you how."

They turned toward the cottage. "Only because you have taught me everything worth knowing."

"There are still a few things left to learn," he said.

She could hardly wait.

Molly added a row of ruched trim around the crown of the hat. The owner of Madam Lupine's Millinery Shoppe looked over her shoulder. "What do you plan to do along the seam?"

"I thought I'd create some red satin rosettes and alternate them with velvet leaves."

Madam Lupine nodded. "Do you have one of each I could inspect?"

"Of course." Molly retrieved the rosette and leaf she'd made the day before.

"*Je les aime*," Madam said. "Though perhaps they should be

a touch larger?"

"I can do that."

"I believe you," Madam said, with her thick French accent. "I've never seen anyone take to hat-making so quickly. Are you sure you've never done this before?"

"I'm sure." Molly didn't dare mention the hats she'd made for the countess. Once her past was out in the open, word might spread and find its way back to the manor. She did *not* want to be found.

"Keep it up, Molly, and I'll give you a full-time position."

"That would be wonderful, my lady."

"My lady?"

"I'm sorry. Madam Lupine."

She had to be careful. Very, very careful. Her new life depended on it.

Epilogue

The carriage stopped in front of the mercantile and Papa exited, then helped Lila down. He retrieved two large boxes from the seat and set them outside the front door. "Are you ready?" he asked.

"They're going to be so excited."

Papa put a hand on the door, then hesitated before opening it. "By the way, Lady Lila, you look stunning tonight. You will certainly be the belle of the ball."

"You look mighty handsome yourself, Lord Summerfield."

"I still can't get used to that title."

Lila leaned close. "Nor can I." She had one more thing to say before they went inside. "Do you realize that all those years ago, Mother was desperate to marry an earl—and it turns out she did."

"I've thought of that. And the fact that you will be living in Crompton Hall—her family home."

"Life does come full circle, doesn't it?"

"Occasionally." He took her arm. "Shall we?"

They entered the store and found Nana and Rose getting ready to close up for the night. Both ladies beamed at the sight of them. "My goodness, Jack. You do look the part of an earl in your dashing tailcoat and patent leather shoes."

He swept his top hat aside and bowed low like a cavalier in a novel. "At your service, ladies."

"And Lila . . ." Nana's eyes filled with tears. "You are a vision."

Lila did feel pretty. Who wouldn't? Her gown was made of

magnolia satin with a golden tint, the bodice embroidered with beads of many colors. The edge of her long train was trimmed with two rows of satin pleats. On her shoulders, embroidered epaulets rested on satin and lisse pleatings above sheer sleeves. A corsage of yellow and ivory satin roses sat on one shoulder.

"I've never seen anything so lovely," Rose said.

"It's the woman inside who makes the costume lovely." Nana ran her fingers along Lila's emerald necklace. "My jewel is wearing her own fine jewels."

"Borrowed from the dowager."

"I'm betting they'll be yours someday."

Lila had a hard enough time borrowing such jewels, much less owning them.

"I am so happy for both of you," Rose said. "You deserve all this—and more."

"Thank you, Rose," Papa said. "I don't deserve any of it but thank God for all of it."

"As do I," Lila added.

"Speaking of what you deserve, where's Joseph?" Nana asked. "I'd hoped he would stop by and show us his finery."

Lila looked at Papa. It was time.

Papa slipped outside to gather the boxes, which were so large he had to turn them on end to get them through the door. "I come bearing gifts." He set them on the counter. "This one is for you, Mother. And this one is for Rose."

Both women were giddy. "I've never been given a gift this large," Nana said.

"Neither have I." Rose pointed at Nana. "You go first."

Nana removed the lid and gasped. Her fingers tittered above the gown as though they didn't know what to do next. They finally lit upon the fringe on the tiers of the skirt.

"Hold it up so we can see," Lila said, though she knew very well what it looked like.

Nana pulled out a sage green ball gown. The weight of its gored skirt make the dress hang like a piece of art. "I've never seen anything so elegant. It's beyond beautiful, but—"

Lila didn't want her to ask the obvious question just yet. "Rose, open your box."

Rose's reaction was the same as Nana's, a gleeful awe at the pink dress with silk flowers along the décolletage.

"I chose the color to match your name," Papa said.

"You chose this? For me?"

"I did."

"And Nana, I chose your dress to match your eyes," Lila said.

"They're absolutely gorgeous," Nana said. "So elegant. But—"

"But nothing," Papa said. "Get dressed. We're escorting you to the ball."

Nana looked at Rose, then both shook their heads. "I don't think so. We don't belong there."

"And we do?" Papa said. "It's a ball to introduce the county to the new Westons of Summerfield Manor."

"But we aren't Westons," Rose said.

"But you *are* an important part of our lives."

Nana looked troubled. "Society people won't want me there. By now they all know that my husband stole you, stole Alexander."

"You raised me to be a fine man. The past has passed. Enough talk. Go get dressed."

They didn't hesitate long and happily headed to the stairs, their arms loaded down with their gowns.

"I'll be up in a minute to help you," Lila called after them. Then she put her arm around Papa's waist. "We did it."

"They were definitely surprised." He kissed her cheek. "This will be a glorious evening."

She shook her head, still unbelieving. "How can this be happening to us?"

"Only God knows."

There was no better explanation.

The ballroom at Summerfield Manor hadn't been used in years. But on this night there was plenty to celebrate.

All the elite of the county were in attendance. Lila couldn't remember most of their names, but they seemed eager to meet the new earl and his family. Grandmamma had done the honors, introducing those gathered to her now completed family. Lila was proud of how easily Papa handled the attention and relieved that even Morgan was making an attempt to be cordial.

As for herself, Lila stood at the head of the room, looking out upon the waltzing dancers. She felt the entire evening floating an arm's length away. The candles sparkling in the chandeliers and sconces were stars in a pulsing sky. The music of the string quartet created a rhythm that was matched by every heartbeat and footfall. The room smelled of perfume, flowers, and a delicious spread of delicacies and sweets. And the swirl of the dancers was mesmerizing, with the men in their dashing formalwear and the women creating a rainbow of bustled gowns, their trains sweeping behind like the feathered tails of showy birds.

Her father danced with Rose, whose cheeks matched her name. Grandmamma danced with her colonel, and Uncle Frederick with Aunt Ruth. Nana was talking with some other ladies her age, and Morgan was surrounded by a crowd of eager young society women. That he was suddenly a "catch" was odd. It would take time for him to embrace his new viscount title, its opportunities, and its responsibilities.

"A penny for your thoughts?" Joseph surprised her from behind, whispering in her ear.

She cupped his head against hers. "'Tis like a dream."

"A good one, I hope."

"Very good now that you're here."

"What could make it better?" he asked as he stood beside her, surveying the scene.

"I can't think of a thing."

"I can."

She looked at him. "You can?"

"Have you noticed there's something we've left undone?"

"I can't imagine what."

He took her hand and knelt before her. Then he reached into his coat pocket and pulled out a ring.

"Joseph . . . " She didn't know what else to say.

"I know I proposed marriage twice before, but now that the road is clear, now that we have our parents' blessing, I want to make it official." He held a ring between this thumb and forefinger. "This was my mother's ring, and now it will be yours. My darling Lila, will you marry me?"

And suddenly, the curtain was lifted and what was a fantasy became very, very real. God's blessings whirled around her.

"Yes," she said, drawing him to his feet. "Yes, Joseph, yes."

The third time was definitely a charm.

THE END

Author's Note

Dear Reader,

Love of the Summerfields was born in Nebraska, in my sister's living room one cold February night. As we talked hour after hour, my handful of ideas turned into many, and Fidelia and Frederick were born, and Lila and Clarissa . . . . It was very much like giving birth. As the mother of my characters, I never know what they look like or even what their names are until they're *here,* and their lives begin.

I live in Kansas, smack dab in the middle of the USA. So why am I writing about manor houses, countesses, and servants in Victorian England? Because I've always had a fascination with all things English. I devour the stories of Jane Austen, Charles Dickens, Elizabeth Gaskell, Anthony Trollope, and John Gallsworthy.

There's a reason for that interest. The ancestors on my father's side were from Kent, England. Job Tyler was born in Cranbrook, Kent County, in 1619. In 1638, at the age of 19, he came to America, to the vicinity of Newport, Rhode Island — before Newport was even named. His great-grandson, David, was a founder of Piermont, New Hampshire, and *his* son fought in the Revolutionary War *against* England. I'm doing further research, but I may even have English roots leading back to a William Tyler from Shropshire in 1543, when Henry VIII was king (no wonder I'm obsessed with the Tudors!)

The whole notion that I can trace my family back over 400 years excites me. How I wish I could talk to them and find out their stories. For stories and family rule my life. As a grandmother I'm very aware of the passage of time and new generations, and I marvel at how each family member has a unique story. And each story contains elements of love, sorrow, joy, anger, frustration, determination, success, and failure. The details of costume and carriage change, but the intrinsic nature of men and women remains timeless. "What has been will be again, what has been done will be done again; there is nothing new under the sun" (Ecclesiastes 3:9).

I hope you've enjoyed your time with the Weston and Hayward families. Please come back and see what happens next in *Bride of the Summerfields*. I will do my best not to disappoint.

Nancy Moser

RUTH'S Fashion

Harper's Bazar 1867-1898, p. 147

English Women's Clothing in the 19th Century, p. 321

Chapter 13: "Ruth walked into her dressing room and found what she was looking for — a gorgeous pink dressing gown edged with Belgian lace. And to wear underneath, an ivory nightgown adorned with rows of tiny pin-tucks on the bodice and embellished with a myriad of pink satin bows."

Chapter 17: "She'd chosen her dress carefully: a moss green gabardine with pleated skirt, bustle, and cuffs. She'd been careful not to be too extravagant, for appropriateness was always the top priority. But this day-dress implied confidence and standing, and if green could ever be considered a color of authority, this dress would do its job."

Victorian Fashions, p. 22

ADDIE'S
Fashion

Harper's Bazar 1867-1898, p. 170

Chapter 14: "Albers fiddled with a pair of satin bows that showcased the curve of Addie's spine, Clarissa adjusted the flowers on a small, flat hat with striped ribbons hanging down the back . . . `"I think the dress is lovely," Ruth said. "A soft blue sprinkled with mauve flowers? And the lace on the neck and shoulders is perfect for a summer garden wedding."

Chapter 15: "The petticoat was fastened, an ivory underskirt was set in place, and an overdress of striped red and white silk was slipped over her head. 'Luckily, this one fastens in front.'"

CLARISSA'S Fashion

Victorian and Edwardian Fashion, p. 65

LILA'S Fashion

Harper's Bazar 1867-1898, pg. 138

Chapter 14: "Clarissa stood near her grandmother, looking lovely in her white batiste dress with layer upon layer of pleats around the skirt. Her blue damask jacket was appropriately adorned with pink roses parading down the front like buttons. Her curved hat was covered with pleated fabric, and pink flowers cascaded down among the ribbons."

Epilogue: "Her gown was made of magnolia satin with a golden tint, the bodice embroidered with beads of many colors. The edge of her long train was trimmed with two rows of satin pleats. On her shoulders, embroidered epaulets rested on satin and lisse pleatings above sheer sleeves. A corsage of yellow and ivory satin roses sat on one shoulder. "

Discussion Questions

If your book club would like autographed book stickers and/or
bookmarks, contact me at:
http://www.nancymoser.com/Contact.html

1.   In Chapter 1, Nana bemoans the loss of her youth, and
      Lila wondered what it was like to grow old; did a person
      feel it come upon them a little at a time, or did they wake
      up one morning, surprised that decades had passed?
      How has growing older come upon you? What is
      involved in the art of aging?

2.   Colonel Cummings appears out of nowhere and sweeps
      Addie off her feet. Do you believe in a love like theirs,
      that never dies in spite of circumstances and time? Do
      you know any couple who've had this experience?

3.   When Lila fell off her horse in Chapter 4, her first instinct
      was to make sure her legs were covered. Yet being
      tangled, she lies back in the grass saying, "I surrender."
      How does this symbolize the struggle of many women in
      Victorian society — and even today? What and why do
      women surrender? Is this a good or bad thing? Later,
      Joseph reveals that this was the first moment he began to
      fall in love with her. Why did it have that effect on him?

4.   The servants at Summerfield Manor are proud of their
      position in the house, and have a hierarchy every bit as
      strict as the hierarchy of the titled aristocrats. Is such an
      order where everyone "knows their place" inevitable in
      any society? What are the pros and cons?

5.   In Chapter 15, Grady and Addie discuss vanity and
      pride. Grady gives credit to *Pride and Prejudice* in the line:
      "Pride relates more to our opinion of ourselves, while
      vanity relates to what we would have others think of us."
      What kind of choices do people make out of vanity, or
      pride?

6.   In Chapter 19 Lila feels a stop in accepting Timothy as a
      beau, and Nana says, "Sometimes I think the stops we
      feel are as important as the starts." (Nana's wisdom is

paraphrased from British evangelist George Müller.) Do you agree with Nana? When have you ever felt a nudge to STOP? Or START? How did the situation play out?

7. Starting in Chapter 19, what do you think about Ruth, Mary, Molly, and Dottie staying quiet about the secret? How is that the right or wrong thing to do?

8. In Chapter 22 Lila and Papa discuss the complicated emotion of love. Who have you had trouble loving? Have you ever felt relief when a loved one died? Why?

9. In Chapter 23, Addie realizes that by taking on Ruth's responsibilities, she prevented her from learning how to do the work. Do you know someone who repeatedly takes over? Are you guilty of letting your strengths prevent others from developing *their* strengths? What is the danger in our strengths? Or . . . what chance to prove yourself would you like to receive?

10. In Chapter 25, Reverend Lyons quotes a verse: "And the truth shall set you free." (John 8: 32) Do you believe this? When has a truth been revealed in your life? What kind of situation would justify keeping the truth hidden? Do you believe the truth always comes out?

11. In Chapter 31 the Haywards find Fidelia's hidden letters with money inside, and get a big lesson on how God uses bad things for good. When has God done as much in your life? Why do you think Fidelia kept all those letters — and the money?

12. Do you want Morgan to marry Molly? Jack to marry Rose? Why or why not? How is it possible within the structure of Victorian society?

13. In Chapter 31 Ruth and Addie talk about regrets: "I will restore to you the years that the locust hath eaten." (Joel 2: 25) What regrets dog you? How can you gain comfort through this verse?

About the Author

NANCY MOSER is the best-selling author of twenty-seven novels, including Christy Award winner, *Time Lottery*; Christy finalist *Washington's Lady*; and historical novels *Mozart's Sister*, *The Journey of Josephine Cain*, and *Masquerade*. Nancy has been married for forty years — to the same man. She and her husband have three grown children, six grandchildren, and live in the Midwest. She's been blessed with a varied life. She's earned a degree in architecture; run a business with her husband; traveled extensively in Europe; and has performed in various theatres, symphonies, and choirs. She knits voraciously, kills all her houseplants, and can wire an electrical fixture without getting shocked. She is a fan of anything antique — humans included.

Website: www.nancymoser.com
Blogs: www.footnotesfromhistory.blogspot.com, and www.authornancymoser.blogspot.com
Pinterest: www.pinterest.com/nancymoser1 (Check out my boards! I have a board for *Love of the Summerfields* that shows some of the real photographs and fashion pertaining to the story, as well as a board on 1880s fashion, History That Intrigues Me, and many others that involve history, fashion, and antiques.)
Facebook and Twitter:
www.facebook.com/nancymoser.author, and www.twitter.com/MoserNancy
Goodreads:
www.goodreads.com/author/show/117288.Nancy_Moser

Excerpt from Book 2
of the Manor House Series:

Bride of the Summerfields

Prologue

Autumn 1881

She wore a wig so no one would recognize her. She wore a simple dress of tan cotton, taking the look of a farmer's wife instead of a titled guest.

Though other villagers smiled and linked their arms sentimentally, she wore a frown and stood alone. Outside the church. Peering in a back window.

The bride, Lila, looked beautiful standing at the altar in her gown of duchesse satin with a pleated edge to the bustled train. The long veil had a scalloped edge, and there were tiny ivory silk roses sprinkled across her shoulders and hair as if she'd just walked through a floral shower.

That could have been me.

"Do you, Joseph Hayden Kidd, take Lila June Weston as your lawfully wedded wife . . ."

He should have been mine.

To be once-engaged then lose a man to another was a dagger to her heart. Yet Clarissa's loss was not confined to love. She had been Lady Clarissa Weston, the daughter of the Earl of Summerfield. She had held that title her entire life, until a forty-year-old secret surfaced, allowing Lila's father — a mere shopkeeper in the village — to step forward as the older brother and rightful earl. His rise shoved Clarissa's family down a branch in the family tree, and elevated Lila to her Lady Lila Weston title.

Clarissa had gained Lila as a cousin and lost Joseph as a fiancée.

She had lost a title, surrendering "Lady" to become a simple "Miss."

And since she'd fled to London, Clarissa had also lost a place in the family.

"I do," she heard Joseph say.

Clarissa shut out Lila's vows and looked at her family who sat in the second row behind Lila's father and brother.

There was her poor father. That he could stay at Summerfield Manor in his demoted position of second son was not surprising. Status had never meant as much to him as it had Clarissa. To Father, the demotion was a relief from the responsibilities that accompanied the title of earl. Clarissa tried not to think less of him for it.

Then there was Mother. Mother had never embraced the countess designation, nor its responsibilities. The demotion from countess to the rather bland title of Mrs. Weston was no strain on her. She had grown accustom to leaving the duties of her position to her mother-in-law, the dowager countess.

Speaking of . . . Grandmamma looked as lovely as ever, if not even lovelier than when Clarissa had seen her last. She sat close to her husband of less than a year, the love of her life, Colonel Grady Cummings. After decades of being married and dutiful to the late Earl of Summerfield, she'd finally been reunited with her Grady. Clarissa envied their happy ending.

The last family member Clarissa noticed was George, her little brother. In the months she'd been hidden away in London, he'd ripened from boy to young man. He'd not minded a whit that he was no longer the heir to an earldom, and that Lila's brother Morgan now held that position. As long as George could breed and train horses, he was happy.

Everyone seemed happy, except Clarissa.

"I now pronounce you man and wife."

Joseph tenderly lifted the veil from Lila's face and touched her cheek with a gentle hand as he kissed her. Then they turned as a couple toward the congregation and beamed as though they had been proclaimed king and queen of the world. Joseph raised Lila's hand to his lips before they started their walk down the aisle.

Clarissa suffered a swell of anger and pain. Why had she come?

Come or not, she couldn't stay a moment longer.

She turned away from the church before the pain within its walls came outside and did her in. For a brief moment she considered lingering, letting her family see her — or letting them think they might have seen her. Yet knowing how the blessings of life seemed to fall upon everyone *but* her, she couldn't take the chance. And so she ran to the train station that would hasten her escape back to London, where she could disappear from the sight and mind of her family yet again.

If only she could forget them as they'd surely forgotten her.

Made in the USA
San Bernardino, CA
16 February 2016